JAN 12

Lillian Lorraine

Lillian Lorraine

The Life and Times of a Ziegfeld Diva

NILS HANSON

Foreword by Richard Ziegfeld

McFarland & Company, Inc., Publishers
Jefferson, North Carolina, and London

LIBRARY OF CONGRESS CATALOGUING-IN-PUBLICATION DATA

Hanson, Nils, 1922–
    Lillian Lorraine : the life and times of a Ziegfeld diva /
Nils Hanson ; foreword by Richard Ziegfeld.
      p.   cm.
    Includes bibliographical references and index.
    Includes filmography.

    ISBN 978-0-7864-6407-4
    illustrated case : 50# alkaline paper ∞

    1. Lorraine, Lillian, 1892–1955.   2. Actors— United States—
Biography.   I. Title.
PN2287.L645H36   2011
792.02'8092—dc23   2011026445
[B]

BRITISH LIBRARY CATALOGUING DATA ARE AVAILABLE

Cover photograph: Lillian Lorraine in fashion publicity shot, 1912

Manufactured in the United States of America

McFarland & Company, Inc., Publishers
  Box 611, Jefferson, North Carolina 28640
   www.mcfarlandpub.com

To the memory of my mother:
she was there through it all.

Acknowledgments

Where did this all begin? Quite simply, from the contents of a musty old theatrical trunk filled with well-preserved theatrical memorabilia from Broadway's golden age of vaudeville and musical theatre. The journey to completion has been a joyful experience of discovery and tangible testimonials of encouragement and friendship.

Midway through this project, I was thrown for a loop by a sudden and severe case of vision impairment. It was Jim Hagadorn who came to the fore with moral and technical support enabling me to complete a first draft of this manuscript. Of equal importance, throughout, he was a superb devil's advocate. Kudos to my nieces Lisa Johnson and Robin Smith. Lisa undertook to edit that first draft and in that process, her constructive suggestions were most gratefully received. Robin unselfishly took time from her professional activities to hunt down Lillian's antecedents in remote Rifle, Colorado, and Pittston, Maine. Also, her diligent scouring of Denver court records has added much to the color and flavor of Lillian's alleged involvement in the Von Phul murder scandal. A hefty thank-you to my friend, novelist James Curtis. Jim has authored books on famed director James Whale, W.C. Fields and Preston Sturgis. He is presently in prepublication of a massive biography on the life of beloved film star Spencer Tracy. Jim's wise counsel throughout this endeavor has been invaluable. To John Griffin, independent film producer, my gratitude for his sharing of research materials utilized in his 1976 A&E *Great Ziegfeld* TV special. I am so very thankful to the last surviving Ziegfeld Girl, Doris Eaton Travis, for almost twenty years of a unique friendship and acceptance into her inner circle of friends and relatives. In her own 2003 autobiography, *The Days We Danced*, she graciously credited me with assisting in her return to show business after an absence of almost seventy years. Thank you to theater and film historian Miles Krueger. He is the definitive human encyclopedia for knowledge of Broadway's musical theater, and his west coast repository of theatrical records and memorabilia is unmatched. I am indebted to Richard Ziegfeld, co-author of *The Ziegfeld Touch*, for his ongoing encouragement and guidance. His generous Foreword to this manuscript was for me a very special treat. Thanks to Amber and Seth Ward and John Forkner for their editorial recommendations which, I believe, greatly enhanced the overall quality of this book. Major credit for making the initial McFarland publishing contact goes to Ziegfeld Club 1st vice-president Patricia Dey. On her own initiative Patricia made the all-important phone call and the rest is history. Many, many thanks, Patti! Thanks also to Paula Lamont for the unconditional use of the Ziegfeld Club archival collections.

Thank you, Earlene Price, director of the New York City Division of Vital Records. To Anthony Roma, managing director for the trustees of New York City's St. Patrick's Cathedral. I am grateful to Robert Taylor, Curator, Billy Rose Collection, New York Performing Arts Library, for often smoothing the way on bureaucratic research paths. To the Shubert Archive under the direction of Mary Anne Chach, which has been most helpful in uncovering long-untouched material from Lillian's first days in the New York theater. The same holds true for

Susan Katwinkel of the Harry Ransom Humanities Research Center, University of Texas at Austin. To Jim Herb, who without fail is always on hand to resolve computer malfunctions—the bane of my existence! Lauren Redness, *Century Girl* author, has been a constant source of encouragement. Dana Amendola, Walt Disney's Vice-President of Theater Operation, has remained a valued friend whose love of the New Amsterdam Theater is to a very large extent shared by this author. Many thanks to Alam of New York Copy Center for photo restoration magic.

David Bartholomew is my best and oldest friend. He has been with me on this project from the very start—begun over ten years ago. His creative mind, technical expertise and compassion have all combined to successfully bring me to the end of a very long journey.

All of this has been a thrilling and challenging endeavor. At times the seas were rough, with accurate navigation almost impossible. Home port was made possible by the aforementioned.

Table of Contents

Foreword

by RICHARD ZIEGFELD

I met Nils Hanson in 1990 as a challenging deadline approached for a biography I was writing on my cousin, Florenz Ziegfeld, the Broadway showman who plays a major role in Lillian Lorraine's story. Nils and I began corresponding about a scandal that had erupted in Denver in 1911: ostensibly, Lillian was a principal in a sexual intrigue gone awry, involving blackmail and murder. Given her history of indiscretions with men and their wives and girlfriends, it did not require a long stretch of one's imagination to believe that she could have been a party to the incident. The historical record, though, was fraught with conflicting information about what happened and who was responsible. I was having some difficulty sorting out the truth and lacked the resources to conduct on-site research. Enter Nils, who, it turns out, had dispatched his niece to delve into the matter on-site in Colorado and was able to settle a number of dilemmas, just in time to help meet my manuscript deadline, including the fact that Lillian was almost certainly not complicit in the crimes that had transpired.

That initial encounter, I've learned over the years, was revealing about Hanson, as man and biographer. He was intent on discovering the truth, regardless of where it led him; delightfully curious about new topics; tenacious, bordering on relentless, in pursuing his goals; and generous in sharing what he learned. Friendship emerged from our mutual interest in the history of Broadway during the early 20th century and, specifically, the relationship among my cousin, the woman whom Flo loved so passionately, and Nils's mother, Nanny Johnson, whom Ziegfeld hired as Lillian's companion.

Initially, Nils exhibited a reverence about Lillian borne of his mother's intimate relationship with this famous actress for whom she was initially a maid but ultimately Lillian's trusted confidante. He was clearly uncomfortable with the colorful side of Lillian's character and seemed disposed to write what I joked with him would perhaps best be described as "the Jazz Age according to Saint Lillian."

As his project evolved over time, Nils discovered the "real" Lillian. He came to terms with the fact that she was, as is true with so many successful public figures (including Flo), riddled with points of brilliance, foibles, and flaws that we would not tolerate in mere mortals. Nils realized that Lillian's passionate exuberance, for good *and* for ill, made her the star she was. And with that dawning recognition, he relaxed about acknowledging that Lillian was, all in one personality, charismatic, memorable, earthy, headstrong, impetuous, sexually alluring, a vixen on occasion, and given to incredibly provocative behavior, even by today's standards. Once, jealous that Flo was dining another woman, she appeared at his table wearing only a fur coat and threatened that if Flo did not do as she wished, she would open the coat on the spot. She was, in a phrase, one of Broadway's most illustrious (and notorious!) shining lights during the era when Broadway ruled showbiz.

Our friendship became richer on other levels as well. We were both writing about subjects

1

with whom we had a relationship, mine by blood (though Flo died long before I was born) and Nils's because his mother was Lillian's devoted friend and because Nils met his subject briefly when he was a child. We shared two challenges that we frequently discussed. One was how to tell a life story passionately *and* honestly when our subjects were people to whom we had ties. The other was how to establish integrity as we told the stories of public figures about whom much had been written that was inaccurate or of dubious origin.

The conventional reliable sources for high-art subjects were not available to either of us. We were dealing with entertainment news outlets fabled for their bias and a willingness to reveal the most scurrilous gossip, including a "rag" published by Ziegfeld's arch-rivals, the Shubert brothers, and a fraudulent memoir, purportedly written by Ziegfeld's first wife. We shared a keen desire to avoid falling into the twin traps of hagiography or what we dubbed the *National Enquirer* school of biography. Balance and intellectual integrity were paramount for both of us.

As Nils began writing, I encouraged him to describe Lillian with all her foibles while still sharing his love for her story and his chief concern — ensuring that she not be forgotten. He struggled for some time with how to handle his original impetus for the book: he had become invested in Lillian's story because his mother had been the star's friend during the turbulent years as Lillian became Broadway's most famous femme fatale. Eventually Nils solved his problem when his friend, W.C. Fields biographer Jim Curtis, suggested Nils interpolate his mother's role and his own experiences, after Edmund Morris's style in the Reagan biography, so readers would experience his sense of discovery.

The backstory on this book is as fascinating as its subject. Nils spent his career in the travel industry, culminating his professional years as a senior executive with Thomas Cook. Meanwhile, a lifelong interest in politics led to associations with two of New York's most colorful politicians, Thomas Dewey and Nelson Rockefeller (Nils took a six-year leave of absence to act as senior staff member while "Rocky" was governor) and to a role as executive assistant to the Republican Party chairman in Westchester County. Thus, Nils came to biography later in life, after departing Thomas Cook, so writing this book presented a significant retirement challenge. His political contacts, though, served him well when he sought access to sensitive source material and to influential public figures.

Nothing prepared him, however, for a series of devastating setbacks. After he had written a first draft, he was revising it, while on the train between Manhattan and East Hampton, for a friend who had volunteered to create an electronic backup. Nils left his seat for a moment and returned to discover that a scoundrel had stolen his attaché case containing the manuscript. He had no backup, not even a photocopy. The desolation I heard in his voice when he reported the mishap was difficult to bear. It took nearly a year before he mustered the resources to begin his project anew. His strength — of character, that is — emerged as he set out to reconstruct Lillian's story. He was progressing reasonably well and had noted that he would soon mail a draft for my review. I was impressed with his recovery from the setback.

Then, in 2005, he reported, in his quiet fashion, no self-pity evident, that lightning had struck a second time. While at a Manhattan traffic light, waiting to cross a busy street, he experienced a severe macular-degeneration incident and found himself completely blind! I remember thinking: "That's it. No way he will ever publish this book. Who is he? Job?" I didn't know Nils well enough. He spent months in New Haven at a veterans' training facility, learning to live independently and to use the specialized computer equipment that allows a blind person to write a book. His courage in living with this challenge has been remarkable. During a recent visit to New York when my wife, Hyon Mi, met Nils for the first time and watched him navigating the tourist-crowded streets near Broadway's New Amsterdam Theatre, the scene of Lillian's apex more than a century ago, she noted: "He's absolutely without fear.

Is he *really* blind?" Somehow Nils rallied from this devastating setback and was making good progress, talking again about sending me a manuscript to read.

Unfortunately, the saga of travail was not complete. Having not heard from Nils for some months, I called to inquire about his progress. Lightning had struck a third time. Both he and his beloved sister had cancer. He endured chemotherapy, radiation, and radical medical experiments. He survived his experience with the medical establishment and finished Lillian's story. And what an intriguing "read" he has to share.

Lillian Lorraine was a beautiful woman who had the good fortune to become a protégé of Flo Ziegfeld, the man who ruled Broadway as no other figure in American theatre has and who, in his own turn of phrase, delighted in "Glorifying the American Girl." Lillian had some talent, though nothing extraordinary, as actress, dancer, and singer, but when Ziegfeld offered her the opportunity, she had the personality — the charisma, grace, and drive — to transform herself into a star who charmed New York theatre audiences and Hollywood film devotees. Her fans reveled in the fact that she was an extraordinary presence in the entertainment world, who wore elegant gowns that emphasized her beauty and sexual allure, and yet in the tradition that came to be known as "the Ziegfeld touch," the showman presented her with an aesthetic integrity on stage that made her as popular with New York society women as with "tired old businessmen" interested in witnessing a little show of flesh. It didn't hurt, of course, that off-stage, Lillian offered spice, including a healthy appetite for sex, and an occasional real scandal. Madonna, you had a model 75 years before your time!

An anecdote involving Flo, Lillian, and Flo's daughter, Patty, crystallizes Lillian's career and life. Because Ziegfeld continued his emotional involvement with Lillian even after he married Patty's mother, Billie Burke, Patty was understandably reticent, almost 60 years after her father's passing, to speak about Lillian. When persuaded to ruminate a bit, she exhibited ambivalence that one could detect without benefit of training as a psychologist, noting with a mischievous sparkle in her eye: "People said Lillian was the world's most beautiful woman. Daddy once observed, after hearing that remark repeated endlessly: 'Yes, *and* the world's dumbest.'" When I chuckled, despite myself, upon hearing the pungent retort, Patty drew back, horrified, explaining she didn't mean to imply that Lillian lacked intelligence. "Daddy" intended, she thought, to say that Lillian incessantly made unfortunate choices: getting mired in scandals with shady characters, drinking too much, and responding so generously when others "touched her" for assistance that she died destitute.

Flo married Billie Burke after his affair with Lillian ended and loved Billie in his own inimitable fashion, but, even so, Lillian's joie de vivre so captivated Flo that, I suspect, he may have loved Lillian more than any other woman, including his wives: after he died, his secretary, Goldie Clough, discovered in his desk an exquisite scrimshaw brooch that contains a nude portrait of Lillian.

Lillian Lorraine burned so bright, so hot in her early years, meteor-like, that it was impossible to sustain the searing heat — figuratively, she crashed to Earth many decades before her physical demise.

Nils Hanson has told Lillian Lorraine's story as only an insider who cares passionately about his subject can, but he has also instilled a measure of objectivity that makes possible a biography rich with historical integrity. He has accomplished the goal he articulated 20 years ago: he has rescued Lillian from obscurity and told her intriguing story movingly and honestly.

Preface

Calvary Cemetery is only ten minutes from Manhattan's tony and fashionable East Side, a vast and sprawling 365-acre Roman Catholic Mecca for over three quarters of a million of the faithful. Were it not for the nearby East River, separating the metropolitan borough of Queens from Manhattan Island, Calvary would have encroached on the sixteen-acre United Nations compound and the posh Sutton Place-Beekman Terrace high-rise condos. The new monolithic 92-story residential Trump Tower might never exist. Calvary would be on its site.

In the spring of 1955, my mother and her friend, Winnie Dunn, stood apprehensively at the edge of an open grave in this cemetery, not an unusual sight either then or today except for the fact that they were not attending an interment. They were witnessing an exhumation. The gravediggers unearthed a pine box that had only one month earlier been consigned to unmarked oblivion together with the earthly remains of twenty other unrelated lost souls in Range 22, Section 14 of the free grave plots—more commonly referred to as a "potter's field." The strapping was secured and the coffin was brought to ground level. Mother and Winnie held hands in a white-knuckled grip that served to underscore the tension evident in their faces. Both my father and Winnie's husband, and a director of the cemetery, stood several feet behind. The men remained silent and respectful in the unfolding drama at the gravesite.

An almost imperceptible gesture from the cemetery's director signaled the diggers to pry open the lid of the coffin. The women, now covering their mouths with their hands, gingerly leaned forward to catch a first glimpse of the corpse which was exposed to the bright daylight of a balmy spring day, May 18, 1955. As one, they turned to face each other and nodded as if to say, "Yes, it's Lillian."

The men joined their wives at the edge of the grave. The cemetery's director remained in the background. The foursome paid their silent respects to sixty-three-year-old Lillian Lorraine, whose snow-white hair was glistening in the rays of intruding sunlight. In repose, the face still was beautiful, with only a suggestion of green mold on the forehead to indicate that the inevitable process of decomposition had begun. Mother and Winnie each carried a single red rose, which they gently placed on Lillian's breast. Then, for the last time, her coffin's lid was resealed.

Exactly one month had passed since Lillian Lorraine's Requiem Mass, attended by only three mourners and presided over by a priest, Father Gerard Micera, who knew only her name on the Certificate of Death: Lillian O'Brien.

Forty-five years earlier, Lillian Lorraine began her eighteen-year reign as the toast of Broadway and more. She was the dazzlingly beautiful embodiment of all that had gone into defining the Ragtime Era as the Wild and Roaring Twenties. It was the time of Prohibition, nonstop free-flowing illegal booze and peephole key clubs. It was a time of glamour, glitz and flappers, and fast-lane living such as the world would never see again. Lillian Lorraine commanded the adulation of thousands, with Broadway her oyster and Hollywood her ultimate pearl. My mother was there through it all.

A reader may quite justifiably enquire what motivated me to resurrect this long-forgotten symbol of a bygone era. My mother and Lillian Lorraine had a close and enduring relationship for ten years and, in absentia, many years beyond. What bonded these two women with so very little in common? One, an immigrant Swedish farm girl; the other, a woman of the world — a glamorous, nationally known figure of the Broadway stage and Hollywood films? The contrast in background and personal lifestyle was incredible. One was a product of ultra-strict Swedish Lutheran upbringing. The other, without need for too much elaboration, was uninhibited and unpredictable in every respect — the exact antithesis. How did Lillian Lorraine happen to be the one exception to escape Flo Ziegfeld's well-known stringent code of unblemished moral and ethical conduct — both on and off stage? All traces of Lillian's presence in the Zeigfeld galaxy had been purged from the National Zeigfeld Club archive. Why? Through the revelations in this book I found the answers.

1

The Trunk

It was one of those old theatrical trunks, the kind you don't see around much anymore—except occasionally in some musty old antique shop or one of those open-air flea markets on streets in the mid-twenties on Manhattan's West Side. It measured two by about three feet and was a murky dark red in color with two-inch wooden reinforcement slats around the sides. What really set it apart from the familiar and ordinary steamer trunk was a curved, hooded top. It was one of a half-dozen or so storage trunks and packing cartons pushed under the attic eaves of my parents' home in Larchmont, New York.

Home was a green-tinted stucco ten-room house with a red Spanish tile roof—really high-style living considering we were in the depths of the Great Depression. It had been designed and built to my folks' specifications and was home to my older brother, sister and me beginning in 1931. By 1978, however, Mother was gone, having passed away the previous year, and Dad was ready to leave behind memories of an idyllic sixty-year marriage for the sun and surf of Florida's Daytona Beach. I can still hear him saying, perhaps by way of self-reassurance, that he was making the right decision: "After all, I'm only ninety, in good shape physically and mentally, and I don't see why I can't stick around for maybe another ten years." (He did just that!) But, prior to his north-to-south exodus, the Larchmont attic remained as just about the last place for cleanup. It was then and there, in the attic, that I came upon the trunk. No one in the family seemed to have any idea what it contained, and besides, they were all busy getting into other things. I unfastened the metal latch, lifted the hooded cover, and was greeted with the pungent whiff of long-undisturbed paper, attesting to my immediate deduction that a good many years had passed since that lid had been raised.

First catching my eye was a large stack of mostly sepia-toned photographs. As I fingered though them, the images were all the same. To be sure, the poses and costumes were varied, but that face—it was the face of an exquisitely beautiful young woman with wide-set eyes, sculpted cheekbones and sensuously shaped lips. The likeness was not at all dissimilar to photographs I'd seen of my mother in her early years. But this was definitely not my mother. This is not to say Mother wasn't pretty, because she was, but these photographs pictured a turned-out glamour queen of the first order.

Her attire was composed of intricately detailed costumes, ostrich-plumed picture hats and an array of diamonds and pearl accoutrements that would surely have been among Cartier's finest. The pictures were only the beginning. The trunk also contained countless folders and envelopes stuffed full of newspaper clippings, showbills and magazine covers featuring, in brilliant colors, that same beautiful face.

Then, suddenly, like the sunrise at dawn, from the distant and cobwebbed recesses of long-forgotten childhood memories, I knew I had seen that face before. I was only five or six years old at the time, but now, some fifty years later, that image came into focus as clear and sharp as any one of those gorgeous photos in the trunk before me. I recalled it was at our home in Larchmont Gardens. She was visiting with my mother. I remember thinking how

Top and right: two views of Lillian Lorraine in the famous Langenberg mystery portrait hat (courtesy Ziegfeld Club Archives). *Left*: 1912 publicity shot of Lillian Lorraine.

very pretty she was. Obviously, at that age I'd not had much experience in this direction, but I do insist the impression was indelibly vivid. I also recall, though somewhat more vaguely, during her visit she was behaving in a rather unusual manner — silly and overly animated. At that specific moment in time, in my wildest dreams, I could never have imagined that sixty-five years later, my sister Marguerite would reveal the existence of audiotape recordings that would spark my immersion into every facet of this woman's erratic and kaleidoscopic passage through life.

As I continued to pore over the contents of the trunk, it became clear I had accidentally stumbled into a treasure trove of theatrical memorabilia and lost splendor dating back to the beginnings of the 20th century. Here, so well preserved in all their magnificence, were photo images of the beautiful Lillian Lorraine. During Broadway's Golden Age of Musical Theatre, Florenz Ziegfeld had dubbed her "the most beautiful woman in the world," and Will Rogers recalled her as the "stunning object of gawkers" as she swept into Broadway's elegant late nighteries.

I needed to know more — about my mother and about Lillian. To begin, I would have to unravel the paradox of just how and why the life of Lillian Lorraine, a worldly and enigmatic darling of old Broadway, became entwined with that of my mother, a pretty and proper staunch Lutheran country girl, fresh off the farm from her native Sweden.

Lillian Lorraine *Follies* publicity shot, circa 1910 (courtesy Ziegfeld Club Archives).

2

The Early Years

Where was I to begin? It wouldn't be easy — so many witnesses were gone — but relatively small as I knew the number had to be, I was certain if I dug deeply enough I could find some surviving peers, relatives or friends. They couldn't all be dead — or could they?

I started simply enough. The New York Public Library for Performing Arts was my opening gambit. Within this library is a major depository of theatrical collections comprising millions of tattered clippings, photographs, recordings and books relating to the Broadway theatre. For me it was an enormous apple orchard, ripe for harvest. I found names in those books and I wanted to trace them. I wanted to talk to people who had known, and even better, performed with Lillian Lorraine. The New York City Hall of Records was another gold mine for birth, marriage and death certification. The Harry Ransom Library at the University of Texas in Austin is a recipient and rich depository of many private theatre collections. It proved to be a truly wonderful resource.

Was there a club or an organization or a building — just something with the name "Ziegfeld"— that was physical, that I could literally reach out and touch? The *New York City, Manhattan Yellow Pages* supplied the answer. There was, and is, a Ziegfeld Theatre on 54th Street between Sixth and Seventh Avenues. A visit to the site bore fruit. Encircling the inner lobby wall space were ten large and lighted display cases, shadow boxes filled with Ziegfeld memorabilia — Marilyn Miller's threadbare and autographed ballet slippers; a lariat spun many decades earlier by Will Rogers; a tattered stovepipe high hat that had once adorned the head of Bert Williams, America's first black comedian to reach national celebrity status, thanks to the theatrical astuteness of Ziegfeld; and, eureka, a shimmering, spangled dress and gold high-button shoes from the person of Lillian Lorraine! In one of the display cases there was a small, printed card —"Courtesy of the Ziegfeld Club." I felt like a gold miner, shaking my sifter and discovering the residue of precious golden nuggets! Again to the telephone book and discovery of a Ziegfeld Club on the fifth floor of the magnificent, Gothic-style Central Presbyterian Church on the northeast corner of Park Avenue and 64th Street.

My next call? The Ziegfeld Club. Little did I know that the offices of the club were rarely open — basically only for occasional social gatherings and monthly meetings of the board of directors. But I persisted and finally got through to the president of the club, Elisabeth Rae Lamont. It was only through Elisabeth's kindness and good auspices that I was able to meet fifteen original Ziegfeld *Follies* girls, two of whom had actually performed with Lillian in the *Follies* of 1918: Grace LaRue Graham — one of Legs Diamond's many mistresses— and Doris Eaton Travis, alive and well at 100+ years at this writing.

The Ziegfeld Club would prove to be of tremendous value as a source of information and leads relating to the Ziegfeld era and, of course, Lillian. The club was the brainchild of Ziegfeld publicist Louis Sobol and Ziegfeld's widow Billie Burke. It was formed in 1936, four years after Ziegfeld's death, to serve as a publicity gimmick to promote Metro Goldwyn Mayer's highly fictionalized and successful musical extravaganza, *The Great Ziegfeld*. At the time of its formation, membership in the club was restricted solely to women who had actually worked in the *Follies* and other Ziegfeld productions. Except for its publicity function for MGM, the club was purely social in nature, hosting parties for Ziegfeld alums to reminisce about the recent glory days of which they had all been an integral part. After the film had been in release for almost one year, Sobol moved to disband the club. But the membership appealed. The women had come sadly to know that many of their peers had fallen on hard times. Too many original *Follies* girls were in dire financial straits, unable to pay for adequate medical care, rent, even food. Thus did Sobol file papers with the State of New York incorporating the club as a charitable organization. It was now more than social; it was qualified to raise and dispense funds for the benefit of *Follies* women in need. The club's mission later broadened to include helping indigent women in all phases of show business.

The degree of my association with the club was initially slight. I was in awe of these stars of yesteryear. But the club obviously needed help: files were in a mess; memorabilia were disorganized. The office needed revamping and organization. My desire to be of assistance overcame my star-struck

Doris Eaton, 1918 *Follies* publicity pageboy shot (courtesy Ziegfeld Club Archives).

reticence. I offered to help. On one hand, a very strong-willed Elisabeth Lamont was reluctant to have an outsider come into what she considered her private domain. On the other hand, she was smart enough to know the club needed management expertise. She accepted my offer of assistance, and as a result, order immediately began to replace chaos. As days and weeks passed, my voluntary involvement with the club's social activities and fundraising functions increased to the point of total immersion. Within a year the club membership created the post of "Administrator," a position I have held under the last three club presidents.

✶ ✶ ✶

But what of Lillian's beginnings, her birth and her early years? Though helpful in so many ways, not a single Ziegfeld club record or *Follies* girl recollection even hinted at Lillian's origin. Within moments of my first involvement with the Ziegfeld Club, I knew this would be the case. To a woman, the *Follies* girls would speak of anyone they could remember — except Lillian. The air turned frigid at the very mention of her name. It would take me years of research, much of it dead-ended, before I was to learn that Lillian was the only *Follies* girl who could — and did — break Ziegfeld's rules of personal and professional conduct for the girls, time and time again, without any penalty at all. She was a Diva in every sense of the word — to the lifelong resentment of her peers.

Thus, I was fresh out of substantive contacts that might lead me to Lillian's origins. I returned to the trunk. It was all I had. I went through its contents again. Instead of skimming,

Grace LaRue posing for "Rag Doll Dance" production number, 1918 *Follies*.

I decided to read every word on every torn and tattered document and photo.

Inscribed on an original 20" × 30" pen-and-ink sketch of Lillian there was a reference to an interview in the April 16, 1911, issue of the *San Francisco Chronicle*. The article was titled "Lillian Lorraine of San Francisco." I stared at the sketch. Something important was here. I sensed it but could not put my finger on it right away. Would the artist Delmue know anything? A call to the newspaper revealed that the article was in the *Chronicle*'s morgue and Delmue was deceased. What was it about the inscription on this sketch? The answer came to me by next morning: The word "of" was the key. Lillian Lorraine *of* San Francisco.

Was Lillian living in San Francisco at the time? Was she born there? My next call was to United Airlines for a ticket to the legendary city of the Golden Gate. I had to see this article. The sketch had come from the artist to Lillian, to my mother, and now to me. It would lead me to my first revelations about Lillian's beginnings. I just knew it.

In the microfilm morgue of the *San Francisco Chronicle*, I soon discovered the article. The sketch and its companion verbiage encompassed one full page. Lillian told journalist Reynaud that she was born in San Francisco on New Year's Day in 1892 and spent the first fourteen years of her life in the City on the Bay. I felt that I had found the beginning point that I was looking for: Lillian's beginning.

On its surface, the interview appeared complete and truthful. Ziegfeld was present. The interview took place in Lillian's San Francisco hotel suite (the *Follies* was playing in San Francisco at the time). Lillian was even able to name the street and house where she was born and lived: 16 Central Avenue, Golden Gate Park West. And she spoke of the school she attended: Sacred Heart Convent, where, she said, "I devoted a considerable amount of time to devising means of escape and just generally getting into trouble." Her story seemed clear and straightforward enough, and certainly Reynaud was known to be a journalist careful about what he committed to print. But I wanted substantiation.

Fortunately, the article showed the names of Lillian's parents: Charles F. de Jacques and Mary Ann Brennan. Lillian told Reynaud that they were of French and Irish descent. However, the 1900 census does not show anyone by the name of de Jacques counted in the entire state of California, and the available San Francisco city directories for preceding years, going back as far as 1888, also do not show anyone with the name C.F. de Jacques living in San Francisco. The census documents do show a single name similar to Lillian's father's name: C.F. Jacques, age 31, living on Russ Street in San Francisco and married to Mary Jacques, born August 1871. But a child was not counted in the Jacques' household.

The Reynaud article contained only scant and passing mention of Lillian's parents or family roots. I learned later that she was always loath to speak of her father in anything but negative terms. To Renaud, she would recount no more about her father than to say that his origins were in St. Louis, Missouri, a fact that I was able to later confirm. This was in sharp contrast to what she would reveal about other facets of her life. Reynaud was quick to observe her willingness to do what so many of her peers would not do; namely, share truly personal tidbits of information. "Miss Lorraine is a recent product of her environment, and not as apt as some of her more news-hardened sisters in pouring her joys, woes, hopes and fears into the complacent ears of this newspaperman," said Reynaud, "and she [possesses] extraordinarily beautiful facial features and other natural physical attributes."

Nothing more was heard publicly of Lillian's father until 1916, when Lillian had already become a nationally known star of stage and screen. On May 16 of that year the *Chicago Tribune* headlined a feature story declaring that Lillian had refused her father's request to pay two hundred dollars toward the burial expenses of her recently deceased paternal grandmother. According to de Jacques, the alternative was interment of his mother in a potter's field grave. The *Tribune* reported, "Mrs. Mary Marshall, paternal grandmother of noted stage and screen beauty, Lillian Lorraine, passed away on April 8th and her son, C.F. de Jacques had sent a telegram to his daughter pleading for two hundred dollars to cover the funeral expenses." Following two weeks of taunting and negative press from the *Tribune*, Lillian's publicist issued a statement on her behalf declaring, "I haven't seen my father since I was six years old. He deserted Mother and me to shift for ourselves and even when dear Mother passed away I heard nothing from him. His treatment of her would not bear printing! The only communications I have received from him have been requests for money. I hardly knew the woman he calls my grandmother. The last time I saw her was at the 1904 St. Louis World's Fair. I'm not at all certain the woman who is dead is really my grandmother." The *Tribune* continued to have a joy ride with the affair. As a rebuttal to Lillian's statement the paper ran a tongue-in-cheek story declaring that a J.F. Ryan from New York City had sent them a check for five dollars with a note stating, "While I'm not hard up by any means, I am still not so affluent that I can spare money easily. This is such a pathetic case that I could not sleep if I should allow this poor woman to be buried as a tramp or pauper while her granddaughter enjoys all the comforts and luxuries that go with a weekly salary of $2,000."

In order to avoid further media bashing and bring closure to the miniature brouhaha, Lillian wired two hundred dollars to the *Tribune*, directing them to "remove Mrs. Marshall's body from Potters' Field and arrange for a proper burial."

Perhaps the tap root of Lillian's animus toward her father rests in celebrated theatrical biographer Charles Higham's *Ziegfeld*, which relates: "At the age of thirteen Lillian had her first affair with a man who had paid her father for the privilege of sleeping with her." It should be noted that Higham never interviewed Lillian and that his reporting of this alleged incident should probably be attributed to the secondhand gossip picked up by Higham from his close friend, Matilda Golden. Matilda, better known as "Goldie," was Ziegfeld's personal assistant and confidante from 1923 to the time of his death in 1932. Her only contact with Lillian had been as the conduit for Lillian's incoming calls on Ziegfeld's private line, a gold-plated telephone. On the other hand, when Lillian asserted her father had flown the family coop when she was six, one must ponder the accuracy of that statement when recalling she also stated the last time and place she had seen her grandmother was 1904 in St. Louis when she was twelve years old. Presumably, de Jacques would have been present as well.

On the maternal side, a small publicity item in the August 22, 1912, *New York Telegraph* did open some doors and shed a modicum of light on Lillian's mother's family background. The *Telegraph* recounted an incident in New York City's Central Park in which Lillian was reportedly thrown from a pony, a gift from an uncle in Colorado by the name of Mars Flitner. This led my niece, Robin Smith, an Aspen photographer and tenaciously superb researcher, to take a short motor jaunt to the town of Rifle. It is a smallish farming community in northwestern Colorado, population 2,200, nestled neatly in the junction of Rifle Creek and the Silt River. Robin's search of genealogical records did indeed confirm that a Mardinboro Flitner had resided in Rifle from 1909 to 1921. Listed as a "rancher" in *E.A. McKinney's Directory*, he was born in Pittston, Maine, July 24, 1880.

Within several months of her Rifle visitation, Robin was on the East Coast delving into Flitner family records in Pittston. It was here she unearthed data on Flitner's seafaring father, David, born in Pittston in 1849. David married Elizabeth Nickles, who had previously been married to a John Brennan or "Brannan." This suggests the strong likelihood that Lillian's mother, Mary Ann Brennan, was born of that first Nickles/Brennan union and the probable conclusion that the State of Maine was the origin of Lillian's maternal forebears.

After my visit to the *San Francisco Chronicle* microfilm morgue, my next stop was Sacred Heart Convent, where I hoped to verify Lillian's allegation that she actually attended the school. Fortunately, the convent was spared from the destructive forces of the great earthquake of 1906, and to this day, the convent stands as operative as it was at the turn of the twentieth century. A Sister Mary Francis answered my ring at the door and extended a warm and gracious welcome. But after hearing the purpose of my quest she sadly opined it would not be at all likely for school attendance records from Lillian's years to have been preserved. Another dead end.

It's probable Lillian never had any formal education whatsoever. According to Lillian, whatever book-learning days there may have been beyond Sacred Heart, they were in the hands of private tutors who, she claimed, accompanied her and her mother on trips up and down the California coast. This does not seem to fit the facts. To begin with, since she had later asserted that her father was not a man of means, it seems likely that, when speaking with Reynaud, she was fantasizing or repeating Ziegfeld's press agent's fictionalized biography of her early background.

Reynaud's interview would be the only published information I would ever locate of Lillian's birth and adolescence. Although it probably is safe to take Lillian at her word that she was born in San Francisco and spent her earliest years there, it is probably also safe to conclude that she embellished her background to better suit Reynaud's audience and the mores of the times. For example, was Lenny Kaye right, in his *You Call It Madness*, when he characterized her as nothing more than a street urchin? Since we do have verification of a census taker visiting a Charles and Mary Jacques for the 1900 census, was a little girl denied the recognition of her natural birthright because Mary Brennan and Charles Jacques were never legally married in the first place?

3

Coast to Coast

Six months shy of the 1906 earthquake, Lillian and her mother packed their bags and departed San Francisco, heading east for New York City and all that it might have to offer a pretty young teenager and her ambitious stage-struck mother. Not a complete stranger to the footlights, Lillian had related to Reynaud that she had made her theatrical debut at the age of four, playing the role of Little Eva in *Uncle Tom's Cabin* at the old Central Theatre in San Francisco. We can assume that Ziegfeld, who was present for the interview, made no attempt to correct Lillian's version of her early theatrical beginnings. Had this been the case, Reynaud would most certainly have raised the point in the interview article.

For the next thirty or so years, Lillian's persona would become more a part of the public domain with each passing day. The foibles and triumphs of her personal and professional life ultimately would become an open book for all the wags to draw upon. And this, of course, would make my task of knowing her much easier.

En route to New York and short on funds, mother and daughter made a stopover in Philadelphia, where, according to noted newsman and TV personality Ed Sullivan, Lillian quickly found employment with veteran cafeman Joe Moss. Joe declared the attractive and personable teen was his "biggest drawing card in many a moon." Lillian enjoyed her newfound success as an entertainer, but the lure of New York and a brighter future won out, and the City of Brotherly Love was soon history. Six weeks after arriving in Philadelphia, Lillian and her mother had already started apartment hunting in midtown Manhattan's far west side.

For their initial financial sustenance in New York City, Lillian wisely capitalized on her already extraordinary natural beauty and handily found work as an artists' model. Within a very short period of time, newspaper photographs and clips began to appear describing her as "the girl who possesses the ideal American face." Her circle of friends and acquaintances included such prominent Manhattan artists as James Carroll Beckwith, Frederick Church, J. Wells Champney, Charles Dana Gibson and matinee idol John Barrymore. Elegant men about town drawn to her included Equitable Life Assurance heir James Hazen Hyde, wealthy socialite Harold Frank Henwood, composer Reginald deKoven, and wealthy St. Louis wine merchant and sometime aeronaut Sylvester Louis "Tony" Von Phul. Another notable friend was model/showgirl Evelyn Nesbitt, the infamous "Girl on the Red Velvet Swing" and the central figure in the 1906 Stanford White-Harry Thaw murder case.

A newcomer into this diverse gathering was a beautiful young Denver socialite, Isabelle Patterson Springer. Her husband, John W., was a powerful player in Colorado political and banking circles. John was middle-aged, affable and extremely proud of his blue-blood lineage, traceable to European nobility. The Springers frequently visited New York, and while there made their home base at Park Avenue's ultra-posh Waldorf-Astoria. The couple easily fit into the social whirl of New York's avant-garde population, concentrated mainly in the fashionable East Side Gramercy Park sector. It was a favorite haunt for artists and "the debonair bounders of New York's Bohemia," as described in writer Gene Fowler's *Timber Line*.

Top left: Glamour shot 1910 of Lillian Lorraine at age 17. *Top right:* Early publicity shot, 1907.

Among Isabelle Springer's new friends were several leading artists of the day. One of the more prominent of her husband's peers was Carl Brabant. Attracted by Isabelle's fine facial features and exceptional good looks, Brabant prevailed on John Springer to allow Isabelle to sit for a portrait. John was at first hesitant, then flattered, and finally acquiescing, he agreed and returned alone to Denver. He thereby unknowingly became the catalyst who would set in motion a series of events that would ultimately end in murder and the scandalous breakup of his marriage.

Isabelle chose to remain in New York several weeks beyond completion of the portrait and quickly became a familiar fixture on the party circuit. In all probability it was here at this time and in this setting Isabelle and Lillian met for the first time. It would be only three years hence when the two women would meet again on Isabelle's home turf, Denver. A tragic murder and scandal of major proportions would transform Isabelle Springer's formerly sedate and elegant socialite existence in Denver into a downward spiral of despair, disgrace and exiled anonymity.

4

Broadway Bound

Lillian was beautiful. New York's glitterati knew it. She knew it. Her demeanor, her dress, her public conduct — all bore evidence of a young lady who knew a lot about herself. At the age of four she had already developed a sense of self-assurance and a kinship with the footlights that other aspiring young girls might not achieve until their late teens and beyond. Lillian's sapphire-blue eyes and dark hair with auburn tints framing a flawless peaches-and-cream complexion complemented her quick wit and outgoing personality. She quickly became the darling of New York's portrait artists and news photographers. As the favorite of the New York art colony, especially those involved in creating advertisements, Lillian's fresh-faced, new-kid-on-the-block image, touted the virtues of everything from Coca-Cola to Mme. Claudine's corset stays. Years later, Lillian would exclaim, "I've never worn a corset in my life!" The public reaction to that declaration was not unlike the response, some fifty years down the line, to Marilyn Monroe's still famous quip in response to a reporter's query, "What do you wear to bed, Miss Monroe?" Her reply, "Why, Chanel No. 5, of course!"

Lillian required no hard sell when a young, up-and-coming theatrical agent, Fred McKay, urged her to capitalize on her newfound public image and accept a minor spot in the chorus of composer/producer Gus Edwards's vaudeville revue, *Schoolboys and Girls*, at Willie Hammerstein's Paradise Roof Garden, a music-hall emporium on the northwest corner of 7th Avenue and 42nd Street. She was more than ready.

German-born Gus Edwards was ready, too. He achieved early fame as an organizer of successful vaudeville acts with special emphasis on promoting the talents of young people, which earned him the nickname of "The Star Maker." He gave starts to Eddie Cantor, George Jessel, Georgie Price, Walter Winchell and the Duncan sisters, to name just a few. Edwards composed "The Modern Sandow Girl" for *The Ziegfeld Musical Revue, Follies of 1907*, the first of Ziegfeld's legendary musical extravaganzas. This song was the musical anchor for the show. Edwards owned the House Melodious, which published his songs, as well as the songs of others, in sheet music form.

A spot in Edwards's act would be Lillian's Broadway debut. Less than three years later, Edwards would become composer and publisher of three of Lillian's first major song successes — "By the Light of the Silvery Moon," "Come On and Play Ball with Me," and "Up in My Aeroplane."

Schoolboys and Girls was a fluffy, summertime escapist offering. Theatre critic Robert Spears, in a June 7, 1907, review, described it as "summer fun on the Paradise Roof with a happy blending of good staging and talented young dancers. A pretty young thing in the chorus line, Lillian Lorraine, is a knockout!" A four-word prediction followed: "She should go far!"

A goodly portion of Spears's enthusiasm was devoted to the general ambiance in the rooftop showplace and what he termed "the over-zealous audience that filled every seat and all available standing room as well." He was enthralled with "the beautiful women in their

Top left: White Studios publicity shot, 1909, Groman unidentified production. *Top right:* Lillian Lorraine, headshot from the Shubert production of *The Tourists,* 1907.

colorful straw hats and flowing summer frocks.... The drinks were cool and the air of June-time relaxation complimented what I am happy to call a jolly good vaudeville show. Everyone seems to feel at home at Hammerstein's whether it be on the Paradise Roof or downstairs in the Victoria Theatre auditorium.... Good humor is evident everywhere with everyone connected with the place, from William Hammerstein, standing at the door, to the young and attractive ushers and usherettes." In closing, Spears lauded Edwards for "having taken good care not to allow his actorines and actorettes too much dialogue thereby wisely leaving the overall emphasis on song and dance."

After Lillian had been in the Edwards show for less than a month, agent Fred McKay signed her for a slightly more important part in the Shuberts' *The Gay White Way* starring Blanche Ring (also a McKay property), Jefferson DeAngelis and Alexander Carr. This led to a still larger role in another Shubert musical, *The Orchid,* starring one of the great clowns of vaudeville, Eddie Foy. Even though, through McKay, she had already appeared briefly in two Shubert shows, she had not yet personally met any of the famous Shubert brothers.

Among Lillian's closest friends at the time was blonde and green-eyed model-actress, Rosemary Reilly. It was through Rosemary's boyfriend, another Shubert employee, that she finally gained entree to Lee Shubert, one-third of the famed trio of theatrical producers. A successful audition followed—the final result of which would lead to a small role in *The Tourists* and a summons that would forever change the course of her life.

In the spring of 1907, following successful out-of-town runs in Boston and Philadelphia, Sam and Lee Shubert brought *The Tourists* to New York's elegant Majestic Theatre at 59th Street and Columbus Circle. Richard Golden, the fifty-four-year-old star, was a highly celebrated song and dance comedian, but he was even better known for co-authoring as well as playing the title role in the 1899 comedy sensation, *Jed Prouty. The Tourists* wasn't one of his creations; it was the work of R.H. Burnside (book and lyrics) and Gustave Kerker (music) that delighted audiences throughout the summer and into the fall.

Through her interviews with Shubert, Lillian found herself cast as one of the five daughters of American millionaire Benjamin Blossom, played by the noted character actor Charles W. Meyers. She had little opportunity to shine in such a limited role, but on a cold night in November of 1907, she shined all she needed to catch the eye of a dapper forty-year-old producer seated in the third row center for an evening performance. His name was Florenz Ziegfeld Jr., and he would change her life. In a 1912 *Green Book* interview,

Majestic Theatre *The Tourists* playbill (left); Lillian Lorraine in costume from *The Tourists*, from Stageland, July 1908 (right).

Ziegfeld recalled this particular evening and his first sighting of 15-year-old Lillian:

> She seemed to have that elusive thing we call personality. She was only a minor member of the chorus, a slender slip of a girl, but she had traces of a peculiar beauty. I found out her name, sent for her and engaged her for my next production... her beauty became the talk of New York.....men about town showered her with diamonds.... It was no unusual thing for her to receive flowers, night after night over the footlights, and then upon taking the bouquets to pieces afterwards, to find a diamond ring or a pin fastened to a cluster of American Beauties.

Suddenly, Lillian Lorraine was on a fast track to stardom as Florenz Ziegfeld's first American-born discovery.

5

The Promoter

Twenty-four years prior to Florenz Ziegfeld's discovery of Lillian, he was already a dedicated connoisseur of the fair sex and a superbly intuitive talent scout. While attending a variety show at Rudolph Aronson's Casino Theatre Roof Garden at Broadway and 39th Street in 1893, Ziegfeld found his first potential headline act. The featured attraction was a German-born strongman billed as the Great Sandow, the possessor of a magnificent and perfectly honed physique. Before the evening was out, Flo, sensing star quality and box office magic, offered Sandow a contract for ten percent of the gross receipts of any Ziegfeld production in which he would appear. The two men struck a deal, and as a direct result of Flo's showmanship genius, Sandow quickly became a national sensation on the American vaudeville circuits. A solid bond of personal friendship developed between Flo and his strongman; for the next three years the two men traveled throughout the United States and Canada, achieving substantial financial success. Then, in 1896, for reasons never publicly disclosed, the relationship suddenly soured. Richard Ziegfeld declares the two men were split over Flo's gambling and disputes about money. The producer and his star attraction, going their separate ways, would never meet again.

His success with Sandow made Ziegfeld a familiar figure in New York City's most exclusive restaurants and chic nighteries. One of the most prestigious and popular of these was Rector's, a swank supper club originally opened as a lobster palace. Its prime location was in the true heart of the new and rapidly mushrooming theatre district between 43rd and 44th Streets and Broadway — a site soon to become an internationally known citadel of the entertainment world: Times Square. With its floor-to-ceiling mirrors, Louis XIV ambiance and subdued décor of lush shades of green and gold, Rector's was so "in" that it required no name identification on its exterior façade. No one ever topped George Rector's own colorful description of his pride and joy property: "It is a full-blown avenue of lobsters, champagne and morning afters!" Allen Churchill, in his book *The Great White Way,* recalled the several commonly used phrases so aptly applied to this favorite watering hole for the beautiful people: "It was Broadway's Supreme Court of Triviality, a Cathedral of Froth, Bourse of Gossip and a Clearing House for rumors of the day."

It was at Rector's in mid–1895 that Flo Ziegfeld had the good fortune to make the acquaintance of the vaudeville comic Charles Evans, one half of the most popular comedy duo in the country, Evans & Hoey. At 30, Evans was already a millionaire, appearing in a show authored by the celebrated playwright Charles Hoyt. Flo had the idea to stage a revival of Hoyt's hilarious comedy, *A Parlor Match,* and convinced his newfound friend, Charles Evans, to accompany him on a European business/pleasure jaunt in search of a French female lead for the show. While in London they made contact with Teddy Marks, who at the time was a leading theatrical agent. Marks urged them to visit the Palace Theatre where, he assured them, they would be enthralled by his newest Parisian import, the adorably cute, wasp-waisted Miss Anna Held.

Flo was immediately smitten by the Polish-born, Parisian-raised soubrette. To his well-practiced eyes, Anna exuded a combination of sex and vivacity he was certain would make her nothing short of perfection for one of the leads in *A Parlor Match*. But one major stumbling block had to be overcome — Anna's unfulfilled contractual obligation with Edouard Marchant of the *Folies Bergère* in Paris.

Flo and Evans embarked on a vigorous campaign to convince Anna they held the key to untold riches and theatrical success beyond her fondest dreams. This, they assured her, could be found only in America. It was a non-stop barrage of phone calls and a startling array of expensive gifts, late-night dining in London's most exclusive eateries, and, of course, breathtakingly magnificent floral arrangements. Anna was duly impressed, but what she didn't know was that Charles Evans, not Ziegfeld, was the "sugar daddy" footing the bill.

The motivation for Flo's recruitment campaign was at first strictly professional, but inevita-

Anna Held, early publicity shot, circa 1907 (courtesy Ziegfeld Club Archives).

bly, it developed into a courtship of personal intensity. It made no difference that Anna, though separated, was at the time still married to Spanish émigré Maximo Carrera and that they were the parents of a young daughter, Liane. Years later, commenting on Flo's amorous pursuit of her mother, Liane would write, "Ziegfeld could find little things to do for a woman that would never occur to another man."

Eventually, Flo and Charles had to return to New York, but following a pattern he would never break — telegraphing those who could fulfill his needs until they acquiesced — Flo suffocated Anna with daily telegrams imploring her to sail for New York at the earliest possible date. Finally succumbing, Anna wired back that she would come to the United States under Flo's personal management if he would send by return wire $1,500 with which she could buy out her *Folies Bergère* contract. Once again, Ziegfeld's chance meeting with Charles Evans at Rector's proved to be the pot of gold at the end of the rainbow. Charles put up the $1,500 and Anna was soon sailing westbound across the Atlantic on the S.S. *New York*. She was on her way to promised fame and fortune.

Awaiting Anna at the S.S. *New York*'s arrival pier in Manhattan was a welcoming delegation headed by Flo and his close friends, Diamond Jim Brady and Lillian Russell. She would also be greeted by a 30-piece band plus a full contingent of the New York press. Anna would soon follow in the celebrity footsteps of that other foreign-born Ziegfeld protégée, German strongman Eugene Sandow, but with vastly different results.

Within three months of her arrival on American shores, Anna had filed for and secured a divorce from Maximo Carrera. She and Ziegfeld were now completely free to carry on their romantic liaison in the very public settings of the Atlantic City Boardwalk, Coney Island, and Manhattan's Central Park. They were regularly seen dining and holding hands at Luchow's and Tony Pastor's.

In the spring of 1897, at the New Netherlands Hotel in New York City, Anna and Flo signed a document declaring themselves to be husband and wife. The unorthodox marriage ceremony, witnessed by Diamond Jim Brady and Lillian Russell, was without benefit of clergy. Although they did remain together as man and wife for almost sixteen years, Flo's insatiable lust for gambling, coupled with incessant philandering, put a constant strain on the marriage, which was at best a shaky affair.

Lillian Russell, circa 1899.

From her first days in America, Anna was kept in the public eye by the Ziegfeld publicists. Although reviews of her first Broadway appearance in *A Parlor Match* were less than glowing, the naughty public image nurtured and encouraged by Flo succeeded beyond all expectations. The fantasy invention of daily milk baths was hot copy throughout the nation, and Anna quickly became a firmly established Broadway celebrity.

The *New York Times* said, "As a spectacle Mlle Held is a success, absolute and complete.... However, her abilities are of the most ordinary kind ... her voice is not sweet or very strong and she uses it with no remarkable skill and would not be a sensation at all if the idea had not been forced upon the public mind that she is—naughty."

Flo had a fanatical conviction that the show was paramount, beyond the demands and obligations of married life, and this did not sit well with Anna. Charles Higham, in his biography of Ziegfeld, wrote of an incident which, if true, shockingly lends credence to Ziegfeld's obsessive state of mind.

During rehearsals for *Miss Innocence* in 1908, Higham reports that Anna became pregnant. At first Flo toyed with the idea of replacing Anna with Lillian Lorraine, but in the end ruled out this option. We can only imagine that he considered Lillian too much of a novice and an unknown quantity to carry the show. Ziegfeld, for the sake of the show, insisted Anna must submit to an abortion. Horrified, she refused. They argued. Flo walked out and, within hours, returned with a seedy-looking doctor reeking of alcohol. The arguing continued and Anna, already in a weakened state, collapsed. The men carried her to the dining room table in their Ansonia Hotel suite, chloroformed her and aborted the child. "Later," Higham reports, "Anna recorded in her memoirs that if she had any respect or love for him, it deserted her at that moment."

The source for the abortion story was most probably memoirs purported to have been written by Anna. But Anna's authorship of the memoirs is highly suspect, according to Richard and Paulette Ziegfeld, co-authors of *The Ziegfeld Touch*. Their investigation of the matter tends to point to Anna's daughter, Liane, as the source. Their conclusion is that the memoir titled *Anna Held and Flo Ziegfeld* was in fact a Liane Carrera hoax.

During casting for *Miss Innocence*, Flo selected Lillian for the role of Angele, the ingénue. In doing this, he unknowingly set in motion personal and professional forces that would set Anna and Lillian on an irreversible collision course.

At the close of each theatre season Flo and Anna would usually set sail for Europe, visiting favorite haunts in London, Paris and Madrid. Flo was well known at the gaming tables in Biarritz, Nice and Monte Carlo, always suffering enormous losses. Anna did not share his enthusiasm for games of chance but was the dutiful wife, bailing her husband out of financial difficulty whenever and wherever the need arose.

6

Ill-Fated Triangle

The year was 1909. Thirty-nine-year-old Anna Held and Florenz Ziegfeld, forty-two, had returned from yet another European holiday. *Miss Innocence* would shortly begin a second season, with radiantly youthful, seventeen-year-old Lillian Lorraine gracing the stage of the New York Theatre as one of seven pretty young things in the "Three Weeks with You" production number. Shortly after the re-opening, Ziegfeld decreed that Lillian's status in the show would be elevated to that of a cast principal. Published reports in trade papers for May of 1909 confirmed what most Broadway wags already knew — that Lillian Lorraine was now under exclusive contract and the personal management of Florenz Ziegfeld. The *Miss Innocence* company publicists were directed to put out the word that any interviews with Lillian were to be conducted separate and apart from any of the other girls of the chorus.

Much to Anna's chagrin, Flo selected Lillian to sing the Nora Bayes/Jack Norworth show-stopper "Shine On Harvest Moon." Anna was fully aware that the song was already well on the way to becoming an American classic and not one to be appropriately or comfortably fit

Edna Chase, Blanche West, Dorothy Follis, Lillian Lorraine, Eunice Mackey, Florence Walton, Ruby Lewis, Elise Hamilton, and unidentified — 1909 "phenom class" of *Miss Innocence.*

Top left: Lillian Lorraine in *Miss Innocence*, 1909/1910. *Top right:* Anna Held, Flo Ziegfeld's first (common-law) wife (courtesy Ziegfeld Club Archives). *Bottom left:* A dapper Florenz Ziegfeld, circa 1910.

into her French-accented repertoire. The song had been originally written and introduced by Bayes and Norworth the previous year in *F. Ziegfeld Jr.'s New Musical Review, Follies of 1908*. Flo, Anna and Lillian were most assuredly not a romantic *ménage à trois* but in every respect a potentially lethal triangle of emotional upheaval.

In the continuing campaign to upgrade Lillian's celebrity status, author Eve Golden writes in her *Anna Held and the Birth of Ziegfeld's Broadway,* "Lillian had been given six costume changes and her own dressing room."

Anna was furious. She'd had enough, and she finally confronted Flo with an ultimatum: "Either she goes or I go!" Her scorn was withering and Flo, realizing he was on the short end of the stick, acquiesced. Lillian was removed from the show. Flo's perhaps too easy capitulation to Anna's demand was at least in part attributable to the fact that this second-year run of *Miss Innocence* would shortly come to an end after twenty-three weeks of good box office returns.

Ms. Golden's analysis of Lillian's public appeal was, "She had only minimal singing skills but her looks assured she would never look for work. Lillian Lorraine was one of those women who'd have been considered a great beauty no matter what era she'd been born into. She had ivory-white skin, auburn-colored hair, china blue eyes and sharp, clean-cut features. While Anna was described as pert and cute, Lorraine was a knockout!"

Within one month of her removal from *Miss Innocence*, Lillian was in rehearsals for Ziegfeld's *Follies of 1909*. It was a production most theatre pundits agree was her breakthrough into the ranks of stardom.

7

The Breakthrough: Up, Up and Away — with Sophie

With the probable exception of Ziegfeld himself, no one could have foreseen the long-lasting impact of what had begun as a daring experiment: *The Ziegfeld Musical Review, Follies of 1907*. The "Follies" concept was the brainchild of Anna Held. She had long been encouraging her husband to take a giant step away from promoting run-of-the-mill vaudeville specialty acts and instead import the legendary mystique and glamour of Parisian night life — a *Folies Bergère* for Americans. "Beautiful women, magnificent costumes and opulently imaginative staging, it will sell," she insisted. Anna prevailed, and Ziegfeld became the trail-blazing promoter of a fresh and fascinating concept for the Broadway musical theatre. He explained this concept in detail in an article titled "Why I Produce the Kind of Shows I Do," published in 1912 in *The Green Book Album*:

Why do I produce the kind of shows I do?

Because the public wants them and is willing to pay exceedingly large prices to get the style of entertainment it most desires. I am not in business for my health. I desire to make money. I have always loved the theatre and its people and I have found it a profitable path of endeavor. I can conscientiously state, however, that while I have made enormous sums in producing musical comedies, I have never willingly permitted the use of any line of doubtful meaning or any situation which might appeal to the prurient.

I am aware that the usual mention of a Ziegfeld show is supposed to indicate a certain style of alluring entertainment. It is true that I endeavor to secure the most beautiful women available for my stage production. Mere beauty alone is not sufficient, however. I endeavor to secure clever people, who can act, or do something out of the ordinary. People with personality of an unusual nature can always secure an engagement with me. In some of my choruses, I have employed girls who afterwards became famous as actresses, artists, singers, or married into society.

While I have produced musical plays for many years, the extraordinary success of the "Follies" of the past few years, has broken all records for myself or any other management. The "Follies" has become such an institution, that it is only necessary to make a mere announcement in the cities we play, to insure [*sic*] an attendance that will tax the capacity of the theatre.

The idea of the "Follies" occurred to me in Paris in 1906. Short burlesque on current offerings, together with a song, a dance, a vaudeville attraction and a beautiful chorus, all presented in quick, rapid succession, with constant change of scene, was the scheme which I evolved, after seeing the fragmentary offerings at several of the Parisian theatres devoted to light entertainment. At the time the New York Theatre roof garden had been operated solely as a vaudeville summer establishment. I arranged with Messrs. Klaw and Erlanger to reconstruct the roof of this immense building and we made it look as much as possible like a Parisian garden. Then, to give a foreign atmosphere to the place, I christened it the "Jardin de Paris," or "Garden of Paris."

The first "Follies" production, "The Follies of 1907," was largely an experiment, as few of my associates and advisers believed this essentially Parisian style of entertainment could be made a success in America. It was in three acts and sixteen scenes and there was absolutely no plot to the performance. I secured well-known artists, furnished them with a background of beautiful girls, gorgeously costumed, made frequent changes of scene, and introduced as many catchy musical numbers as possible. It was one continuous maelstrom of mirth, one act following another in such quick succession that the audience had constant variety. Then, to cap the climax, I had the entire chorus of sixty-four beautiful girls, dressed as drummer boys, line up on the stage, all beating snare drums. To the astonishment of the audience, they marched down a flight of steps from the right hand side of the stage, up the right aisle to the rear of the auditorium across the rear of the theatre, and down the other aisle to another flight of steps, and thence to the stage.

This was an innovation and it made a great hit with the audience. The drummer girls were the big feature of "The Follies of 1907."

At the end of the summer season, we had played to such great receipts that we decided to move to the Liberty Theatre and see if New York audiences would continue to appreciate the "Follies" in the winter time. But here again, the wisest managerial calculation proved wrong. New York paid nearly $20,000 a week to see the "Follies" as a roof garden show, but they ignored it absolutely as the attraction at a regular theatre.

I and my associates were in dismay. It looked as though the only possible field for the "Follies" would be as a summer diversion in New York. Mr. Erlanger suggested that we experiment in at least one [other] city and I took "The Follies of 1907" to the National Theatre in Washington late in September. Washington paid nearly $17,000 to see the "Follies" and we sold out at every performance. From that time on, it was the same story in every city on the road....

...I attribute the phenomenal success of these entertainments, the past five years, to the fact that the public had grown sick and tired of the conventional plots of the ordinary musical comedy. For over a generation, librettists have stuck to the same old stories, in which a tenor makes love to a soprano, while there is a low comedian to inject necessary humor. It makes no difference whether the scene is on a mythical island, in some strange kingdom, or amid what surroundings the librettist may choose — the plots are always the same. For this reason I boldly discarded every pretense of plot.

Critics still come to a performance of the "Follies," sit through the sixteen or seventeen scenes carefully, and then go away, only to write the next day that "there is no plot to the show."

Of course there is no plot. That is the secret of my success with the "Follies.".…

...I do not produce the "Follies" to please the critics. I produce these shows for the public. It is quite a custom for the critics to find fault with my productions, but this does not affect the attendance in the least. Once in a while I am fortunate enough, however, to please the critics also.

Professional critical appreciation is naturally very dear to the heart of a producer who, for the last five years, has been accused of exploiting beautiful women merely to draw dollars to the box office. Yet it is not the beautiful women of the "Follies," who draw the audiences. If mere beauty alone could draw an audience, every musical show ever produced would be a success, because it is always possible to engage beautiful girls. The supply seems unlimited. In the big extravaganzas, it is no unusual sight to see three times the number employed in the "Follies" and yet these big extravaganzas do not always succeed. Therefore, the question of beauty alone must be eliminated.

This means that the real success of a production must depend upon the question of whether or not it is clever and entertaining. And to my knowledge, no production of the "Follies" has ever been accused of being dull.

Evidently the public, which pays its good money, believes the same thing, for the profits of the "Follies" in the past five years have been over $700,000. This year will probably be the greatest season this style of entertainment has ever known and the profits are likely to reach the $1,000,000 mark.

That is why I produce the kind of shows I do.

Through one century and into the next, the Ziegfeld trail has led from Broadway to Hollywood, Las Vegas, Atlantic City and beyond. The girls are still beautiful, the costumes, although scantier, are magnificent, and the staging so innovative that Joseph Urban might well be applauding from his grave.

It was June 14, opening night for the 1909 *Follies*. After only two years, the Ziegfeld shows had become a New York institution. Word of mouth, combined with excellent advance notices, guaranteed this third edition of the series would be another blockbuster hit. First-nighters included New York's fun-loving mayor, Jimmy Walker; Diamond Jim Brady and his constant companion, the still beautiful Lillian Russell, music hall queen of the late 1800s; Edward Windsor, Prince of Wales, young and handsome bachelor heir to the British throne; prize

Sheet music cover, "Play That Fandango Rag," 1909 *Follies.*

fighter Jack Dempsey; and the list goes on. Proper attire for the festive evening was white tie and tails for the gentlemen and bustled evening gowns for their bejeweled ladies. The cream of New York society, politicians and sports figures—all gathered together for the show of shows on the roof garden of the New York Theatre — re-christened by Flo "Le Jardin de Paris."

The cast was a constellation of well-established headliners, as well as many newcomers who would be the stars of tomorrow. Husband and wife team of Nora Bayes and Jack Norworth were riding high on the success of their co-written hit, "Shine On, Harvest Moon." Then there were Billy Reeves, Bessie Clayton, Annabelle Whitford and Harry Kelly. Heading the list of new names was, of course, Lillian Lorraine and another vivacious and beautiful youngster named Mae Murray, who had just previously been the White Pirroutte in *Miss Innocence* and, prior to that, Vernon Castle's original dancing partner in the musical comedy *About Town*. Mae Murray continued with the *Follies* until 1916, when Paramount Pictures chieftain Adolph Zukor lured her to Hollywood and a hugely successful career in silent films. She became, in the words of author Eve Golden, "one of the most glamorous and eccentric movie queens of the twenties."

The year 1909 was a particularly eventful one; the *Follies* debut and departure of Sophie Tucker, a woman who would go on to become one of America's best-loved entertainers, occurred within the space of two short months. Tucker had originally been spotted on the vaudeville circuit by Marc Klaw, one-half of the Klaw & Erlanger financial team that backed Ziegfeld. Klaw convinced Ziegfeld to hire Sophie, and at the Atlantic City opening, she was an immediate sensation. In her 1945 autobiography, *Some of These Days* she wrote, "I had them eating right out of my hand!" This instant and spontaneous acclamation proved to be the downfall of her *Follies* career. Sensing the presence of a rival with whom she had no desire to compete, Nora Bayes served notice to Flo that either Sophie Tucker be dismissed from the company or she, Nora, would leave the show. In an effort to placate Bayes, Flo removed Sophie

from six production numbers and left with only one song, "The Jungle Queen." It had been a last-minute insertion into the show, seeking to capitalize on President Theodore Roosevelt's recent and highly publicized African safari. Flo had directed the songwriting team of Harry Smith and Maurice Levi to come up with a light and witty song featuring wild animals and African natives fleeing the fearless and formidable figure of the American president. With a monkey, lion, tiger, ostrich, elephant, giraffe and Sophie in a leopard-skin toga, the number was first performed for the Atlantic City opening, and it was an overwhelmingly successful hit. Weeks later, on Broadway, Roosevelt, already a friend of Flo's, attended the New York premiere and thoroughly enjoyed the parody of his hunting prowess.

Sophie Tucker posing during a brief stint in the 1909 *Follies* in Atlantic City, New Jersey (courtesy Ziegfeld Club Archives).

In her early vaudeville days Sophie had been known as

"a coon shouter," which, according to Jerome J. Wolbert of the University of Chicago Mathematics Department, was "a person who engaged in a form of entertainment arising from black culture that made its way to the white man's world." Coon songs involved whooping and hollering as loudly and creatively as possible. The name "coon" at the time was a commonly used racial slur. This was the milieu in which the up-and-coming Lillian Lorraine found herself: highly charged with flaring political and racial overtones.

In the chronicle of her career, Sophie described the Ziegfeld *Follies* as "a class act. It offered Americans a form of entertainment they could only find in Paris and at ticket prices that lifted the form of variety theatre way out of the vaudeville class." She observed, "Never in my life have I seen so many beautiful girls! Their perfect figures left you breathless. The Queen of the Venuses was Lil-

Nora Bayes, publicity shot from 1909 *Follies* (courtesy Ziegfeld Club Archive).

lian Lorraine, petite and exquisite with her auburn hair, perfect complexion and enormous brown [actually, they were blue] eyes. A girl with looks of that nature didn't have to do anything in order to get the center of the stage....an eyeful of her knocked you cold!" Recalling the Atlantic City opening night, Sophie referred to the black tie audience as "one that puts you on your mettle and challenges you to do your best. It's as stimulating as a new love affair....and, what receptions they gave the stars that night! The house buzzed with enthusiasm when Lillian Lorraine swung out over the audience on a rose covered swing; her beauty dominated the whole stage."

The climax of Nora Bayes's continuing displeasure with Ziegfeld is related in Anthony Slide's *Encyclopedia of Vaudeville*. Flo wanted Nora to dress in tights and sit astride a pink elephant. He warned that her refusal would mean the sequence would go to Lillian Lorraine, "the prettiest little thing I've ever seen!" Nora refused and the threat was made good. With one last tantrum, Bayes quit the show, never again to appear in a Ziegfeld production. Nora's husband, Jack Norworth, singer and songwriter with the *Follies*, exited with her.

Ziegfeld sued for breach of contract and sought an injunction to prevent Nora and her husband from working elsewhere unless he was fairly compensated. In the subsequent court hearing, Nora accused Ziegfeld of partiality to Lillian. Flo's capricious, quite innocent and offhand "prettiest little thing" remark came back to haunt him. While seated in the witness

Sheet music cover of the classic, "By the Light of the Silvery Moon," 1910.

chair he was asked by Nora and Jack Norworth's attorney, William Klein, if he had actually made such a remark. With just a moment of hesitation, he responded, "Well, I guess I might have — because, you know it's true!" Nora further complained that when she was on stage the house lights were full and the air circulation fans were left running. She contended that when Lillian took the stage it was in a spotlight with house lights down and fans turned off. Accord-

Sheet music cover for "Up in My Aeroplane," from the *Follies* of 1909.

ing to the *Morning Telegraph*, "Young Miss Lorraine was present throughout the proceedings, seated demurely and looking very pretty in a conservative but highly stylized navy blue with white trim tailored ensemble." Though she was subpoenaed as a witness for Ziegfeld, and though she might have been the innocent cause of all the trouble, she was never called to the stand. The case dragged on interminably for almost two years and culminated in a permanent injunction prohibiting Bayes and her husband, Jack Norworth, from working with another producer until the termination date of their original contract with Ziegfeld.

Nora's *Follies* replacement, Eva Tanguay, was well aware of the goings-on that had pre-cipitated Nora's departure. She picked up the same cudgels in demanding for herself the one surviving Sophie Tucker number, "The Jungle Queen." This brought to a crashing finale Sophie's very brief stint as a Ziegfeld showgirl. For Ziegfeld, this was a grievous error in judg-ment since Sophie, on her own, went on to become the legendary "last of the red hot mamas."

For her first *Follies*, Lillian was a featured principal in no fewer than nine production numbers, ample evidence of Flo's determination that his newborn star be more than a passing fling. Lillian enjoyed a reunion with her songwriter friend Gus Edwards when she introduced his "Up in My Aeroplane." A picture of loveliness, she captivated the audience as she circled overhead in a double-winged airplane, showering fresh rose petals on the cheering playgoers. The production number was truly a crowd pleaser. Equally important as an enduring symbol of that era was another Gus Edwards-Edward Madden favorite, "By the Light of the Silvery Moon." It was first introduced the prior year by the popular vaudevillian, Georgie Price, and it was Lillian's good fortune to reintroduce it in the *Follies*. According to David Jasen's *Tin Pan Alley*, it was she who helped boost its sheet music sales to what was then a phenomenally staggering figure of well over two million copies.

Variety, the Bible of the show business world, lauded Lillian as "the first real dazzler," and *Vanity Fair* joined the chorus in declaring, "Lillian Lorraine charms the crowds who are lucky enough to get to the Jardin de Paris....she looks as though she has come to stay."

All in all, it was a good year for a youngster from San Francisco who, on one cold and blustery night, had just happened to catch the eye of a certain gentleman seated in the third row center of the Majestic Theatre.

8

Affair of the Necklace

By 1909 Lillian's comings and goings became almost daily grist for the gossip mills. Early on, the usual source was the Ziegfeld public relations machine, but now, more often than not, it was attributable to her own reckless and frenetic lifestyle. Although her professional conduct was not yet in question, often erratic and blatant disregard for convention in her personal life was beginning to create the image of a beautiful seventeen-year-old celebrity whose life was spinning out of control.

On May 23, 1909, the *New York Telegraph* devoted considerable space to a charge by Lillian that her chauffeur, one Charles Brockway, had absconded with a $10,000 diamond necklace. When reached for comment, he expressed surprise and declared his innocence. In spite of this, within hours he was apprehended by law enforcement officials and taken into custody. Uncharacteristically, Lillian avoided the press and refused to discuss the case. On arraignment, Brockway vehemently protested his arrest and insisted the whole affair was nothing more than a minor misunderstanding. "I don't think Miss Lorraine really meant to make a charge against me," he declared. "I have been in her company many times and we've even been together on trips to Atlantic City." His lawyer claimed that Brockway and Lillian had together gone to a loan shop, pawned the necklace and received $2,700.

The story took on a new dimension when the name of Boots Durnell was injected into the scenario. He was a well-known turfman, and when not patronizing the betting windows of the local race tracks, he was regarded as a *bon vivant*. The Durnell and Lorraine paths had crossed several months earlier in Rector's. Friends told Lillian that in addition to knowing a good horse when he saw one, Durnell was no slouch in the terpsichorean department. Soon, Boots and Lillian were the center of attraction, tripping the light fantastic in local night spots.

"L'affaire necklace" began to take on comic overtones when a *Brooklyn Eagle* reporter jokingly suggested the situation was analogous to an incident some 120 years earlier when the ill-fated French Queen Marie Antoinette and Swedish Count Axel Von Fersen had similar problems with a diamond necklace. Two women, driven by emotion and whim to extreme behaviors, Lillian and Marie Antoinette, ultimately both fell victim to scandals involving necklaces. In the case of the queen and the count, however, the repercussions were far more serious: Von Fersen was forced to flee for his life, and the Queen lost her head to the guillotine on the Place de la Concorde. The word now was that Durnell had somehow inveigled Lillian into parting with the necklace to raise bail money for the release of Brockway, who was said to be facing a charge of vehicular homicide.

The fiasco was growing more ridiculous by the day. Finally, Lillian marched herself down to the Jefferson Market Court and withdrew the charges against her hapless ex-chauffeur, but not before announcing to waiting reporters that she did indeed lose the necklace and had withdrawn the charges only to put an end to the ongoing negative publicity. In deference to her wishes, Magistrate Timothy Hornell ordered the release of Brockway.

In *Ziegfeld*, Charles Higham's account of the incident adds spice and sex to the story.

Higham alleges Lillian was involved in an unsavory sexual relationship with Brockway, and that one night when she was out on the town, dancing with Flo at Rector's, Boots Durnell cut in on them, offering to teach Lillian one of the latest dance crazes. High-stepping her away from Flo, Boots told her that unless she could produce $3,000, Brockway would be arrested on a bad debt charge. Durnell's chauffeur drove her back to her hotel, where she was confronted by four men, one of whom presented himself as a police officer, who showed her a warrant for Brockway's arrest. She handed over the necklace to the three men, who immediately disappeared and pawned it. The police officer and his warrant, it turned out, were fakes. Lillian, furious at being taken, called a detective friend, Val O'Farrell, and had Brockway recharged. "Police traced him to a 54th Street rooming house," wrote Higham, "where, it was discovered, he was operating as a clairvoyant." Brockway was arrested, tried, found guilty and subsequently served time in the New York City Tombs. Higham did not tell us why the lovely Miss Lillian was not upset with Durnell's role in the scam. Maybe she was.

Flo's propensity for romantic dalliances had long been a plague on his already unraveling marriage to Anna Held — and now, with his increasing public attention to Lillian, tongues began to wag. The *New York Review* on August 27, 1910, was the first of the metropolitan New York dailies to take aim and fire:

> Is there any element of secrecy in Mr. Ziegfeld's attentions to a certain young woman who he has done his best to raise to theatrical prominence? How can any mystery exist when said young woman has openly used Mrs. Ziegfeld's (Anna Held) limousine and has accompanied Mrs. Ziegfeld's husband to first nights and has been seen with him in many public places, including moonlight trips in roller chairs on the Atlantic City Boardwalk? Mr. Ziegfeld's declarations of personal rectitude given out in Paris are laughable, indeed, in light of the fact that he even permitted the Other Woman to see him off on the boat when he left American shores to explain it all to dear Anna who at the time was sojourning on the French Riviera.

It should be noted that the *New York Review* was owned by Ziegfeld's arch rivals, the Messrs. J.J. and Lee Shubert. This, plus the fact that Flo had lured Lillian from the Shubert chorus organization two years previously, accounts for an absence of objectivity whenever the *Review* published gossip concerning Flo Ziegfeld and his new love interest.

9

Enter Bert Williams, Fanny Brice and the Blonde Venus

In the early months of 1910, Ziegfeld introduced and promoted a talented quartet of *Follies* newcomers: Bert Williams and Fanny Brice, each already a seasoned comedian; Vera Maxwell, a graduate of choreographer Ned Wayburn's musical reviews; and Lillian Lorraine. They would be the stars of the 1910 *Follies* in which Lillian burst on the scene as a personality to be reckoned with for twenty years to come.

Born in St. Croix in the Virgin Islands in 1874, Williams was the first man of color to be signed for a principal role in any Broadway show. He had come up through the ranks in early vaudeville, and from his first appearance in the *Follies of 1910*, it was widely predicted he had the talent to be one of the greatest comedians the musical comedy stage had ever produced. Reasonably well-educated, Williams was trained first as a civil engineer, but by 1895, at the age of twenty-one, he was already following his natural bent. He was touring with a musical group. Ziegfeld came to know Williams for his excellent sense of timing, pantomime and mimicry, honed during his many years on the road as a minstrel and vaudevillian. Commenting on his close association with the song "Nobody," Williams said, "Before I got through with it I could have wished that both the author of the words and the assembler of the tune had been strangled to death. I had to sing it, and month after month, I tried to drop it and sing something new, but I could get nothing to replace it and, besides, the audiences seemed to want nothing else."

The soulful melody and plaintiff lyrics depicting a shuffling black hobo with no hope for the future would be forever linked to the Williams persona. It was his signature song.

> I ain't ever done nothing to nobody
>   I ain't ever done nothing to nobody, no time
>   And until I get something from somebody, sometime
>   I'll never do nothing for nobody.

Bert's tenure with Ziegfeld was of nine years' duration, longer than any other *Follies* principal. He was a loner, though, often depressed and seldom mixing with fellow cast members except Leon Errol, who was his sidekick in many of his comedic skits, and Lillian Lorraine, with whom he developed a platonic friendship. Press reports in 1912 headlined the news that Bert and Lillian were leaving Ziegfeld and would be appearing together in a London music hall revue, but this did not come to pass. However, Bert did finally leave the *Follies* in 1919 and started touring nationally as a featured solo artist.

Williams's Achilles heel was that "old devil, John Barleycorn"; additionally, he was a heavy chain smoker. While performing at Detroit's Shubert Theatre, he collapsed on stage, and after a short hospitalization, he canceled his remaining tour bookings. He returned to New York, where at the relatively young age of forty-eight, he died on March 4, 1922 — only three years after leaving the Ziegfeld fold.

* * *

Fanny Brice began her spectacular show business career at the age of fourteen, singing for nickels and dimes in amateur contests at Keeney's Theatre in Brooklyn, New York. Even as a child, Fanny knew her calling in life would be centered in the world of entertainment.

Her brother, Lew Brice, in an interview with Fanny's oral biographer, Norman Karkov, reminisced he couldn't recall a time when Fanny wasn't performing. "Her first, her very first act," he said, "was a show she conceived, produced, directed and starred in. Admission was a penny and the theatre was a shed behind the tenement in which we lived."

From her first appearance at Frank Keeney's, she began winning one amateur contest after another. Inasmuch as she had never been a model student, quitting school was not a difficult option. This enabled her to pursue a full-time career in show business. Before long she was earning between sixty and seventy dollars a week in prize money. When performing would hit a slow period, Fanny had no qualms about working as a ticket taker or a floor sweeper in a movie house at the corner of Third Avenue and 83rd Street in Manhattan.

First *Follies* principal actor of color, Bert Williams (courtesy Ziegfeld Club Archives).

Fanny's professional breakthrough into authentic burlesque and vaudeville came about as a result of another contest win at Hurtig & Seamon's Harlem Opera House. It was at this stage in her career she discarded the family name of Borach, which she felt did not have the desired charismatic ring. She adopted the name "Brice," taken from a longtime Irish friend of the family.

Fanny's lifelong nemesis was her inability to master the art of the dance. She often indulged in self-ridicule, insisting she was the "proverbial two-left-feet girl." In spite of this, Joe Hurtig hired her for the chorus line in his new show, *Transatlantic Burlesque*. One special night, Fanny lucked out. The leading lady was indisposed; Fanny took over and she was a sensation. Consequently, Hurtig extended her contract for the remainder of the season. Seeking to broaden her horizons, Fanny arranged to meet with another producer, Max Spiegel, who was casting for a new musical comedy, *College Girl*. For her audition she sought the help of a friend, a little-known but up-and-coming songwriter by the name of Irving Berlin. He played two original compositions for her — "Sadie Salome" and "Grizzly Bear." The Salome number he sang with a Yiddish accent. "That's it!" Fanny gleefully declared. The following day, she auditioned with Berlin's version of Salome and had Spiegel convulsed with laughter. On the spot, he signed her to an eight-year contract with the guarantee her salary would be close to $100 per week — at the end of the eighth year.

Broadway's Columbia Theatre was the first house constructed primarily for burlesque and it was here, in *College Girl*, that Ziegfeld first set eyes on Fanny. He was immediately struck by her flawless sense of timing and the rapid-fire delivery of heavily slanted ethnic comedy. Her routine was hilarious and for the audience, it was non-stop laughter. Before leaving his seat, Flo was determined to break the Spiegel contract and secure Fanny for the 1910 *Follies*. Turning his lawyers loose, Ziegfeld quickly found a loophole. Spiegel had signed her when she was seventeen — a minor. That was all Flo needed, and the deal was done! Fanny had finally realized her childhood dream. Eddie Cantor recalled, "Fanny had never wanted anything so much as to work for the Great Glorifier." In Cantor's 1934 *Ziegfeld, The Great Glorifier*, he said, "[Fanny is] not only the best comedienne of her time, but I will say Fanny is among the first three funny women of the world, at any time."

Fanny was now in the big time and literally overnight exposed to a strange and entirely new world of class and elegance. The transition from vaudeville comedienne did not come easy. One of the first of her newfound friends was Lillian Lorraine, and that first year, while on national road tours, Flo arranged for the two women to be roommates. Herb Goldman, in his *Fanny Brice: The Original Funny Girl*, writes, "Clothes were all important to the women in show business. Audiences wanted to see gorgeous costumes, but where Sophie Tucker and others knew the value of a great stage wardrobe, Fanny thought of clothing as an emblem of success ... she wore clothes that loudly proclaimed her new status in the Broadway theatre." Goldman relates one incident in which Fanny, on a dinner date with Flo and Lillian, "wore an ostentatious, sapphire blue satin dress, an orange coat, and a big blue hat topped with a vegetable garden and ostrich plume. The ensemble did little more than make Ziegfeld lose his appetite. He finally asked Lillian to show Fanny how to dress, giving her $250 for that purpose." Lillian was already an acknowl-

Comedienne Fanny Brice, in her first *Follies*, 1910 (courtesy Ziegfeld Club Archives).

edged fashion trend-setter both on and off the stage. In later years, Fanny recalled, "Lillian never wore any makeup. Everything about her was glowing and fresh, a sort of blooming newness like you see in a very young girl. Her hair rolled off her forehead in simple lines and swung into lovely folds. I've never seen a woman in the theatre with so little artificiality."

Following Ziegfeld's death in 1932, and the end of any authentic *Ziegfeld Follies*, Fanny transferred her comedic talents to the then most popular medium of audio communication, the radio. She achieved phenomenal success as Baby Snooks, a role she developed in 1934. For observers with long memories, the Baby Snooks character was a veiled take-off from a Gus Edwards/Lillian Lorraine "Kidland" production number in the 1910 *Follies*.

In spite of her revitalized and newfound success on the airwaves, Fanny did not forsake live theatre or films. Her Hollywood career, with only two exceptions, was limited mostly to cameo roles in big, splashy MGM musicals and comedy short subjects.

Fanny was married three times. After suffering a debilitating stroke, she died in 1951 at the age of fifty-nine, one of the truly great comediennes of the twentieth century.

* * *

Vera Maxwell was a native New Yorker, star-struck at an early age and possessing an inborn love for dance. Forbidden by her father from taking dancing lessons, she taught herself in front of the full-length mirror in her bedroom. He mother was an alcoholic and a difficult personality, at best, and offered but scant support for Vera's show-business aspirations. By the age of fourteen, her father had lost his fortune, plunging the family into near poverty, and Vera struck out on her own — dancing in a traveling show across America. This led to a part in a featured act with Ned Wayburn, then to the touring company of the 1909 *Follies* and ultimately to the 1910 *Follies* on Broadway, where she remained until 1916.

With the other three members of the quartet, Williams, Brice and Lorraine, Vera became a sensation. Her extraordinarily beautiful features prompted Ziegfeld to proclaim her the "Blonde Venus." The following year he dubbed Lillian Lorraine "the most beautiful woman in the world." Both tag lines would remain with the two women throughout their long professional careers. After leaving the *Follies* in 1916, Vera teamed with Wallace McCutcheon, performing exhibition ballroom dancing throughout the United States and abroad. She opened and operated several cafés and nightclubs before retiring from show business completely in 1928.

Vera Maxwell never married, but she was close to her goddaughter Vera Ialenti, who recently donated a large and priceless pastel portrait of her godmother to the National Ziegfeld Club.

Long an active participant in the charitable endeavors of the New York chapter of the Ziegfeld Club, Vera Maxwell was sick for years before she died of throat cancer at the age of 58 in 1950. Until the very end, she was never aware of the nature of her illness.

That Bert Williams, Fanny Brice, Vera Maxwell and Lillian Lorraine went on to greater fame as solo artists beyond the *Follies* once again affirmed Ziegfeld's stature as Broadway's premier showman and star-maker.

10

The Ziegfeld Follies of 1910— Atlantic City and Beyond

Ziegfeld previewed all of his *Follies* at Nixon's Apollo Theatre in Atlantic City before taking them to Philadelphia for polishing and finally to Broadway. Atlantic City in 1910 was a far cry from today's East Coast Mecca of gambling casinos, posh hotels and musical extravaganzas. It was a small and sleepy hideaway coastal resort for the rich and famous, situated midway between Washington and New York. Atlantic City's main attractions were the celebrated boardwalk and miles of magnificent white sand beaches. It was here that the 1910 edition of the *Ziegfeld Follies* made its pre-Broadway debut.

Public relations hype was the order of the day. Ziegfeld and his publicists scored a major coup when Lillian Lorraine and six of the Annette Kellermann chorus girls descended on the nearby sedate Gold Coast community of Deal. The September 1910 *Green Book* published a full account of the beach invasion and subsequent frolic. Under the headline, "Follies Girls at Deal," the story read as follows:

Flo Ziegfeld nearly caused a panic at Deal Beach on the Jersey Coast one day this summer by interpolating Lillian Lorraine and six of his Annette Kellermann girls in the cast that regularly gathers to bathe in front of the Deal Casino. The majority of the patrons of the Deal Beach & Pool Club are wealthy merchants and their families who live in the magnificent homes that dot the coastline for miles. The younger men of this set are among the most reliable patrons of Ziegfeld's *Jardin de Paris*; although until his arrival with his troupe of scantily clad Diving Venuses, they had been compelled to worship from afar.

Behind the invasion, of course, was a carefully laid press agent's plot but the effect of the *Follies* girls, clad in their clinging costumes of silk, upon the scions of New York's wealthiest bankers was so disconcerting that the press agent also lost his head and the proposed story vanished somewhere in the surf.

Miss Lorraine, the leading woman of the *Follies* company, was dressed for the occasion in a bathing suit of white that never was intended for publication or general circulation. Behind her trouped the Annette Kellermanns and, as they dashed towards the surf, fully fifty young men disporting themselves in the high tide, nearly swallowed the Atlantic Ocean. Miss Lorraine, who is an excellent swimmer, plunged into the surf and the Diving Venuses went tumbling right after her. When they all emerged a moment later and walked back toward the crowd that lined the beach, a gasp went up that might have been heard above the roar of the ocean from Asbury to Seabright.

Immediately thereafter, the Ziegfeld troupe departed. It is not recorded that they left by request. It is merely suggested that opposition was too strong from the heiresses accustomed to having all of the attention during their morning dip. The spectacle also was too much for the male patrons. Bathing for the day was suspended. Hereafter, when Ziegfeld desires to wash his flock, he will either have to hire his own ocean or outfit his charges with bloomers or hoop skirts.

Although it was a financial smash, the 1910 *Follies* opened on Broadway to less than glowing notices. One reviewer wrote, "The stupid visual imitations of a number of public persons served no useful or other purpose. They are simply in very bad taste.... The return of [Theodore] Roosevelt with which the piece ends, was simply stupid."

In the *Metropolitan,* highly respected critics Edwards and Smith referred to the three previous editions as "almost ranking with Manhattan Beach and Coney Island as places to go. They travestied the events of the year and were models of stage management, but that was all in the past." The widely-read twosome had more harsh words for this latest edition of the *Follies.* "It is a burlesque show not worth the price of admission." Of Lillian, now in her second edition, they scathingly wrote, "Even her loveliness does not make up for her inability to act or sing." Of Bert Williams they were somewhat kinder but certainly not glowing: "He was as good as ever but has nothing new to offer." Summing up, they declared, "It is a pity!"

Never overlooking an opportunity to lampoon their nemesis, the Shubert Brothers' *New York Review,* commenting on Flo's publicity hype for the *Follies'* mid-western premier, unsheathed a quiver of poisoned darts, declaring, "If Chicago really likes the *Follies of 1910* as well as Mr. Ziegfeld's press agents insist that it does, then indeed the taste of that city has sunk to a sub-cellar level of meretricious tawdriness. This piece, in common with all the Ziegfeld shows, is nothing more than an appeal to common lewdness. It is an exhibition of female nakedness allied to salacious suggestion. To the healthy mind, it is revolting. To the nostrils of the clean it bears a stench more nauseating than that arising from the Stockyards, of which Chicago is so justifiably proud."

Lillian Lorraine with child actors from "Kidland" production number, 1910 *Follies* (courtesy Ziegfeld Club Archives).

A far friendlier reception awaited the company on its arrival in the City of Brotherly Love. That city's leading dispenser of news, the *Philadelphia Inquirer,* was lavish in its praise when it declared, "It may be asserted without fear of contradiction, that this latest review is the best of the series and that its stay here (at Chestnut Street Opera House) will be rewarded with large audiences.... It is a marvel of harmony, color and texture.... There were so many good things during the evening that to particularize would take up columns of space...."

On June 21 the *Follies of 1910* opened on Broadway at the *Jardin de Paris* to a wildly enthusiastic packed house. Fanny Brice, the irrepressible crowd-pleaser, stopped the show with her ragtime presentation of Marion Cook and Joe Jordan's "Lovey Joe" and was further rewarded with twelve encores. The spontaneously enthusiastic reception given Bert Williams was a clear and positive signal of audience acceptance of a major black artist in an otherwise all-white cast of performers.

Gerald Bordman, in his *American Musical Theatre,* lauded Fanny and Bert as "probably

the two finest performers Ziegfeld ever presented. Both had an almost incredible range, from hilarious ethnic travesty to broad, human pathos."

Lillian Lorraine was described as "a vision of beauty as she was carried out over the audience on a trolley fixed across the roof. One woman was heard to exclaim that Lillian's exquisitely embroidered black silk hose must have cost as much as $50!" Actually, Ziegfeld bought the stockings in Paris for $275.

Lillian's standout song success was "Swing Me High, Swing Me Low," the sheet music of which became an immediate best seller. From the same show, she scored again with another popular favorite, her Lake Killarney number, Gus Edwards's "Sweet Kitty Bellairs." Audiences ooed and ahed over Lillian's spectacular entrance, in which she rose through the stage flooring on a specially constructed elevator lift and then rode up the center aisle on a live pony. Capitalizing on the Deal beach incident, in the Diving Venuses production number, Lillian and comedian Billy Reeves scored heavily when

Top: Lillian Lorraine as the Hen Pheasant with unidentified actor, 1910 *Follies* (courtesy Ziegfeld Club Archives). ***Bottom right:*** "Kidland" production number publicity shot, *Follies* of 1910 (courtesy Ziegfeld Club Archives).

Sheet music cover, "Kidland," 1910 *Follies*.

he jumped to the stage from an elevated parquet seat and grabbed Lillian, with both ending up in a water tank.

The financial success of the 1910 edition was in keeping with returns from the previous three years. Flo's gamble on Anna Held's brainchild *Folies Bergère* concept had paid off, and he was now widely acknowledged to be the master entrepreneur of the Great White Way. His reckless disregard for soaring production costs and an almost studied absence of financial

AT HOME

CHESTNUT STREET OPERA HOUSE

NOVEMBER 21ˢᵀ TO DECEMBER 17ᵀᴴ
Including Thanksgiving Week

Ziegfeld Revue
Follies of 1910

SURPASSES ALL MUSICAL ENTERTAINMENTS
I HAVE EVER PRODUCED

F. ZIEGFELD, JR.

SECURE SEATS EARLY
MATINEES WED. & SAT. EXTRA MAT. THANKSGIVING DAY

Lillian Lorraine

Top left: Ziegfeld gave Lillian Lorraine this $275 pair of Parisian-made stockings in 1910 (courtesy Ziegfeld Club Archives). *Top right:* Eddie Cantor headshot, *Follies* of 1918 (courtesy Ziegfeld Club Archives). *Bottom:* Postcard from *Ziegfeld Revue, Follies* of 1910, Chestnut Street Opera House.

restraint was staggering; but the finished product was always a dazzling display of ostentatious opulence and feminine pulchritude that has never been surpassed on any Broadway stage. In his *Ziegfeld, The Great Glorifier,* Eddie Cantor perhaps summed it up best: "When Flo put on a show, Art triumphed and Business held the bag. Sometimes there were process servers in front of the New Amsterdam, posing as ticket speculators because Ziggy had an almost pathological disregard for piling up debts. He never really intended to deprive any creditors and paid when he could."

Sheet music cover, "Swing Me High, Swing Me Low," 1910 *Follies.*

With respect to Flo's lavish lifestyle, Cantor continued, "He was always putting on a show and no emperor entertained his guests more generously than Ziggy did his public. He knew that the flower of Art was an exotic plant that flourishes best in luxurious soil. He erred on the side of having too much rather than too little. Throughout his entire show business career, Flo never settled for anything less than the best."

Bon vivant and man about town, Flo was fortunate that when in need he could turn to his coterie of well-heeled friends. They were primarily people of not only means but equally important, influence in a variety of high places. His financial backers ran the gamut from the immensely wealthy railroad equipment tycoon James Buchanan ("Diamond Jim") Brady to the shadowy and unsavory crime lord Waxy Gordon. Additionally, always on call were longtime business associates and theatre chain magnates, Marc Klaw, Abe Erlanger and Charles Dillingham. Not to be overlooked were longtime friends Charles Evans and the legendary queen of the music halls, beautiful Lillian Russell.

All told, 1910 was a banner year for Florenz Ziegfeld. Bert Williams, Fanny Brice, Vera Maxwell and Lillian Lorraine were firmly established as major stars of the Broadway musical theatre. Now in its fourth year, the *Ziegfeld Follies* would become a must-see Broadway institution for the next 21 years, to be terminated only by Ziegfeld's death in 1932.

11

Enter Nanny Johnson,
My Mother

By 1910, Flo was hopelessly and madly in love with seventeen-year-old Lillian Lorraine and sorely in need of some womanly advice and counsel. He turned to an old friend and confidante, the matronly and beloved stage comedienne May Irwin. May's tremendous popularity had carried over from one century to the next, and in 1912 she was the first prominent American stage personality to appear in the then infant medium of silent motion pictures.

Flo was a frequent house guest at May's summer home in the Thousand Islands, and it was on one of those visits he agonized with May over Lillian's continuing refusals to take seriously his proposals of marriage and, equally frustrating, his inability to contain Lillian's unbridled and frenetic passion for life on the fast track. She was carousing with a class of people he considered, at best, unacceptable. He also complained she was becoming much too familiar a fixture in late-night haunts along the Rialto. Flo was truly at his wits' end and enthusiastically reacted to May's suggestion that a compatible companion be found, a catalyst to serve as a moderating, steadying influence on his young protégé.

May had, that very summer, employed as seasonal help in her island sanctuary a young, strikingly pretty Swedish immigrant by the name of Nanny Johnson. The personable, petite and blue-eyed brunette quickly endeared herself to May and her husband and manager, Kurt Eisenfeldt. So it should come as no surprise that May soon envisioned in Nanny the ideal solution to Flo's emotional dilemma. Here was a high-spirited and fun-loving girl, literally fresh off the farm, who didn't smoke, drink, curse or carouse, the exact antithesis of Lillian Lorraine. May wasted no time in promoting Nanny as the hoped-for stabilizing influence on Flo's new love interest.

Never one to procrastinate, May set into motion a series of personal encounters that would have a lasting effect on the lives of the three protagonists of this book — Lillian Lorraine, Florenz Ziegfeld and my mother, Nanny Johnson. Over ninety years later it is not incorrect to include a fourth component with that trio— this writer.

May Irwin's introduction of my mother to Flo and eventually, through him, to Lillian, provided the incentive and personal motivation for the relating of this story. My objective was now clear — to bring these people back to life and let them live again in the readers' minds. I determined if I could somehow, with help from the relatively small number of surviving Ziegfeld players, dig deep enough, I could theoretically restore flesh and bones to a select number of men and women long ago consigned to history as phantom figures from an era of long-forgotten lost splendor, and, at same time, know more about the duality of my mother's early life.

The setting was the Irwin summer retreat. Ziegfeld was again a house guest. Following one of May's gourmet supper parties, she, Flo, and husband Kurt moved to an outside veranda for after-dinner coffee, liquors and, for Flo, a cigar. The server was Nanny Johnson. Flo,

Top left: Nanny Johnson (Elsie Hanson) portrait, upon first arrival to the U.S. from Sweden, 1903. *Top right:* May Irwin, the 20th century vaudeville headliner and confidante of Flo Ziegfeld, and one-time employer, as well, of Nanny Johnson.

always the connoisseur of feminine beauty, was not unaware of Mother's wholesome and attractive physical attributes. Also, one can safely surmise he would not have been oblivious to the strong physical resemblance between Lillian and this Swedish damsel now offering a sugar for his demitasse.

My mother recalled she was still standing, listening intently, as Flo eloquently proposed that she consider joining his theatrical family as a personal assistant to his newest star creation, Lillian Lorraine. Mother, very much an adventuresome free spirit, was sorely tempted, but images of family and friends back in Sweden came sharply into focus. Their dire warnings of the pitfalls and temptations with which she would be confronted could not easily be dismissed, nor could she erase the teachings of her strict Lutheran upbringing, coupled with the Old Country belief that anything connected with "theatre" was something all decent and God-fearing people should avoid.

Flo was at his persuasive best as he proffered a new life of adventure, glamour and excitement. She would be free of the confines which had governed her life in Sweden and even, although to a lesser extent, here in America. Sensing Mother's mental turmoil, May gently interjected herself into the conversation and suggested, "Nanny need not make an on-the-spot decision and should perhaps take some time to reflect on Mr. Ziegfeld's proposition." Mother gratefully thanked them both and retired to do just that.

Over the next several weeks, among her mostly young Scandinavian friends, Mother began to drop hints that she was having second thoughts about what course of action she should follow. Unanimously, they urged her to forget her misgivings and take the job. The last obstacle to her weakened resistance was removed after a heart-to-heart private discussion with May's husband. Kurt Eisenfeldt liked my mother and was eager to help her improve her station in life. As devoted wives are wont to do, May confided to Kurt the details of her privileged conversation with Flo and, according to Mother's taped reminiscences, Kurt in turn shared them with her.

Two months later, at another Irwin dinner party, this time in May's New York City home, Ziegfeld was again a dinner guest. Before the evening was over he once more approached

Mother, suggesting a get-to-know-each-other meeting with Lillian at her suite in the Ansonia. Within days the meeting took place. The two young women hit it off immediately. Overnight, a little country farm girl from Sweden was catapulted into a lifestyle of sophistication and show business glitz —far beyond the stretches of anything she had ever known.

Thus began a nearly ten-year relationship in which the two young women, physically almost identical, would become as close as sisters. First as a maid, then secretary, and finally confidante and best friend, Mother was an integral part of Lillian's life during the Ziegfeld years and even — in absentia — at the time of Lillian's tragic decline and death.

Nanny Johnson came from Hallaryd, a small farming hamlet in south central Sweden. Both parents passed away when she was still a child. Foster parents were good to her, but dreams persisted of a far-off land where "streets are paved with gold." Still in her teens, Mother made it known she wanted to visit her older sister, Sigrid, who was already happily settled in the Massachusetts town of Winchester. Hallaryd locals shook their heads and cautioned, "America is the gateway to Hell!" Not one to be easily discouraged, Mother and a school chum, Ruth Carlson, purchased steerage class steamship passage for $2.00 and set sail from Gothenburg to New York. Eleven days later they disembarked at the Castle Gardens Immigration Processing Center at the southern tip of Manhattan Island. Within two days, Mother was reunited with Sigrid in Winchester.

Lillian Lorraine (left), Elsie (in Lillian's outfit, right), French Lick Spa, 1912.

All of a sudden there were no more farm chores. Everything had changed — now there were new friends, party socials and visits to nearby Boston. It didn't take long for Mother, on a restrictive visitor's visa, to decide her next trip to America would be on a permanent immigration visa. This she accomplished when she and Ruth returned in 1907. Rather than again take up residence in New England, for a little bit more of the same in terms of environment and social circles, Mother decided to remain in New York City and seek employment.

In her audiotaped reminiscences she explained her decision to forego a return to Winchester. It was a move to assert her independence from the influence and strictures of a Scandinavian culture she had chosen to leave behind. To live in Winchester would not achieve that purpose — even in the local Lutheran church, the service was still conducted in the Swedish language. How could she become "Americanized" under those conditions? The answer was,

Ziegfeld Follies of 1910, "Teddy Roosevelt" production number, Lillian Lorraine garbed in American flag (courtesy Ziegfeld Club Archives).

of course, that she could not. She therefore elected to make her stand in New York City, which, even at that time, was known as the melting pot of the world.

In those days there was a considerable demand for foreign domestic help, more commonly known as "house servants." Consequently, there were many ethnic employment offices anxious to supply that demand. Mother applied to one of those agencies and quickly found kitchen work at St. Joseph's Roman Catholic Seminary in Yonkers, a Westchester County suburb of New York City. Several weeks later, she moved on to work as a domestic for the Hammerstein family at their estate in Oyster Bay, Long Island. It was there she attracted the attention of May Irwin, and eventually Ziegfeld and Lillian.

The hectic and glamorous pace of life in Lillian's shadow exceeded all expectations. Mother's baptism of fire on the Ziegfeld payroll came early on. Lillian and Flo had gotten into a violent exchange of epithets. The intensity and volatility of their relationship was occasionally reflected in public displays of mutual recriminations and ill-tempered histrionics. Flo's artistic flare-ups were not uncommon, and as for Lillian, Marjorie Farnsworth, in her *Ziegfeld Follies*, wrote, "Lillian's laughter at the world was the laughter of compulsive despair. She had a mania for speed and gay parties and a reckless insouciance that sometime bordered on psychotic."

Lillian fled this latest altercation to Boston with a former society matron, retained by Ziegfeld as a chaperone/companion prior to Mother's coming on the scene. Unfortunately, that matron's zest for high living and "John Barleycorn" was comparable to Lillian's. In recalling the incident, Mother jokingly explained how she got drawn into it:

We lived in the Ansonia, as did Flo and his wife, Anna Held. Soon after Lillian had left for Boston, Flo called and asked if I knew where she was and when I told him he firmly directed me to go up to Boston and bring her back. Well, seven hours later I got off a train at Boston's South Station and taxied over to the Hotel Touraine. Lillian's so-called chaperone was drunk and after a lot of cajoling on my part, Lillian agreed to return with me to New York. Flo sent the chaperone packing, and I ended up with one more job title.

One of Mother's most indelible impressions from those early days was an occasion where she came face to face with President Theodore Roosevelt. Never content to rest on his laurels, Flo sought to recapture the success of his Teddy Roosevelt parody in the 1909 *Follies*. For 1910, in a production number titled "The Return of Roosevelt and his Rough Riders," popular comic Harry Watson was cast as the president and Lillian was the Goddess of Liberty. As was the case the previous year, the president was again in attendance on opening night at the New York Theatre. Flo and Lillian had on at least one occasion visited at the president's Sagamore Hill home, so it wasn't too much of a surprise to hear he was in the audience. At intermission Flo told Lillian the president would be coming backstage after the closing curtain. Mother was in the dressing room with Lillian, and I can still hear the excitement in her voice when she speaks on the tape, "You can't imagine how thrilled I was over the prospect of seeing the great American president. When he came to the door with Flo, I almost collapsed! I left the three of them alone but, my goodness, he was a handsome hulk of a man — much more attractive than his photographs."

12

PR Woes and the Denver Caper

After four successive hit seasons, the *Ziegfeld Follies* was literally a household name, as was its founder and namesake. Ziegfeld's publicists made certain there would not be many days go by without some newsprint mention of their boss, his shows or one of his star creations.

Three blocks south of Flo's New York Theatre office, his arch rival Shubert Brothers were ensconced in their own headquarters on the third floor the magnificent 45th Street Lyceum Theatre. Lee and J.J. Shubert held the upper hand over Ziegfeld in the field of public relations—namely through their ownership of the widely read theatrical trade paper, the *New York Review*. On the other hand, Ziegfield was the undisputed master of Broadway extravaganzas, surpassing the Shubert endeavors season after season. The Shuberts' ongoing campaign of harassment and negative hyperbole against Ziegfeld had been refueled this year when Flo announced that Anna Held would soon embark on a "farewell tour" and, at its completion, retire in Europe. The *Review* had this comment: "Anna Held has been Ziegfeld's one excuse for his managerial existence and, because of his alliance with Anna, personal as well as business, he has been permitted to gamble on credit and run up debts which he would subsequently repudiate by stopping payment on settlement cheques....Is Ziegfeld going to let his meal ticket get away from him? Oh, no! Miss Held will not retire—not if Ziegfeld can help it."

Within days of that story, the Shuberts had another field day when Flo's brother, William, was arrested in Chicago and charged with obtaining money under false pretenses from playwright Myron Fagan. It was alleged that William had swindled Fagan out of $1,500. William was released on bail furnished by his father, F. Ziegfeld Sr., and since there was no follow-up media coverage on the story, it can be assumed a quiet settlement was effected.

The extended national tour of the 1910 *Follies* opened at Denver's Broadway Theatre, directly across from the Brown Palace Hotel, in the early spring of 1911. The original New York cast was on hand, headed by Lillian, Fanny Brice, Bert Williams, Bessie McCoy and the Dolly Sisters. Gene Fowler recalled opening night as "a gala occasion for Denver society." Among the groups occupying boxes in the grand show palace was the foursome of Mr. and Mrs. John Springer and two friends, Frank Loveland and New York/Denver socialite, Frank Henwood.

Mrs. Springer is the same Isabelle Springer referred to earlier as an acquaintance of Lillian's, going back to the 1906–07 Gramercy Park days of artists and models. Reporting on the opening night festive air, a *Denver Post* society writer described Isabelle as "breathtakingly lovely in a lace tea gown covered by an opera coat of mousseline and edged with maribou." Of John Springer, the columnist wrote, "he was so entranced by the beautiful girls on the stage that he had to be pushed back in his seat for fear of him falling out of the box."

The day after the opening, Sylvester Louis (Tony) Von Phul, a well-known wine merchant, playboy and balloonist, arrived in Denver and checked himself into the Brown Palace. In his *Ziegfeld* biography, Charles Higham suggests that both Frank Henwood and Tony Von

Phul had previously been recipients of Lillian's "favors" in New York City. In addition, as it was later revealed, Isabelle, while married to John Springer, had also been involved in illicit affairs with Henwood and Von Phul. Also, it became known Isabelle had foolishly written self-incriminating love letters to Von Phul, who was allegedly blackmailing her for their return.

Isabel asked Henwood to intercede, and try to get the letters back from Von Phul. Von Phul refused, and over a two-day period Henwood and Von Phul had several heated discussions regarding the matter. On the afternoon of May 23, in Von Phul's hotel room, there was a physical confrontation: Von Phul struck Henwood with a shoe tree and further threatened him with a revolver to his stomach. Later that evening, Henwood, seething with anger, went to police headquarters and reported the incident to Denver Police Chief Armstrong. At the outset he declined to provide specific names, but when pressed, he revealed Isabelle Springer was the *femme fatale* in the middle. He urged the chief to run Von Phul out of town before he would be forced to kill him or before the situation got so out of hand that John Springer would learn of his wife's infidelities. Chief Armstrong refused to take any action unless Henwood would agree to file a formal charge of assault. Henwood declined, walked to a gun shop and purchased a .38 caliber revolver.

Follies showgirl Eleanor Dana O'Connell, 1920 (courtesy Ziegfeld Club Archives).

The following evening, May 24, Henwood invited the Springers to his box at the Orpheum Theatre. Von Phul, on the same evening, was enjoying the *Follies* at the Broadway. Shortly after 11:00 p.m. Henwood left the Springers at their suite in the Brown Palace and went downstairs to the bar with the revolver concealed in his hip pocket. Von Phul entered the bar one-half hour later and sidled up to Henwood. Angry words were again exchanged, culminating in Von Phul's driving a short blow to Henwood's chin, knocking him to the floor. There is much blurred and conflicting testimony as to exactly what next transpired. However, witnesses claim Henwood pulled out his revolver and fired, not stopping until the gun cylinder was empty. Other patrons tried to dodge the flying bullets but two of the onlookers could not escape. George Copeland, owner of the Copeland Sampling Works in Victor, Colorado, was shot just below the knee and unexpectedly died the next day following an operation on his leg, which had become infected. Tony Von Phul was immediately removed to St. Luke's Hospital and even at the point of death would only say, "I hold no grudge against Henwood. He was a good sport but I didn't think he'd let a woman come between us." His reference to "a woman" gave birth to a rumor that the female in question must have been a Follies girl. Von Phul died the following morning at eleven o'clock. Isabelle Springer's name never passed his lips.

Ziegfeld and his fellow New Yorkers awoke the next morning, May 26, to a glaring *New York Review* headline proclaiming, "Lillian Lorraine Was The Actress in Denver Shooting Scrap." The sub-heading went on to say, "Follies Prima Donna Had Been Much In The Company of Von Phul & Henwood Before The Former Was Killed." Buried in small-type text: "A prominent society woman of the Denver social set figured with Lorraine in the shooting fray." Charles Higham's account of the affair has Ziegfeld taking the first available train for Denver, removing Lillian from the scene and entraining to Atlantic City and rehearsals for the 1911 *Follies.*

Murder charges were preferred against Henwood, and four days later, Gene Fowler reported that "the first bombshell directly involving the Springers was exploded in the form of a divorce petition filed against Isabelle." The news media was in a feeding frenzy as rumors began to fly that Springer's divorce action was based on charges of illicit intimacy between his wife and the deceased Von Phul. It was further revealed that "a cache of love letters substantiating the affair was found among the dead man's personal effects." These letters, of course, were Isabel's.

Denver's politically ambitious district attorney elected to prosecute Henwood by first charging him with the death of Copeland, the innocent bystander hit by a stray bullet, and holding the Von Phul murder charge in abeyance. He was obviously trying to shield the influential John Springer by excluding all testimony pertaining to Isabelle's extramarital activities with Von Phul. Eventually, following two lengthy and tedious trials, Henwood was twice found guilty and sentenced to prison for life. After serving ten years he was freed on parole but within a few months was again behind bars, convicted of a sex felony in New Mexico, where he died in 1929.

An exhaustive search of the grand jury proceedings and local newspaper files revealed that at no time was the name of Lillian Lorraine introduced into the judicial proceedings. Needless to say, there was no retraction of the Lorraine involvement allegation from Shubert's *New York Review.* There is even some doubt as to the veracity of the report concerning Ziegfeld's train trip to Denver.

Isabelle Springer, disgraced and ostracized from the Denver social scene, fled to New York City and the familiar haunts of her earlier escapades. She sought and found employment as an artists' model. Her new lifestyle eventually led her down the path of alcoholism and drug addiction. No longer a belle of the ball, deserted by her former Gramercy Park gay blades, she lapsed into abject poverty. Gene Fowler reported that she died in 1922 at the age of sixty-three in New York City's Welfare Hospital on Blackwell's Island. The cause of death was listed as "narcotics." Fowler's report continued, "An actress who had once been a Springer houseguest in Denver read of her death in a small newspaper notice. The actress claimed the body and saved it from burial in a Potters' Field free grave." It was none other than Lillian Lorraine who reclaimed Isabel. This comes to us from Eleanor Dana O'Connell, the late president of the Ziegfeld Club, who said, "It was common knowledge amongst our girls that Lillian, without a doubt, was Gene Fowler's unnamed actress." This was a grim foreboding of the identical incident that would occur 33 years later, when my mother reclaimed Lillian Lorraine from another potter's field only five miles from the Blackwell Island site.

Dana O'Connell wasn't through yet. With a toss of her well-coifed blonde curls, a twinkle in her brilliant blue eyes, and the suggestion of a sly, I've-got-a-secret smile, she glanced around as if to see if anyone else could hear her. She looked me squarely in the eyes, lowered her voice, and continued, "I'll tell you something else the Shuberts never got hold of. Lillian's close friend Lu Martell told me, even though all of the *Follies* company was housed in local Denver hotels, and even though Ziegfeld's publicists hushed it up, it was an open secret that Lillian had been the Springers' houseguest up to the night Tony Von Phul was shot."

13

Anna-Liane-Flo: The Ansonia

Mr. and Mrs. Florenz Ziegfeld (Anna Held) were among the original tenants of the magnificent, baroque Ansonia apartment/hotel located at 73rd Street and Broadway. The Ansonia, completed in 1903, was—and still is—one of New York City's finest beaux arts architectural gems. It has twenty-five hundred rooms, sixteen floors, and magnificently sculpted cupolas on each of its four corners. The Ansonia was home to many of the most illustrious figures in the world of arts and entertainment and is richly deserving of the Landmarks Preservation Commission's descriptive phrase, "Joyous exuberance profiled against the sky."

It was the year of our entry into the new millennium when a call came into the Ziegfeld Club office from that very same Ansonia. The caller was Alexandra Yu, president of Film History Limited, and quite coincidentally a thirty-year resident of the Ansonia. Alexandra is a woman of considerable charm, seemingly boundless energy and an acutely inquisitive mind, and is presently writing the history of twenty-five of her favorite elegant New York City landmarks, the Ansonia being one of them.

"Mr. Hanson," she began, "I need some help with photographs and personal anecdotes...." To my amazement and delight, the subjects of her search were Flo Ziegfeld, Anna Held, Lillian Lorraine and Billie Burke. Within minutes I was on the receiving end of a personal invitation to inspect the former Ziegfeld Ansonia apartment, number 8–41. The Lorraine suite, smaller in size, was only two flights up the handsome green marble staircase—apartment 10–41. I couldn't believe my good fortune, but here it was, a golden opportunity to feast my eyes on the fabled inner sanctum of Florenz Ziegfeld. The entire building was in the throes of a complete restoration, yet the indomitable Mrs. Yu had somehow inveigled permission from the contractors for us to tour the apartment.

Within twenty-four hours of Alexandra's phone call, she and I were ascending to the Ansonia's 8th floor in one of the six well-preserved, original and ornately opulent elevators. Entering the apartment I caught my breath at the first sighting, and for the next twenty minutes the muffled exclamations of wonder were too profuse to number.

The all-white entry is a miniature rotunda with a frescoed domed ceiling supported by six columns with Ionic capitals. Its hardwood floor is dappled with inlaid and delicately subdued floral designs. The plaster-of-Paris ceiling moldings are again subdued and tastefully classic. Five handsomely paneled doors lead from the receiving rotunda into the private living quarters—bedrooms, parlors, an oak-paneled library and dining salon, a music room, and finally, a large kitchen and butler's pantry—more than adequate for large-scale entertaining. The focal point of the exquisite music room is six stately French doors overlooking the convergence triangle of Broadway and 72nd Street with its glass-canopied subway entrance dating back to the turn of the century.

As we left the apartment I half whispered to Alexandra, "Oh, if only those walls could talk!" Her eyes rolled upward before meeting my gaze. She smiled knowingly, and responded, "Yes, indeed! I know exactly what you're thinking!" If I interpret the look she gave me, I don't

Postcard of Ansonia Apartment Hotel, New York.

think I am in error assuming we both had in mind confirmation or repudiation of the 1908 Anna Held abortion allegation.

Oh, were it only possible to have seen the apartment that Lillian and my mother lived in. But is wasn't to be so, nor is it now.

Thanks to Liane Carrera's 1954 *Anna Held and Flo Ziegfeld*, there is yet another story

Ansonia Hotel, early residence of Ziegfeld, Anna Held, Lillian Lorraine and Elsie, 73rd Street and Broadway, New York City (photograph taken by author circa 1990).

which those Ansonia walls could affirm or deny. Liane recounts an incident which, if true, may well have been the proverbial and final straw that broke the camel's back — specifically, her mother's marriage to Flo Ziegfeld.

When Anna Held divorced Maximo Carrera, their daughter, Liane, was passed off to a Spanish convent boarding school. In 1911, Liane was living with Flo and Anna in their luxurious thirteen-room Ansonia apartment.

One Sunday afternoon, Flo, Anna and Liane had been out for a drive in Flo's chauffeured Bentley limousine. Upon their return to the Ansonia, Flo announced he would take Anna's poodle for a Broadway promenade. Anna returned to the apartment, but Liane chose to accompany her stepfather. They had walked no more than a block when Flo suggested Liane return to the Ansonia. Several minutes later, Flo, too, had returned, but he didn't notice Liane lingering in one of the lobby alcoves. She observed the elevator which he had just entered was not stopping at their eighth floor. It was continuing on to the tenth floor. Never overly fond of her stepfather, Liane wasted no time in reporting to her mother that Flo had left her and was now "seeing that nasty woman on the 10th floor!" Anna queried, "What nasty woman?" and Liane countered, "Why, that chorus girl who was your understudy; the one who wears the same kind of dress as you on the stage, except it was white." Anna responded with another question. "How do you know that woman is her?"

Precocious Liane had all the answers. "From the servants, of course. She is awful and they all feel sorry for you."

Anna snapped back, "The servants are meddling in things that are none of their business. I don't believe a word of what you just said."

Undaunted, Liane exclaimed, "Maman, if you don't believe me, come and see for yourself."

In her book, Liane tells us that ordinarily Anna would have had only contempt for this affair between Flo and her understudy, but the idea that he had settled Lillian (and incidentally my mother as well) in the same apartment building was too much.

During one of Anna's extensive national road tours, Flo had indeed installed Lillian and my mother in a five-room suite on the Ansonia's tenth floor. Flo would later declare that by keeping Lillian in close proximity, it might serve as a modifier to her flamboyant lifestyle and continuing association with individuals not to his liking.

In her written account, Liane continued:

We went up two flights of stairs, and, sure enough, the girl had managed to get a suite on the tenth floor that corresponded to our own.... Mother told me to run back down and wait for her in front of our apartment door.... She could hear laughter...then, Flo appeared in the doorway holding the dog on its leash.... With him was that woman, 'en deshabille!' He gave her a prolonged kiss and promised to come back soon...then, he turned and found he was facing Mother...she poured out her disgust to the very dregs as Flo very bravely slipped away.

With reference to this incident, Eve Golden opines, "The only accounts of Anna's discovery of Lillian's Ansonia apartment are in Liane Carrera's various memoirs and must therefore be viewed with appropriate caution."

For whatever reason, Anna had had enough and, according to Liane, returned to their own apartment and packed some bags. One hour later she and Liane were checking into the Savoy Hotel. The next morning, Flo sought them out, pleading with Anna to consider what it would do to his reputation if the press learned the true reason for their separation. Anna did return to the Ansonia, but only long enough to have her trunks packed and bid a few farewells. Prior to embarking for Europe on the French liner, *La Savoie*, Anna tearfully confided to her close friend, Irene Smith, "I am leaving Flo to Heaven and Lillian Lorraine!"

14

Canadian Getaway

From his first visit to May Irwin's Thousand Island summer retreat, Ziegfeld set his mind to one day acquiring his own north country hideaway. In 1908, he did locate and purchase a remote Canadian campsite in New Brunswick, about 160 miles north of Quebec City.

The 1911 *Follies* at the Jardin de Paris ran from late June to early September. At the close of the New York run, Flo, Lillian and my mother entrained for a one-week holiday at Kit Clarke's Island Canadian camp. With them was Flo's close friend and fishing companion, Henry J. Siegel, co-owner of Siegel & Cooper, at the time the largest women's dry goods department store in New York City. Siegel's unique blend of expertise in both merchandising and artistry led him to a special appreciation for architecture which was further shaped by his heavy involvement in the 1893 Chicago World's Fair. Employing the architectural firm DeLemos & Cordes (who would later design Macy's), Siegel oversaw the construction of what would become a stunning example of the American beaux-arts style which still stands to this day on Sixth Avenue and 18th Street.

Mother recalled:

The Canadian camp was not an easy place to reach. At one point we all had to wear high leather boots for trudging through some pretty dense woodland that eventually led into the campsite. Neither Lillian, myself or Henry Siegel's companion brought any makeup or dressy clothing so it was a wonderfully relaxing week. All we did was swim, fish, play cards and indulge ourselves with some pretty tasty food cooked up by the Canadian guides who had accompanied us. Lillian and I shared a cabin sparsely furnished with only two cots, two chairs, a table and one kerosene lamp." After a brief second of hesitation she continued in firm tones, "No matter what some people might have thought, Flo Ziegfeld never came near our cabin any night during that entire week." Sharing a room with Lillian was the exception to the general rule. Mother always was given her own room at the Ansonia and private accommodations on the road.

It was during the Canadian vacation that Lillian confided to Mother, "You know, Nanny, Flo has been after me for more than two years to get married. In a way, I do love him, but he is twenty-five years older than I am and that makes him old enough to be the father I never had. He's done more for me than any other man in my life, but I can't bring myself to use that as an excuse for marriage. It just wouldn't work."

In her taped memoirs, Mother recalled an incident from some months earlier that she felt had a direct bearing on the subject of Lillian and Flo's personal relationship:

Lillian was scheduled for a publicity photo sitting with the White Studios in midtown Manhattan on Fifth Avenue. Flo insisted on coming along with us and patiently sat through the two-hour session, occasionally offering advice or a suggestion as to how a certain shot might be set up. Lillian had several costume changes and when the photographers were finished, she got back into her street clothes and was ready to leave when Flo said something to the effect [of], "Hold on, Lillian. I want a shot of us together." I think Flo was trying to impress her with the seriousness of his marital intentions. Lillian is pictured, seated demurely on a beautiful, silk damask, gold-gilt love seat with Flo behind her, arms outstretched in an obviously protective, "this is my property" stance. The two of them looked for all the world like a blissfully happy married couple.

Top: Florenz Ziegfeld, Lillian Lorraine, Nanny Johnson, Henry Siegel and friends in repose on Kit Clark's Island, 1912. *Above left:* Close friends Lillian and Nanny at Camp Ziegfeld, 1912. *Above right:* Elsie, Lillian and Canadian guides on picnic excursion, Kit Clark's Island, 1912.

Sheet music cover, "Bumble Bee," 1911 *Follies.*

That particular photograph has been published many times over the years, and it should be noted here that never before or after is there any recorded evidence of Florenz Ziegfeld posing for a formal studio portrait with one of his stars.

With some humor, Mother related another incident at the camp when Ziegfeld and Lillian got into a tiff because she wouldn't camp out overnight in a tent. "She had always been terrified

of bugs and spiders, so in spite of all Flo's teasing, she just wouldn't give in."

Along the Rialto it had long been common knowledge that Flo and Lillian were engaged in a serious and long-term relationship, but Lillian never agreed to making it completely monogamous. Much to Flo's dismay, whenever they had a spat Lillian would accept invitations from other admirers — a practice which continued throughout their tempestuous four-year tryst. In his *Scandals and Follies*, Lee Davis writes, "By 1911, [Ziegfeld] was insanely in love with Lillian Lorraine and would remain so, to one degree or another, for the rest of his life, despite her erratic, irresponsible, often senseless behavior, her multiple marriages to other men, his own two marriages, and his need for all his adult life to sleep with the best of the beauties he hired."

As they had done the previous two years, for the second week of their vacation break, Flo, Lillian and Mother spent

Top: Nanny Johnson at Ziegfeld's Camp, Kit Clark's Island, Canada, 1912. *Bottom:* Lillian and Nanny on horseback, French Lick Springs Spa, Indiana, 1912.

Top left: A rare example of Florenz Ziegfeld in formal offstage pose with one of his actresses, Lillian Lorraine, 1910. This outfit can also be seen worn by Nanny Johnson in photograph taken at French Lick Spa, which speaks to the closeness of two women. *Top right:* Lillian Lorraine out "stumping" at Ziegfeld Camp, 1912.

time at Indiana's prestigious French Lick Spa and Resort. It was another period of rest and relaxation, with mineral baths and horseback riding being the order of the day. (This latter activity was a first for Mother, but before the week was out, she had become an accomplished equestrienne.)

Returning to New York, Ziegfeld took the 1911 *Follies* on the road, with the first stop at Chicago's Colonial Theatre. Once again, this time by their own choice, Lillian and Fanny Brice were roommates, and now Fanny happily realized that her social standing was on the upswing, as evidenced by invitations to join Flo and Lillian for dinner and evenings on the town. According to a Fanny Brice biographer, Herb Goldman, it was in Chicago that Fanny had the first serious sexual affair since her ill-fated 1909 marriage to Frank White, a barbershop concessionaire in upstate New York. The new man in Fanny's life was Fred Gresheimer, a tall and handsome Adonis. Throughout the Chicago run, Freddy was Fanny's constant suitor, and when the company did finally depart for New York, Fred continued his courtship via the U.S. mails. Fanny foolishly shared the content of Freddy's letters of endearment with Lillian, who, after seeing a photograph of Freddy in bathing attire, began to exhibit more than a passing interest in Fanny's new beau. Soon, Freddy arrived in New York, and it wasn't too long thereafter that he and Lillian discovered their mutual attraction for each other. It was inevitable that the jilted Fanny would exact her revenge over what she considered to be Lillian's betrayal of their friendship.

The *New York Review* on June 8, 1911, carried a front-page story with headlines declaring, "Lillian Lorraine and Fanny Brice Fight on Roof Stage. Patrons in Front Heard Signs of the Lively Scrimmages."

"When the scrimmage was ended," the story went on to say, "Miss Lorraine's raiment was in rags, her face and her hair bore sundry marks of the conflict, and she had reached a state of hysteria which made it necessary for her to be carried bodily to her dressing room."

and friends
Long Beach, Long Island, New York
August 19th 1912

Top: Beach frolicking (left to right): unidentified companion, Henry Siegel, Nanny Johnson, Lillian Lorraine, and Flo Ziegfeld, Long Beach, Long Island, New York. *Bottom:* Lillian Lorraine primping under scrutiny of Nanny Johnson, French Lick Spa, 1912.

Top left: Equestrienne Lillian Lorraine, French Lick Springs, 1912. *Top right:* Morning "spruce-up" — Lillian Lorraine with Nanny Johnson, Kit Clark's Island, 1912. *Bottom left:* Style setter Lillian Lorraine, French Lick, 1912. *Bottom right:* Lillian lapping up some sun, Lake Edward, Kit Clark's Island, 1912.

It was reported the altercation began when Fanny, accidentally or on purpose — we don't know — stepped on the train of Lillian's dress as she was about to make her stage entrance. Lillian retaliated with an expletive which triggered Fanny into high gear. Witnesses said that Lillian's wardrobe was "in a state of demolition," and they unanimously declared Fanny to be the victor. Herb Goldman's take on the incident was that there had been bad blood between the two stars for some time and that in all likelihood the fracas had been precipitated, at least in part, by the Freddy Gresheimer situation. Lillian absented herself from the show, declaring her defection to be a two-week vacation. *Variety* reported on July 29 that her two-week leave

Top: Nanny Johnson (white hat), Lillian Lorraine (bottle to mouth) and friends "cutting up" with the guides, Ziegfeld Camp, 1912. *Bottom:* "Dining Room," Ziegfeld Camp, 1912.

had expired and no one really expected to see her back in the *Follies*. Her songs and dance numbers were already being distributed among other principals. Lillian, however, did return and played out the full season of the 1911 edition. Her major song hit, "Row, Row, Row," was a one million-plus best seller, but it was Bert Williams and newcomer Leon Errol who walked away with the critics' kudos for their Grand Central Terminal skit.

By the time work began on the 1912 *Follies*, Lillian's increasingly bizarre behavior was causing friction between Ziegfeld and Abe Erlanger, one of his chief financial backers. Erlanger,

Top: The rejuvenating atmosphere of Lake Edward, Ziegfeld Camp, 1912. *Bottom:* Lillian Lorraine admirers, Long Beach, Long Island, New York, 1915.

who, it so happened, was a friend and confidante of Anna Held, despised Lillian for her role as the other woman in Flo and Anna's marital woes. He served notice on Flo that he would not tolerate any shenanigans from Lillian and that if she did not shape up, he demanded that she be fired from the company.

The crisis came to a head, indirectly, in connection with a new song that had been written for Lillian by the twenty-six-year-old composer Gene Buck and his collaborator, Dave Stamper. The song title was "Daddy Has a Sweetheart and Mother Is Her Name." During a dress rehearsal run-through of the number, Lillian failed to appear on stage as scheduled. Gleefully seizing the opportunity to make good on his threat, Erlanger sharply queried Julian Mitchell as to Lillian's whereabouts. Mitchell was responsible for staging the production and told Erlanger that Lillian was having a problem with a costume change. Erlanger rose up from his seat and shouted, "Tell her she's through and the song as well!" In spite of his prestige, his background of over eighty successes in Broadway musical theatre, and his close relationship with Ziegfeld spanning almost two decades, Mitchell was unable to reverse Erlanger's decision to dismiss Lillian.

Lillian departed the *Follies* in the company of the song's composer, Gene Buck. They took Buck's song to William Hammerstein, who happily embraced the twosome and the song. He immediately signed them for his new music hall review at his 42nd Street Victoria Theatre of the Varieties, a premium vaudeville emporium. In addition to his contribution of music, Gene Buck took over set and costume design for Lillian's numbers. Her act was an unqualified hit, running for seven weeks, and "Daddy Has a Sweetheart" became a sheet music sensation with sales of over one million copies. Almost equal in popularity and sales was Lillian's rendition of "Some Boy," another of the Buck/Stamper collaborations.

How did she do it—make the jump, literally overnight, to vaudeville headliner from *Follies* principal? How did she perform her songs—with animation? Standing still? Was it that her style was unique for the times? The December 25, 1912, issue of the *New York Telegraph* relates it all: "Miss Lorraine first has a song that the title on the program says is 'Want to Go Into Opera,' in which she describes herself as a girl with a mission, who, not having received an operatic contract, is prepared to entertain in vaudeville, and she entertains when she is just explaining her purpose. Her second song, sung in a gown designed on the old-fashioned hoop skirt plan, is a gem of sentiment, in which Miss Lorraine charmingly emphasizes that 'Daddy Has a Sweetheart and Mother Is Her Name.' It is in this style of song that Miss Lorraine undoubtedly excels."

> Daddy has a sweetheart and he's head and heels in love,
>   I have often watched him kiss her,
>   While the moon peeped from above,
>   Each day he loves her more and more,
>   And she loves him the same,
>   Daddy has a sweetheart and Mother is her name.
> — The Penn Music Company, 1912

The *New York Telegraph* article continued, "Following this she has a costume that rather indicates she might be an Indian maiden. She has one song, 'Some Boy,' that seems hardly in keeping with her personality. It is more fitting to one of the coon shouting comediennes, but it does deserve to show that Miss Lorraine has versatility."

> Take it from me that I'm crazy 'bout my boy, He brings me joy,
>   He is so grand, and Got a heart that's full of sympathy, And it's
>   beating all the time for me, When he looks into my eyes, I'm
>   hypnotized, He kisses me like the hero in Three Weeks, It
>   burns my cheeks, And when he speaks 'bout Lovin,' baby, then

Left: Autographed picture to "Nanie" [*sic*] (Elsie) Johnson from *Follies* dancer Ann Pennington. *Right:* Songwriter and Lorraine collaborator Gene Buck (courtesy Ziegfeld Club Archives).

> I'm gone, that's all, For his lovin' ways I'm bound to fall, That
> man of mine he's cert'nly some boy.
> — The Penn Music Company, 1912

"Her fourth number," the *New Telegraph* reports, "is 'Row, Row, Row,' in which she appears as a Summer girl, but such a Summer girl as has only been seen in the pictures of artists until Miss Lorraine flashed upon the gaze of Hammerstein audiences."

> Young Johnnie Jones he had a cute little boat,
>   And all the girlies he would take for a float.
>   He had girlies on the shore,
>   Sweet little peaches by the score,
>   But Johnnie was a Weisenheimer you know,
>   His steady girl was Flo,
>   And every Sunday afternoon,
>   She'd jump in his boat and they would spoon.
>   And then he'd row, row, row,
>   Way up the River he would row, row, row,
>   A hug he'd give her,
>   Then he'd kiss her now and then,
>   She would tell him when,
>   He'd fool around and fool around and then they'd kiss again,
>   And then he'd row, row, row a little further he would row,
>   Oh, oh, oh,
>   Then he'd drop both his oars,
>   Take a few more encores and then he'd row, row, row.
>   — Harry Von Tilzer Publishing Company

The *New York Telegraph* concluded, "Miss Lorraine, when first she walks to the footlights, instantly wins her audience. This favor she retains by her grace, the sweetness of her voice, and an interesting repertoire that, with the exception of one exceedingly popular number, was written especially to suit her personality." Consider the frolicsome, witty, and promiscuously suggestive lyrics from "Row, Row, Row." Do they not seem to have been written for Lillian?

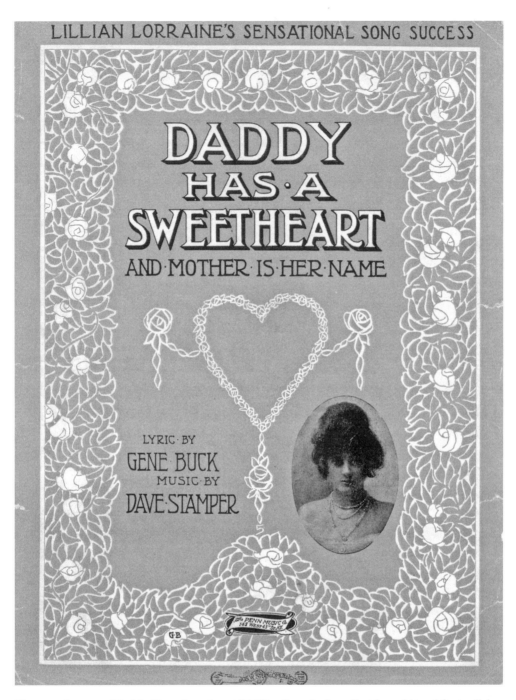

Sheet music cover, "Daddy Has a Sweetheart," Lillian Lorraine's earliest huge hit and first collaboration with lyricist Gene Buck, 1910.

"Her costumes, too, are gorgeously becoming," the *New York Telegraph* reported. The *New York Times* said, "A feature of her act, not to be passed over lightly, was the gowns worn by Miss Lorraine. There was a new one for each song and the wonder was how she managed to get into such elaborate costumes in the almost unbelievable short time between the last chorus of one song and the 'vamp' of the next."

There was, however, another side of the coin. *Variety* staff writer Dash, on December 27,

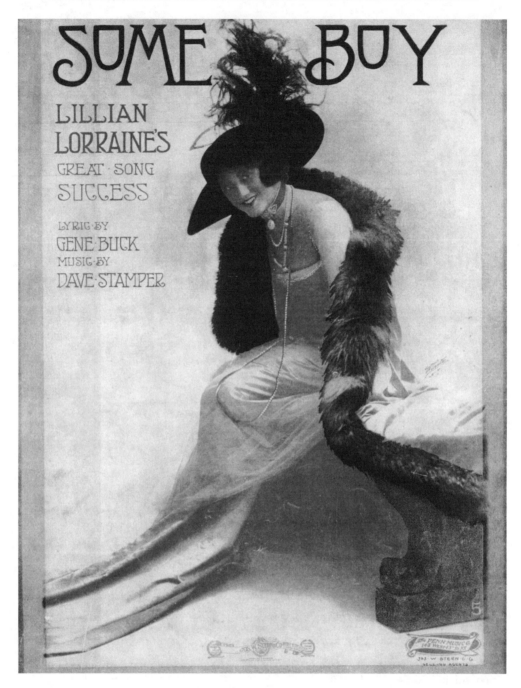

Sheet music cover for "Some Boy" (1912).

said, "The house did big business. Lillian was given about one-half the credit while the popular juggling act Ching Ling Foo took down the rest. There is little question that some of the business will trace to the singer and there are many who will undoubtedly go in to see her again this week, for she has clothes for the women and 'cooch' for the men." (According to Niva Inc.'s communications website, "*Cooch* is a variant of hoochie coochie, the term for pseudo-

Sheet music cover, "Row, Row, Row," 1912 *Follies.*

Oriental, sexually suggestive dancing; the term originated at the 1893 Chicago fair, probably as an English corruption of a foreign term.") In this review *Variety* castigates her lack of professionalism, and at the same time praises her performance. Early in the review Dash says, "She acts as though she takes but little interest in her work and it must be so or she would be more the finished performer by this time." One might assume, however, that Lillian was bored

Left: Lillian Lorraine from *Over the River,* in which she starred with Eddie Foy at the Globe Theatre, 1912 (courtesy Ziegfeld Club Archives). *Right:* Lillian Lorraine in full-length fashion shot, 1912.

with the material at hand, since at no other time has there been a published description of such demeanor in her stage career.

Taking particular note of her wardrobe, *Variety* said:

> The yellow gown and a big black picture hat are the features of the first number. Not to be overlooked is the opera cape nonchalantly thrown over the piano and on which all women's eyes are riveted during the entire song. In a crinoline gown, the singer looks dainty and sweet and the song does the rest. In the third number, Miss Lorraine kicks up the big fuss. It is something about my man who kisses me like a lover — not on the cheek and there's an 'oh' and an 'ah' in it which when combined with a 'cooch' movement would make the girl in blue turn over. It had the house at Hammerstein's ohing and ahing right along with her. This 'cooch' alone could have gotten two more hold-over weeks at Hammerstein's and perhaps draw an offer from the Palace in London.

This should have come as no surprise to Mr. Dash, for Lillian was well-practiced in the art of "cooching." She had been using "cooch" techniques throughout most of her stage career.

Lillian and Gene Buck's successes at Hammerstein's Music Hall did not go unnoticed in the Ziegfeld camp. Flo, who had reluctantly agreed to Erlanger's termination of Lillian and Buck, was elated as Erlanger, with a dollar sign in both his eyes, was forced to eat crow and rehire the twosome at the close of their Hammerstein engagement.

Lillian's return to the Ziegfeld fold was short-lived. On March 26, 1912, she stunned her Broadway cronies with the announcement of her marriage to Fred Gresheimer, Fanny Brice's ex-love interest. At the time, she was co-starring with comedian Eddie Foy in the Ziegfeld-Charles Dillingham production of *Over the River* at the Globe Theatre.

The wedding news was broken by Lillian in a telephone call to a friendly reporter with the *New York Evening World.* The following day's headline declared, "Lillian Lorraine Phones She's Wed to a Millionaire. She's Quit the Stage." Once again ready to pounce, Shubert's *New*

Sheet music cover, "Ring Ting a Ling," from Charlie Dillingham's *Over the River* with Eddie Foy, 1912.

York Review gave the story an entirely different slant: "Ziegfeld Faints at News of His Star's Wedding!"

Lillian, at 20, was still in many ways a little girl. This is blatantly evident when one reads the transcript of her conversation with the *Evening World* reporter:

Mr. Gresheimer was introduced to me last summer in Atlantic City...he was in his bathing suit and

looked perfectly grand...he offered to teach me how to swim and in five minutes he had me pad-
dling around like a little tadpole...he had proposed to me every week, either by mail, telephone or
telegraph. Yesterday we were lunching with a friend of mine, Mrs. Lancaster, and Freddy suggested
we jump over to Jersey City, get a license and have it over with.... He just happened to catch me in
the mood and off we went.

"I suppose Mr. Gresheimer has lots of money," suggested the reporter. He wrote, "The
beauteous one rapturously gurgled, 'Oodles, and oodles and oodles of it!'" She concluded the
conversation by announcing, "I'm not going to act any more and I'm packing up now to go
to Europe for my honeymoon."

The wedding news, coupled with Lillian's second defection from the show, threw not
only Ziegfeld into a tizzy, but Abe Erlanger, Marc Klaw and booking agent Pat Casey as well.
Days later, according to Charles Higham, Flo and Fanny Brice consoled each other — he standing before a large photograph of Lillian on the mantle. Fanny said, "He [Ziegfeld] could not
bear to be alone." For her part, she admitted she'd been charmed and "fascinated by Freddy's
demeanor and extensive vocabulary but I was never in love with him."

The gala wedding supper took place at Rector's. Freddy, in jovial spirits, announced to
the gathered guests that his name was really Gresham but Lillian was equally emphatic in
declaring it was still Gresheimer. The following day, March 27, Lillian, in an interview with
Hearst's *New York American*, continued her foolish banter: "This is the first time I've been
married so I don't know too much about such things." Of the wedding she said, "We took a
taxi cab and went to Jersey City. I don't know exactly what the place is called but it is a big
building that has a dome and we had to sign a paper.... I don't know if they asked my husband
if he'd been married before.... He has been divorced, or is a widower."

Two days later, on March 29, the *New York Telegraph* was headlining, "Maybe, Lillian,
There's a Rival?" Florence McCauley (believed to be her stage name) of San Francisco, an ex-
chorine, wired the *Morning Telegraph* stating, "Was married to Fred Gresheimer, August 13,
1907 in Jersey City. Have been separated past two years. No knowledge of any divorce having
been granted." The wire was signed Gertrude McCauley Gresheimer.

Five days had elapsed when, on April 4, Freddy's attorney, Charles S. Wharton,
announced, "Fred M. Gresheimer has not married Lillian Lorraine or any other woman
recently. His suit for divorce was filed in circuit court on December 28, 1911 charging his wife
[McCauley] with desertion as of December 15, 1909."

The affair was now a major fiasco and the press was having a field day. Ziegfeld gleefully
took the occasion to announce that Lillian would be rejoining the cast of *Over the River*. But
from her suite in the Nevada, Lillian countered by declaring, "I can't tell you a thing about
it until three o'clock tomorrow and then everybody will know what I'm going to do." That
statement elicited a choice slice of tongue-in-cheek sarcasm in the closing sentence of the
press report: "Isn't the uncertainty simply maddening!"

Within one week Lillian was back with Ziegfeld and *Over the River*. The show received
lukewarm to scathing notices. The *New York Review* opined,

Without Lillian Lorraine to stare at, *Over The River* would be a hard sentence!... Poor old Eddie
Foy cannot help being dreary in the hashed-over relic that Willie Collier really played, being a
comedian instead of a clown.... Somebody might have carelessly mistaken Foy for a comedian in
the past but *Over The River* deposits him in the sawdust with a sickening thud. The exhibition is a
monument for the eternal glorification of Collier.... Not that Lillian Lorraine sheds any heaven sent
talents over the occasion. She just drawls a few lines in her usual would be tough manner. The girl
is amusing with her mixture of physical refinement and mental toughness but her personality is so
well cared for she looks as though she feeds on olive oil and cream. There is considerable of the
persian kitten to Lill — purr, scratch and all. Her drawl of south of someplace takes the curse off
the coarseness and, blended with panache velvet beauty, the result is diverting.

15

A Split and Trouble in Paradise

On the Ziegfeld home front, on April 15, 1912, national wire services carried a news item announcing that Anna Held had filed suit for divorce from Florenz Ziegfeld on grounds of adultery. New York State Supreme Court Justice Julian Bischoff appointed Edward Whitaker as referee to take testimony in the proceedings. The *New York Times* reported that in her deposition Anna had named several correspondents, and although relevant court transcripts are no longer accessible, Charles Higham categorically states that Lillian was among those named.

At the time, New York State requirements for a divorce action on grounds of adultery was documentation and positive proof of certain acts of misconduct. Even though Flo and Anna had never been formally wed but had agreed in their 1897 informal exchange of vows to live together as husband and wife, Referee Whitaker found the marriage to be legal under the provisions of New York State Common Law.

In the suit Anna cited specific incidents of Flo's infidelity with a "Mary Ann Brennan" at the Ansonia on April 1, 1910, and previous to that, on April 2, 1909, with a certain "D.E. Jacques." Of course, the Brennan name referred to Lillian's mother Mary Ann, and D.E. Jacques, to her father Charles de Jacques. Lillian was known to use the name Brennan throughout her life to avoid public notice of her many comings and goings in the New York area. The *Morning Telegraph* reported, "In spite of Miss Held's divorce action, relations between the estranged couple are friendly."

Ziegfeld's comments on the divorce action appeared to confirm this assertion when he said, "I have no desire to discuss my personal affairs in the newspapers. My personal relations with Miss Held cannot concern the public. Of her, I can speak in only words of the highest praise, both as a woman and an artist. I believe that she plans to retire from the stage — at least as far as America is concerned, and if she does the American stage loses one of its greatest drawing cards. Anna Held is one woman in a million!"

Very shortly thereafter, Anna sailed for Europe on the French liner *La Savoie*, and at the time of her debarkation, she offered some choice comments during a shipboard news conference. When queried as to any future marriage plans, presuming the divorce action would be successful, she coyly responded, "Who can tell?" To another query, "Would you consider remarriage with Mr. Ziegfeld?" To this she replied, archly, "Poor Florenz. He looked so forlorn. I just might give him another chance." She terminated the interview by explaining she was in a state of mourning over the recent death of her "little doggie, General Marceau. He ees dead, you know. Zee poor leedle General Marceau swallowed a balloon and zen he eat a British lion.... Zey keel him!"

Public airing of Flo and Anna's marital strife had barely disappeared from the headlines when the Gresheimer-McCauley matrimonial problem reappeared to complicate Lillian's life. McCauley publicly disputed Freddy's assertion that he had been "a kind, loving, faithful and indulgent husband, providing for her and that she willfully deserted him." She went on to declare, "All my married life I was obliged to earn my own living with the full knowledge and consent of my husband and whenever I was absent from him it was with his full knowledge and agreement." She further contended she had saved him from arrest on bogus check passing charges. As if she had not already spewed enough venom, she further asserted she had been forced to sell her jewelry to cover Fred's losses at the race track. Her allegations went on and on and if only a smidgen of the charges were true, any reasonable person would conclude Fred Gresheimer was a bounder and con artist of the first order!

Across the country, when news of "millionaire" Gresheimer's marriage to Lillian hit the Los Angeles press, a restaurant keeper, John Brink, notified the local police that Fred had not only "welshed" on a $400 IOU, but he had also received cash on a bogus draft written against his father's Chicago bank account — a draft which was subsequently dishonored.

In his court papers, Brink described Fred as about twenty-eight years old and from a reputable Chicago family background. His father and uncle operated a prestigious men's clothing establishment at Clark and Lake Streets. As a young man, Fred had fallen into disfavor with his family for writing bank drafts on nonexistent accounts. The *Morning Telegraph* described Fred's acquaintances and friends as "tin horn gambler sorts and women of similar rating." In spite of all the negative press reports, Lillian turned a deaf ear to the frequent entreaties of friends and peers that she leave Fred and immediately file for annulment of their marriage. My mother was one of the most vociferous advocates of such action, but even now, close as she and Lillian had become, her urgings went unheeded. Lillian insisted, "Things will work themselves out. There are just an awful lot of jealous people out there!"

Lillian signed again with Ziegfeld for the 1912 *Follies* and shared top billing with Bert Williams, Leon Errol and Bernard Granville. It was the last year the *Follies* would be presented at the Jardin de Paris roof of the New York Theatre, at the time known as Ziegfeld's Moulin Rouge.

Bert Williams, now a popular and established *Follies* regular, gave voice to three well-received songs—"My Landlady," "You're on the Right Road but You're Going the Wrong Way," and "Blackberrying Today"—all Williams classics done in his inimitable droll style. Leon Errol shared comedy honors with Bert and brought the house down when he appeared on stage costumed in the garb of a horse who had "become too sophisticated for Broadway after midnight."

Lillian, too, was on the receiving end of critics' accolades. The *New York Globe* wrote, "She was very much improved, very pulchritudinous and full of good humor.... She has learned to make her songs effective and her tripping of the light fantastic with Harry Watson was the best dance of the whole evening."

By the summer of 1912, the first public cracks in the Lorraine-Gresheimer mating began to appear in the press. Headlines declared, "Ziegfeld Star Who Lived with Seaside Adonis a Week Wants Liberty!' When queried by reporters for the true status of her marriage, Lillian responded with an uncommonly terse "No comment!" It was, however, common knowledge along the Rialto that Lillian and Fred Gresheimer no longer shared the same bed and were actually living apart.

Yet another disruption in the Ziegfeld constellation of stars soon developed. The *New York Times* reported on February 15, 1913, that Lillian and Bert Williams would not continue with Ziegfeld in the new edition of the *Follies* and that both had signed contracts to appear in an American revue in Great Britain at the London Opera House. Of special note is the fact that Williams was guaranteed by Opera House manager Bert Fischer that he "would be treated just like a white man and that no prejudice would be shown because of his color." This would be a significant departure from still highly prejudicial conditions within the United States with which Bert Williams had to deal every day of his professional life.

Lillian was already in rehearsals in New York with Gus Sohike for a musical act, specially

Left: In fashionable repose, circa 1912. *Right:* Lillian Lorraine in full-length ermine cloak, publicity shot, 1912.

created for her, which would include a large backup chorus of pretty British girls and handsome young British men.

My mother was elated at the news of the London show. "Of course, I was very happy with this turn of events," she recalled.

> I would naturally go along with Lillian and once we got settled in London rehearsals I would take a quick run up to Sweden. Then, out of a clear blue sky, on a Sunday morning, Lillian told me we would not be going to England. She gave no reason and said she just didn't want to go. I got kind of angry about it — well, not really angry, but I was disappointed. I came right back at her and said I was going to Sweden, anyway. She just looked at me for what must have been a full minute and then, very sweetly, sort of pleaded, "But you will come back to me? Just tell me how much it will be, and I'll pay your steamship fare."

"So," Mother continued, "Lillian paid for the whole trip, first class all the way. I never told her, but I exchanged my ticket for two in second class and took my friend Ruth Carlson along with me. We didn't stay very long in Sweden, because nobody could talk about anything other than the war they thought was coming. We got back to this country just in the nick of time." World War I did, in fact, break out the following August as the result of the assassination of the heir to the Austro-Hungarian throne.

Mother did return to Lillian and by now her presence had become almost indispensable to Lillian's well-being — not only as a personal assistant but close friend and confidante. In New York and on the road, every night Lillian was on stage, mother arrived early at the theatre to organize costumes, makeup and all necessities for the evening's performance. Lillian would seldom have dinner before going on stage, preferring instead late-night supper parties with friends. Mother recalled, "One night Lillian had four dinner invitations and didn't accept a single one. She had me tell whoever was calling that she was busy with rehearsals. Just the two of us went out to a nice restaurant and enjoyed a good, leisurely supper." This was not an unusual practice. The two women slipped away out of the public eye for quiet late-night suppers on numerous occasions.

In addition to canceling out the London booking, Lillian, at the instigation of a jealous Fred Gresheimer, sent word to Ziegfeld that she would not be available for the 1913 *Follies*, which was scheduled to make its New Amsterdam Theatre debut on June 13 of that year. Located on 42nd Street, just steps west of Broadway and Times Square, the magnificent 1903 New Amsterdam show palace would be the home of the *Ziegfeld Follies* for the next fourteen years.

Flo was unaccustomed to cast defections, and losing both Lillian and Bert Williams, two of his biggest drawing cards, he found himself forced to scurry for new and well-established star caliber performers. For Williams's replacement, he quickly moved to exercise an option he held on the services of popular blackface comedian Frank Tinney, a longtime favorite on the national vaudeville circuit. With respect to Lillian, as late as April 26, trade papers were reporting that she and Ziegfeld had resolved their past differences at a small, private dinner party in Yonkers at the Park Hill Inn — a romantic, old-world-charm hideaway on the Hudson River overlooking the spectacular New Jersey Palisades. According to the *New York Review*, the Park Hill Inn could be reached only by high-powered cars and was, the paper reported, "a particularly appropriate spot for Ziegfeld and Miss Lorraine to renew their collaborative efforts by entering into a new and mutually advantageous contract. The friends who brought the two principals together on that evening felt they had performed a valuable service in the best interests of Broadway musical theatre."

However, before the ink could dry, something went terribly wrong. In less than two weeks, on May 7, there appeared a small item in *Variety* announcing that Lillian and Gresheimer had been remarried in Hoboken, New Jersey, by Justice of the Peace Gerald Rudolf, on April 25 — only two days after the Ziegfeld/Lorraine reconciliation dinner party. Once again, Gresheimer interfered and influenced his wife against any further association with Ziegfeld. Flo, forced to again move quickly, sought out and signed Jose Collins, a popular British music hall import who just happened to be a Lillian look-alike. Collins had previously been under contract to the Shubert Brothers, appearing with Al Jolson at the Winter Garden Theatre.

In 1997, Nona Otero, a Ziegfeld Club vice-president and former *Follies* dancer, revealed Ziegfeld's standard ploy for stealing talent from the Shuberts and others. Nona had briefly worked for the Shuberts before joining the *Follies*. "All I can say about them is that they were lousy penny-pinchers and cheapskates. They wanted quality but never wanted to pay for it." Therefore, when Flo offered considerably more money and the role of a featured principal in the new *Follies*, it was sufficient incentive for Jose to switch her allegiance to Ziegfeld and share the New Amsterdam stage with other principals Leon Errol, Elizabeth Brice, Stella Chatelaine, Frank Tinney and Nat Willis. She was featured in four major production numbers— originally created for Lillian — but was still apprehensive as to the longevity of her *Follies* career. The show opened in mid–June with Jose receiving good notices. Yet, within a month, rumors had begun to fly that Ziegfeld had convinced Lillian to reconsider and return to the *Follies* under his personal management. The reaction from the notoriously temperamental Collins was immediate and vehement. In a hastily-called news conference she made it abundantly clear that whatever advantage there was to being a featured principal in the *Follies*, she intended to retain that status, undisturbed by Lillian Lorraine or anyone else! The issue became moot when Lillian made it equally clear the rumors had no basis in fact, and she was through with the *Follies*.

The Collins tenure with the *Follies* company was, in fact, short-lived — only that one 1913 season — but not because of Lillian Lorraine. In 1914 she met and married Leslie Chatfield, an officer in the Australian army, and with the outbreak of war, the newlyweds sailed for England. She returned to the British stage and he joined the East Lancashire 66th Regiment. In 1917 his name appeared on the British War Office list of casualties. While Chatfield was absent from Britain in the European theater of war, Jose became romantically involved with a series of wealthy British men about town. During the 1917 Christmas holidays word was received that Chatfield was not dead but had in fact been a prisoner of war. On his return to England, he found his marriage was irretrievably finished. Jose went on to marry a member of the House of Lords, a nuptial bond that also was of relatively short duration. Next, she turned again to the military and married a Captain C.B. Kirkland. She remained in England for the rest of her life and died there in 1958 at the age of seventy-nine.

From Hammerstein's "Whirl of the World" show, circa 1913 (courtesy Ziegfeld Club Archives).

Meanwhile, in 1914, Lillian signed with the Shuberts to star in their production of *The Whirl of the World*. At her seductive best, Lillian introduced the one million-song-sheet-seller "Smother Me with Kisses." In spite of her success with this song, the high quality of Lillian's performance in the rest of the show was lacking and had not seemed to improve with time. On January 10, a New York critic wrote, "Neither can Lillian Lorraine [sing] who might be contracted for to show herself and her clothes only. It was a pity what Miss Lorraine did to Irving Berlin's latest song, 'This is the Life.' It was a real Berliner."

By January 24, another critic wrote:

The Whirl of the World is, in a word, a good, brisk performance, replete with specialties which have been melded with admirable skill, so that the general effect is remarkably smooth and harmonious and the three hours and a half taken for the performance pass so amusingly that the audience is content to remain seated to the final curtain.

The beauty of the production is Miss Lillian Lorraine, who wears her many magnificent costumes with the immodesty for which she is deservedly famous. It is always to be regretted that Miss Lorraine finds it necessary to sing. She has neither the personality nor the voice to fit her for this form of entertainment. Her only gift is that of her youth; her only triumph the parade along the familiar Winter Garden runway which brings the audience in close touch with the chorus and proves that Miss Lorraine is remarkably pretty and young even at close range. The runway this year is very busy indeed. During Miss Lorraine's singing (?) of "Little Miss U.S.A." a canopy is formed over the heads of the audience by red, white and blue streamers, held at one end by the ladies of the chorus and at the other by the gentlemen, who are standing in the aisle.

Charles Darnton of the *New York World* wrote:

First of all let me warn you that the Winter Garden, with the beauteous crop of maidens it's sprouting, is no place for a man with a weak heart. It is so gorgeous and so generous in its display of femininity that if you happen to be sitting in the centre of the house you look up to see nothing but stars—star-eyed goddesses drawing star-spangled banners above your dizzy head.

There's something new on the runway. Charmers raise starry parasols over you, while smaller though no less charming maidens carry the flowing stripes up two aisles until you find yourself playing George M. Cohan beneath a glorious canopy. You feel you could go to war under the circumstances—provided you were given such dazzling company. From the point of view I was only too pleased to take, I must say I have never seen an array of beauty to equal that at the Winter Garden. It didn't matter so much that Lillian Lorraine shouted "Hello, Little Miss U.S.A.," as that the various members of the Chorus Girls' Union who followed her were so well worth looking at that I closed my ears—but didn't shut my eyes. Take my word for it, the chorus, not the musical play is the thing to look out for at this Garden of girls. Pretty little things brush past you, while others not so little—but oh, Maxine!—walk right over you. It is only at the end of the performance that these sirens of the board-walk go too far by becoming so—let us say Oriental—that you feel every little movement of theirs isn't wholly above criticism. The whirl of girls is worth all the songs Miss Lorraine can't sing. It is enough for her, perhaps, to wear costumes that would shame the noonday sun in Paris.

In contrast to the foregoing negative critiques, Lillian did seem to have some friends in New York's Fourth Estate. The *New York Review* headlined on January 17, "Lillian Loraine [*sic*, throughout] Comes to Her Own at Winter Garden, Her Success Stamps Her as Musical Comedy Artist of First Rank." The review read:

Lillian Loraine has made a more distinct impression at the Winter Garden than any other woman who has appeared there since its opening, except Gaby Deslys.

For the first time the real quality of Miss Loraine as a musical-comedy artist has had an opportunity for display. Heretofore in the various *Follies* of Ziegfeld she has been under a handicap which prevented the development of her natural talent or the best reflection of her individuality.

Many of her costumes in the Winter Garden vie with those of Gaby herself, and she wears them with as much distinction and chic as is characteristic of the famous Parisienne in her finest sartorial moments.

It must be with bitter envy that Ziegfeld views the immense success of Miss Loraine at the Winter Garden, not only because she is doing far finer work than she ever did for him but also because former Winter Garden favorites whom he has engaged to bolster up his attractions, such as Frank Tinney and Jose Collins, have never since had the same success which marked their careers at the big theatre at Broadway and 50th Street.

The fact is that the prestige and glamour of the Winter Garden does for actors what no other management or productions can do. It is easily in a class by itself, not being approached by any other theatre or by any other class of entertainment in America.

It should not be overlooked that this review comes from the theatrical trade paper owned by the Shuberts. Could it be that the true motivation for the review's praise of Lillian was an indirect but obvious slap at Ziegfeld and his longtime and never-disguised personal relationship with Lillian?

16

Ziegfeld vs. Gresheimer

Rumors of yet another Ziegfeld/Lorraine reconciliation rumor gained impetus when Flo and Lillian were seen together outside of Louis Martin's restaurant on the southwest corner of Seventh Avenue and 43rd Street. As one story goes, Lillian was seated in a taxicab outside of Martin's and Flo, at curbside, was talking with her through the cab's open window. Suddenly, Fred Gresheimer approached and struck Flo on the head with a walking stick. The identity of the assailant became clear when Lillian was heard to scream, "Oh, Freddy! Don't, don't!" Ignoring her plea, Fred then cut loose with a right arm swing, catching Ziegfeld on the right side of his jaw. Fred, too, was heard shouting, "Say, don't you know that this woman is my wife!"

Another version of the incident, as reported in the *Evening World*, had Flo and Lillian dining together in Martin's when Fred entered the restaurant in search of her. In their attempt to escape, Flo and Lillian slipped out a back door onto Seventh Avenue. Having already spotted them, Fred was quick to follow, and when catching up to them on the sidewalk, accosted Ziegfeld. Although this version was not verified by any of the principals, the *World* went on to report "eye witnesses to the affair declared that, Mr. Ziegfeld and Miss Lorraine did indeed emerge together from the rear door of the restaurant and on their heels came a wildly excited young man, brandishing a walking stick in a threatening manner."

Ziegfeld repaired to the Ansonia to attend his wounds. Lillian and Fred walked quickly to their Long Acre Square Hotel, only one block away on the southeast corner of Broadway and 42nd Street. When contacted by reporters, the couple refused to make any comment. For his part, Ziegfeld, when interviewed at the Ansonia, declared, "After he hit me, Gresheimer jumped into a cab and drove away with Miss Lorraine. I had no chance to get at him and I have no idea what motivated his attack on me."

Incredibly, the following day, Lillian was again in the headlines, charging her husband with theft and assault. She claimed he had torn a $5,000 solitaire diamond ring from her finger and pawned it. Further, through her attorney, Herman Roth, she charged that following his attack on Ziegfeld, Fred had "jumped in the cab, throttled her and directed the driver to take them to Ravenhall's at Coney Island," not to their Long Acre Square Hotel as originally reported. She said he kept her captive there until her cries for help frightened him enough to flee the scene. According to attorney Roth, Lillian then repaired to Long Beach to avoid any further confrontations with Fred. That same night she was seen out on the town, winning a turkey trot dance contest with an escort, whose identity was unknown to the paparazzi of that day. On the dance floor and over her shoulder, Lillian called to a friendly reporter, "I feel invigorated enough now to go after my husband!"

This public display of irrational and silly carryings-on now appeared to be manifesting itself as a constant in Lillian's personal and public life persona.

On July 17, 1913, the *Morning Telegraph* reported that Lillian, her attorney and my mother, amidst a swarm of popping flash bulbs, arrived at the Criminal Courts Building in lower

Manhattan. Judge Richard Turner presided over a hearing in which Lillian brought charges of assault and larceny against Fred Gresheimer. Sensing another round of scandalous headlines, reporters eagerly awaited the conclusion of Lillian's testimony, following which they had been promised an eyebrow-raising statement. Lillian was happy to oblige, and in the huge courthouse rotunda, she held court with the waiting press.

Dabbing a tear or two from her eyes, Lillian began:

> Because too much false gossip has been floating up and down Broadway, I would like to tell the true story of the brawl outside Martin's Restaurant last Saturday evening. I thank you all for giving me a chance to tell my version of what really happened.
>
> I was dining at Martin's with a friend known by my husband for quite some time. When he was out of town Fred had never before had any objection to my taking dinner with him. We had just left Martin's when my escort spotted Mr. Ziegfeld also coming out of the café. Mr. Ziegfeld stopped to talk with us and, all of a sudden, Freddy appeared and began to attack not my escort, but Mr. Ziegfeld, after which he dragged me into a taxicab and threatened me with a beating if I cried out. He told the driver to take us to Ravenhall's in Coney Island. He forced me to stay there with him until Monday morning, when he finally agreed to bring me back to the Long Acre Square hotel. He left me there and I haven't seen him since. If I know Fred, he's probably down in Atlantic City and won't be back until he runs out of money!"

As opposed to media stories, Lillian's version of the now scandalous incident does not appear to stand up to eyewitness statements.

Lillian wasn't the only one doing the turkey trot to dance away her stress. Reporters caught up with Ziegfeld on the roof of the New York Theatre and asked for his comments on Jose Collins's earlier ultimatum on the subject of Lillian's possible return to the *Follies*. Instead of a verbal response, he moved onto the dance floor and took chorus boy Wallace McCutcheon's place as partner to Joan Sawyer in the fancy turkey trot and tango competitions. He called back to the befuddled reporter, "No comment!"

Not withstanding Flo's and Lillian's terpsichorean dexterity, some Americans did not share their enthusiasm for these latest dance crazes. Echoing what was surely a minority point of view, *Evening World* columnist Nicola Greeley-Smith described the dance movements as "products of the fashionable and decadent society now causing so much excitement in modern Babylon.... Here in Babylon we have an unmistakable passion for the grotesque, particularly the grotesquely immoral!"

Lillian continued her pursuit of Freddy by going to the West Side Court with attorney Roth. There she petitioned Magistrate Corrigan to issue an arrest warrant for Fred charging him with theft of the aforementioned diamond ring and many other expensive baubles which she claimed had somehow disappeared from her jewelry box dating back to the time she and Fred had become man and wife. In addition to the theft charges, Lillian and Roth filed an affidavit for separation, charging Fred with "cruel and inhuman treatment and habitual drunkenness."

Continuing to serve as a gadfly on Ziegfeld's back, the *New York Review* on July 5 published an hilarious editorial on the subject of the recent fiasco at Martin's:

> Behind the Ziegfeld-Lorraine-Gresheimer imbroglio, which resulted in fastidious Flo being soundly thrashed by Gresheimer when he found the *Follies* manager in company with his wife, and in Mrs. Lillian Gresheimer swearing out a warrant for the arrest of her husband on the charge of Grand Larceny, are some facts of little interest to those who like to keep up with the doings of the Rialto fast set.... That Ziegfeld should finally have been pummeled for his attentions to another man's wife does not in the least astonish those who have watched his career as a boulevardier.... What may be news to all, save the intimates of those directly concerned, is that the costly bauble was a gift to Miss Lorraine from Ziegfeld.

With the probable exception of Lillian Russell, there were few actresses who could rival Lillian

Lorraine's collection of expensive adornments, which at one time were reported to be valued in excess of $100,000.

The ring that Freddy allegedly tore from Lillian's finger was a large diamond with a solitaire cut. It was eventually recovered by Lillian and presented to my mother several years later as a wedding gift, and it is still in our family's possession. Oh, that I could have been there to see the expression on my staunch Swedish conservative father's face at the prospect of his new bride possessing such a magnificent and permanent reminder of her earlier years with Lillian. I know Mother must have been flabbergasted, and at the same time deeply touched, for she knew that Lillian's gifts to others, whether money or jewelry, always came from a special place deep in Lillian's heart.

17

Catch-Up Time
on the Rumor Mill

After the earlier confrontation at Martin's and an absence of almost two months, Freddy Gresheimer did turn up in Manhattan. With a warrant out for his arrest on the Ziegfeld assault charge, he voluntarily turned himself in to a Detective Raynes from the district attorney's office. He was immediately incarcerated in the Men's House of Detention, then and now more commonly known as the "Tombs." By way of explaining his two-month absence from New York City, Gresheimer said, "[I have] traveled extensively, first going to Canada, thence to Detroit, from Detroit to Chicago, from Chicago to Boston, and from Boston to England."

Lillian's assertion that he wouldn't be back until he was broke appears to be not too far from the truth. Needless to say, Gresheimer ultimately was indicted on charges of grand larceny. There is no public record of a trial or subsequent sentencing. It would be a period of years before Freddy reappeared in Lillian's life.

Less than six weeks after the Gresheimer-Ziegfeld altercation, Flo was again front and center in another humiliating incident involving Lillian. This time the event occurred at the Tourelle Ballroom in Long Beach, New York, and is chronicled in the *New York Review* of August 27, 1913:

> Florenz Ziegfeld, Jr., has a very sore nose as a result of a tweaking given his organ of smell at Long Beach on Tuesday night by an irate gentleman who did not care for the brand of manners exhibited in public by the manager of the *Follies*. A large number of men and women witnessed Ziegfeld's discomfiture and applauded the action of the one who gave him the lesson in deportment. The man in question, who occupies a high position in the vaudeville field, was dancing at the Tourelle Ballroom with Lillian Lorraine when Ziegfeld put in an appearance. All Broadway and Long Beach knows that Miss Lorraine had been under Ziegfeld's personal management for almost five years and had been featured by him in just about as many editions of the *Follies*. Neither was it any secret that she had long been the recipient of marks of his favor. These facts are said to make Ziegfeld intolerant of all others who smile upon the actress.
> When he saw the vaudeville man dancing with Miss Lorraine, he approached them and said in a voice loud enough for many other dancers to hear, "How much are you giving her for that dance — one hundred dollars?"

Ziegfeld's caustic remark, according to a commentary in Allen Churchill's *The Theatrical 20s*, may have had some substance in fact. Churchill described Lillian "as probably the first of many *Follies* girls to demand that a man give her a present — before — taking her out!" Lillian was on public record as facetiously declaring, "I have no problem with accepting expensive gifts from my gentlemen friends."

Actually, it was not an uncommon practice for any high-flying *Follies* girl to expect an expensive bauble or hundred-dollar bills just for stepping out with a gentleman admirer. Dimple-kneed darling and longtime *Follies* principal, fleet-footed tap dancer Ann Pennington, in an interview with Stuart Oderman published in the May 1986 *Films in Review,* said, "Being courted and being chased are two different things.... We were pretty expensive girls, but, at the same time, we were very nice and wholesome. We never took advantage of any man who did not show us the jewelry first. If he came backstage with diamonds, it was every girl for herself. A lot of those girls had collections of both men and diamonds. It's okay if you know how to handle it, I guess.... I don't go along with this 'Women's Lib,' Stuart, honey. Any woman can get whatever she wants out of any man. All she has to do is treat him kindly.... Once she does that..." Her voice trailed off, she pushed back in her chair, closed her eyes and the interview was over.

Returning to the Tourelle Ballroom account, the *New York Review* continued:

Miss Lorraine's partner halted for a moment and in response to what he regarded as Mr. Ziegfeld's snide reference to one hundred dollars, said, "Kindly desist from addressing me. I don't know you. People hearing you speak to me like that would think I am a friend of yours. If you have anything to say to me, come on outside after the dance." And with that, off he Turkey Trotted again with Miss Lorraine, leaving Ziegfeld standing flushed and uncomfortable in the middle of the dance floor. When the orchestra ceased playing, Miss Lorraine joined some other friends while her dancing partner went outside. There, he came face to face with Ziegfeld. Reaching out a strong right hand, he took the *Follies* manager's proboscis between his thumb and index finger and gave it a mighty twist which drew forth a flow of blood and a howl of pain which brought many other dancers to the scene.

"If you ever dare speak to me again, I'll use my fists instead of my fingers." Leaving Ziegfeld applying his handkerchief to his smarting face, he returned to the ballroom and began another Turkey Trot with Miss Lorraine.

According to records kept by a man who makes a specialty of Broadway brawls, Ziegfeld has yet to come out first in any street fight.

* * *

During the 1912–1913 time frame, Lillian completed her first dabble in the new entertainment medium of silent motion pictures. For the week of December 13–20, the Lyceum Theatre in Stamford, Connecticut, advertised the showing of a film titled *The Flowers in Japan*, a Kinemacolor production starring Lillian Lorraine. There is no information available as to where the film was made — Astoria, New York, or Hollywood — the two major filming sites at the time. An exhaustive search of film archives on both the east and west coast was unsuccessful. The Lyceum Theatre poster advertisement is the only printed evidence that the film even existed. This poster is on display in the lobby of the Lyceum Theatre to this very day. Various sources, including the usually reliable Bible of the film industry, *Motion Picture Guide*, credit Lillian with other movie roles, such as *The Face at the Window* (1912), *The Immigrant's Violin* (1912) and *The Old Parlor* (1913), but these credits are not substantiated, as were her major successes, *Neal of the Navy* (1915) and *Should a Wife Forgive* (1915). However well-known Lillian was in the northeastern United States, she would probably not have been as well-known elsewhere and would therefore not have enjoyed the same billing or status in pictures. This would suggest that her roles would not have been publicized. It would be another three years before Lillian would achieve national prominence as a major star of stage and screen.

* * *

On December 12, 1913, international wire services carried a dispatch from Paris reporting the suicide of Evelyn Nesbit, Lillian's friend from Gramercy Park soiree days. The front-page news, as reported in the *Morning Telegraph,* was a shocker not only to Lillian, but even the most jaded of Broadway's gossip wags. It was reported in lurid detail that Evelyn Nesbit Thaw had shot herself through the right temple and her body was found on her hotel room bed by a maid who claimed to have heard the gunshot. Within hours, it developed, the story was a hoax—100% pure fabrication. Red-faced *Telegraph* executives were forced to beat a hasty retreat and issue a full retraction and apology for erroneous reporting.

The last quarter of 1913 was a busy time for Lillian, now coming into her own as a solo headliner with Hammerstein, the Shuberts and the Keith Orpheum vaudeville circuits. Anna Held had returned from Europe and embarked on a national road tour, teasing the press with intimations she might still harbor romantic feelings for her "Ziggy."

Flo, however, was now involved in a short-term romantic dalliance with British songstress Ethel Levy. At one point, the rumor mill had them married and, when queried on the subject, Flo mischievously responded, "Ask the lady." Ethel, in turn, made short shrift of the story by

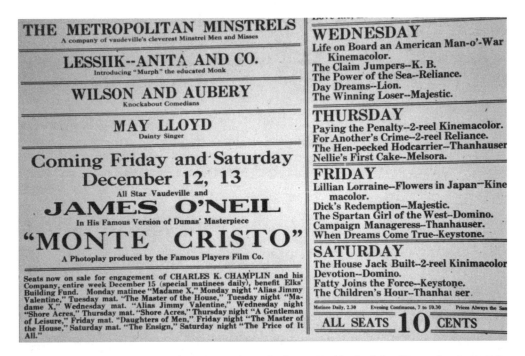

THE METROPOLITAN MINSTRELS
A company of vaudeville's cleverest Minstrel Men and Misses

LESSIIK--ANITA AND CO.
Introducing "Murph" the educated Monk

WILSON AND AUBERY
Knockabout Comedians

MAY LLOYD
Dainty Singer

Coming Friday and Saturday
December 12, 13
All Star Vaudeville and
JAMES O'NEIL
In His Famous Version of Dumas' Masterpiece
"MONTE CRISTO"
A Photoplay produced by the Famous Players Film Co.

Seats now on sale for engagement of CHARLES K. CHAMPLIN and his Company, entire week December 15 (special matinees daily), benefit Elks' Building Fund. Monday matinee "Madame X," Monday night "Alias Jimmy Valentine," Tuesday mat. "The Master of the House," Tuesday night "Madame X," Wednesday mat. "Alias Jimmy Valentine," Wednesday night "Shore Acres," Thursday mat. "Shore Acres," Thursday night "A Gentleman of Leisure," Friday mat. "Daughters of Men," Friday night "The Master of the House," Saturday mat. "The Ensign," Saturday night "The Price of It All."

WEDNESDAY
Life on Board an American Man-o'-War Kinemacolor.
The Claim Jumpers--K. B.
The Power of the Sea--Reliance.
Day Dreams--Lion.
The Winning Loser--Majestic.

THURSDAY
Paying the Penalty--2-reel Kinemacolor.
For Another's Crime--2-reel Reliance.
The Hen-pecked Hodcarrier--Thanhauser
Nellie's First Cake--Melsora.

FRIDAY
Lillian Lorraine--Flowers in Japan--Kinemacolor.
Dick's Redemption--Majestic.
The Spartan Girl of the West--Domino.
Campaign Manageress--Thanhauser.
When Dreams Come True--Keystone.

SATURDAY
The House Jack Built--2-reel Kinimacolor
Devotion--Domino.
Fatty Joins the Force--Keystone.
The Children's Hour--Thanhauser.

Matinee Daily, 2.30   Evening Continuous, 7 to 10.30   Prices Always the Same

ALL SEATS 10 CENTS

Opposite page and above: Alhambra Lyceum (Stamford, New York) schedule of December 8–10, 1913, mentioning Lillian Lorraine in "Flowers in Japan" in Kinemacolor — Hollywood's first attempt at color photography.

emphatically declaring, "No, we are not married!" Her denial did not discourage the *New York Review* from pursuing the matter and reporting the couple engaged with plans to marry by the end of November when Ethel would have completed a theatre engagement in London. The story had really begun to gather momentum but was again squelched by Ethel, who declared she was through with Ziegfeld because she was not at all certain he had given up his romantic interest in Lillian Lorraine, then headlining the bill at the Colonial Theatre.

On December 27, police were called to Lillian's suite at the Hotel Wentworth on West 46th Street. She told officers she had returned to the hotel at 10:30 P.M. on Christmas night to find her suite had been ransacked, with furs and a considerable amount of jewelry missing. My mother was out of town for the holidays and when contacted by police was unable to shed any light on the situation.

Reading of his estranged wife's misfortune, Fred Gresheimer rushed to the Wentworth and phoned Lillian, offering to be of assistance. Lillian responded cheerfully, "Oh, indeed you can. I've been wondering where you were. Just wait where you are for a moment." Within minutes, Mother appeared in the hotel lobby, smilingly walked up to Fred and handed him a long blue envelope which he opened immediately. Glancing at the contents he quickly realized he'd been duped. Lillian was finally successful in having him served in her suit for legal separation and now, he charged, "She tricked me!"

At the time, Lillian was in rehearsals for her opening at the Shuberts' Winter Garden Theatre. Some reporters felt she had used the robbery ploy not so much to get Fred out of hiding but purely and simply as a publicity stunt for her new revue. Her response was, "Absolutely not. Everything was stolen when I was out for dinner on Christmas night. I suppose that's what comes from keeping jewelry in a hat box. I guess I'm just too careless!"

At just about the same time, Anna Held was also having problems with the law. She was

Sheet music cover for "Cutey Boy" (1913).

served with papers charging nonpayment of a $2,400 decorator's bill and another writ attaching her salary for $5,000 and alleging breach of a management contract.

It seemed the New York media never got enough where these two women were concerned. No matter how trivial or ridiculous the event, the news hawks were always eager to set the type.

18

Live Reflections

There have been so many occasions during the research and writing of this book when I wished that I had queried my mother about her life in the theatre. In my younger days I knew that she was somehow once connected to the theatre, but it was not a part of her life that was openly discussed in our family. Besides, I did not give any thought to much beyond the present, and with getting on in life: the Marines, school, career — these were the matters I was focused on. Only after my mother's death and my discovery of the trunk did I come to realize how much I did not know — and wanted to know — about my mother and this woman, Lillian Lorraine, who was at the center of my mother's life for so many years.

The audiotapes recorded by my sister have been invaluable, but revealing as they are, they raise more questions than they answer — questions relating to enhancement of specific reminiscences, clarifications, explanations and personal observations. One of my chief regrets is that my interest in Lillian Lorraine did not develop until almost forty years after her death in 1955. In the late 1940s and early 1950s she was living in New York — and so was I!

And so, in my capacity as administrator for the Ziegfeld Club, I persisted at every opportunity in my questioning of the very few remaining "original" *Follies* girls who could and would speak freely of those golden days with the authority of firsthand knowledge and personal experience.

One rainy afternoon in 1996, while waiting in our Ziegfeld office for a car service to take her home to Rego Park, our club president, *Follies* dancer Eleanor Dana O'Connell — with just a little prodding from me — reminisced about Lillian. "You know," she said, "Lillian never had any real appreciation for the value of money and the security it could bring in later years. In her glory days, Lillian had lots of money and she helped plenty of our people through some pretty tough times. Sometimes it was cash and other times it was jewelry. I have to say she was generous to a fault."

My introduction to another *Follies* original, Muriel Harrison Merrill, was purely by chance. Barbara Bonard, the formidable and dynamic ex-board chairwoman for the Ziegfeld Girls of Florida, had invited me to attend her club's annual fundraising extravaganza at the posh Boca Raton Country Club. It was there, on a typically bright and balmy day in February of 1997, I first set eyes on Muriel. She was animatedly holding court at a table barely ten feet from my own. I asked my hostess, "Barbara, who is that adorable creature in white?"

"Oh, why, that's Muriel Harrison Merrill. She's our oldest member, and hold on to your hat, my friend, she's in the opening number of our show. Just wait until you see her snap open that little white parasol and go into the cakewalk routine she did in the 1918 *Ziegfeld Follies*." With the mention of "1918" I almost flipped. That little old lady must have at least known and probably worked with Lillian Lorraine. How lucky could I get? I had stumbled across another real live original Ziegfeld Girl, especially one who might have actually worked with Lillian.

Muriel Harrison Merrill was just a wisp of a thing. She couldn't have been more than

Left: **Muriel Harrison Merrill, 1918.** *Right:* Eleanor Dana O'Connell, *Ziegfeld Follies* headshot, ca. 1921–23 (courtesy Ziegfeld Club Archives).

five feet tall, but what a love! She was ninety-seven years old and cute as a button. From her well-coiffed powder-white wig to her dainty, spotless white linen pumps, just a hint of lip color and eye shadow accenting her china-blue eyes, she looked like a miniature Dresden doll.

Surprisingly at such an age, Muriel lived alone in a tiny one-bedroom second-floor apartment at the Marion Towers complex in North Miami Beach. The living room was tastefully furnished with a white wicker sofa, chairs, tables and enough incidental accoutrements to make for a truly cozy ambiance. A proliferation of photographs in white wooden frames covered most of the available wall space and, hello, it didn't take me long to spot a familiar image with upswept hairdo and the inscription, "To my pal, Muriel—Lillian—July 7, 1918."

Over the course of three years and several return visits, I developed a close friendship with Muriel. Her hearing was impaired but her mind was as sharp as the proverbial tack. What tales she did spin with relish as she gently moved back and forth in her white wicker rocker! For my part, I kept my mouth shut and just listened as she talked and talked and talked. I instinctively knew it had been a very long time since anyone had been willing to sit and listen to this precious little lady's reminiscences from the days of her youth and glamorous past. I wasn't just being polite—as much as she obviously enjoyed talking, I enjoyed listening.

When I mentioned the autographed photo of Lillian, she volunteered, "Everybody liked her and I guess there were plenty who envied her as well. She was fun and easy to work with and even though I was only a specialty dancer, she, as a principal, always treated me as though we were equals."

Muriel also told me, "The girls and boys in the chorus always knew they could count on Lillian to help them through whatever financial problem they might have at the moment. She really was a soft touch and, I'm sorry to say, in most cases, memories were short when it came to payback time."

Muriel was popular with many of the big spenders of the day and likened Lillian's generosity to a philosophical point of view often expressed by Diamond Jim Brady. "What the hell," he would say, "it's a lot easier for me to make big money than it is for the average man on the street. Why shouldn't I help along a little bit, even if some make an easy mark of me. I know that many times my leg is being pulled, but did you ever stop to think it's sometimes fun to be a sucker — especially one who can afford it."

At the time of my last meeting with Muriel, she was in an exceptionally playful and candidly expansive mood. She exhibited undisguised glee, resurrecting tales of her days as a much sought-after beauty by the stage-door Johnnies gathered at the 41st Street address of the New Amsterdam Theatre. The details of one affair, in particular, I think bear sharing.

Only eighteen and strikingly beautiful, Muriel caught the eye of young Irving Fields, a Chicago multimillionaire and scion of the Marshall Fields department store dynasty. A year-long romance came to a bittersweet end when Irving's mother sent for Muriel and handed her a check for $10,000 in exchange for a promise to end the affair with Irving. Then, with a chuckle, she said, "I took it and ran. After all, we'd been going together for almost a full year and I didn't see any engagement ring on the third finger of my left hand! At the time, Irving was pretty upset but it wasn't long after our breakup that he took up with Jenny Dolly — you know, one of the Dolly Sisters. I don't know if his mother tried to buy Jenny off, too, but they did marry and, after not too long a time, divorced. Jenny sadly ended up committing suicide."

Muriel, at the time the oldest surviving original Ziegfeld Girl, passed away in a Florida nursing home in 2001 at the age of 101.

A 1919 *Ziegfeld Follies* alumna, Betty Dalton Baruch, told me in 1995:

> You know, Lillian Lorraine was such a gorgeous creature that men were falling all over themselves just to get a smile or a quick wink of recognition. She also had a big following with women because of all the big stars on Broadway at that time, Lillian was the ultimate fashion plate and a much-copied trend setter. Why, she's even credited with being the first celebrity to wear an ankle bracelet as part of her beach bathing attire. Her collection of jewelry was exquisite and, why not! After she split up with Mr. Z., she had suitors coming out of the woodwork. My husband's brother, Sailing Baruch, was just one of them and the family was so upset they tightened the purse strings, exiled him to Florida and told him to not come back soon! Another man who was crazy about her was Jules Glenzer, a Cartier senior executive. And then there was Park Avenue socialite Edward Thomas and Coca-Cola's Joe Whitehead from Atlanta. Oh, yes, for awhile Lillian had it all, but in the end, she had nothing."

Quite by accident, Dame Good Fortune smiled on me once again, as well as on another New York *Follies* original. I found Grace LaRue holed up in a tiny one-room apartment in the Hotel Lucerne, a baroque and stately edifice of red sandstone and mortar, truly an architectural relic of a bygone era. The Lucerne occupies the northwest corner of Amsterdam Avenue and Seventy-Ninth Street on Manhattan's Upper West Side. It is to this historic landmark I was one day summoned by a Columbia University undergraduate. The young drama student, a part-time Lucerne resident, had befriended another of the hotel's guests, ninety-seven-year-old Grace LaRue Graham. This student had seen my name and Ziegfeld Club association in a news release pertaining to one of the club's charity benefits. She called because she felt Grace was in need of assistance, and she wanted to make sure that we, the Ziegfeld Club, knew about her. Seventy-seven years earlier, Grace LaRue had been a glorified acrobatic dancer in the *Ziegfeld Follies of 1918*. Like some others of her peers, she had fallen on hard times.

A knock on the door of room 307 at the Lucerne Hotel elicited a whispery, yet somehow friendly, "The door's not locked, come on in." In the dimness of a poorly lighted room my eyes focused on an army cot in which lay the wizened, white-haired figure of a very old lady — the subject of the drama student's earlier call and summons for help.

Although it was mid–July and nearing the noon hour, Grace LaRue was still bedded with a tattered, soiled coverlet pulled up to just beneath her toothless mouth. As I approached her, she smiled timidly, patted the edge of her cot and bade me to sit. As I looked around the one-room flat, there was not even so much as one chair on which I might otherwise have sat.

She was still smiling as her next words jolted me into action: "Forgive me for not getting up, but I am so terribly cold." To me, the temperature in the room felt warm and the air was close and heavy, but she was indeed trembling like a fragile leaf in a late autumn breeze. I looked around the room for a blanket, but there was none to be found. I covered her with a frayed woolen coat I discovered in a tiny closet; this served as a quick-fix remedy to her discomfort. The room was a mess of clutter — newspapers, magazines and soiled TV dinner trays. Stained walls of peeling paint were covered with dozens of Scotch-taped images of every conceivable breed of cat one could imagine. For years she'd had feline companionship, until sanitary conditions became so much of a problem the hotel management had to step in with a "No Pets" edict. One wall, however, was devoted to photographs of Grace in her glory days of youth and physical beauty. There were also snapshots of a daughter and grandchildren who, I soon learned from the hotel management, no longer cared. Although her pride dictated to the contrary, the hotel manager told me no one had visited or telephoned Grace in many years.

Minutes after revealing my Ziegfeld Club affiliation, Grace's demeanor transformed, which was a joy to see. The initially shy and questioning suggestion of a smile now expanded and the face glowed with a relaxed flush of expectancy. The Ziegfeld Club was able to help Grace, and during the ensuing months we two developed a bond of trust and friendship. Grace now seemed to be completely at ease with a new friend. She spoke freely and expansively of her early childhood and the adored mother who, when Grace recovered from malaria, put her into dancing school in Jacksonville, Florida — more for reasons of rehabilitation than for a future professional career. Then there were the teenage years as an acrobatic dancer with a Southern vaudeville troupe. It was not long before Grace and her mother made a decision to secure an agent and travel north to New York City.

I was certain we were now getting into territory that was of prime interest to me. With her permission, I had the good sense to record and film our meetings, thereby preserving a verbatim account of just how Grace LaRue landed a chorus spot in the 1918 *Ziegfeld Follies*. It is a gem of dialogue well worth recounting here. I sat in amazement as she recalled with absolute clarity this particular incident from her life that had occurred some eighty years before:

> I simply answered a call to the New Amsterdam Theatre. There were about twelve other girls on stage with me and we all had our turns at a one-minute buck and wing. When we had finished, Ned Wayburn, the show's dance director, asked me to come back the next day to meet Mr. Ziegfeld. It was made clear the invitation did not include my mother or my agent and I was, of course, petrified!

As she spoke, from her facial expressions and mannerisms, it was obvious she was reliving the incident.

> The next day, at the appointed time, and dressed to the nines, I was back at the theatre and ushered up to Mr. Ziegfeld's second-floor office. He was sitting at his desk and on the wall behind him there were beautifully framed pictures of some of his most famous stars— Nora Bayes, Bessie McCoy, Olive Thomas, Fanny Brice and Lillian Lorraine. I thought to myself, gosh, will I ever be up there with those people?
> At first, he didn't say anything at all. He just looked. Then, after a minute or so of unimportant chit-chat, he asked to see my legs. Coyly, I raised my skirt to just above the ankles. He'd gotten up from his desk to look and said, "Higher, higher." I think I blushed a little bit and raised the skirt another level to my knees. This still wasn't enough for him and he suddenly came around the desk,

grabbed my skirt and pulled it up over my head! Thank goodness my mother had warned me about his reputation with women. When he saw I was wearing knee-length bloomers he broke out laughing and said, "Well, young lady, you certainly came well prepared for any emergency, didn't you! You've got a job. Report for work tomorrow." And that, my friend, is how I got into the *Follies*!

I like to believe my bi-monthly visits to the Lucerne were bright spots in Grace LaRue's normal, everyday placid existence. Aside from Meals on Wheels deliverymen and hotel maintenance personnel, there was an obvious deficit in outside human contact. So sad. Through the good offices of the national Ziegfeld Club, I was able to arrange a small monthly stipend that continued until the time of her death in 2000 at the Mary Manning Walsh Nursing Home in New York City. Her burial was generously arranged for by the late Tom Dillon, then president of the Actors' Fund of America. She was interred at the fund's Kensico Cemetery plot in Valhalla, New York.

Since these Ziegfeld women, Dana, Betty, Muriel and Grace, were either specialty or chorus dancers, they were not much involved in the swirling circles of people that Lillian Lorraine and other *Follies* principals, Florenz Ziegfeld, and my mother worked and played with day-to-day. As a result, my mother was no more than a vague memory to them — a pretty, dark-haired Swedish lass frequently in the backstage company of Lillian.

19

Enter Billie Burke and the Ghost of the New Amsterdam

New Year's Eve of 1913–14 marked a dramatic turning point in the often turbulent four-year Ziegfeld-Lorraine relationship. Jack Rumsey's Sixty Club, downstairs in Time Square's elegant Hotel Astor, was the setting for a fancy New Year's Eve masquerade ball. During the last weeks of December 1913, Flo and Lillian had once more reconciled. New Year's Eve, in costume, he as a tramp, she as a shepherdess, they arrived at the Sixty Club twenty minutes before the midnight witching hour. Anna Held was in attendance also. After divorcing Ziegfeld and traveling to Europe, Anna had returned for an American tour earlier in the year, and was once again living at the Ansonia in the apartment she once shared with Ziegfeld. She attended the party in the company of good friends Diamond Jim Brady and Lillian Russell.

The evening soiree was a star-studded gala with Broadway's elite making the most of their entrances down the grand staircase. Among the two hundred celebrants were Ethel Barrymore, Laurette Taylor, Diamond Jim Brady and Lillian Russell, Anna Held, Gene Buck, J.J. and Lee Shubert, and, in their party, a young and pretty blonde dancer, Marilyn Miller.

Minutes before midnight, Flo and Lillian, for some unknown reason, in plain view and hearing of the celebrity assemblage, erupted into a violent quarrel. Flo, who had been mincing no words, quickly regretted his harsh outburst, but not soon enough to deter Lillian from walking out on him. He then also beat a hasty retreat back to the Ansonia, hoping to find Lillian and patch up whatever the particular problem might have been. After phoning several of Lillian's favorite late-night haunts to no avail, he shed his tramp costume in favor of white tie and tails and returned to the ball and a chance encounter that would forever change his life.

Rejoining the merrymakers on the dance floor, he reached for the hand of a pretty, twenty-nine-year-old redhead and danced her away into the crowd of happy revelers. The dance was a Paul Jones and the young lady whose hand he had taken was Billie Burke.

* * *

Billie was born in Washington, D.C., in 1884. At an early age she moved with her parents to England, where her mother decided Billie was to study acting and singing. By the age of eighteen, Billie, guided and mentored by famed producer Charles Frohman, was well on the way to becoming a popular figure in the London musical and legitimate theatre. At Frohman's urging, she returned to America in 1907 and was an immediate success in her Broadway debut with John Drew in *My Wife*.

In New York for New Year's Eve of 1913, Billie was hosting a bon voyage party for her friends, British actor Forbes Robertson and his wife, who would shortly return to England. Unattached and very single, Billie's escort for the evening was the noted author Somerset Maugham. Sometime after two o'clock on the morning of New Year's Day, Billie suggested the party move on to the festivities at Jack Rumsey's Sixty Club. As she relates it in her auto-

Left: In such a shepherdess costume, at the Hotel Astor's 50-50 Club, Lillian Lorraine split with Ziegfeld, following his introduction to (right) Billie Burke (courtesy Ziegfeld Club Archives).

biography, *With a Feather on My Nose,* Billie, descending the grand staircase on Maugham's arm, noticed a slim, tall man in evening dress—as opposed to the mostly costumed assemblage. He, too, had noticed Billie and inquired of Gene Buck as to her identity. In addition to being strikingly pretty, Flo would later learn Billie had not only social standing but a country-house estate in tony Hastings-on-Hudson—facts that Flo did not discount as he shortly embarked on a nonstop, whirlwind courtship. It was the Anna Held campaign all over again, but this time with a new leading lady.

* * *

Charles Frohman was deeply disturbed by what he perceived to be Billie's more than passing interest in a man he considered to be a philanderer of the first order. "Billie," he implored, "this has got to stop. He's still in love with Lillian Lorraine and still sees Anna Held. Both those women live at the same hotel he does. What do you think of that!"

Billie stubbornly defended Flo and politely, but firmly, suggested her personal relationships should not be his concern. She did not want to offend Charles because, after all, it was he who had early on "seen the possibilities of her charm, beauty and daintiness." No question about it, he had successfully guided her career to its present impressive status.

Lillian's reaction to the budding romance and ultimate marriage, according to one source, was not benign acceptance. In *Ziegfeld,* Charles Higham relates that one night the two lovebirds, Billie and Flo, were dining at the New Amsterdam Aerial Roof Garden when Lillian arrived, dressed in a floor-length sable coat. Walking unsteadily to their table, she glared at Flo and said, "I want to talk to you for a minute." Embarrassed and attempting to put her off, he responded that at that moment it was impossible and he would see her later. She insisted he leave the floor with her and upon a second rebuff, she countered, "If you don't, I'm going to throw off this coat in front of your face and I don't have a stitch on!" Flo, again according to Higham, took Lillian by the arm, escorted her down to the street level, placed her in a taxi and instructed the driver to take her home.

The fur-coat incident was never attributed to Lillian by any source other than Higham, which could lead one to believe the real source for the tawdry episode may very well have been a passage in ex-*Follies* girl Louise Brooks's *Lulu in Hollywood*. Brooks, a notorious iconoclast, was featured in the 1925 *Follies* and was later successful in films. Her nonconformist lifestyle on Broadway and in Hollywood was not at all unlike Lillian's. They were both free spirits with little regard for professional discipline when it did not suit their own purpose. Brooks wrote:

> There are two categories of celebrities that readers and writers appear to dote on. They are the tramp-type woman star, delineated by her outrageous conduct, and the drunken actor whose cruel antics are considered hilarious. In the first category is the star who goes into a smart restaurant clad only in a mink coat and a pair of slippers. Beneath the coat she is naked and the question is, how is it known—her nakedness? Does she take the coat off? Journalists refer to the mink coat anecdote as a "possible" item. It could happen; it probably has. But not to a star with the eyes of the press upon her. No documentation ever confirms this anecdote.

Additionally, Billie Burke's own words in *With a Feather on My Nose* refute the veracity of the sable coat episode. She unequivocally stated, "I never met Olive Thomas or Lillian Lorraine or Anna Held, and for obvious reasons. But they were all beautiful women and no man could be blamed for loving them." However, Billie did send flowers and gifts during Anna's final illness, according to Flo's cousin Richard Ziegfeld. Regarding Lillian specifically, Billie wrote, "Of all the girls in Flo's life I think I was most jealous of Lillian. I think he loved her."

Aside from herself and their daughter Patricia, Billie had singled out the three most important women in her husband's life. Of Anna and Lillian, much has already been written. Let us now consider Olive Thomas.

The Olive Thomas ascendancy into the Ziegfeld galaxy of stars was meteoric, both as brilliant and as brief as the heavenly journey of a shooting star. She was a Ziegfeld Girl at seventeen, a glamorous movie queen at nineteen, and a corpse on the slab of a Parisian morgue at twenty-two. It is a pity modern-day theatre enthusiasts know her best as the "Ghost of the New Amsterdam Theatre." She is remembered today more for the circumstances of her death than for her exceptional beauty or any positive contribution she made in the world of entertainment.

Olive was born in 1898 into conditions of near destitution in the small steel town of Charleford, Pennsylvania. She lost her father in early childhood and watched her mother slave at menial jobs to support herself, Olivia, and two siblings. Eventually, the family moved to McKees Rocks in suburban Pittsburgh. Olive, still only a teenager, was forced to seek employment, thereby negating any opportunity for a normal education. Desperate to leave behind the impoverished living conditions at home, she sought to escape through marriage to a nondescript local businessman. After two unhappy years, Olive left her husband and moved to metropolitan Pittsburgh, where, capitalizing on her physical attractiveness, she found immediate employment as a department store model. Within three months she was again on the move with her sights this time set on New York City, and she had no problem securing work as a photographers' model. At the urging of one of her photographer friends she answered a chorus call notice at the New Amsterdam Theatre for the *Ziegfeld Follies*. She successfully auditioned and was signed for the 1915 edition as well as the 1915–16 *Midnight Frolics* on the New Amsterdam Ziegfeld Roof.

Olivia was frivolous and temperamental, but her beauty—not her intellect—gained her rapid favor and a following among high-society playboys and well-heeled Wall Streeters. But she was in the *Follies,* and so it was inevitable that she would end up in the arms of Flo Ziegfeld. Friends and associates of the producer felt he had not been so smitten since his long and tempestuous affair with Lillian Lorraine. At the time, Billie Burke was on the West Coast making films, thereby providing favorable conditions for Flo's amorous extramarital pursuits. Eventually, though, word got back to Billie, and she quickly issued an ultimatum which effectively ended the affair. She told him to sever his relationship with the Thomas woman, or else he would be the recipient of divorce papers.

Late in 1916, twenty-year-old Jack Pickford entered Olive's life. He was the high-strung wastrel brother of Hollywood's reigning movie queen, Mary Pickford. Handsome and precocious, young Jack had achieved some degree of success in silent films, and from the age of fifteen his romantic dalliances and exploits with beautiful showgirls were the talk of the town. In her 1997 *Pickford: The Woman Who Made Hollywood,* Canadian author Ellen Whitfield relates a rumor that Jack at fifteen had been sexually involved with Lillian. Not too risky an assumption, since both of Jack's marriages were to Ziegfeld Girls. However, with no basis in truth, this rumor should be evaluated as just that and nothing more. On the other hand, Jack's fascination with the

Jack Pickford, younger brother of Mary, spouse of Olive Thomas, then Marilyn Miller, circa 1923 (courtesy Ziegfeld Club Archives).

beautiful and childishly naïve Olive Thomas was intense and substantiated by a very public courtship, which eventually culminated in a stormy three-year marriage, replete with numerous trial separations and reconciliations.

In the late summer of 1920, Jack and Olive sailed for Europe in one more attempt to salvage their rocky marriage; it was intended to be a second honeymoon. Instead, it turned into a continuous bacchanal of wild parties, heavy drinking and cocaine abuse. According to Jack Pickford, in the early morning hours of September 4, either by accident or intent, Olive swallowed a fatal dose of bichloride of mercury. Doctors were summoned to the Pickfords' Ritz Hotel suite, and Olive was immediately removed to the American hospital in the Parisian suburb of Neuilly, where she succumbed on September 10, 1920. The highly toxic concoction that killed Olive had been prescribed by Pickford's personal physician to treat Pickford's syphilis.

The circumstances of the twenty-two-year-old actress's death have always been shrouded in mystery, with speculation ranging from accidental poisoning to suicide and even murder at the hands of her jealous husband she had been threatening to leave. The Parisian medical authorities conducted a cursory autopsy, but there was no attempt by the medical authorities or the Paris police to attribute the cause of Olive's death to anything other than the inadvertent ingestion of a fatal dose of bichloride of mercury. They simply accepted Jack Pickford's version of the events immediately preceding Olive's taking of the lethal elixir. Jack returned to New York with Olive's body, and following funeral services at a packed St. Thomas Fifth Avenue Episcopal Church, Olive was interred in a small, single-casket crypt at Woodlawn Cemetery in the Bronx — less than a three-minute walk from where the mausoleum and final resting place of Marilyn Miller, Pickford's second *Follies* conquest.

The mystery surrounding the exact cause of Olive's demise encouraged the yellow press to speculate on the precise nature of Jack Pickford's role in the tragedy. According to Richard

The New Amsterdam Theatre 1925

New Amsterdam Theatre marquee, 42nd Street, New York, 1925 (courtesy Ziegfeld Club Archives).

Ziegfeld it was rumored that Jack was involved in drug dealing, that he was syphilitic and had transferred the disease to Olive, and that he was primary beneficiary in a newly purchased insurance policy taken out on Olive's life.

Over the eighty years since her death, the New Amsterdam Theatre has become the focal point for allegations of ghostly sightings thought to be Olive, returning to haunt the stages she had graced with her youthful beauty in the *Follies* and *Midnight Frolics* of 1915–16. Night watchmen and theatre custodians swear they have seen what appeared to be a white-shrouded female figure, a ghostly apparition, hovering about in dark recesses of the theatre. Dana Amendola, Disney Vice-President and General Manager of the New Amsterdam, has told me his tour guides are constantly besieged by their listeners for additional details on the Thomas phenomenon. The ghost lives on.

20

Lillian, on Her Own

It was early January of 1914. Europe was bristling with rumors and threats of a major military conflagration among the last great empires of Austria-Hungary, Germany and Russia. The United States was blissfully remote in the grips of political and philosophical isolation. But Broadway, America's premiere entertainment Mecca, was vibrant and thriving with a record number of big-name stars lighting up theatre marquees from 42nd Street to Columbus Circle: Eva Tanguay, Eddie Foy and the 7 Little Foys, Dainty Marie and Lulu Glaser. The Messrs. Shubert were presenting Al Jolson in *The Honeymoon Express*; Gus Edwards was always presenting something new at the Astor Theatre Building; Frank Fogarty was hitting his stride as *The Dublin Minstrel*; William Montgomery and Florence Moore were vaudevillizing musical comedy; London's Bonita and Lew Hearn were at the Gaiety; Eva Davenport had opened *The Ceiling Walker*; Melville and Higgins had the audience in stitches in *Putting on Airs*; Maurice and Florence Walton were tripping the light fantastic with their program of original dances; and Jim and Bonnie Thornton had a major hit with their *Survival of the Fittest*.

Fresh from her 1913 vaudeville triumphs as a headline attraction at Hammerstein's Victoria Theatre of the Varieties, the Shuberts Wintergarden, the Colonial Theatre and finally the Palace Theatre, Lillian Lorraine signed for the principal role in a new musical extravaganza, *The Whirl of the World*. The all-star cast included Bernard Granville, Trixie Raymond, Ralph Herz, Juliette Lippe and the outrageously funny Jewish comic, Willie Howard.

Reviews were generally good, with most critics agreeing *The Whirl of the World* was "extravagant, in people, production and costuming."

Of Willie Howard, one critic wrote, "And the comedy hit is a Jew comedian, which is almost a paradox. But this Hebrew comedian is a comedian who can commede and sing. He is Willie Howard, as far removed from those with 'The Pleasure Seekers' as that show is now distant ... with its mob of Jew comedians and unfunny comedy." Needless to say, in today's climate of ethnic sensitivity, such a commentary would not be likely to see the light of day, although this critic might not have been referring to the cast's Jewishness so much as the characters they portrayed.

The Shuberts' *The New York Review* was inexplicably generous to Lillian but could not resist using its praise of her as a double-edged sword to snipe at Ziegfeld: "For the first time, the real quality of Miss Lorraine as a musical comedy artist had an opportunity for display. It must be with bitter envy that Ziegfeld views the immense success of Miss Lorraine at the Winter Garden, doing far finer work than she ever did for him. He had stifled her natural talent and the best reflection of her individuality."

Lillian delivered the lyrics of Harry Carroll's and Alfred Bryan's "Smother Me with Kisses and Kill Me with Love" in her typically sensuous style — and this guaranteed the song would be a solid million-copy best seller. From the chorus of this number:

Smother me with kisses, hon,
   And kill me with love,

Broadway theater guide from *The Morning Telegraph*, 1914.

Wrap yourself around me like a serpent 'round a dove,
'Cause I love it,
Oh! How I love it,
And it fills my heart with joy,
Just take it from me,
I am crazy 'bout you, boy,
Love me like the vampire Mister Kipling wrote about,

Love me with a burning flame that never will go out,
Kiss me honey, till I lose my breath,
Go 'way, doctor, it's a happy death,
Smother me with kisses, hon,
And kill me with love.
— Shapiro, Bernstein & Co, Inc., Publishers, 1914

Inasmuch as she was no longer under Ziegfeld's personal management, Lillian signed with one of the youngest and most successful of Broadway's agent-managers, Frederic Edward

McKay. First a Boston newspaper drama critic, then a theatrical agent, McKay arrived in New York at the age of twenty-four and quickly became a popular figure in Gotham's young Bohemian set. As he was attending a performance of the musical comedy *The Defender*, his fancy was struck by an ingénue in the company by the name of Blanche Ring. Her one big solo number was "In the Good Old Summertime," and this, together with McKay's personal guidance, made her name marquee-friendly within less than one year. Blanche was for the most part under contract to the Shuberts and became a stellar attraction in their constellation of performing artists. Nevertheless, on frequent occasions she was the recipient of stern admonitions from the brothers Shubert, who were critical of what they considered to be excessively high travel expenses while on tour as well as her disregard for budgetary restrictions in costume selections.

Olive Thomas in Ziegfeld debut appearance, *Midnight Frolic*, 1915 (courtesy Ziegfeld Club Archives).

Blanche Ring was a tireless and highly vocal activist for women's rights and the Equity Chorus Girls' Association. In this latter role, she was the subject of another, very strong Shubert reprimand. J.J. Shubert wrote:

My dear Miss Ring: I have been told by various girls of our company that there has been a propaganda started, emanating from you, to make every one of our chorus girls a member of the Equity Chorus Girls' Association. This is not in the spirit of our understanding when we fixed up our past differences. I wish that you would let our girls alone and strictly attend to your own business. If you do this, that is all we shall desire of you. Our girls are satisfied and we do not want any agitation that will be the cause of disrupting our organization.

In 1908, Lillian Lorraine had been a lowly member of the Shubert chorus in *The Gay White Way* starring Blanche Ring. Now McKay, as Lillian's agent, signed a contract on her behalf with the Shubert Theatrical Company calling for her to star in a new musical comedy entitled *A Trip to Washington*, scheduled for a Washington, D.C., premiere in the early part of 1915.

Prior to going into rehearsal for the new show, Lillian was signed to appear in a William Hammerstein revue at the Victoria Theatre, a magnificent 1899 edifice on the northwest corner of 42nd Street and 7th Avenue. Even in those long-gone days, police censorship of the entertainment industry was very much in evidence. Therefore it came as no great surprise when the *New York Telegraph,* reviewing Lillian's December 16 opening, took note that

> the presence of a representative of the New York City Police Department on Thursday night, taking stenographic notes during Lillian Lorraine's songs caused William Hammerstein his greatest anxiety. Consequently, those who attended the performance yesterday afternoon with the expectation of hearing Miss Lorraine sing the widely discussed "Put, Put, Put" number were disappointed, for Mr. Hammerstein had ordered the number stricken from her repertoire. The song and its refrain ostensibly alludes to the put-put sound of a motor boat. But the references to the young woman aboard the launch, and the owner's deportment with her, have been causing even the Victoria's audience to gasp.

Although readily acknowledging its box office appeal, Hammerstein had no wish to be involved in a legal hassle with the law and did not reinstate the number.

The adverse publicity had not escaped the watchful eyes of the ultra-conservative J.J. Shubert and gave him cause to reflect on the wisdom of going forward with *A Trip to Washington.* Consequently, McKay, again signing for Lillian, agreed to cancellation of the contract, by mutual consent, for the enormous compensatory fee of one dollar.

21

Ziegfeldian Potpourri

Billie Burke and Florenz Ziegfeld were married on April 11, 1914, four months and eleven days after their first meeting at Jack Rumsey's Sixty Club. According to daughter Patricia, born on October 24, 1916, the first thing her mother did upon taking up residency at the Ansonia was to clear the Ziegfeld suite of stacks of Lillian Lorraine photographs.

Billie had every intention of continuing her professional life in the theatre. Flo, of course, assumed that she would willingly put furtherance of her career under his personal management. However, Flo had not taken into account the depth of Billie's loyalty to her longtime friend, confidant and mentor, Charles Frohman. Billie's relationship with Frohman came to a tragic halt on May 7, 1915, when a German U-boat sent a single torpedo crashing into the hull of the SS *Lusitania*, taking the luxury passenger vessel and over 1,000 souls to the bottom of the sea. One of those passengers was Charles Frohman. Billie was devastated and mourned long and hard over the loss of her dear friend.

The impact of Frohman's death — the loss of his theatrical genius on the international theatre community — was severe, and was perhaps best described in the *New York Review* of May 15, 1915:

> The theatre world of America and, indeed the world, sustained an irreparable loss when Charles Frohman and the other victims of [German aggression] went to their deaths with the sinking of the *Lusitania* last week off the Irish coast. It remained for Mr. Frohman, a true American, standing calmly, waiting his end on the deck of the stricken vessel, to utter the finest piece of philosophy to come from the lips of man concerning the impenetrable eternal mystery of death.
>
> With the waters of the Atlantic lapping the deck of the shattered liner and scenes of tragedy and agony being enacted all around him, Mr. Frohman tried to calm the nerves of fellow passenger Rita Jolivet, standing by his side, when he said, "Why should we fear death — it is the most beautiful adventure in life." It was a simple but supremely eloquent observation.

Obviously, Miss Jolivet was one of the few lucky survivors.

* * *

The year 1914 started out as a singularly bad one for Flo Ziegfeld and a number of the men and women in his inner circle of friends and associates. First, Anna Held found herself in trouble with the law when she was charged with defaulting on a contractual agreement. The threat of incarceration hung over her head unless she paid the $5,000 fine which had been awarded against her. Next, it was Lillian's turn when she was called to appear before the New York State Supreme Court to explain why she had not paid a paltry $125 judgment for non-payment of the rental fee on her safe-deposit box. The *Morning Telegraph,* with tongue in cheek, editorialized, "With all her jools, which the cruel knaves of the city are constantly striving to annex, Lillian has forgotten to pay a little bill of $125. What a shame!"

Flo, too, found himself the subject of a legal judgment. His honeymoon was rudely interrupted when a heartless process server delivered a summons charging he had defrauded Harry B. Smith by refusing to pay $4,340 in royalties allegedly due him from Ziegfeld's 1909 production of *Miss Innocence*, which starred Anna Held and introduced Lillian Lorraine. Smith claimed Flo had failed to pay him five weeks' worth of royalties at the rate of 3 percent of gross receipts. Not anxious for any audit of his income records or any further negative press, Flo settled out of court with a full payment of $4,340.

Another of Flo's confidantes, James Buchanan Brady (Diamond Jim), was having serious medical problems with his stomach, which would soon lead to his demise. Previous surgery at Johns Hopkins in Baltimore, to which he had recently endowed $25,000, was not the success it was originally thought to be.

Evelyn Nesbit Thaw was feeling the long arm of the law, not in New York, but in Richmond, Virginia, where she was appearing in *Marietta*. She was placed under arrest for "a performance outraging public decency and to the detriment of public morals. Additionally, she is charged with being a common nuisance to all the citizens of this commonwealth." After hear-

Billie Burke Ziegfeld and daughter Patricia, circa 1913 (courtesy Ziegfeld Club Archives).

ing arguments for both sides, the court ordered the charges dismissed and the immediate release of Evelyn from custody. That same evening she returned to *Marietta*, and without a single change in its content, performed the original program to a packed house and thunderous applause.

With Lillian out of Ziegfeld's life — at least publicly — Anna Held and Flo were again on speaking terms, and Anna returned to his personal management of her career. Amid much Ziegfeldian public relations fanfare, Anna opened in a highly touted musical revue at the Colonial Theatre in New York City. One critic drubbed her performance, calling it "a frost" and causing her great humiliation over the loss of the always prestigious top billing. Another reviewer administered the *coup de grace* when he wrote, "It would seem that vaudeville audiences no longer care for Anna's trademark rolling eyes and wriggling hips!"

Ironically, on March 15, 1915, it was Lillian who followed Anna into the Colonial, but she did not fare any better with the theatre critics. A feud with the *Morning Telegraph* over alleged nonpayment of an advertising bill led that news outlet to blacklist her name from any future mention in that paper. Following a financially successful Colonial run, Lillian opened a new revue at Hammerstein's Victoria. On March 27, 1915, the *New York Review* declared the *Telegraph* had lifted their boycott of Lillian just long enough to describe Lillian as "an onion in a bed of roses." Lillian's good-natured rejoinder, "I'm an onion, am I? How nice. I must be going strong!"

On another front, the *New York Star* took Lillian to task on grounds of what they determined to be "racial prejudice." They wrote, "Miss Lorraine has her own company of colored musicians who are seated behind some palms and unseen by the audience. They are good musicians and Miss Lorraine need not be ashamed to show them." Commenting on her performance, they wrote, "She noticed that her first two songs were not received with too much enthusiasm and decided to cut loose. Or, it may be that she lost her bearing and forgot where she was playing because during the delivery of her last number she indulged in some 'cooching,' a throwback to an undulating 1911 dance form."

Billie Burke had a 1916 fling with law enforcement. It was charged that her car had knocked down and run over thirteen-year-old Helen Neville in the Harlem section of New York City. Although Billie was not in the car at the time of the accident, she was nevertheless charged and named the offender in the $15,000 action that followed. Process servers were unsuccessful in their efforts to locate and serve Billie and were finally forced to petition New York State Supreme Court Justice Pendleton for permission to serve her through the mails. Since there was no further publicity on the matter, it is reasonable to assume an out-of-court settlement must have been effected.

As for Lillian and my mother, they soon would be entraining for the West Coast and new and exciting adventures in what was rapidly emerging as the film capital of the world: Hollywood.

22

Hollywood Beckons

It was late spring of 1915 — the first World War was raging in Europe but along Gotham's Gay White Way, rumor mill speculation was rife to the effect that Lillian Lorraine was deserting Broadway's bright lights and was in the midst of contract negotiations with certain motion picture impresarios. The word on the street was that she would soon be Hollywood-bound for the starring role in a screenplay by Douglas Bronston from an original story by William Hamilton Osborne. With the European war threatening to engulf the entire world, patriotic fervor was at a high pitch in America, and Osborne's saga, a fourteen-chapter serial, took full advantage of the prevailing national mood by utilizing the U.S. Navy as a focal point of the photoplay.

It had been almost two years since Lillian's initial forays into the increasingly popular medium of moving pictures. Her previous five years on Broadway and road show touring throughout the country had made her a nationally recognized stage presence and, in the eyes of Balboa Pictures chieftain H.M. Horkheimer, a sure-fire bet as a big-screen box office attraction.

Less than a month after the first stories of Lillian's rumored defection appeared in newsprint, the Horkheimer Brothers confirmed that Lillian had indeed been signed for the lead role in Osborne's *Neal of the Navy*. By the first week in June, she, with my mother in tow, entrained for the West Coast. After a six-day journey in a luxurious double-compartment drawing room, they arrived in Los Angeles and were met by the Horkheimer Brothers, floral bouquets and a bevy of studio publicists.

According to Jean-Jacques Jura and Rodney Bardin, co-authors of *Balboa Films: A History and Filmography of the Silent Film Studio*, shooting on *Neal* began on June 19 with Lillian cast as the film's heroine, Annette Illington, a girl whose life had been fraught with terror, threats of kidnapping, and even worse. William Courtleigh Jr., in his first major film appearance, played the title role of Neal Hardin, an apprentice seaman who, through acts of daring heroism, works his way up to the rank of ensign. The supporting cast included character actors William Conklin, Ed Brady and Henry Stanley.

The serialized story begins with five-year-old Annette Illington (not played by Lillian) surviving a shipwreck. Her father, not so fortunate, is lost at sea but not before entrusting his daughter with a map of the treasure-rich lost Isle of Cinnibar. The second episode jumps thirteen years and shows the orphaned Annette hiding and evading a band of villainous pirates in search of her and the map. Now a grown woman of 18, Annette (played by Lillian) eventually meets and comes under the protection of Ensign Neal Hardin and the U.S. Navy. Through the subsequent twelve episodes of the film, Lorraine's and Courtleigh's characters romp their way from one cliff-hanging crisis to another.

One film reviewer credits the Osborne story with being "made of the stuff that contains every element of human appeal, love, fear, hatred, suspense and survival. The Balboa-Pathé release is a production that is by far the most virile, red-blooded installment I have ever

viewed." In the early scenes, authentic footage of a volcanic eruption is used, suggesting the disastrous and terrifying 1902 Mount Pelée tragedy on the Caribbean island of Martinique. Shipboard mutinies, fires and perilous diving from high cliffs keep the excitement level high throughout the picture.

One segment of the film called for Annette to be chased by the pirate horde to the edge of a cliff overlooking the sea. To escape capture she must dive into the swirling waters below. The actual location for the jump scene was the famous La Jolla Cliffs in Southern California. Lillian, while being an accomplished swimmer, had a phobia of heights, so the call went out for a stunt double. My mother, a natural-born daredevil and very much at home in the water, ended up as the Lorraine stand-in who made the dive into the pounding surf, twenty-five feet below.

Although Lillian did not appear in the first episode, there was an additional two hundred feet filmed for private viewing by exhibitors in which Lillian is featured as the best-dressed woman on the American musical comedy stage. She is seen in a magnificent collection of frocks and gowns successfully highlighting her legendary beauty and fashion-plate status. Double exposure in the footage simultaneously shows her in five different poses. Exhibitors previewing the film applauded the sequence as a remarkably clever device to introduce the star

Top: Pathé's *Neal of the Navy* poster. *Bottom:* Pathé star souvenir pennant.

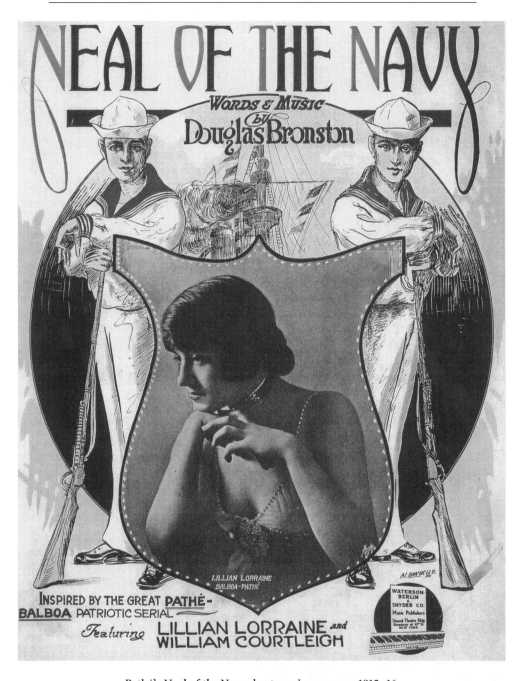

Pathé's *Neal of the Navy* sheet music cover, ca. 1915–16.

who would hopefully soon be causing their cash registers to jingle. Lillian's co-star, William Courtleigh Jr., began his acting career at the age of five in his father's East Lynn stock company. He left the theatre after another five years and returned to Chicago for a resumption of his education, ending with the completion of one year at the University of Chicago. After working with a number of stock companies in Chicago, Atlanta and New York, he finally arrived in Hollywood, where he had several minor movie parts just prior to his casting as Ensign Neal

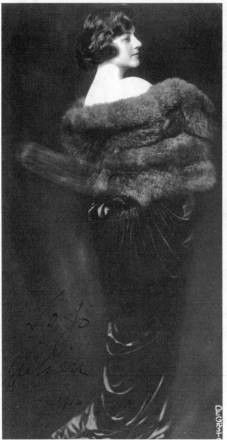

Hardin. It was during filming of *Neal* that the twenty-three-year-old actor met, fell in love with, and married Balboa starlet Ethel Flemming. In their appraisal of his acting talent, *Variety* wrote, "He greatly resembles his distinguished actor-father and comes across as a clean-cut boy with a good face. There isn't much question about him being in line to become a screen favorite."

Initial reviews of the early episodes were excellent, and according to figures obtained from Pathé-Frères, who released the picture, *Neal of the Navy* was the most successful serial yet put out, having broken all booking records as of that reporting period. As the weeks went on with the release of each new episode, the former exuberance of reviewers was muted and eventually replaced with severely critical notices. The explanation may be found in the Jura-Bardin book on the history of the Balboa Studio. They state, "According to Marc Wanamaker, author and film historian, Harry Harvey (the film's director) was offered a bonus of $500 if he could make the serial in twelve weeks. He completed eight episodes in six weeks and finished the rest before the deadline. The rapidity of the production showed and Pathé barely accepted the hastily made episodes because of their poor quality." *Variety,* which reviewed each episode as it was released, in discussing the later installments said, "Audiences applauded only when the American flag was portrayed [on the screen at the end of each episode]."

In anticipation of high revenue yields, and weeks prior to the completion of *Neal*, the Horkheimers moved to exercise their option with Lillian for a two-picture deal. She signed for the lead role in a Joseph E. Howard original melodrama first titled *The Lady of Perfume*, then *Should a Woman Forgive?* and finally, more appropriate to the story line, *Should a Wife Forgive?*

Lillian was cast in the femme fatale role of LaBelle Rose, a cabaret dancer, described by film

Top: Pathé and Balboa sketch, supplement to *Motion Picture News*, 1915. *Bottom:* In a pre-film publicity reel for *Neal of the Navy* in 1915, Lillian Lorraine was photographed in a series of elegant gowns to highlight her well-established reputation as a fashion plate.

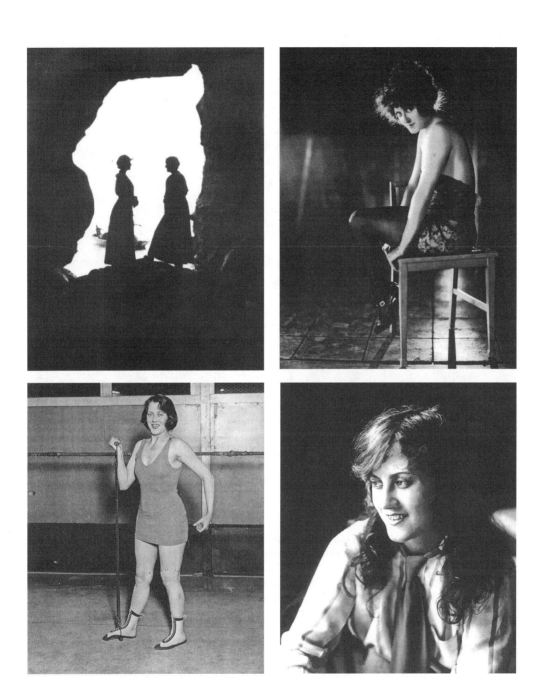

Top left: Nanny Johnson and Lillian Lorraine in silhouette at the LaJolla Caves during filming of Balboa-Pathé serial thriller, *Neal of the Navy*, 1915. Nanny doubled for Lillian in a third-episode sequence calling for Lillian to dive into the ocean from a rocky promontory. *Top right:* The original pose used in a *Rio Rita* publicity shot. *Bottom left:* Proof that actresses of all eras have been concerned with their fitness and figures (courtesy Ziegfeld Club Archives). *Bottom right:* Lillian Lorraine headshot from *Neal of the Navy.*

critic Hanford C. Judson as "a woman utilizing all the vapors, whims and petulances of a Gypsy trollop with a heart that is cold and calculating in a voluptuous body." LaBelle entices a young married man into an adulterous relationship. The wronged wife discovers her husband's infidelity and turns him from their home. In the last scenes, a gunfight takes place between LaBelle's married lover and a jealous suitor. LaBelle, the unintended victim, is mor-

The Bystander, September 27, 1916   561

The Super-Scooter
AN AMERICAN NOTION THAT MAY COME OVER AND HELP US

LILLIAN LORRAINE

Was born in San Francisco in 1892—and only four years later made her stage debut as "Eva" in "Uncle Tom's Cabin." Soon after going to New York—at the age of fourteen—she appeared with Eddie Foy; later with Blanche Ring and Jeff De Angeles and Anna Held—starred in "The Follies of 1912." Her beauty, talent—the way she wears her clothes—make her a favorite. Equitable.

Copyright 1916, by A. Manford Stryker, Chicago.

As a means to "hustle"—the American desideratum—the Auto-push-mobile is the latest scream. It is run by a small gasoline motor, and a very respectable speed can be got out of it, besides any amount of amusement. It is naturally beloved of stage favourites, since its novelty is in itself an advertisement, and Miss Lillian Lorraine and Mr. Dickinson are evidently alive both to its delights and its uses.

Left: Promotional card for Lillian Lorraine as fashion plate: Balboa/Pathé, 1915. *Right:* A flirtatious Lillian Lorraine and Mr. Dickinson ride tandem on "super scooter," 1916.

tally wounded, but not before having penned a note suggesting suicide in repentance for her past sinful life. Both men are thereby exonerated of murder and go their separate ways. In the case of LaBelle's married lover, the question is intentionally left hanging—should a wife forgive?

Two endings were filmed. In the first LaBelle dies, and in the second, LaBelle becomes a nun. For the final cut, the director opted for the more sensational of the two, the shooting death of LaBelle. The *Rochester Express* in its review noted, "Gunplay in the last act is so frequent that one is given cause to wonder what has become of the National Board of Censorship's ruling on murder and suicide in full view of the audience."

Should a Wife Forgive? was eleven weeks in production, five reels in length and contained four hundred scene settings. For the most part it was filmed at the Balboa Studios in Long Beach, but many interiors were shot in the elegant Long Beach and Pasadena private residences of Lillian's movie colony friends. The film opened to mixed notices, with *Variety* reporting, "Lillian Lorraine is the star and shows some stunning clothes. It is evidently firmly planted in her mind that clothes will help her gain a reputation on the screen as a fashion trend-setter such as she enjoys along Broadway.... It is not a wonderful picture by any means since it has a story that dates back many moons. Lillian Lorraine's portrayal of the cabaret dancer gives ample evidence of her ability to play highly emotional roles. It is not a brilliant performance but certainly adequate to the demands of the part she has been given."

With reference to the supporting cast, the trade paper continued, "Henry King, later to become a very successful director at 20th Century-Fox, and Lew Cody as the two suitors are capable actors but neither one is the sort Lillian Lorraine would fall in love with." Mabel Van Buren, as the wronged wife, is lauded by *Motion Picture World* for a "performance not so artistic as Miss Lorraine's but far more pleasing. It is one that rings true emotionally and is full of dignity."

It was during the final two weeks of filming when national wire services reported

Top: Lillian Lorraine with Pathé Pictures co-star William Courtleigh Jr. and his new bride, starlet Ethel Fleming. *Neal of the Navy*, Hollywood, 1915. *Bottom:* A pre–*Neal of the Navy* fashion publicity shot.

Fred Gresheimer, the proverbial bad penny, had been indicted by a San Francisco Grand Jury on charges of grand larceny. He was charged with obtaining money under false pretenses from Dr. Karl Mack, director of the Boston Symphony Orchestra. Freddy had assured Dr. Mack the money would go into a support fund for *The Fatherland*, a conservative, San Francisco based, pro-German publication. In the trial that followed, the magazine editor, George Sylvester Vierick, denied ever having authorized Fred to collect funds on the publication's behalf. Fred was found guilty of fraud and sentenced to eighteen months in San Quentin Prison.

Opposite page top: Undated fashion shot. *Opposite page bottom left:* Foxtail publicity shot, 1920. *Opposite bottom right:* Lillian Lorraine on the cover of *The Photo-Play Review*, 1915. *Above:* Lillian Lorraine and co-star Lou Cody in publicity still for Equitable's *Should a Wife Forgive?* ca. 1915–16. *Right:* Lillian Lorraine test-driving a new fad, the "Auto-Push-Mobile," for a Hollywood publicity shot, Long Beach, CA, 1916.

Should a Wife Forgive ad, from ***The Moving Picture World***, Nov. 6 (year unknown).

When approached by reporters for an update on the status of her marriage to Gresheimer, Lillian responded, "Yes, he is still my husband but we have not lived together as man and wife for quite some time. As soon as I have completed this picture I fully intend to reactivate my original suit for divorce, and this time, if he chooses to contest it again, I don't think any judge will take the word of a convicted felon against mine." When one acid-tongued news-hen asked if the title of her latest film might be applicable in the present situation, Lillian curtly replied, "Don't be ridiculous!"

I conducted an exhaustive search of private collections and film archives in the hope of turning up footage of either of the two Lorraine films. I was ultimately rewarded at the Library of Congress, where one badly deteriorated 35mm first reel of *Wife* was discovered and very graciously transferred by the library staff to VHS tape for my own private collection.

After completion of the filming of *Should a Wife Forgive?*, Lillian motored to her native San Francisco to again begin divorce proceedings and take one full month for rest and relaxation. Her co-star William Courtleigh and his new bride also traveled north to the Golden Gate Exposition. During the next two years, while under contract with Famous Players, Courtleigh achieved some minor success in films, particularly in supporting roles with Ethel Barrymore and H.B. Warner. In March of 1918, while playing in the Philadelphia stage production of *Blind Youth*, he was stricken with plueropneumonia and succumbed at the age of 26. His sudden and unexpected demise cast a pall of sadness over his many friends and peers in the theatre community. It was a tragic end to career most observers believed was on the brink of major stardom. Courtleigh's remains were brought to New York, where final services were held at Campbell's Funeral Home on upper Broadway. Lillian was still in San Francisco, but it can probably be assumed that my mother, who had preceded Lillian's return to New York and who had been befriended by Courtleigh during the film's production, would certainly have attended the funeral and been among the mourners.

23

The Broadway Fast Track and Ziegfeld's Frolic

The Hollywood of 1915 was a peaceful village not too many years removed from sheep, goats and pigs wandering along dusty and unpaved streets. Then the film moguls, based for the most part in the New York area, searching for permanent sunshine, took over and Hollywood changed forever, becoming the make-believe capital of the world. To Lillian's way of thinking, however, the fledgling Tinseltown community could not begin to compete with New York and the glitter of Broadway's Gay White Way. She yearned for the footlights, the infectious enthusiasm of a live audience, and of course the glitzy intimacy of familiar after-hours nightclub haunts. So it was that, after her one-month sojourn in San Francisco, Lillian rejoined my mother, who had preceded her to New York, and reopened their Hotel Savoy apartment.

On November 29, 1915, the *New York Times* published an extensive obituary reporting on the death in New York of the noted German portrait artist Gustave C. Langenberg. It was a death that, according to the *Times,* brought to light a romantic anecdote concerning Lillian and the late artist, the details of which, at that time, she claimed little or no familiarity with. The artist had been an avid equestrian and did a considerable amount of painting as he toured much of the civilized world on horseback — thus he was dubbed "the painter on horseback." As a portrait artist he had been commissioned to paint President Woodrow Wilson, Kaiser Wilhelm II, and the internationally revered stage luminary Sarah Bernhardt.

Aside from Lillian, the central figure of the story was an unidentified stranger who disappeared almost as mysteriously as he had initially come on the scene. He had approached Langenberg at his New York City studio, almost a full year before the artist's demise, and commissioned Lillian's portrait for an agreed price of $10,000. He brought with him a photograph of Lillian which he said he had purchased in Paris. He said he had never met the object of his infatuation but was smitten with her image in the photograph and would soon attempt to arrange a meeting with her. Leaving a good faith payment of $1,000 and declining to identify himself, he told the artist he could address him as "Doctor." With the exception of some minor touches of color to the facial features, the portrait was complete at the time of Langenberg's death. The *Times* article continued, "The portrait Langenberg had titled *Meditation* was found hanging on a wall in his West 55th Street studio. The mystery doctor never returned to claim the painting. It is a beautiful work, showing Miss Lorraine, wearing a Leghorn hat, pensively looking down at a stream below. Langenberg had hoped one day to meet Miss Lorraine and induce her to sit for him so that he might add the remaining color tones to the face." The whereabouts of this portrait are, to this day, unknown. In today's markets of specialty buyers of one-of-a-kind paintings, this original Langenberg oil would be enormously valuable.

Despite its generally unfavorable notices, *Variety* reported that final box office figures on

Neal of the Navy had, as originally forecast, set a record for any serial picture thus far released, and *Should a Wife Forgive?* was also doing well. Yet all was not milk and honey between Lillian and the Horkheimer Brothers, producers of both films. On her return to New York, Lillian contacted her attorney, Nathan Vidaverf, and although she was already appearing at the Winter Garden in the Shuberts' *Passing Show of 1916*, she found time to file charges against the Balboa Amusement Producing Company for $4,637, which she alleged she had personally advanced to them on a thirty-day promissory note. On the expiration date, payment was requested and allegedly refused. An affidavit of service shows it was served on E.D. Horkheimer, secretary and general manager, at the Hotel Astor in New York City. The matter never went to trial since the Horkheimers eventually chose to settle out of court. *Variety* did

Odds and Ends of 1917.

not disclose the reason for Lillian's advance to the Horkheimers, and it did not disclose the terms of the settlement.

After an absence of several seasons, Lillian's return to the musical comedy stage in *Odds and Ends of 1917* at New York's Palace Theatre was greeted with positive notices all around. Her leading man was popular Jack Norworth, former husband of Nora Bayes. Jack and Nora had co-starred in the 1908 *Ziegfeld Follies*, one year prior to Lillian's arrival on the Broadway scene. In one number in *Odds and Ends of 1917*, in a complete departure from her traditional glamour attire, Lillian surprised and delighted the Palace Theatre audiences when she came on stage in the garb and makeup of a scrub woman, trading rapid-fire repartee with Norworth in a sassy Irish brogue. Fanny Brice, watching the performance from a box seat, gasped in amazement at what she termed "Lillian's remarkable transition from glamour queen to a polished comedienne." Before the final curtain, Lillian had reverted to what her adoring fans liked best, returning to the stage in an exquisite gown of shimmering silver with a cleverly bifurcated skirt under a tunic upon which hundreds of sparkling sequins had been applied. Another crowd-pleaser was a high-fashion, tailor-made khaki outfit with bellows pockets and flared skirt. The *New York Times* reported on June 17, "Miss Lorraine's vacation has agreed with her. She has kept her beauty and there is a tremendous improvement in the singing quality of her voice and comedic sense of timing." The same review made casual reference to a secondary cast member, song and dance man George White. He would very shortly emerge as a phenomenally successful producer of high-end musical revues. *George White's Scandals* would become a Broadway institution in the 1920s, and, with its glorification of American Beauty showgirls, strong competition for the *Ziegfeld Follies*.

Taking note of the teaming of Lillian Lorraine and Jack Norworth, *Variety* wrote, "If there ever were two entertainers better suited to each other in talent and temperament, they have yet to make their presence noted to the variety boards. As for *esprit de corps,* it isn't possible for two real siblings to behave so well toward each other — and really mean it."

Jack Norworth and Lillian Lorraine from *Odds and Ends,* 1917 (courtesy Ziegfeld Club Archives).

Lillian's romantic dalliances had again become juicy morsels for media wags. For example, *Variety* erroneously reported in July of 1917 on the "imminent wedding of Lillian and Frank Moran, a contender for the Heavyweight Boxing Championship." Moran had been seen in her company quite often on the late-night party circuit, but that particular rumor came to naught as Lillian continued her frivolously promiscuous ride on the merry-go-round of non-monogamous sexcapades.

By the end of 1916, Flo Ziegfeld's *Follies* was in its ninth year and continued to reign supreme as the ultimate symbol of undisputed excellence in Broadway musical theatre. Having left the *Follies* four years earlier, Lillian, too, was now a firmly established star of stage and screen and, most recently, a headliner on the supper club cabaret scene.

Ever the innovator, Ziegfeld was expanding his horizons and literally reached for new heights when in 1913 he opened his *Midnight Frolic* on the New Amsterdam roof. It was a counterpoint to the existing Aerial Roof Gardens restaurant. It was Ziegfeld's response to the new craze of upscale cabaret supper clubs springing up all over the midtown theatre district. The entertainment was an informal cabaret mix of music, dancing girls and stand-up comedy.

Vaudeville entertainment was a marked contrast to the lavish extravaganzas taking place in the magnificent "downstairs" 1800-seat auditorium of the New Amsterdam Theatre. Many of the *Follies* headliners moved upstairs to the *Frolic* following their appearances in the regular 8 o'clock show. Olive Thomas, Eddie Cantor, Will Rogers, Pearl Eaton, Fanny Brice and Bird Millman, the high-wire queen, were among the *Frolic* regulars. Glass catwalk promenades were suspended from the ceiling and movable arms extending from the presidium into the audience provided a sense of intimacy not possible to affect in the larger auditorium.

To supplement his own creative genius and instinctive good taste, Ziegfeld brought in and utilized the considerable talents of Joseph Urban, a Viennese-born artist and architectural set designer. In 1917, Ben Ali Hagan, the already well-established portrait artist, was engaged to introduce and stage his personal trademark "living statues" tableaux. They were composed of scantily clad, but always in good taste, motionless showgirls, bathed in subdued, pastel-colored lighting. The effect was breathtakingly beautiful. At just about the same time, the brilliant choreographer and stage director Ned Wayburn came on board and is credited with the creation of the famous Ziegfeld Walk. Doris Eaton Travis, at one hundred and one years of age, the oldest surviving *Follies* principal and specialty dancer, clearly recalled and demonstrated for me the precise movements involved in the execution of the Ziegfeld Walk: "One hand is placed on the hip and the other hand is raised over the head. A step forward is taken with one foot, followed by the other foot drawn alongside of the first. Following a brief hesitation, the walk continues. Walk, hesitate, walk, hesitate. It can be performed without raising the hand and without placing the hand on the hip, such as when the performer is carrying a prop or balancing a cumbersome headdress."

In 1962 noted theatre historian Robert Baral, in his authoritative

Will Rogers, 1918 *Follies* (courtesy Ziegfeld Club Archives).

Bible of show business, *Revue*, complements the Eaton description with his own interpretation of the walk. "It was a combination of Irene Castle's flair for accentuating the pelvis in her stance, the lifted shoulder, and a slow, concentrated gait. A girl would enter into the spotlight very quietly — and with no visible smile proceed down the runway, a slight suggestion of a smile would then appear as she reached center stage and turned her full allure on an appreciative audience." The walk creator, Ned Wayburn, was ultimately responsible for choreographing eleven editions of the Ziegfeld *Midnight Frolics*.

Although he had briefly appeared in the 1915 *Frolic*, Oklahoman Will Rogers officially joined the *Ziegfeld Follies* in 1916. In the 1917 edition, Will stunned the wealthy New Amsterdam patrons with a tongue-in-cheek parody of his employer. Ziegfeld was made the butt of Will's earthy and down-home brand of humor. Suggesting that Flo might be looking for him to invest in a future Ziegfeld production, Will twanged, "Before I would put a dollar into any show that he produces, I'd get myself examined by a lunacy commission, yes I would!" With Flo in the audience, he continued to taunt, "I understand that Billie Burke is going to have a theatre of her own here in New York. It looks as though Billie has fallen for Flo's hokum because if it is true, it will be built with her own coin and you can bet on that." According to Ned Wayburn, many of the company cast members had serious doubts as to whether or not Will would be on the next Ziegfeld payroll.

In April of 1917, Flo was deeply saddened by the loss of his longtime friend and confidant, "Diamond Jim" Brady. The multimillionaire had been a stalwart supporter for almost a quarter of a century and Flo would sorely miss his wise counsel in affairs of finance as well as the heart. Brady's estate was estimated to be in excess of five million dollars, although his executors claimed it had been diminished by at least one fifth due to depreciation in the stock holdings. An interesting tidbit appeared in the *New York Review*, which reported the existence of a second and secret will awarding one hundred and fifty thousand dollars to the Dolly Sisters, Rozika and Janzieka. Both girls had been featured dancers in the 1911 *Follies*, and soon thereafter became international favorites in music halls throughout Europe. Brady's two siblings were named in the first will but for considerably less money than had been anticipated. They unsuccessfully initiated legal proceedings to set aside many of Diamond Jim's specific bequests, including his bequest to the Dolly Sisters, on the grounds that prior to drawing the will, their brother had suffered "mental aberrations."

One year later, fresh from her triumph in the Shuberts' *Odds and Ends of 1917*, Lillian would be enticed back into the Ziegfeld fold as a major principal attraction in the *Midnight Frolic* as well as the *Follies* itself.

In the waning months of 1917, Flo was to hear more sad news. Anna Held was seriously ill. She was touring the country with a new musical comedy, *Follow Me,* when her failing health forced closure of the show in January of 1918 and her immediate return to New York for medical attention. She took up residence at the Hotel Savoy, which ironically, as in the Ansonia days, just happened to be the home port for my mother and Anna's ex-nemesis, Lillian Lorraine. With the exception of Lillian Russell, a friend from her earliest days in America, Anna refused all visitors.

With Anna now for the most part bedridden, her malady was diagnosed as terminal myeloma, an incurable disease of the bones. She died a painful death at the age of forty-five on August 12, 1918. Although thousands attended her high requiem mass at St. Patrick's Cathedral, Flo Ziegfeld, who, as was widely publicized at the time, dreaded any symbolism depicting the finality of death, was not among the mourners. He never attended funerals. Anna's body was interred at Gate of Heaven Cemetery in Hawthorne, New York.

24

The Follies of 1918

It was 1918 and America was still at war, but an allied victory was clearly in sight. My mother was in her tenth year with Lillian —first as a maid, then secretary, and finally, close friend and confidante. It was from this relationship that my mother's American first name was born.

When I once overheard my mother's sister, Aunt Sigrid, call my mother Nanny, I asked Mother why. She told me her name from the old country was Nanny, and that a woman here she once worked with told her the name Nanny reminded her of a nanny-goat. Until then I had no idea that my mother ever had a first name other than Elsie. As I later learned, Mother changed her name from Nanny to Elsa, and Elsa yielded the nickname Elsie, which she used throughout her life. The woman my mother referred to as her employer, of course, was Lillian Lorraine. Mother said that Ms. Lorraine good-naturedly teased her until she changed her name to Elsa. It was about the time that Mother met my father that Elsa became Elsie. As I have written earlier in this story, I regret not caring enough to ask more about my mother's past, and that of Lillian, instead of accepting the fact that such matters simply were rarely discussed. The theatre and Lillian Lorraine held no particular interest for me.

When not touring with Lillian, Mother had her own social life, which was centered in New York's Scandinavian community, then contained pretty much in the Bay Ridge section of Brooklyn. It was at a Swedish Engineers Club dance that she met a fellow Swede, George Hanson. Following a two-year courtship, they married at the Episcopal Church of the Transfiguration at 29th St. and Fifth Avenue in Manhattan. This church is around the corner from the famed Marble Collegiate Church, and became known as the "Little Church Around the Corner" when, at the turn of the last century, a Marble Collegiate minister refused to conduct funeral services for an actor and said, "Take him to the little church around the corner." The Little Church was also the home of the nonsectarian Episcopal Actors' Guild, a charity for down-on-their-luck actors, which is still in existence today.

Mother remained with Lillian throughout my father's courtship and their first year of marriage, until the end of 1918 when she and my father decided to begin a family. Mother would stay home, which was the norm for mothers at the time. Lillian, then twenty-eight years of age, would go on to sign for the final time in a Ziegfeld production.

But during 1918 Mother was still with Lillian and Broadway was humming. Show business pundits were agog and many an eyebrow was raised in wonder with the announcement that Lillian Lorraine would be re-signing with Ziegfeld and his *Midnight Frolic* on the New Amsterdam Roof. After all, hadn't Lillian proven her stage and screen box office appeal independent of Flo's guiding hand? And hadn't the flame of their past romantic partnership been extinguished with his marriage to Billie Burke some five years earlier? Even more of a surprise was a second announcement declaring that Lillian would, after a six-year absence, sign on as one of the stars of the 12th edition of the *Ziegfeld Follies*. It was obvious that Ziegfeld was assembling an all-star cast of established headliners and box office giants for the 1918 *Follies*. In addition to Lillian, the formidable roster would include Will Rogers, Eddie Cantor, W.C. Fields, Ann Pennington, Frank Carter, Savoy & Brennan, Dolores, the Fairbanks Twins, Bee Palmer, Martha Mansfield, Marie Wallace, and a blonde, blue-eyed dancer by the name of Marilyn Miller. This 1918 *Follies* signaled Marilyn Miller's *Follies* debut as well as Lillian Lorraine's final *Follies* appearance. Lillian would return to Ziegfeld only one more time, a brief appearance in *Ziegfeld Girls of 1920*.

Marilyn Miller was a Shubert property discovered by Lee Shubert on the stage of a London music hall. She was known as a tap and ballet dancer, but her tap-dancing skills certainly were not in the class of Miss Twinkle Toes, Ann Pennington, and her proficiency as prima ballerina was far below that of her eventual successor Mary Eaton. The qualities that Shubert recognized and that swiftly catapulted Marilyn to co-stardom in the 1918 *Follies* were her natural beauty, youthful spirit and ability to grip an audience's heart. Captivated by her physical attributes and youthful freshness, her former employer Shubert had been quick to recognize a hefty box office potential. He immediately signed her to an exclusive agreement, countersigned by her mother. Within two weeks Marilyn was on her way back to the United States and the Broadway stage.

Lillian Lorraine in a fashion publicity shot, 1912.

While Marilyn was appearing in Shubert's *The Passing Show* at the Winter Garden, in the audience on one particular evening was Mrs. Florenz Ziegfeld, Billie Burke. She was thoroughly taken with Marilyn's freshness and what she described to Ziegfeld as Marilyn's *joie de vivre*. Two days later, as a result of Billie's persistent prodding, Flo was in a Winter Garden orchestra seat, first row center. Before the final curtain had fallen he was determined to move heaven and earth to sign Marilyn for the 1918 *Follies*. As a starter, as was his *modus operandi*, he offered more money, but there was still the annoying hurdle of a Shubert contract. Flo retained the services of Jacob Malawinsky, a high-powered theatrical attorney. Together they devised a scheme to provide Marilyn an escape hatch by charging the Shubert contract was null and void due to the fact that when she signed, Marilyn was a minor. Even though her mother had co-signed as the "guardian," the agreement lacked the additionally required signature of Marilyn's stepfather, Caro Miller. (The omission was not accidental. The two women had wanted to foreclose any possibility that Caro might at some future date make a claim against Marilyn's earnings.)

The Shuberts were furious and unleashed a scathing attack on Ziegfeld through the pages of their *New York Review*, declaring, "He's at it again. One of his favorite indoor sports, corralling talent that has been discovered by other managers." Fully aware of sure defeat on legal grounds, they decided against contesting Marilyn's defection. Instead, they issued a snide, sour-grapes statement declaring, "The Messrs. Shubert feel that Miss Miller's services are not worth fighting for and will permit her to go her way without the publicity she and her new manager expected and craved.... Moreover, the Shuberts feel quite capable of developing any one of a score of their chorus girls, as they did Miss Miller, whom they found dancing in an all-night club in London and who, until given her big chance by them at the Winter Garden, had never appeared in a first class New York production." Adding one last barb, they said, "If the actress and her mother considered the contract invalid, they were not averse to receiving the goodly amount of money weekly which its terms called for, and they were quite satisfied with it until Ziegfeld, on one of his customary hunts for other people's ideas, offered them a larger salary." They went on to cite other instances of Ziegfeld's alleged piracy as manifestations of his inability to develop his own talent. Among those he was accused of pilfering were Bert Williams from Comstock and Gest, Nora Bayes from Lew Fields, Will

Elsie Johnson in White Studio fashion shot.

Rogers, the Pony Ballet, Jose Collins and, of course, Lillian Lorraine from the 1909 Shubert production of *The Tourists*.

The pre–Broadway opening of the 1918 *Follies* took place in Atlantic City's Apollo Theatre on June 14, and according to all accounts, the venerable old show palace was taxed to capacity with an audience mix of celebrities, theatre owners, and an unusually large contingent of New York City first-nighters.

To ensure that this 12th edition would be the most technically advanced production to date, Ziegfeld leaned heavily on his already tried and proven stalwarts Joseph Urban and Ned Wayburn. Urban is credited with the design and painting of the twenty lush scene settings. Staging and choreography were in the hands of the incomparable Wayburn. The music was by Louis Hirsch and Dave Stamper, with lyrics supplied by stalwarts Gene Buck and Rennold Wolf. Commenting on Lillian's return to the *Follies*, Rennold Wolf wrote:

Lillian Lorraine is as quick and active as one of those snappy little fighting planes. She is all over the Metropolitan District doing something to make folks talk. Lillian couldn't be quiet or com-

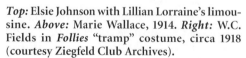

Top: Elsie Johnson with Lillian Lorraine's limousine. *Above:* Marie Wallace, 1914. *Right:* W.C. Fields in *Follies* "tramp" costume, circa 1918 (courtesy Ziegfeld Club Archives).

monplace if she tried. She lives fully and zestfully at racing speed. She puts paprika on mustard and the intensity of her nervous organization shows in her work. She gives it an exotic and feverish allure that the highly-strung theatre goer delights in. Lillian expresses the zip, zest and high spots of New York life under forced drought.

The *New York Star* was not far behind Rennold Wolf when it reported, "It isn't at all an accident that Lillian Lorraine is a star. With her, part of the business is a campaign carefully mapped out and faithfully executed. The rest just comes naturally!"

Before re-signing with Ziegfeld, Lillian had committed to play the Century Grove Theatre

Top left: Marilyn Miller "on her toes" for a 1918 publicity shot (courtesy Ziegfeld Club Archives).
Top *right:* Lillian Lorraine curtain call, New Amsterdam Theatre, circa 1918 (courtesy Ziegfeld Club
Archives). *Bottom left:* As the "Evening Star," 1918 *Follies* (courtesy Ziegfeld Club Archives). *Bottom
right:* Lillian Lorraine in a portrait by photographer Alfred Cheney Johnston, circa 1918, her last year
in the *Follies.*

Sheet music cover for 1918 *Follies*, featuring Marilyn Miller in her first *Follies* and Lillian Lorraine in her last.

under the personal management of Elliott, Comstock and Gest, but somehow Ziegfeld managed a breach of contract without penalty by giving the trio an option on Lillian's services at the end of the present *Follies* run.

During the previous ten years, Lillian had performed in numerous spectacular venues throughout the country, but nothing could compare in grandeur to the New Amsterdam The-

atre. Ziegfeld had moved his *Follies* to the New Amsterdam in 1913, but in 1918, it was a new venue for Lillian. Years later Mother reminisced about the special thrill that she and Lillian felt when they first approached the theatre's 41st Street stage door. Lillian's personal maid, Cora, and her publicist accompanied them. It was a special local media event, as well, attested to by the presence of half a dozen newspaper photographers recording the affair for their local dailies.

* * *

In 1990, I, too, approached this same stage door for the first time. The entrance had aged, but had not

Top: Lillian Lorraine (front) in "Spring Drive" production number, a Ziegfeld *Midnight Frolic* staged on the roof of the New Amsterdam Theatre, 1918 (courtesy Ziegfeld Club Archives). *Right:* Lillian Lorraine takes a bow in the 1918 *Follies.*

been altered since the day my mother, Lillian and their entourage stepped through it. The theatre faced the wildness of 42nd Street. The stage door was in the rear, opening onto a desolate 41st Street. From Broadway to Eighth Avenue, 42nd Street had become a seedy promenade for the scum of New York. Pimps, prostitutes, adult bookstores and peep shows dominated both sides of the street. Drug dealers blatantly flaunted and plied their stock in trade. Knifings were nightly occurrences. Eighth Avenue from 42nd to 50th Streets was known as the "Minnesota strip" because Minnesota was where so many of the blonde, blue-eyed teenagers who worked for the pimps came from.

It was along 41st Street, halfway between Seventh and Eighth Avenues, that I, accompanied by a friend in the New York City Police Department, and a friend of his, a New York City building inspector, had made our way to the theatre stage door. With more than just a slight shiver of anticipation, I found myself about to enter the long forgotten and forsaken inner sanctum of the *Ziegfeld Follies*, the *Midnight Frolic* and the *Nine O'Clock Revue*. Since my involvement with the Ziegfeld Club, I craved the opportunity to see this place firsthand, knowing what had transpired here, and what my mother had seen and been a part of. Public access to the theatre had been strictly prohibited, and it was only through the good graces of my NYPD friend, and his friend, that my dream was finally becoming a reality.

Inside, past the watchman's post, up a few steps, and through a long, narrow corridor with a ceiling so low that we had to stoop in some places, we found ourselves on the theatre's stage. Beams of light from our flashlights scanned the cavity where 1,800 seats once accommodated New York City's high-fashion theatre goers. Seats and carpeting were gone. Even the boxes that had held the popular box seats had been ripped from the walls and carted off. The architectural grandeur of hundreds of plaster of Paris friezes and sculptures depicting Shakespearean and mythological figures, along with Hoffman's tales of the Vienna woods were naught but crumbling reminders of what had once been. The roof had been removed and never replaced twelve years prior during an aborted attempt at restoration by the Nederlander organization. Snow, rain and city soot had seeped into every crevice and ravaged the building, top to bottom. Only the jade-green terra cotta balustrades and staircases were still intact and seemed untouched by time and Mother Nature. In the presence of an audience comprising only city rats, snakes and other lower creatures skirting filthy pools of liquid, my friends and I were on stage in a grim and ghostly emptiness.

It was impossible in this musty temple of decay to imagine Lillian Lorraine dancing and singing on this very stage, or my mother watching from the wings. Never would I have thought that in the span of six years I would be instrumental in bringing five of the remaining live *Follies* girls to this stage to be introduced by Mayor Rudy Giuliani and then to see them dance and strut at Disney's gala white tie re-opening of the completely restored New Amsterdam Theatre. No expense had been spared to restore the theatre to its 1903 grandeur and glory.

The theatre had been acquired by New York State as part of its plan, in partnership with New York City, to reclaim the block from the criminal and undesirable elements which had been present for so long on this fabled section of 42nd Street. The Disney organization was solicited to restore the theatre, and in 1994 Disney formally agreed to take on the task of rehabilitating the building, supported by $26 million in low-interest loans from the city and state, and $10 million of its own money.

To oversee, manage and preserve the authenticity and legacy of their new flagship show palace, Disney recruited Dana Amendola, a young and vibrant New Englander from the Westbury Music Fair on Long Island. His love of the theatre and dedication to preserving the cultural heritage of the Ziegfeld era has stood him in good stead to the present day. He is truly a remarkable custodian of all that might otherwise have been lost. On a cold winter's morning in 1995, Dana called me and asked if I knew whether there were any *Follies* girls still alive and able to appear at the gala opening of the theatre scheduled one year hence. Of course, I knew. Of course, they appeared. One even performed a physically demanding version of the Charleston; it was 92-year-old Doris Eaton.

* * *

By the time Lillian and my mother were everyday regulars at the New Amsterdam, Ziegfeld, always the promoter, was stretching the limits of promotion. A release from New York City Fire Commissioner Thomas J. Brennan read "This theatre, under normal conditions, with every one of the 1800 seats occupied, can be emptied within three minutes." If you have ever been in the New Amsterdam Theatre, you know that Brennan's statement was more promotion than truth.

Another announcement alerted theatre patrons to a sale in the ladies' cloak room of sets of five Blum and Wentzel postcards, and in the men's smoking lounge, a set of seven cards— all for ten cents. The rationale underlying the decision to offer fewer cards to the women is a mystery. With respect to a special production number titled "Under the Sea," the 1918 Playbill notation read, "Owing to the mechanical massiveness of this scene it can only be exhibited advantageously at the beginning of the performance, 8:20 sharp!"

Ticket scalping for the top Broadway shows was becoming more and more a major headache. Ziegfeld met the issue head-on, with full-page advertisements in every metropolitan daily, declaring that his management "was making every effort to confine the sale of all *Follies* seats, including the *Midnight Frolic*, directly to the public from the New Amsterdam box office." By so doing, he said, "We will prevent tickets from falling into the hands of hotel agencies or speculators. This will enable the theatre-going public to secure good seats without extortion. I am certain this can be accomplished if the public will do their share by stamping out profiteering. I know this menace can be successfully eliminated." In large, bold print he concluded his message by offering the sum of one thousand dollars to "any person who will give me conclusive proof that collusion exists between speculators and any employee of this theatre."

Ziegfeld was determined to outdo everything that he had done before, by assembling in this 1918 *Follies* edition the largest, most impressive collection of creative and performing artists ever to appear under the roof of the magnificent 42nd Street emporium. Production costs were soaring and Flo's extravagance could not be contained. Robert Baral reported the 1918 *Follies* cost had exceeded what at that time was considered a staggering ten thousand dollars. But one major headliner was missing from the cast line-up — Fanny Brice.

In his *Fanny Brice: The Original Funny Girl*, Herbert Goldman writes that Fanny's two-year contract with Ziegfeld had expired and the prospect of another *Follies* failed to excite her. She was, on the other hand, anxious for a solo starring vehicle and jumped when A.H. Woods offered her the lead role in *Why Worry?* It was a three-act melodramatic farce by the writing team of Montague Glass and Jules Eckert Goodman. There had been some gossip that Fanny's absence from the 1918 lineup was due to a continuing feud with Lillian Lorraine over the Gresheimer affair. Scott Margolin, Fanny Brice historian, says "no" to that theory, declaring the two women had long since patched up their differences and mutually concluded Freddy Gresheimer was nothing more than a worthless, first-class bounder.

Twenty-year-old Marilyn Miller, the one principal newcomer to the star-studded cast of headliners, had already had several seasons of impressive work with the Shuberts, but it was the *Ziegfeld Follies* that catapulted her to a permanent berth in the galaxy of Broadway greats. Irving Lewis of the *New York Telegraph* raved, "Delightful, dainty and accomplished in her every number is Marilyn Miller, a new acquisition in the *Follies*. Light as a feather and blithesome as a spring breeze, Miss Miller stands out resplendently."

Top: Lillian Lorraine (center) and chorus in Irving Berlin's "Blue Devils of France," 1918 *Follies* (courtesy Ziegfeld Club Archive). *Bottom:* A classic photograph: "Any Old Time" production number with W.C. Fields, Will Rogers, Lillian Lorraine, Eddie Cantor, and Harry Kelly, 1918 *Follies* (courtesy Ziegfeld Club Archives).

With Lillian, Marilyn and the statuesquely beautiful showgirl Dolores heading up the glamour contingent, Ziegfeld balanced that formidable array of feminine pulchritude with the masculine, earthy appeal of Will Rogers, his lariat and homespun humor. Will, Eddie Cantor, W.C. Fields and the hilariously funny team of Savoy & Brennan excelled at regaling audiences with their own individualistic brands of mirth.

With World War I in its final months, Ziegfeld sought to honor our French ally in a production number titled "The Blue Devils of France." Lillian, in a glamorized haute couture version of a French military uniform, sang the title song by Irving Berlin and was supported by a chorus line of twenty-four *Follies* lovelies. Almost eighty years later, one of those twenty-four lovelies, Muriel Harrison Merrill, when she was ninety-nine years old, recalled to me in her tiny Miami Beach apartment, "Lillian was always a happy-go-lucky cut-up. She was constantly doing things to taunt Mr. Ziegfeld. One night, in the Blue Devils number, she came on stage with two of her front teeth blacked out — just to shock and annoy him. We all knew she could have married him at any time but she wouldn't have any part of it. Gosh, she lived so recklessly!"

There is no evidence to support the rumor mongers' contention that Flo and Lillian had rekindled their amorous relationship, but his continuing obsession with her is proven by the fact that even at twenty-six years of age she was the featured principal in five of the twenty production numbers of the 1918 *Follies*. In "Any Old Time at All" she was courted and serenaded by Will Rogers, Eddie Cantor, W.C. Fields and Harry Kelly — all four men, appearing either together or individually, for the first time ever on stage in formal attire of top hat, white tie and tails. A classic photograph of that quintet has frequently been reproduced over the years as an example of Ziegfeld star power in that era.

Eddie Cantor, in a 1934 *Colliers* interview, said, "Lillian Lorraine was one of the most fascinating women ever to appear in a Ziegfeld show and one of the very few to whom Ziggy was thoroughly attached." In his later memoirs, Cantor reminisced about what he termed "Lillian's tragic downslide." He wrote, "She had the world at her feet. There wasn't anyone or anything she couldn't have but she self-destructed and threw it all away."

Commenting on another of the 1918 *Follies* principals, Irving Lewis in the *New York Telegraph* wrote, "Sprightly Ann Pennington is as refreshingly graceful and cunning as ever. Garbed in more or less scanty but bewitching raiment, she does an Indian dance, an Oriental dance and an hilarious prairie frolic with Will Rogers."

The Eaton sisters, Pearl and Doris, also newcomers to *Follies* company, danced in the chorus of the production number "The Blue Devils of France." Pearl was first, hired in the dual capacity of both performer and assistant to choreographer Ned Wayburn. For Doris, it was a case of pure luck and happenstance. On one very special day, fourteen-year-old Doris chose to tag along with her older sister to the New Amsterdam and sit in on rehearsals. Seated quietly in the wings just off-stage, minding her own business, she suddenly found herself the focus of attention when Wayburn spotted her and queried, "Who is that girl?" Pearl was quick to respond, "Why, she's my little sister, Doris." With a longer second glance, Wayburn continued, "She's a pretty little thing. Can she dance?" With Pearl's reply in the affirmative, all that was left was for Doris to race home to get her mother's permission, and almost within the blink of an eye she was off and running as a real live Ziegfeld Girl. Because she was underage and had dropped out of school, in order to stay one step ahead of the Geary Society for the Prevention of Cruelty to Children, Doris assumed the name of Doris Levant, then Lucille Levant, and finally at age sixteen, she happily reassumed her true identity as Doris Eaton.

Doris, whom I ultimately met, laughingly has recalled to me, "Yes, that's the way it was, but, you know, there was something strange about Mr. Wayburn. He was a large man, not fat, but tall and muscular, and in all the time I knew him I never saw him dance a step! Very strange, indeed."

Our paths first crossed in 1992 as the result of a story in the pages of the *New York Times*.

Lillian Lorraine headshot, "Blue Devils of France," 1918 *Follies.*

The news article that caught my attention concerned a woman, eighty-eight years of age at the time, who had the distinction of being the oldest graduate in the illustrious, century-old history of the University of Oklahoma — not to mention her election to the prestigious national honor society, Phi Beta Kappa. My eyes focused on a past and present pairing of photographs. The first, a head shot of a pretty young damsel adorned in a gypsy-like bandana, and the second, a handsomely beautiful, white-haired woman. The accompanying news story intrigued me enough to read on — and so began an odyssey that was to have a profound effect on the future course of my own life.

As the *Times* story unfolded, Doris Eaton Travis emerged as a woman who had packed an extraordinary amount of diversified living into her eighty-eight-year journey through life. With her husband, Paul, she was the mistress of the Travis Ranch, an 880-acre spread on the outskirts of Norman, Oklahoma. Prior to her marriage, Doris had owned and successfully operated eighteen Arthur Murray dance studio franchises in and around Detroit, Michigan. In the thirties she was a headliner in legitimate theatre. In the late twenties to the early thirties, she was a featured principal in silent films produced not only in fledgling Hollywood, but also in New York, the United Kingdom and Egypt.

What really exploded off the printed page was the account of her still earlier life and musical comedy debut in the *Ziegfeld Follies of 1918*. Immediately, I sensed the possibility of opening another door into the life of Lillian Lorraine. The sun had not set on that day before I had composed and posted two letters— one to Doris Eaton Travis and the second to the University of Oklahoma requesting that they forward the Travis letter to wherever she might be residing. Three weeks later, I received a letter from Doris. She answered my most burning questions: What memories might she still have of the 1918 *Follies* and did she know Lillian?

"Well, you know," she wrote, "I was only fourteen years old and just a dancer in the chorus. Miss Lorraine was one of the stars of the show and principals did not usually mix with the company's supporting cast. I can tell you she was very beautiful and it was common knowledge that at one time her personal relationship with Mr. Ziegfeld was very close, and, yes, I had heard that occasionally there was a drinking problem. I do recall one incident in the "'Garden of my Dreams' number that she lost her footing and had to be helped back up by Frank Carter." (Much to the dismay of a jealous Ziegfeld, Frank Carter would be the first husband of Marilyn Miller.) Robert Baral, in his *Revue*, described that number as "the real song hit of the show, sung by Lillian Lorraine and Frank Carter against a magnificent Joseph Urban backdrop of a huge Japanese flower bowl replete with a miniature arched bridge and stunted Japanese cherry trees. It was a show stopper!"

Sheet music cover, "My Pony Boy" from 1909's *Miss Innocence,* starring Anna Held and featuring ingénue Lillian Lorraine.

I called Doris after I received her letter. Of course, we discussed Lillian and the "Garden of My Dreams" production number that Doris had written to me about. She told me:

The scene opened with Lillian seated on the bridge and at the last part of the song she was to rise and walk down to center stage. One night, as I was standing in the wings with the other chorus girls awaiting our cue, we watched Lillian approach the bridge. We noticed she was a little

unsteady in her walk and she missed her footing stepping up onto the bridge. A watchful stagehand dashed to her rescue and helped her to get in place just before the curtain went up. However, in his haste he failed to notice that Lillian's headdress, which was eight inches tall, was by this time slightly askew. Frank Carter, who had come on stage to join her in the song, was alert to the situation and helped her get off of the bridge and join him for the rest of the number downstage. We were all glad when the curtain came down, but all through it, Lillian never missed a note. Frank was relieved to turn Lillian over to the faithful stagehand who was there to help her get to her dressing room.

From the time of this call to Doris to the present day, I treasure what has become a wonderfully warm and close friendship. She likes to joke about our relationship: "Nils Hanson is the one who put me back into show business and now he's my New York agent!"

In the final analysis, the 1918 *Follies* went down in musical theatre record books as one of the great extravaganzas of Broadway's Golden Age — only to be surpassed the following year by the 1919 *Follies*.

Opposite top: Lillian Lorraine and Frank Carter in "Garden of My Dreams," a "bump in the road" for Lillian in the 1918 *Follies* (courtesy Ziegfeld Club Archives). *Opposite bottom left:* Doris Eaton Travis with Lillian Lorraine dinner dress and Dean Ellis oil portrait, circa 1997. *Opposite bottom right:* Lillian Lorraine in costume from 1918 *Follies* number, "Garden of My Dreams" (courtesy Ziegfeld Club Archives). *Top:* Initial collage for sheet music of "Garden of My Dreams" production number, from the 1918 *Follies* (courtesy Ziegfeld Club Archives). *Bottom:* Doris Eaton Travis and author Nils Hanson, 2008, in a dressing room at New Amsterdam Theatre, for "Broadway Cares: Equity Fights AIDS" (aka "The Easter Bonnet Competition").

25

Ziegfeld's Roof Garden and Lillian's Blue Devil

With more than a decade of highly successful *Follies* under his belt, Ziegfeld in December of 1918 offered his devoted followers a new concept in evening entertainment — the *Nine O'Clock Revue*. According to Burns Mantle of the *New York Times*, "It was two Frolics for the price of two Frolics! . . . The first of the Frolics begins shortly after nine o'clock and runs until ten. The patrons then dance for half an hour until the second Frolic starts at 10:40 and continues until after eleven. There is another period devoted to public dancing after which the original Midnight Frolic begins. Those partygoers not able to remain for the midnight show reluctantly vacate the dance floor and their tables to accommodate the late night revelers."

Ziegfeld preceded the summer season of 1918 on the roof garden with his Annual *Follies* Frolic Ball, a money-raiser for the company's Sick and Needy Fund. The elegantly printed invitation read,

The Meeting Place of the World
Ziegfeld Roof
Atop New Amsterdam Theatre, New York City
Follies-Frolic Ball
Of 1918
Florenz Ziegfeld, Junior
Presents
A Combined Performance of the
Ziegfeld Midnight Frolic
And
Ziegfeld Follies of 1918

The *Ziegfeld Follies* of 1918 at this ball probably was cast as a mix of performers from the 1917 *Follies*, which had just completed its final road tour, and the 1918 *Follies*, which was coming off previews in Atlantic City in preparation for opening in June of 1918. This formula had been used in the previous year.

Art Hickman's band was imported from California to supply the dance music. Utilizing the colloquial speech patterns of a southern Negro of the time, one reporter described the Hickman rhythms as heard by

the dark-hued elevator runner, peering around the edge of his car last night, listening to the impulsive and syncopated beat emanating from the Ziegfeld Roof dance floor. Reluctantly, he would close the door, returning patrons to the main lobby, then head back up with a fresh load and another opportunity for an extended dally at the top. As the itchy feeling subsided in his legs, he closed the door again and exclaimed, "Boy, that sure is a shame, shutting off the music like that. I sure love that jazz music and they certainly don't get any uninterrupted work out of me, long as they have that band! Some folks suggest I oughta leave the outer door open but then some one of them dancers might go crazy with the music and fall down the shaft and that would just spoil my evening!"

Publicity ad for *9 O'Clock Revue* on the New Amsterdam roof.

Art Hickman's jazz band performing on roof of the New Amsterdam, 1917 (courtesy Ziegfeld Club Archives).

Victor Kiraly, business manager of the roof enterprise, gleefully expressed the view, "No one could resist that Hickman outfit. I'm not much on dancing myself but even my toes were tapping. The waiters were constantly showing signs of animation and became positively rhythmical when serving the French pastry desserts."

In his description of the performing artists appearing at this fundraising ball, Burns Mantle wrote, "Among the stars who came trailing glory were the Misses Delyle Alda, Fanny Brice, Dolores, Mary Eaton, Lillian Lorraine and Marilyn Miller. Their male counterparts were Eddie Cantor, W.C. Fields, Bernard Granville, Eddie Dowling, Van & Schenck, Carl Randall and Bert Williams."

Unfortunately for the Sick and Needy Fund, Flo, always the super-showman and sparing no expense, dug deeply into the cache of money that had been subscribed. The interior of the roof was entirely done over in hues of rose and gold. The girls' costumes, again according to Mantle, "however much they may have cost, looked like a million dollars and the playbill of principals read like a Sunday night benefit for a popular war fund."

The audience of high-society blue bloods enthusiastically tapped tiny wooden mallets on table tops as Bert Williams offered his classic, "Nobody." The eight-inch-long mallets were supplied by the Ziegfeld organization for audiences to use in lieu of applauding with their hands. They were inscribed with the words "Ziegfeld Roof" and they were unique to this particular venue. To this day, they are highly valued memorabilia collectors' items often seen on modern-day eBay auctions.

One of the Ball's special highlights was Frank Carter's rendition of "The Motor Girl," supported by a dozen chorus girls made up to represent various makes of cars. Evan Burrows Fontaine executed an exciting South American dance; Fanny Brice acted out her hilarious travesty of a movie queen vampire; Georgie Price was in top form with his inimitable imitations; Bessie McCoy Davis performed her legendary "Yamma, Yamma Man," a number dating back to the earliest *Follies*; and Lillian Lorraine revived her popular Irish scrubwoman

Publicity still from *Little Blue Devil,* with Lillian Lorraine (top) and Winnie Dunn (second from left) (courtesy Ziegfeld Club Archives).

parody, Tipparary Mary. Lillian shared center stage with Pearl Eaton, eldest sister in the Eaton family clan.

Town Topics on January 2, 1919, carried a tantalizing tidbit of gossip concerning Lillian's continuing, insatiable zest for life on the fast track. "She has been giving a series of holiday parties which are making even the most hardened Broadwayites sit up and take notice. Last summer at Long Beach, Lillian made things hum but her party on New Year's Eve was one of the gayest affairs which theatredom has seen in many a day. We hear a prominent broker is quite attentive to Lillian. As he is a bachelor and one of the most successful plungers on the Street, perhaps we shall hear something interesting in the future."

On January 6, 1919, Lillian signed for the title role of Paulette Devine in *The Little Blue Devil.* Her co-star was good friend and popular leading man Bernard Granville. Lillian's performance in the out-of-town previews garnered glowing notices in the October 22, 1919, *Philadelphia Record*:

> The surprise of the evening was the ability displayed by Lillian Lorraine in the title role. Not only has this girl improved her voice, but she enacts the part with all the snap and dash that it requires. It is a typical musical farce with all the old ingredients served up in approved popular style. There is the heroine Little Blue Devil of the title, a celebrated actress hired to impersonate the wife of a young man who hopes thereby to seek business advancement. There is the employer, a hypocritical old fellow who loves the ladies, and there is the usual mixture of pursuing wives and lovers with a peppy chorus to help keep things gay."

The show was equally well received on its November 3 opening at the 47th Street Central Theatre, west of Broadway. Another reviewer reported, "Lillian Lorraine romps into the situation with zest and contagious spontaneity, aided by a girlishly pretty chorus of bare-ankled pretties, handsome young men and a dimly lit bedroom scene. They razzle dazzle through three acts of nonsense. Lorraine acts so well that she will doubtless promote herself out of the realms of musical farce."

In the chorus of "girlishly pretty" young ladies was Winnie Dunn, a cute and perky dancer who would befriend Lillian and be an integral force in Lillian's and my mother's lives for the next twenty-five years.

In 1998, the Ziegfeld Club president, ninety-three-year-old Dana O'Connell, told me that when she first met Winnie Dunn, both were performing in George White's *Scandals*. "Winnie was a deeply religious girl, very prim and proper, and she really didn't mix very much with the other girls in the show. She wasn't snooty or anything like that, but I would say she was a little on the shy side, and she lived at home with her parents. Off stage, she was a plain dresser, very sweet and not at all a typical show business type. I wouldn't call her pretty, but she really was cute."

Louise "Lu" Martell was another of the *Scandals* girls who was close to Winnie and Lillian. Lu had known Lillian for several years and it was through her that Winnie and Lillian became fast friends. Lu lived in New York City's Hell's Kitchen, a seedy, low-rent area on Midtown Manhattan's west side, and was not unfamiliar with the lively local bar scene. She told Winnie of one particular night when Lillian had been out on the town bar-hopping and drinking more heavily than usual. At one of the local nighteries her drink order was refused and she was asked to leave the premises—which she did. Outside, while attempting to hail a taxi, she slipped, fell into the gutter and was unable to get up. Dana clearly recalled Lu's telling her that someone had called the Ziegfeld office and had been told Mr. Ziegfeld himself would come immediately. Dana continued, "I wasn't there so I can't verify whether or not the incident really did happen, but if it did, I think it would be far more likely Mr. Ziegfeld would have sent someone from his staff."

Dana, Winnie and Lu shared a dressing room in the *Scandals*, and it was there Winnie constantly expressed concern over Lillian's problems with alcohol. She was often seen to shake her head and wonder aloud, "I honestly don't know where that poor girl is going to end up. She's got the world on a string, but I don't know how much longer she'll be able to hold on."

While the majority of New York dailies carried positive notices for *The Little Blue Devil*, the *New York American* was a shocking exception. Its review was probably the most brutal and scathing media attack to which Lillian had ever been subjected. In part, Hugh Donaldson wrote:

Lillian Lorraine, whose chronic incompetence covers such a wide field, was the Blue Devil of the title. It is always interesting to observe any person so completely unskilled in everything she is called upon to do.... She dances without grace and sings without voice, but her burlesque scene did prove to be a surprising bit of real artistry.... Apparently, other than the star herself, it is Miss Lorraine's back that is featured in the Shimmy show, a pretty, gleaming back that holds the spotlight in a jazzy, shimmy wiggle from shoulders to waist.... Muscle dancing was performed much better years ago when first introduced to America on the midway of Chicago's World's Fair. It was a performance of skill compared to Miss Lorraine's shimmy version.... The hoochey-coochie is not so far beneath the shimmy for Miss Lorraine to turn her dazzling back upon it.... They are both especially vulgar if not in degree, in kind.

Obviously, the risqué nature of the show had not found in Mr. Donaldson a very appreciative viewer.

When a *New York Sun* reporter queried Lillian for comment, he wrote the following account of her response:

"Well," declaimed the daring Lillian, wriggling herself into the minus-quantity gown she's wearing with so much sartorial success and so many press notices, "When will people stop being so squeamish about the human body? It is beautiful, isn't it? I suppose there are still a few antediluvians who think they have to sleep with windows closed and heads under the blankets to keep from catching a cold. But why bother with these evil-minded fossils? They'd find something wrong with the Madonna if you give them enough rope. I don't think it's anyone's business whether or not I can draw both of my stockings through my pinkie ring at once."

The *Sun* reporter concluded, "Miss Lorraine can afford to be defiant. She has the sort of back that would convert the most solemn-visaged of carpers."

In another interview, sounding not unlike the product of a press agent, Lillian ventured to express some views on the virtues of American chorus girls as opposed to their British counterparts. Basing her views on impressions gained during what she claimed to be several trips to England, she said:

Lillian adorned in an immense amount of georgette crepe for the "Telephone" production number, *9 O'Clock Revue* of 1920, Lillian Lorraine's last professional association with Ziegfeld (courtesy Ziegfeld Club Archives).

Much of the charm of American girls is their ability to project a vision of dash and good-natured high spirits over the footlights to an appreciative audience. Too many chorus girls in other countries seem to think that glamour alone is all that should be expected of them. I think the American male theatre-goer admires a girl who not only has physical attributes pleasing to the eye, but can also interest him as a real person with a lot more than glamour and glitz under the grease paint. I think he also appreciates a girl who can show she is getting a lot of fun out of what she's doing up there on the stage. I felt the Englishmen preferred a girl who was more the poseful and reposeful type.

On March 8, 1920, Ziegfeld opened a new edition of the *Nine O'Clock Revue* on the New Amsterdam roof, and the next week followed it with an equally new *Midnight Frolic*. It had been eleven years since Ziegfeld had first presented Lillian to his Broadway audiences in *Miss Innocence* and now, at twenty-eight, she was still a major box office draw. Theatre critic Rennold Wolf described *The Ziegfeld Girls of 1920* as a "brilliant review with Lillian Lorraine scoring high marks for a vast improvement in the quality and force of her voice and the trimness of her figure. She is radiant as a picture in a series of exquisite garbs."

The *Star Gazer* rapturously declared:

Miss Lorraine is one of the stage celebrities without whom the annual Ziegfeld *Follies* or Frolic would be incomplete. Not only Broadway, but that mysterious district known as "the road," agrees that hers is the beauty and talent that goes far toward making a tremendous success of the Ziegfeld entertainments. Do you know that Lillian Lorraine is worshiped by the humblest attaché of every theatre in which she appears — both in New York and on the road — just as she is idolized by every member of the Ziegfeld companies to which she contributes her beauty and talent? I might tell many instances illustrating her goodness of heart but I know she abhors the idea of such facts becoming public. She is indispensable and that is a fact she cannot deny.

26

Detour and Scandal on the Fast Track

In the spring of 1920 Lillian's personal lifestyle was again up for public scrutiny. The *New York Herald* headlined, "Off Stage Gayety Laid to Actress," and of course this was Lillian. The complainant and source of the story was Ralph Becker, representing the Century Leasing Company, landlords of the apartment house into which Lillian had recently moved. In the legal brief presented to the West Side Court, Becker charged that since the time Lillian had taken occupancy of an apartment at 114 West 58th Street, there had been no peace for the other tenants. The complaint charged that Lillian was entertaining groups of friends on an almost nightly basis and that the parties were lasting well into the early morning hours, "a time when even actresses are supposed to be entertaining thoughts of retiring." In his presentation, Becker told Magistrate Isaac Levine that unless the condition was corrected many tenants were threatening to withhold their rent payments and still others were planning to vacate and seek quarters elsewhere. When Magistrate Levine asked for details, Becker responded, "Midnight revelry is not a strong enough term for what has been going on. Some of our tenants are even getting indigestion because of the racket, and let me tell you, your honor, there isn't a phonograph that could take a record of the conversations coming out of that apartment! I've been doing nothing but listen to complaints since Miss Lorraine arrived on the scene." Having heard enough, Levine issued a citation charging Lillian with maintaining a public nuisance. She chose not to contest the court's action, paid a two-hundred-dollar fine, and moved to new quarters at the Walton Hotel.

The incident, however, was not the end of Lillian's problems with law enforcement this year. Her automobile had been impounded the previous day by a deputy sheriff, and in order to regain possession, she was forced to satisfy a two-hundred-dollar judgment in favor of Frederick Kupper, owner of a parking garage in Long Beach, where Lillian had sojourned the previous summer.

By fall of this same year, Lillian had permanently severed her professional connection with Ziegfeld, and anxious for a change of pace from musical revue, she signed with the Selwyns to appear in *Sonny*, a new comedy by George Hobart. The play premiered in Washington, D.C., with Emma Dunn, Robert Ames and Lillian sharing top billing. It opened to lukewarm notices and consequently had a run of only seven weeks. Emma Dunn was the critics' favorite, with Lillian's performance rating only a three-line mention as "the girl of the footlights who handles Broadwayese with facility."

Lillian returned to New York from Washington. One month after her twenty-ninth birthday, personal tragedy struck. It was the third of February, 1921, sometime after midnight. My mother was awakened by a call from Marie Wallace, a *Follies* girl and close friend of Lillian and my mother. Mother's professional relationship with Lillian had ended in 1919, but she and Lillian continued to stay in touch. Mother had been Lillian's closest friend and confidant

146

for more than a third of Lillian's young life, and Lillian needed her now. Lillian told the police to get hold of Marie Wallace, who was living at the Monticello Hotel in Manhattan. Marie would be able to let my mother know without involving law enforcement in Mother's home life.

Lillian had been leaving a late-night soiree at the Fifty-Fifty Club at 129 West 50th Street. While walking to a waiting car, she slipped and fell on an icy sidewalk and was immediately brought to her apartment at the Walton Hotel. Within minutes, and in excruciating pain, she was rushed by emergency ambulance to Stern's Sanitarium at 365 West End Avenue. Neither her personal physician, Doctor Philip Grauseman, nor Marie Wallace would divulge any details of what the national wire services were already reporting as "a mysterious accident." At an early morning press conference, Doctor Grauseman did reveal that Lillian had suffered a serious fracture of the fourth and fifth cervical vertebrae of the spine. Rumors as to the "real" nature of the accident were rampant: *Billboard*, a theatrical daily, was reporting that hospital attendants were leaking stories to the media that Lillian had not only sustained the spinal fractures but was partially paralyzed, having lost the use of both arms. In the following days, conflicting versions of the accident surfaced on news wires throughout the country. It was widely speculated that Lillian had not slipped on the ice, as originally reported, but had, in fact, after a night of heavy drinking, fallen down a flight of stairs at the nightclub. Other reports had her in a plaster cast and that she would remain so for the next twelve months. The one commonly held belief was that she would never be physically able to return to the musical comedy stage.

Tabloid gossip sheets declared that on the night of the accident, Lillian was in the company of Joe Welling, a lightweight prize fighter, and that their engagement was to have been shortly announced. When questioned by reporters, Welling refused comment. The only persons with visitation rights were my mother, Marie Wallace, and Lillian's good friend, producer Charles Dillingham. Years later, in a taped conversation with my sister in 1975, Mother, always Lillian's champion, did not discuss the specifics concerning the night of February 3 other than to declare the simple fact that Lillian had slipped on the ice. As the days went on following Lillian's injury, everyone around her was circumspect when questioned by reporters, indicating only that Lillian was resting comfortably, was in good spirits and was bursting with confidence that she would have a speedy and complete recovery.

Prior to the accident, Lillian had been scheduled to open a vaudeville engagement the week of February 11 in Yonkers. This was to be followed with two weeks at the Coliseum in upper Manhattan's Washington Heights, and then a return to the historic Palace Theatre on Broadway.

Charles Higham, in his book *Ziegfeld*, alleges that Flo made an unannounced, secret visit to Lillian's hospital room. That Ziegfeld visited Lillian at Stern's, there can be no question for I was told by Lucile Layton that she was present at the time of Ziegfeld's visit. Ned Wayburn had urged Lucile to visit Lillian, and when she arrived, Ziegfeld was already there. It could hardly have been a secret visit, as Higham suggests. How would Higham have known, unless the affair had been whispered in his ear by Ziegfeld's secretary, Matilda Golden? More likely, Higham's use of "secret" is hyperbole, meaning discreet. Ziegfeld did conduct himself with more discretion in these years than ever before.

Probably, Ziegfeld did not want the press to know he was visiting Lillian for fear that it would be inferred they were still a romantic item. Flo was now a happily married man with a five-year-old daughter, and contentedly ensconced in Billie's 22-acre Burkeleycrest estate in Hastings-on-Hudson, a posh and sleepy Hudson River enclave in rural Westchester County, New York. No longer maintaining his Ansonia residence in New York City, Flo had become a regular suburbanite commuter, thereby eliminating much of the after-show partying and philandering of his previous lifestyle. He now lived the life of a country squire and was in no way anxious to revive rumors of his former romantic relationship with Lillian Lorraine. No doubt, however, the flame he once carried for Lillian had not extinguished entirely. For one thing, he showed up at the hospital. Further, according to Flo's confidante, Matilda Golden (Goldie), Flo paid many of Lillian's medical bills and incidental expenses before, afterward, and until the time of his death.

Higham suggests that Lillian told Ziegfeld that she was on the verge of bankruptcy and had several suits pending against her for unpaid restaurant and clothing bills. Higham also suggests that when Ziegfeld inquired as to Freddie Gresheimer's whereabouts, Lillian said that as far as she knew he was still serving jail time in the Tombs. Flo paid her bills, but cautioned that for the sake of his own marriage they should not be seen together again.

The first truly encouraging reports on the progress of Lillian's recovery came from her old friend Fanny Brice, who was also in Stern's, where she had just given birth to a son, William Fallon. Scott Margolin tells me that Fanny chose the names "William" and "Fallon" as a gesture of gratitude toward the defense attorney who had represented her husband, Nicky Arnstein. Nicky had been arrested and charged with embezzlement of five million dollars in bonds. There was, however, a subsequent falling-out between Fallon and Arnstein, and Arnstein, with a new attorney, was eventually convicted and jailed.

While in Stern's, Fanny told reporters that Lillian had come to her room "with a brace on her head, a cane in her hand and a cakewalk in her stride, and she is just as beautiful as ever!" Within three months of the accident, Lillian's doctors were issuing glowing bulletins on the progress of her recovery and even going so far as to predict that with another two or three months of rest and intense therapy she would be strong enough for discharge. Miraculously, it was only one month later when Lillian, with a nurse and chauffeur in tow, met reporters and set off on a two-hour drive from 72nd Street, down Broadway to Times Square, up to Columbus Circle, through Central Park and back to Stern's. Photographs of Lillian standing on the running board of a Rolls-Royce touring car appeared in newspapers from coast to coast.

All told, it was just a little over one year of hospital confinement when Lillian and her doctors announced she had beaten the odds. She was feeling one hundred percent fit and ready for a Broadway comeback. Very soon after her discharge, she returned to Hollywood to film *Lonesome Corners*, perhaps to work first without the strain of a nightly stage performance. Edgar Jones starred in, produced, directed, and wrote *Lonesome Corners*, a rustic comedy-romance, with a theme remarkably similar to an abbreviated version of George Bernard Shaw's *Pygmalion* and the modern-day *My Fair Lady*. The cast included Henry Van Bousen, Edna May Sperl, and Walter Lewis. Lillian, in the supporting role of Martha Forrest, had bottom billing. The lackluster box office record of the film matched Jones's fifty-nine-film record of Class B films, most of which were one-reel westerns, but this did give Lillian an opportunity to get back on the work track and to reinforce her financial position.

Shortly thereafter, she signed with Arthur Hammerstein for the title role in *The Blue Kitten*, a musical comedy based on the book by Otto Harbach and William Gary Duncan. The *pièce de résistance* was music by Viennese composer Rudolf Friml. The all-star supporting cast included Victor Morley, Joseph Cawthorn, Robert Woolsey, Marion Sunshine, and my old friend from the Lucerne Hotel, Grace LaRue. It was a reunion of sorts, since Grace and Lillian had played together in the 1918 *Follies*. Grace had since that time formed a close friendship with Hammerstein and remained under his personal management until her retirement in the late twenties. Grace coyly suggested to me that she and Hammerstein spent many an intimate evening together when he traveled to New York from his home base in Chicago.

I recall with a considerable amount of pleasure, from my 1998 Hotel Lucerne video and

LILLIAN LORRAINE Whose Alluring Beauty Again Charms All New York.

Unidentified magazine sketch in tribute to Lillian Lorraine's starring role as Arthur Hammerstein's *The Blue Kitten*, 1921.

audio tapings, several amusing anecdotes dealing with Grace's social and personal life during the *Follies* years and before her involvement with Hammerstein.

In the teens and early twenties of the previous century, the "stage-door Johnny" phenomenon was at its height. The "johnnies" represented almost every walk of life, from both married and single Wall Streeters to wealthy college preppies and dapper lords of the underworld. One of those in the latter category, the notorious mobster Jack "Legs" Diamond, took a shine to Grace, showering her with attention in the form of exquisite floral pieces, expensive jewelry and nights out on the town. She described "Legs" as more of a gentleman than some of the Park Avenue playboys of the "wham, bam love 'em and leave 'em" school of after-dark

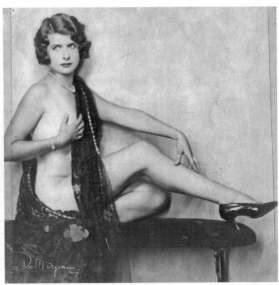

Left: Alfred Cheney Johnston publicity shot, 1920 (courtesy Ziegfeld Club Archives). *Right:* Grace LaRue in a risqué-for-the-times publicity shot, 1918.

shenanigans. With a raspy chuckle, Grace recalled how Diamond, always concerned for her well-being, often queried, "Do you have anyone whose legs need breaking?"

It was with genuine relish that she spun a tale of her encounter with one of the biggest names in the underworld:

> I remember one night when some of us girls were sitting in on a backroom meeting at Jack's Hotsy Totsy Club and Al Capone, in from Chicago, was there too. Just to be friendly and make conversation I asked him how he had gotten the scar on the side of his face. Boy, did I ever get hustled out of there in a hurry! You can guess why Jack Diamond never took me to another one of those meetings. Even though it was Prohibition, the Wall Streeters would take us out to some pretty nifty private clubs for a nice evening of dinner and dancing and afterwards, especially if our escort was married, he would hail a taxi and slip us a one-hundred-dollar bill to get home. I would usually ride the cab for one block, then hop out and take the subway home for all of five cents! The ninety-five dollars I saved was enough to take care of home groceries for a couple of months!

At the time, Grace was living at home with her mother and was the provider.

At ninety-nine years of age, Grace was still able to recall with a remarkable degree of clarity an incident during the run of *The Blue Kitten*. She had been talking with Lillian about the plight of a seventeen-year-old dancer in the company by the name Jeanne Dixon. (Grace was not one hundred percent certain of the girl's name.) The young dancer had been impregnated by a college preppie playboy who, upon learning of Jeanne's "condition," dropped her like the proverbial hot potato. In order to keep her job she knew it would mean an abortion, which she could not afford. In Grace's presence, Lillian called the youngster into her dressing room and, probably as a result of Lillian's Irish Catholic upbringing, convinced her to have the baby and leave the show for whatever time she needed. Removing a beautiful diamond bracelet, she gave it to the girl with the assurance that it would bring more than enough money to see her through the pregnancy and beyond. Grace continued, "They can write whatever they want about Lillian, but by gosh, when the chips were down, she was always there with a helping hand, and do you know what, she never looked to be paid back! I don't think she ever forgot her early struggles to hit the big time."

Cartoon clipping of *The Blue Kitten*, 1921.

The Blue Kitten was well received by the critics, with most of them waxing enthusiastic about Lillian's miraculous return to musical comedy. Lillian's character, Totoche, was the bright star of the Blue Kitten Café's cabaret. James Whitaker, in his *Evening Telegraph* review, wrote, "On the occasion of Miss Lorraine's first entrance, the audience rose in spontaneous rapture and hailed the miracle."

James E. Dean, in an Associated Press article for the *Colorado Springs Telegraph*, summed up the show. "The Blue Kitten is a satire on the tipping habit. By night ... [Cawthorn's character] is a porter in a café (the Blue Kitten). By day he is a gentleman of leisure at a chateau at Fontainebleu. His wife and daughter think his wealth is derived from his position as a night editor on a Paris newspaper."

Responding to the first news of Lillian's pending comeback, the doomsday wiseacres scoffed, "They never come back!" But the *Star Gazer* extolled her return: "Lillian fooled us all. She came back with a bang and a great many playgoers are going to agree she is as fascinating in her work as when she first flashed into prominence via 'the swing number' in the 1910 *Follies*."

Much was being made of Lillian's beautiful but scanty stage attire, described in a Steven Rathbun piece in the *Sun*, "Miss Lorraine's back was a high spot of the evening at the Selwyn. It was more beautiful than her thirty- or forty-thousand-dollar fur coats. When she initially appeared in her backless, almost frontless first act gown one could judge quite critically that the recent accident had not marred her beauty." Rathbun concluded his commentary with one swift and sour barb: "She handled her songs well but would it be too much to ask this prima donna, the queen of all showgirldom, to act?"

Alan Dale in the *New York Review* also picked up on the "back" theme: "Talk of back to nature and all that sort of thing. Miss Lorraine seemed determined to do the stunt. She has a very wonderful back, sleek and glossy, with neat and tidy cervical vertebrae and she carefully prepared it for its night out. It is an amiable back, unostentatious, though it is a back that renders more clothes unnecessary."

Burns Mantle in *The Evening Mail* commented, "Miss Lorraine seems entirely recovered from the accident which has kept her off the stage for many months and her fans present at the Selwyn last night were eager to welcome her back, bare or otherwise."

The January 14 *Herald* declared, "Lillian Lorraine, who is more statuesquely beautiful in face and figure, delighted her admirers by returning to the stage in seemingly perfect health, singing and dancing with her usual high level of energy."

However, we see a new side to Lillian via backstage interviews during *The Blue Kitten*'s run. And so did Charles Bamfield Hoyte. In the *Metropolitan Guide* he tells us:

> The precarious pastime by which one judges an actress across the footlights has its dillusionment. Manner, voice, style, height, smile, personality — all these ingredients of an estimate may so easily be dissipated by a single step from audiences to dressing room. On the stage, Lillian Lorraine has a peculiar style of willowness which accentuates her height. Perhaps it is those gorgeous gowns deleted with becoming taste in the region of the back. Perhaps it is her manner of carriage. Perhaps the projection of the personality at work behind the footlights. We will not hazard guesses. We will confine ourselves to the statement that in the dressing room Miss Lorraine seems a different person.

In one backstage interview, Lillian said, "But it is only on the stage that I am carefree now. I know that the persons who make up the audience want their cares washed away, so I laugh with them and [entertain them] ... but when the curtain goes down, the many serious thoughts which came to me during my illness crowd in upon me and I am filled with the seriousness of life."

And to Hoyte, she revealed, "I came back to the stage with an entirely new outlook on things. We are apt in our everyday life, to take too much for granted. We take the good fortunes that come to us as a matter of course. This sort of thing, where we become really acquainted with suffering, turns one's mind into a more serious trend, and is quite apt to make you philosophize a little."

Hoyte also tells us, "In bringing the knowledge of this experience back to her work, Miss

Lorraine admits it has developed a desire in her to undertake some really serious dramatic work."

Lillian told Hoyte, "I have never undertaken serious drama. I'd really like to try it. It's so very difficult, somehow, for a star of musical comedy to become the star of anything else. The public grows to expect you to sing a little, dance a little, and entertain them. Entertain them and that's about all. Perhaps I would find the drama was not my field but I should surely like to try it."

Sadly, Lillian just could not follow through on either her reflections or her resolve for a new life and career path. She did not have Ziegfeld, except for his occasional telephone calls and financial help. In the absence of my mother's tempering influence Lillian could not maintain the discipline required to achieve her goals. As a result, her efforts were short-lived. Her wants and her wishes were never realized. It was not long before she returned to her old self-destructive ways, best described by Marjorie Farnsworth in her *Ziegfeld Follies: A History in Text and Pictures*: "Lillian lived in the grand manner and laughed at the world.... But Lillian's laughter at the world was the laughter of compulsive despair. She had a mania for speed and gay parties and a reckless insouciance that bordered on the psychotic and it was not long before this girl, born in San Francisco under the name of Mary Ann Brennan [actually Lillian's mother's name], became known in the public prints as a 'broken butterfly.'"

The Blue Kitten ran the full season at Forty-Second Street's Selwyn Theatre, closing in May of 1922. Lillian's "high level of energy" seemed to have spilled over once again into her personal life as newspapers reported she had been named "co-respondent" by Mrs. Gladys Wagner in her suit for divorce from her husband Charles. He was well known in the Rialto district as "Billy Lloyd," a principal stockholder in the fashionable Maurice nightclub. A May 26 boudoir raid was the sordid culmination of an investigation into Wagner's extramarital activities. In the filed affidavit, private detectives swore they had trailed Wagner from the nightclub to Lillian's apartment at 120 West 71st Street. Waiting until three o'clock in the morning, the detectives raided the apartment, finding Lillian and Charles in scanty attire and greatly surprised by the intrusion.

Seven weeks earlier, Lillian had given what was described as a "hilarious party" at the Maurice, and soon thereafter Charles Wagner disappeared from his own home and turned up living at Lillian's West 71st Street address. Because of a locked and chained front door, one of Gladys Wagner's five detectives had to gain access to the apartment by scaling the outside wall and entering through an open window. Charles awakened the neighborhood with his shouts of "Murder! Help! Police!" Lillian, believing the intruders to be revenue agents, screamed, "Charlie, save the hootch! Don't let them take my hootch!" Throughout the early morning melee, a scorned and vengeful Gladys Wagner and her maid, Lulu Caldwell, observed the fiasco from the sidewalk immediately outside the apartment. Lillian's concern for the "hootch" was understandable and came as no surprise since raids by police and federal agents were commonplace events at the many private after-hours peephole clubs mushrooming all over New York City.

In an interview with reporters covering the pre-divorce hearings, Gladys Wagner gave the following account of the infamous raid. She said her husband "had been caught wearing a pair of pajamas that once were white but now looked as though they had been used to clean a gas range." She exclaimed to the amused reporters, "My God, I don't care so much about finding those two birds together, but to think of those dirty pajamas that I always kept so clean, well...!" Her divorce suit called for alimony plus five thousand dollars in legal fees and another thousand for the detectives. Wagner, in turn, denied all charges of misconduct and further declared himself to be penniless. He claimed that he had recently given his wife $16,000 for safekeeping even though his nightclub had recorded a loss of $47,000 in the last season.

He further alleged that she had deposited the money in her personal account and then proceeded to spend most of it on furs and other expensive extravagances.

Broadway Brevities ran a scathing yet satirical account of the Lorraine/Wagner imbroglio in which they described Lillian as the "amorous albatross of inland liaison." The magazine's appetite had been whetted and they happily went on to revive ancient history with a rehash of another salacious incident which had occurred some four years earlier, when Lillian was caught up in a similar situation at her Ansonia apartment with Joseph L. Pani of swanky Westchester County. Pani was best known for being the man who coined the familiar candy slogan, "Happiness in every container." His wife had filed suit for alienation of affection to the tune of one hundred thousand dollars. The media accounts of the Pani raid were very similar to those described in the Wagner affair: "Lillian, in her earlier phase of nonchalant gayety and vitality, just laid back and laughed at the detectives and the irate, wronged wife bringing up the rear guard of the sortie."

Lillian's personal life was once again hot copy and, as before, became the property of newspaper gossip wags. Ghosts of her life on the fast track continued to plague her in the person of two process servers at the Selwyn's 42nd Street stage door. There was the little matter of a three-year-old unpaid bill from Reisenwebers, one of Lillian's favorite Columbus Circle haunts. The theatre tabloid *ZITS* headlined their story, "Lillian Lorraine Had to Bend an Elbow Often to Run Up a Bill Like This!"

The following year, 1923, Lillian was the headliner at the Beaux Arts Club, pulling down a salary of one thousand dollars per week. The *Morning Telegraph* reported on March 16 that Lillian had caused the arrest of not only Charles Wagner, but his brother Louis as well. According to the complaint, Louis was employed at the Club Maurice as secretary and treasurer. Lillian charged that both brothers had misappropriated checks due her from an earlier engagement at the Maurice. The amount was sixteen hundred dollars. Lillian, smartly dressed and wearing no jewelry, was seated in the front row of the courtroom. Unsmiling, she sat calmly with her eyes fixed steadily on the two brothers. As the proceedings progressed, the brothers countercharged that it was Lillian who owed them the money in question. After a one-week recess the case came before Magistrate Michael Corrigan. With no public explanation, the charges were dropped and the case dismissed. Exactly why Lillian initially filed the charges was a mystery and only served to focus additional attention on her increasingly bizarre patterns of behavior.

Three months later, Lillian took up residency at 38 West 72nd Street. It was not long before she was back in newsprint as a result of neighbors' complaints to police about excessively noisy festivities in the Lorraine abode. Again, according to *ZITS*, residents in the next door building insisted they did not question Lillian's right to have parties but did draw the line when those parties commenced in earnest at a time when "decent and law-abiding citizens should be donning their nighties!" The unhappy neighbors continued, "We would be pleased had the fair actress raised her own voice in a lilting lullaby, but, instead, it was her gentlemen guests whose voices usurped the evening air waves."

The *ZITS* story concluded, "This week the actress crammed her many portmanteaux with oodles of feminine finery and is seen no more in the fashionable upper Broadway environs."

27

Marilyn Miller and Frank Carter
— Broadway's Golden Couple

In late 1920, Ziegfeld was riding high with the success of *Sally*, his new Marilyn Miller venture. The void in his superstar lineup created by the departure of Lillian Lorraine after 1920's *Glorifying the American Girl* was now filled by Lillian's 1918 *Follies* co-star, Marilyn Miller. For Lillian, the undercurrents of a downswing were already in play and soon to follow: her less than inspiring performance in *Sonny* that garnered only mediocre notices; her tragic fall in February 1921; a winning performance in *The Blue Kitten* that was offset by innumerable legal problems, created by her willful and freewheeling personal lifestyle, that were driving her closer and closer to the brink of financial and emotional bankruptcy.

As for her *Follies* successor, the critics were ecstatic in their praise of Marilyn Miller and box office business for *Sally* was boffo — going through the roof! However, Flo's personal relationship with Marilyn was at a dangerous boiling point. Throwing discretion to the winds, Marilyn, now an established star, was publicly accusing Flo of attempted seduction as well as conducting indiscreet affairs with girls in the chorus.

In her autobiography, *The Ziegfelds' Girl*. Patricia Ziegfeld recalls a shocking incident that took place during the run of *Sally* when, as a young child, her father took her backstage at the New Amsterdam to meet Marilyn. The public persona of Marilyn as a sweet, demure and delightful young lady was, at least in Patty's mind, shattered when she and Flo made their appearance at Marilyn's dressing room door. They were met with a barrage of foul language, the likes of which Patty had never before heard. "Hello, you lousy son-of-a-bitch! Hello, you no good bastard!" Marilyn was on a tear as Flo tried to pacify her by explaining he had brought his daughter backstage specifically to meet her. He remonstrated how many nice things he had told Patty about her. Marilyn sarcastically retorted, "To the point of nausea!" Flo continued to explain it was Patty's first visit backstage to any show, to which Marilyn caustically snapped, "How thrilling!" The cause for Marilyn's tirade soon came to the fore when she exclaimed, "You know God-damned well what's bothering me! It's this piece of crap you call a costume. As far as I'm concerned you can just take it and shove it! I'm asking you for the last time, Buster, what about the costume?" Realizing the situation was clearly out of control, Flo said they would talk about it another time and, taking Patty by the hand, beat a hasty retreat. Marilyn had the last words, shouting after them, "We'll damned well talk about it now!"

Most of the so-called pundits in the know were convinced there had been a short sexual assignation between Flo and Marilyn — probably in 1918 when she first came under his management. His infatuation with the dancer was deep, and for a time he showered her with expensive gifts, not at all unmindful that in her he had a gold mine and was not about to chance losing her back to the Shuberts.

Two years earlier, in 1916, Marilyn had been dancing at the Shuberts' Winter Garden in

Show of Wonders. A young song-and-dance man, Frank Carter, was in the same production. Although their first personal encounter was at that time, they did not become a serious item until both were appearing in separate feature roles in the 1918 *Ziegfeld Follies.* In that show, Frank and Lillian Lorraine sang a duet titled "Garden of My Dreams," singled out by critics as the outstanding number in the production. Frank and Marilyn had begun seriously dating and also worked together selling Liberty Bonds for the war effort. Warren Harris, author of *The Other Marilyn*, said the two lovebirds sold over one and one-quarter million dollars'

worth of bonds in one day from a specially-constructed booth in Times Square. Opposition to the budding romance came from Marilyn's mother and stepfather, both of whom disliked Carter, believing him to be a scheming opportunist. Flo, too, was reportedly jealous of the younger man's amorous attentions to Marilyn. Eddie Cantor, also in the 1918 *Follies*, had befriended Frank and encouraged the affair, as had songwriter Gene Buck — much to Ziegfeld's chagrin. The couple signed for the 1919 *Follies* and formally announced their engagement in May of that year. One month later, without consulting even their closest friends, Frank and Marilyn eloped to Maryland and were married. Ziegfeld was furious and immediately terminated Frank from the company, vowing that he would never work in another Ziegfeld show. Marilyn threatened to quit the *Follies* but thought better of it when Flo's attorney raised the specter of a breach of contract suit.

Rare photograph of *Follies* star Marilyn Miller and actor-husband Frank Carter, 1920 (courtesy Ziegfeld Club Archives).

Frank Carter was twenty-eight, boyishly good-looking, with dark brown hair and smoldering brown eyes. He and Marilyn had become Broadway's dream couple — she the golden princess and he, the handsome Prince Charming who had captured her heart.

Frank was born in Fairbury, Nebraska, in 1891 and before he was in his teens had made his vaudeville debut in a sketch titled "Aunt Jerusha." Show business was in his blood, and at fourteen, with a lilting soprano voice, he arrived on Broadway as a "song seller" with George M. Cohan Productions. With a change in his voice and more than just a small amount of ingenuity, he joined a carnival as a daredevil high diver. An injury caused him to rethink his career path, prompting him to add to his repertoire acrobatic and ballroom dancing. Before long he was a regular with Hammerstein's. He toured throughout England and France, and it was during this time he was romantically linked with Lucy Weston, a well-known songstress in British music halls. It was rumored the two were married but factual evidence of the alleged nuptial does not exist. The year 1914 marked Frank's return to the United States and a contract with the Shuberts for their Winter Garden production, *Dancing Around*. Within two years he was a principal player sharing top billing with the popular Duncan sisters in *Doing Our Bit*. In 1917 he was signed by Ziegfeld for the 1917 *Midnight Frolic* with the 1918 *Follies* to follow. At this juncture the ill-fated Carter-Miller saga took center stage.

Word of Ziegfeld's contentious and abrupt dismissal of Frank in 1919 did not escape the Shubert Brothers' ears. They immediately signed him for the lead in their new musical comedy, *See Saw*. The critics were lavish in their praise of both the show and Frank's performance, resulting in the extension of his contract beyond the New York run and for the road company tour. The closing night of *See Saw* was May 8, 1920, in Wheeling, West Virginia. Anxious to join up with Marilyn, who was also on tour, Frank set out for Philadelphia that night with fellow cast members Frank Esdale, Guy Robertson and Charles Risdale in a newly purchased ten-thousand-dollar Packard touring car (a surprise for Marilyn). Driving all night, near Grantsville, Maryland, traveling at what was then considered an abnormally high speed of 65 miles an hour, Frank misjudged a curbing on the National Pike. He slammed on the brakes, spinning the car out of control and crashing it into an embankment. Crushed between the seat and the steering wheel shaft, Frank was instantly killed. Esdale sustained a broken collarbone and four fractured ribs, while the other two passengers escaped unharmed. Frank's body was immediately removed to the morgue in Cumberland, awaiting instructions from next of kin.

That same morning, on her arrival in Philadelphia, Marilyn was told Frank had been in a serious automobile accident, but it was not until her arrival in Cumberland that she was told of his death. It had fallen to the unscathed survivors, Robertson and Risdale, to break the news that her twenty-eight-year-old husband of eleven months was dead. Thus, after less than a year of marriage, Marilyn was a widow and Broadway mourned the end of what had been billed the fairy-tale love match of the Great White Way.

Doris Eaton, then a specialty dancer in the 1919 *Follies*, vividly recalls the *Follies* company entraining from Chicago to Philadelphia and, upon arrival in that City of Brotherly Love, Marilyn's notification of the accident. "It was horrible," Doris told me,

> and of course, none of us knew anything other than Frank had been seriously injured in an early morning automobile accident. We were all aghast. We had known and loved Frank and our hearts went out to Marilyn. I knew most of her dance routines and with one day's notice was told I would be her replacement for at least a two-week period. The critics and audiences were very kind, especially when I took to the stage with an exact replica of Marilyn's "Mandy" costume and soft shoe dance routine.

On May 11 in New York City, a massive outpouring of the theatre community and high public officials attended services at the Frank E. Campbell Funeral Home, then located on upper Broadway. Among these many friends and mourners were my mother and Lillian Lorraine, Frank's co-star in the 1918 production number "Garden of My Dreams." Consistent with his well-known phobia relating to death, Ziegfeld did not attend. A private interment followed at Woodlawn Cemetery in the Bronx. Sixteen years later, Marilyn would be laid to rest alongside Frank in the beautiful white marble, Grecian temple mausoleum she'd had constructed following Frank's death. It was intended for only the two caskets, and in accordance with Marilyn's instructions, upon her death, the crypt was to be sealed forever.

28

Lillian Faces Financial Ruin and a Fleeting Comeback

In 1921, while recuperating at Stern's Sanatorium, Lillian's financial underpinnings were given a hard knock. In a July 16, 1924, interview with Ruth Dayton of *The American*, Lillian declared she had lost ninety thousand dollars at the hands of fraudulent stockbrokers. She said, "I lost most of my securities at the time of my accident. I thought I was making thousands of dollars investing in longs and shorts. I was flat on my back in a cast for almost six months and by the time I was able to get around again and pay attention to my finances, everything was gone — including the brokers! I wasn't alone — several of my friends met with the same fate."

By the beginning of 1923, Lillian's economic status hit rock bottom. Her medical expenses had been astronomical. The long months of confinement and rehabilitation at Stern's had been an enormous drain on an already precarious financial condition caused by a decade of unchecked extravagances and wanton behavior. Her physical recovery and triumphant return to the stage were hailed by the media as both medical and show business miracles, but in spite of such glowing reports, she refused to heed the counsel and warnings of well-meaning friends, my mother included, to temper her lifestyle and start planning and saving for her later years.

Before long she was at the door of a notorious loan shark, Solomon David, associated with the firm of Sperry and Yankauer at 150 West 42nd Street. Her magnificent cache of jewelry was all that remained for collateral. Still, she would not face reality. She continued her compulsive excesses. By July of 1923 the loan money had been spent, her remaining assets were wholly depleted and her liabilities were over twenty-six thousand dollars, which, based on average annual inflation since that time would amount to over $300,000 in today's money. Julian Haman, an attorney friend with the firm of Gilbert & Black, finally convinced Lillian that she was left with no recourse other than to file a petition for bankruptcy in Manhattan District Court. In addition to personal loans, other debtor items included ongoing physicians' fees, bills for high fashion clothing and stacks of long-overdue extended credit notes for everyday living expenses.

One might think that to bolster her financial status Lillian would have returned to the lucrative field of films. But because of her ever increasingly erratic behavior, movie producers probably no longer considered her a bankable commodity. Also, on her own, Lillian's background suggests that — without knowing it — she sorely missed the steadying presence of my mother and the guiding hands and professional expertise of those who initially brought her to the peak of stardom: her own mother, Joe Moss, the Shuberts, and Ziegfeld. When the chips were down, she needed them, and they were no longer available to her. Thus, it seems that she chose to remain on the turf most familiar to her: namely, Broadway.

Lillian's popularity as a headliner was luckily still at a high mark, thereby enabling her to make a fresh start and to try to repay those creditors most dear to her. She was frequently the featured attraction at the Gold Room atop the Beaux Arts Building at 80 West 40th Street, and was a repeat wee-hours favorite at *Larry Faye's Follies* at 247 West 54th Street, the former home of the Automobile Club of America. At the time, it was the most elegant and most popular night spot on Broadway. Not since Ziegfeld was forced to close down his *Midnight Frolic* due to Prohibition was there anything else to compare to the late-night entertainment being offered at the Faye show palace. Faye's overhead was not in any way comparable to that which was required to support Ziegfeld's commitment to the chic and opulent shows that his audiences had over the years come to demand and expect. For Ziegfeld, the full effects of the Volstead Act were in high swing, causing Ziegfeld to rethink the profitability of his New Amsterdam Roof enterprise. Prior to Prohibition, the *Midnight Frolic* had been extremely successful as an upscale cabaret supper club featuring not only his beautiful showgirls but after-theatre repast, music and public dancing. Now a major money-making ingredient, liquor, was missing, and for the first time since its opening in 1913 and at least for the time being, the lights went out on the Ziegfeld Roof and Aerial Gardens.

In his review of *Larry Faye's Follies* opening night, columnist Dayton Lewis wrote:

> Faye's Follies reminds me of the dazzling cabarets we now see only on a movie screen but seldom in real life. Like other nocturnal playgrounds, its dance floor is built for stationary calisthenics—not dancing! Texas Guinan, undisputed Queen of the Nightclub scene, was on hand to chaperone the chorus beauties and the indomitable Lillian Lorraine was the clear favorite of the evening. She sang songs but all one could gather is that they were in English or American. We were in the 99th row, you know. Anyway, those down front thought Lillian was awfully good and to us, she was radiant!
>
> Last night the Broadway mob was on hand with its usual display of bad manners. Tables were everywhere except on the bass drum. Those who went to be seen—ostentatious first nighters and society's circus set, many of whom actually paid the opening night's admission price of eleven dollars per head—and those who went to see the midnight cuties, had a gay old time elbowing their way about and squeezing into *Lobster Palace* chairs.

Lillian was not yet wholly free of her legal or, it seems, social entanglement with Charles Wagner. On the night of January 14, 1924, Lillian, Wagner and Gladys, his estranged wife, all happened to be in the same cabaret but at three different tables. Observing Lillian making her entrance with a group of friends, Wagner approached her indicating he would like to talk with her. With obvious disdain she brusquely suggested he go over to his wife's table and talk with her. Gladys, apparently feeling no pain and still smarting over her estranged husband's recent defection, picked up a bottle and threw it in the direction of her two antagonists. Wagner, in an attempt to prevent Lillian from leaving, picked up her mink coat and fled to an upper story of the club. Police were called to the scene and very quickly Wagner found himself to be the center of their attention. A club bouncer had retrieved the fur coat and returned it to Lillian, who immediately proceeded to leave with her friends. On her way to the exit she saw Wagner still engaged in heated conversation with the police and, true to form, injected herself into the fracas in an attempt to assure the blue jackets that everything was all right. Apparently they were not convinced and proceeded to bundle Lillian, Gladys and Wagner into a paddy wagon and a ride downtown to appear before a night court magistrate. Charged with disturbing the peace in a public place, the unhappy trio of defendants breathed a collective sigh of relief when the weary judge threw up his hands and told them all to "go home and sleep it off!"

The good news in the spring of 1924 was U.S. District Court Judge Learned Hand's announcement of Lillian's discharge from the bankruptcy for which she had filed the previous July. As a result of her highly successful appearances at *Ted Lewis' Frolic* in Boston, Ciro's, the Gold Room and Philadelphia's Art Studio Club, where she was the highest paid entertainer to date, her financial position had considerably improved—at least temporarily.

The *Morning Telegraph* reported on September 14, 1925, that Lillian had married again, and that this time the groom was not Fred Gresheimer. The alleged husband was Andrew Brown, an unsavory character, presently free on bail following a conviction on charges of blackmailing several persons in the theatrical company of *Broadway Brevities*. His under-appeal sentence was for two years in an Atlanta penitentiary. Although the couple had been seen together on a dance floor, the rumored marriage was nothing more than idle gossip.

However, one month later, in October of 1925, Lillian's unfortunate penchant for uncon-ventional involvements provided more salacious copy for scandal-hungry gossip mongers. Katherine Frey, wife of wealthy turfman and sometime bookmaker Charles Frey, filed a one-hundred-thousand-dollar alienation of affection suit against blonde showgirl Wilda Bennett, who was appearing in *Say It with Music* at Irving Berlin's recently opened Music Box Theatre. At a court hearing, Katherine declared she had recently filed for divorce on advice of her attorneys, who had recommended such action to counter an earlier suit by her husband. In the petition for divorce she had not named the co-respondent, but now declared the unnamed woman was Lillian Lorraine. When queried by reporters, both Wilda Bennett and Lillian refused to comment. Following two weeks of legal maneuvering, an out-of-court settlement was reached, thereby robbing the scandal sheets of what had promised to be another messy chapter in the life of a very tarnished Broadway beauty.

29

Dimming Footlights and the Bessie Poole Affair

There is no public record of Lillian's personal or professional life during 1926. She had disappeared from public view, except for an occasional sighting in a New York nightspot.

Lillian celebrated her thirty-fifth birthday on January 1, 1927. Incredibly, after years of fast living, she was still an extraordinarily beautiful woman and time was overdue in collecting its toll. Admiring heads continued to turn wherever and whenever she appeared in public. She was a handsomely mature woman when she signed with producer Laura Wilck for the female lead in *Get Me Into the Movies*, a new three-act comedy by Charlton Andrews. At the outset, Bertram Harrison, the stage director, was wary of Lillian's casting. The scandals in her personal life and breaches of professional discipline were an open book — but, in the end, it was her still-potent box office appeal and proven ability to handle comedy that won out. Wilck had assembled a first-class roster of thespians, including Donald Macdonald, Elizabeth Murray and Wilfred Lytell. A decade earlier, Lillian's widely acclaimed youthful radiance had been a key to critics' forgiveness of what some had termed her less-than-brilliant acting and singing abilities. Now, at thirty-five, *Get Me Into the Movies* would either be Lillian's theatrical swan song or a golden opportunity to prove her detractors wrong. Fans and friends alike held their collective breath and hoped for the best.

Get Me Into the Movies opened for out-of-town previews at the Parsons Theatre in Hartford, Connecticut, on March 7. The Hartford press was generous with its praise of Lillian's comedic and witty portrayal of Fame Dawson, the nation's $10,000-a-week movie queen sweetheart. "The play is a laugh a minute tour de force with Miss Lorraine and Donald Macdonald, a Theatre Guild protege, shining examples of just how funny high comedy can really be. They are in top form!"

Regrettably, I am unable to share any of the purported high comedy lines of this script with the reader. Following an exhaustive search from the U.S. Copyright Office to the revered halls of the New York Public Library for Performing Arts archives, I must conclude that all copies of the pre–Broadway script and Broadway script (with revised title) appear to have been remaindered to obscurity.

Ten days following the opening of the play in Hartford, and immediately prior to a scheduled Broadway opening, *Get Me Into the Movies* opened at the tony Westchester County Mamaroneck Playhouse. The theatre was exactly three miles from our Larchmont Gardens home. Midway through the run of the show, Lillian decided to visit my mother. I was five years old, almost six, at the time.

In retrieving the memory of my only contact with Lillian Lorraine from so far into my past, I ask acceptance for the literary license I am about to take with respect to the exact details of this experience.

I was waiting on our front lawn for the famous person that my mother said would be visiting when a big chauffeur-driven black limousine pulled up in front of our small stucco cottage on Harmon Drive. I had never seen such big car. A uniformed chauffeur assisted a woman from the rear seat of the car and accompanied her up the walkway to our front door. I wondered why it was necessary for the chauffeur to assist the woman. To my childish mind it appeared that she required the assistance because of an unsteady gait. Of course, at the age of five, with my upbringing, I had no way of knowing that she probably was in a state of intoxication.

Lillian Lorraine at age 35 (courtesy Ziegfeld Club Archives).

Mother and Lillian embraced each other and seated themselves in our living room. They talked, but to me, Lillian's tone of conversation sounded silly. She wore lipstick but not a lot. Today, I would call it discreetly applied. She smelled good. I remember thinking that she was the prettiest woman I had ever seen. I must have been gawking during the few moments I was with them, and before I knew it, my mother excused me from the room. I didn't feel hurt. In fact, I was glad to leave the two grown-ups. I remember happily going into the yard behind our home and playing in a big sand bank that was there.

It was many decades later, when I listened to the taped conversations between my mother and my sister, that I learned that my father did not want his children exposed to Lillian, whom he perceived as an alcoholic. Ultimately Mother and Dad agreed it would be in the best interests of my sister, my older brother Raymond, and me, if this were Lillian's final visit to our Larchmont home. I am sure it must have involved much soul-searching and wringing of hands for my parents to reach this decision. Mother could never have been described as a timid soul. Quite the contrary, like Lillian, she was, from childhood to her death, a free-spirited and fun-loving individual; however, one major difference was that Mother was tempered by the ever-present ingredients of Swedish Lutheran upbringing, discipline and good common sense. Mother's acquiescence to my father's exhortations was, for her in this particular case, a normal response: family comes first.

To the best of my knowledge, this was the last time any of us ever saw Lillian alive again. Furthermore, the starring role in *Get Me Into the Movies* at the Mamaroneck Playhouse was in every sense Lillian's swan song in legitimate theatre.

The play did not open in New York in the spring of 1927 as previously scheduled. Rather, it arrived at the Earl Carroll Theater one year later, completely reworked with a totally new cast and a slight change in the title. Apparently, this overhaul was not successful, since the run of the show was only 32 performances.

For almost a year, Lillian's name and image were absent from the New York dailies, but this hiatus ended when national wire services ran feature stories with headlines proclaiming, "Once Darling of Broadway Dying in Poverty," "Once Pet of Gay Broadway Now Near Death," "Former Follies Girl Nearly Destitute Goes Under Knife."

Lillian had been stricken with a ruptured appendix while visiting a friend at 162 West 56th Street and was immediately removed to the Park West Hospital. Emergency surgery was performed by Dr. Harry Gilbert, her longtime friend and personal physician. Her condition

MAMARONECK
PLAYHOUSE

THURSDAY, MARCH 17th, 1927

LAURA D. WILCK

Presents

A Farce in Three Acts

GET ME INTO THE MOVIES

By CHARLTON ANDREWS

Staged by BERTRAM HARRISON

Reservations for Vaudeville **and Broadway**
Attractions on Sale One Week in Advance

TELEPHONE 2200

Donald Macdonald. Lillian Lorraine. and Wilfred Lytell

LAURA D. WILCK

Presents

GET ME INTO THE MOVIES

A Farce in Three Acts

By CHARLTON ANDREWS ·

Staged by BERTRAM HARRISON

Setting by YELLENTI

CAST

In the Order of Their Appearance

JIM JACKSON	Robert Ritz
MRS. STARBUCK	Elizabeth Murray
JOHNNY LORING	Donald Macdonald
DOROTHY GRAY	Ruth Mero
MRS. PRINGLE	Jean Newcombe
MRS. CALKINS	Frances Neilson
BENJAMIN ROTH	Harry Hanlon
COUNT HENRICO MARDONES	Wilfred Lytell
QUEENIE QUAINT	Lillian Ross
DOLORES CALKINS	Gladys Frazin
FAME DAWSON	Lillian Lorraine
CICELY ARNO	Joan Blair
TONY BADURO	Marshall Bradford
SERGEANT SMITH	Jack C. Grey

Gowns, wraps and hats by Hadley Leon, New York.
Thor Electric Vacuum Cleaner used.
Murphy door bed used.
Polo Costume by A. G. Spalding & Brothers.
The wraps of Miss Lorraine and Miss Ross in the second act are from the
fabrics of Haas Brothers, New York.

ACT I.—Johnny Loring's apartment in Hollywood. Morning.
ACT II.—The same. That night.
ACT III.—The same. The next morning.

EXECUTIVE STAFF FOR LAURA D. WILCK.
Company Manager .... JOHN R. WILLADSEN
Press Representative .... F. M. O'CONNOR
Stage Manager .... HARRY HANLON
Ass't. Stage Manager .... JACK C. GREY

Wurlitzer Organ—At the console, ARTHUR BELICH.

OVERTURE:
George White Scandals by Ray Henderson

Lucky Day
Tweet Tweet
The Birth of the Blues
The Girl is you and The Boy is me
Black Bottom
Sevilla

EXIT MARCH:
Just a Little Blue--Lapham

Get Me Into the Movies program, Mamaroneck Playhouse, March 17, 1927.

was at first reported as "critical but not life threatening." Then, later the next day, a hospital bulletin stated that after a slight rally her condition, aggravated by the onset of peritonitis, had taken a turn for the worse. At the time, the miracle healing drug of penicillin had just been developed, but it was nowhere near being available to the medical community for use in treatment of infections. The tabloid *New York Daily News* was the first to report that Lillian

Lillian Lorraine nude, baked on ivory, framed in Tiffany. Piece commissioned by Florenz Ziegfeld (courtesy of Mary Ann Alfond).

was penniless and that Dr. Gilbert had performed the surgery on a gratis basis. Contrary to former *Follies* Girl Grace LaRue's inference that "no one extended a helping hand [to Lillian] when needed," the *News* reported flowers and offers of financial assistance poured into Lillian's hospital room.

Several days later, Flo Ziegfeld returned from his Quebec hunting and fishing campsite and, according to Marie Wallace DeSylva, he discreetly visited Lillian's hospital room. Marie told my mother he and Lillian laughed till they both cried when he told her that not too many hours before, while he was while en route to Grand Central Station, U.S. Customs officers confiscated his cache of Scotch whiskey during a railroad inspection stop at Rouses Point, New York. Flo had wrongfully and unhappily assumed he would be given a "courtesy of the port" clearance from a customs search since he and his camping guest, Dr. Jerome Wagner, were traveling in a private railroad car owned by U.S. Steel magnate Leonard Replogle.

Commenting to author Charles Higham on the hospital visit, Matilda Golden, from her Santa Monica home in the 1970s, said, "The worst part of this wretched business was that Ziegfeld still loved Lillian. To the end of his life he kept a pair of exquisite miniature nude paintings of her in his desk drawer. He would constantly take them out, look at them, and his eyes would fill with tears. Then he would say, 'If only she had not drunk, had not married badly, had not...' He would mutter a few more grim words on the subject, replace the paintings and close the drawer." After his death, the miniatures, baked on ivory and sealed in Tiffany brass frames, came into the possession of Goldie, and upon Goldie's death, her niece, Mary Ann Alfond of Marblehead, Massachusetts. Efforts to secure them for the Ziegfeld Club Archive Collection have to date been unsuccessful.

Another *Follies* girl, Peggy Fears, told Higham, "Ziegfeld would sometimes put his hand on my face and look into my eyes, which were just like Lillian's, and say, *Don't drink as she did, don't go with bad men, don't dissipate.* Then, with a sigh, he would say, *Lillian wouldn't* listen to me." Peggy Fears was signed by Ziegfeld for his 1924 *Follies* and ultimately she became a close friend of both Flo and Billie Burke.

Marjorie Smith, a columnist for the *New York Evening Graphic,* writing of Lillian's financial plight, described her as "forgotten, ill, penniless and even forsaken by her current boyfriend, Dapper Dan Collins—one more example of Lillian's notoriously poor judgment in the choice of men friends and lovers." The caption under Lillian's front-page photograph described Collins as "an international crook, heartbreaker and shadowy figure in the underworld."

On September 21, 1928, Lillian called reporters to her hospital room and cheerfully announced there was a strong possibility she would be rejoining Ziegfeld and performing in the next season's *Midnight Frolic.* She added, "If I do decide to return to the *Frolic* it won't interfere with my comeback on the legitimate musical comedy stage. The *Frolic* doesn't come to life until after the theatre closing hour, so, I'll be able to do both." The *Brooklyn Citizen* reporter quoted Lillian as saying, "I feel thankful to friends who thought I was in need and sent me checks. I have asked my doctor to return all the checks. I am not destitute at all, nor friendless. I have loads of friends, plenty of funds, and I might say, I'm rich in pride, too."

Lillian Lorraine orchestrating a press conference to announce plans for a "hoped for" return to the Broadway stage under Ziegfeld's personal management, while recuperating in Manhattan's Park West Hospital from an undisclosed illness, 1928.

To the reporter from the *New York Daily News*, Lillian said, "Just think, this is my second close call. You know, when I was stricken so suddenly, I almost stayed in an isolated Cape Cod town, away from medical attention. The last time I miraculously escaped death was seven years ago when I slipped and fell on some ice, injuring my neck and my back. I know my life is charmed and like a cat, I have seven more lives to live!" As if to prove her point, two weeks later she left the hospital, surrounded by an entourage of friends, her doctor, a nurse and several large floral bouquets. As she was about to enter a waiting Rolls-Royce limousine, she turned to waiting photographers and exclaimed, "Well, does this look like I'm a pauper, huh? Well, does it?" With that said, she was whisked away to her apartment suite at the Dorset Hotel, 30 West 54th Street. However, her hospital room comments concerning a possible return to the Ziegfeld fold were apparently wishful thinking, since nothing developed on that front.

Barely a week had passed when Lillian's Dorset Hotel apartment became the setting for the opening act of another headline-grabbing sensation. Bessie Poole, also a former *Follies* girl and Lillian's house guest at the Dorset, became the central and tragic figure in a late-night drunken brawl at Chez Florence, an after-hours speakeasy reputedly owned by Tommy Guinan, brother of the celebrated nightclub queen, Texas Guinan.

When she first arrived on the Broadway scene, Bessie Poole was a star-stuck sixteen-year-old high school dropout. According to biographer Simon Louvish in his *W.C. Fields: The Man on the Flying Trapeze*, Bessie made her Broadway debut in the 1915 *Ziegfeld Follies.*

Fields, also in the 1915 edition, until that time had earned his stripes primarily as a juggler touring vaudeville. With Ziegfeld, he rapidly established himself as a versatile and multi-talented comic, and as such, was given star billing in all future *Follies* through his last in 1925. As his source for exactly when and how Fields and Bessie became romantically involved, Lou-

W.C. (signed "Bill") Fields, *Follies* of 1918 (courtesy Ziegfeld Club Archives).

vish quotes former *Follies* dancer Faye O'Neill. She and Bessie were in the opening "Birth of Elation" chorus for the 1916 *Follies*. "W.C. was watching from the wings," she said. "Their eyes met and that was the beginning of a relationship that would last for the next ten years. You must understand, Bessie had long, beautiful legs and was so fresh and attractive."

It was clear to everyone in the company that Bessie was Bill Fields's girl. Faye O'Neill recalled, "I remember the night Bessie went to the hospital for what we thought was an appendicitis operation. I asked Bill how she was ... he laughed and said, *Operation, hell — she had a turkey in the oven!*"

That same day, August 15, 1917, Bessie gave birth to William Rexford Fields Morris. The name Rexford was taken from Bessie's brother, who lived in Boston at the time. W.C. had taken an apartment for Bessie under the name of Morris at the St. Nicholas Hotel, and the name of the father on their child's birth certificate was given as William R. Morris, an actor. While there was no DNA testing available in 1917, the heavy preponderance of circumstantial evidence leaves very little doubt that Bessie's child was Fields's son.

Why all the subterfuge relating to this child? Fields, a devout Roman Catholic, was married and a divorce was out of the question. Consequently, Bessie, although madly in love with him, never had any illusions as to a future relationship that would encompass a matrimonial state of bliss.

Bessie was not from a wealthy family and had very little money of her own, and at that time, the stigma of bearing an illegitimate child was something to be kept under wraps. Reluctantly, she gave the infant to a Mrs. Rose Holden, the sister-in-law of Lillian Lorraine's close friend, Lu Martel. At the time Rose lived on West 130th Street in New York City. She did not tell the boy who his biological parents were until he was seventeen years old and a junior in high school. For young William's first ten years, W.C. paid monthly support but there is no evidence to suggest that he took more than a cursory interest in the boy's upbringing.

On the other hand, Fields did maintain a good relationship with Bessie's parents. According to Bessie's mother, Mrs. Bessie Adelaide Witherell, W.C. and Bessie teamed up in vaudeville skits between their stints in the *Follies*. During their frequent stage appearances in Boston they made a point of visiting with the Witherell couple in Onset, Massachusetts, for dinners of sautéed sea scallops and clams.

By 1927, Fields had left the musical comedy stage and was a contract player with Paramount Pictures. During a filming in Los Angeles, he broke his neck in a fall on the set. Bessie was in New York City at the time. Their relationship, although not monogamous on his part, was now of ten years' duration but wearing thin. A split was imminent.

Several of Fields's biographers have speculated and advanced various theories as to the precise circumstances of their breakup. However, the only definitive and factually researched account is that of noted author James Curtis in his widely acclaimed and best-selling 2003 biography, *W.C. Fields*. Curtis writes:

> Bessie Poole read of Fields' injuries in one of the New York dailies and wired her concern. He had kept her afloat over the years with a series of $500 checks, but had ignored her pleas since her return from Europe. Then their ten-year-old son was hospitalized in November 1927 and, after covering $100 of Mrs. Holden's expenses out of her own pocket, Bessie traveled to California for a "show-down" with the father. Armed with a sheaf of letters he had written over the years, she got a lawyer and threatened to sue him in open court if he didn't make good on his responsibilities. Fields retained an attorney of his own and dictated an affidavit which included, in part, the words: "W.C. Fields is NOT the father of my child." Upon a negotiated payment of $20,000 ($13,000 in cash and a note for the balance), Bessie relinquished all claims and walked out of Fields' life forever.

She was heartbroken, destitute, and by this time, having kept up for ten years with W.C.'s well-known appetite for distilled spirits, she was a confirmed alcoholic. She was still very much in love with Fields, but believing she had no alternative means of support, she signed the affidavit and received the twenty-thousand-dollar settlement.

The altercation at the Chez Florence, which brought Bessie back into this chapter of Lillian's life, occurred in the late hours of October 6, 1928. Early that evening, Bessie joined Lillian and two of her friends for dinner at Dinty Moore's restaurant. One of the men was Joseph Whitehead, a Lillian beau and a top executive with Coca-Cola; the other man was Whitehead's Orangeade counterpart, Robert Neilly.

Following dinner the foursome returned to Lillian's apartment at the Dorset, where they were joined by Whitehead's brother-in-law, Edwin McCarthy, a shipping corporation executive. During a discussion of where they should all go for a night on the town, McCarthy suggested the Chez Florence. Lillian, less than a week away from her recent hospitalization, declined to join them but said she would await their return later in the evening.

Sensational press accounts of the brawl at Chez Florence were worthy of today's supermarket tabloids in both front-page appearance and substance. But the press accounts were inconsistent, and witness statements were tainted, thus making it difficult for law enforcement authorities to piece together just exactly what precipitated the conflagration. Witnesses declared that Bessie and her three companions were in high spirits when Robert Neilly showed signs of passing out. Someone poured spirits of ammonia in a glass and held it under Neilly's nose. Bystanders claim Bessie started screaming, "Stop, you're burning him!" As she tried to push the glass away, Tommy Guinan and two of his cohorts joined the melee. Whitehead and McCarthy, who had momentarily left the table, returned to find a disheveled Bessie, bleeding profusely from the nose and charging that Guinan had punched her. Guinan countercharged that Bessie had been out of control and tipped over the table, spilling its contents on the floor. At that point, he said, someone took a swing at him and he, in turn, retaliated. Whitehead's version was that he and McCarthy were attempting to protect Bessie when club personnel moved in and began pummeling both himself and McCarthy. Finally, Bessie, in shambles, left the club in the company of Whitehead and McCarthy. Resolving to let the matter drop, at least temporarily, they returned to Lillian's suite at the Dorset. Bessie retired to a bedroom and the two men left immediately for their own hotel. Bessie, still agitated and in a considerable amount of pain, told Lillian that it was Tommy Guinan who had attacked her and struck the blow to her nose.

No further importance would have been attached to this incident were it not for the tragic sequence of events during the next thirty-six hours.

The next morning, Sunday, Bessie penned the note to her mother revealing the existence of her grandson, his whereabouts and his true parentage. Throughout the day, Bessie's level of discomfort became more and more acute, prompting Lillian to summon her personal physician, Dr. Harry Gilbert. After examining Bessie he administered a sedative, but by Monday afternoon she was suffering with intense abdominal pains, crying out, "Oh, Lillian, I'm going — I know I'm going!" It was 4:00 p.m. and Dr. Gilbert was again summoned. He ordered her immediate removal to the Park East Hospital, where she lapsed into a coma. Within hours she lay on the medical examiner's marble autopsy slab at the Bellevue Hospital morgue.

The case would now become a *cause celebre* and that same evening at the Dorset, in the presence of four witnesses, Dr. Gilbert told a reporter from the *New York Graphic* that Bessie's nose had been fractured, that he wasn't afraid of anybody and would tell the truth about what he had observed concerning Bessie's condition at the time of his initial examination. Astonishingly, within twelve hours, Gilbert had recanted his earlier statement and now said, "There were no marks of violence on her body and she did not indicate she had met with any violence." One must surely draw the conclusion he had been gotten to! On the death certificate, he gave as the cause of death as myocarditis — an inflammation of the myocardium, or heart muscle. Gilbert went on to tell reporters that Bessie had been suffering from alcoholism and had been in that condition for several days.

A sampling of newspaper headlines the following morning made it clear that a major scandal was brewing over the cause and exact circumstances of Bessie's sudden demise. Involvement, although indirect, of a famous actress, two prominent married corporate executives, and a well-known nightclub figure gave the affair just enough tang to prompt an official criminal investigation by New York County District Attorney Joab S. Banton. The sensational nature of the case gave Banton the spark he needed to provide new impetus to his already well publicized campaign against nightclubs he described as "haunts of the underworld and by-products of Prohibition."

Rumors were rampant that organized crime figures had become involved in a cover-up of the Poole affair. The October 10 *Evening Graphic* headlined, "Reprisal Hint in Girl's Death; Bessie Poole Was Told She Would Be Taken for a Ride!" Assistant District Attorney Ferdinand Pecora said, "Police reports dismissing Miss Poole's death with the glib phrase *heart failure* will not end the investigation."

For the most part, persons who witnessed the assault on Bessie appeared anxious to avoid publicity. Few, outside of the principal figures, could be found. Tommy Guinan readily admitted his presence in the club on the night in question but denied having any financial interest in the club. His version: "Me and my friends had just dropped by for a little refreshment and we walked right into a battle spinning around Bessie Poole. I tried to mix in as a peacemaker and you know what a peacemaker usually gets! In the argument, Miss Poole had tipped over a table and somebody made a pass at me. I guess I retaliated. I may have crowned somebody, but certainly not Bessie Poole — not a woman!"

Whitehead and McCarthy admitted that Bessie had been drinking before entering the club but stuck to their original statements denying their immediate presence when Bessie was struck. They also reiterated their charges of having been pummeled by club employees but could not specify their assailants by name. Lillian's deposition, taken at the Dorset, repeated the assertion that Bessie, within minutes of her return to the apartment, had fingered Tommy Guinan as her assailant. Certainly, Guinan's cohorts must have "gotten" to Dr. Gilbert and caused him to completely reverse his testimony of the evening's fateful events.

Whether or not alcohol poisoning was a contributing factor to Bessie's death, no determination could be made because her body had been removed to the Plaza Funeral Chapel and was already three-quarters embalmed when the District Attorney's office ordered an investigation and the autopsy report.

Bessie's parents were charging their daughter had been murdered, but as suddenly as the story had broken on the front pages, it disappeared. In bitter frustration, the district attorney issued a terse, one-paragraph statement declaring that neither enough evidence nor witnesses could be found to bring the case before a grand jury and the case would therefore be closed.

In my research efforts to secure copies of Lillian's statements in court transcripts and depositions relating to Bessie's death, I wrote to my friend Carl Vegari, then district attorney for Westchester County, requesting his intercession with Robert Morgenthau, his New York County counterpart. The end result was a stone wall of silence from the Morgenthau office.

The sad conclusion to the Bessie Poole saga was written off in a *New York American* final headline: "Liquor Killed Ex-showgirl — Not Beating!"

W.C. Fields died on Christmas Day of 1946. It was during the court hearings on Fields's controversial last will and testament that William Rexford Fields Morris presented the court a claim for a share of his father's estate. He submitted a handwritten letter from Fields to Mrs. Holden asking her to keep him apprised of any address changes so that he could keep up the monthly support payments. Additionally, to bolster his claim, Morris produced a "deathbed" letter from Bessie to her mother. It read, "Darling Mother, I don't expect to die but in case anything should happen, I have something to tell you. I have a son, ten years old, who now lives with a Mrs. Rose Holden, but I want you to take him and bring him up. W.C. Fields is his father. He is named William Rexford Fields Morris. He was born here in New York and I fully believe that Bill will take care of him, but in case he does not, why make him?... I did not tell you before because I know you could not do any good...."

A bizarre and sad incident, illustrative of Fields's continuing efforts to deny having fathered his progeny, Morris, is recounted in author James Curtis's biography of Fields. Curtis attributes this account to Eddie Sutherland, a performer/actor turned director who worked with and knew Fields quite well. Sutherland stated:

> [Fields] had a very formal Norwegian butler, and he used to play tennis with his pal, Sam Hardy. They'd summon the butler for a drink by tooting on a Halloween horn. It was that kind of establishment. This particular day, the bell rang at the gate, and this was quite a trek down to the gate, and down went the butler and he came back and said, "Your son is here to see you."
>
> "Tell him to go away!" said Fields.
>
> He went down again, came back, said, "Mr. Fields, he came all the way from the east to see you," and prevailed on Fields to see him. Now, Fields had no feeling about this boy at all. He was a stranger. How could he have much feeling about him? So they brought up the son. Fields got to questioning him. . . . Finally, he said to the son, "Will you have a drink?" The kid said, "Yes, thanks." So Fields's ears perked up a little bit. He thought, "At least he's human." He said, "What'll you have?" The son said, "A Coca-Cola." That set Mr. Fields on a flat spin. Finally he said, "You say you're my son. Where are your credentials? Show me something." So the kid pulled out his driver's license. Fields said, "Get out of here!" and threw him right off the place and never saw him again.

His disdainful and abrupt dismissal is illustrative of the dark side of his personality similar to his sarcastic dismissal of Bessie's pregnancy — "a turkey in the oven."

At the conclusion of the hearing, although he never secured legal recognition of his paternal heritage, Morris was awarded fifteen thousand dollars as a special payment out of W.C.'s widow's entitlement.

In the whole of the sordid Poole/Fields affair, Lillian Lorraine was the only honorable player. She never buckled to the criminal elements, and she never changed her story about the true identity of Bessie's assailant and injuries.

30

End of an Era and Beyond

When the smoke had cleared and the media furor over Bessie Poole's tragic end had subsided, Lillian's friends discerned a subtle but definite change in her mental state as well as her outward demeanor. The frenetic pace of life appeared slower and the giddiness was replaced by a more introspective pattern of public behavior. Her financial position was again on a downslide, and had in fact deteriorated so badly she was forced to leave New York and take up residence in less costly Atlantic City. Although Ziegfeld was always in and out of financial straits, he continued to provide Lillian with a small stipend to the end of his life, according to Matilda "Goldie" Golden, his loyal personal assistant. Goldie only revealed such intimate details about her employer after his death in 1932.

During the course of one of her lengthy interviews with Charles Higham, Goldie spoke of the frequent telephone calls Lillian would make to Ziegfeld, identifying herself as "Mary Brennan," her mother's maiden name, a practice she followed more and more often in the ensuing years. "He always took her calls on his gold-plated private phone in a small room behind his office in the newly built Ziegfeld Theatre. Patiently, he would listen to her often sad stories of a physically painful and lonely existence." Lillian had never fully recovered from the 1921 back injury, which was now aggravated by a progressive arthritic condition. Goldie said Lillian's calls left Ziegfeld despondent, and by 1928 he finally asked her not to put the calls through any longer. As far as is known, there was afterward no direct communication between Flo and Lillian.

Throughout the twentieth century's teens and twenties, Flo Ziegfeld reigned supreme as the most successful, innovative and entrepreneurial producer in musical theatre. His Broadway productions and touring companies saturated New York and major cities all over the country. Aside from the *Follies* and *Midnight Frolics*, there was a wide variety of hit shows including *Kid Boots*, *Louie XIV*, *Rio Rita*, *Rosalie*, *The Three Musketeers*, *Whoopee*, *Sally*, and ultimately the Ziegfeld masterpiece, *Show Boat*. In spite of these successes, by the end of 1928, storm clouds had begun to gather and were rapidly casting a pall of gloom over both live musical theatre and vaudeville alike. It was becoming increasingly obvious that the new medium of talking pictures would become major competition not to be underestimated. Al Jolson's *The Jazz Singer* revolutionized the film industry with astronomical box office returns, and in 1929 Ziegfeld finally succumbed to the industry he had previously held in contempt, joining the fray with his sound production of *Glorifying the American Girl*. It was a splashy musical version of the rags-to-riches success story of a typical Ziegfeld *Follies* chorine. The film was shot at Paramount's Astoria, Long Island, studios, and it starred Mary Eaton, the beautiful blonde dancer Flo had groomed and successfully promoted as Marilyn Miller's *Follies* successor. For additional star power, popular twenties crooner Rudy Vallée held a cameo role. Other notables included Eddie Cantor, Helen Morgan, and, in a walk-on, New York City's flamboyant and dapper chief executive, Mayor Jimmy Walker. With a brazen display of arrogance and a blatant disregard for public opinion, Walker "walked on" with his mistress showgirl,

Betty Compton, on his arm. The movie was only moderately successful, but happily, it is available on videotape and DVD for future generations.

Returning his attention to the legitimate theatre, Ziegfeld imported to New York the British actor Noel Coward and his play, *Bitter Sweet.* He also had his American productions of *Simple Simon* and *Smiles,* the latter starring Fred Astaire, Fred's sister Adele, and Marilyn Miller. It was triple-threat casting, but in the end, only moderately successful. In July of 1931 Flo produced what would be his last *Follies.* It featured Gladys Glad, Helen Morgan, Ruth Etting, Harry Richman, Dorothy Dell and dancer Hal LeRoy. Flo was still struggling to stay financially afloat, and much to his and Gene Buck's delight, the *1931 Follies* enjoyed a reasonably successful four-and-a-half-month run.

The stock market crash of 1929 had been a devastating blow to the entertainment industry, and to Flo Ziegfeld in particular. He had been financially wiped out, and in order to survive, he was forced in 1932 to seek and accept financial backing for *Hot Cha* from two notorious crime figures—Dutch Shultz and Waxey Gordon. Eddie Cantor had already advanced one hundred thousand dollars, which was paid back, but the show never did achieve mega-hit status. This, in spite of an all-star cast headed by comedian Bert Lahr, "Mexican Spitfire" Lupe Velez, tap-dancer Eleanor Powell, and the handsome matinee idol Charles "Buddy" Rogers, who would later marry movie queen Mary Pickford.

Diversification was the order of the day and Flo, having tried his hand at films, now proceeded to get his feet wet in radio with *The Follies of the Air.* Eddie Dowling, old friend and ex-*Follies* principal, was chosen as master of ceremonies. He was eleventh in a family of fourteen children and made his stage debut at fifteen. His early years were spent in vaudeville and New England summer stock companies where his expertise was in song and dance. In 1914, he met, fell in love with and married Scottish-born comedienne Ray Dooley. It was in the 1918 *Ziegfeld Follies* that Dowling met and formed a close and lasting friendship with Lillian Lorraine.

In New York and on the road tour with *Hot Cha,* Flo was driving himself to the point of physical exhaustion. A serious and debilitating attack of the flu brought urgent pleadings from wife Billie Burke and daughter Patricia to join them in California for extended rest and rehabilitation. Finally acquiescing, Flo left New York and entered a private sanitorium in New Mexico. After a brief period he joined Billie and Patty in California, but before long he was diagnosed with pleurisy. He was again hospitalized, this time in Santa Monica, where his condition continued to deteriorate. The pleurisy had developed into a lung infection, necessitating his transfer to Cedars of Lebanon Hospital in Hollywood. During a recent conversation with Ziegfeld's daughter, Patricia (Patty) Ziegfeld Stephenson, I learned that Flo rallied, and his wife Billie felt confident enough to return to work at RKO, where she was appearing in Katharine Hepburn's *A Bill of Divorcement.* On the eve of July 22, 1932, Billy, Patty and Flo were so happy about the improvement in Flo's condition that all three celebrated with dinner and champagne in his hospital room. Flo's ever-present valet Sidney oversaw the affair.

After dinner, Patty went to a movie, and then to the family residence in the Brentwood section of Los Angeles. Billie returned to RKO to do some retakes. Later that evening, each of the women was called and told that Flo's condition had seriously worsened. They should return to the hospital immediately. Patty was contacted at home. Billie was reached at the studio. Patty told me she arrived at about 10:20 p.m., shortly after her mother, who preceded her by only a few minutes. Sadly, they were too late. According to Patty, Flo passed away at approximately 9:40 p.m. He had been stricken with a coronary thrombosis. But he did not die alone. His trusted and loyal valet, Sidney, was at his bedside.

Patty recalled: "Daddy was cremated and a funeral service was held at the Kirk of the Heather Chapel in Forest Lawn Cemetery where he was buried. The general public was allowed in and the chapel was packed. In the 1960s, I transferred Daddy's ashes to Kensico Cemetery in Valhalla, New York. They were placed in my mother's family plot which already contained the remains of my maternal grandmother, Blanche. Mother joined Daddy at Kensico in 1970."

Dorothy Killgallen, the Hearst newspapers' syndicated café society doyenne, was the first to contact Lillian Lorraine with the news of Flo's death. After a pause of shocked disbelief, Lillian spoke touchingly of the man who twenty-three years earlier had plucked her as an unknown teenager from a Shubert chorus line and within one year had created a star:

> God knows, I'm far from perfect. I've made lots of bad choices of the men in my life but Flo Ziegfeld was the only man I can honestly say I both loved and respected. If we'd married it probably wouldn't have lasted and that would have been mostly my fault. Flo was decent and caring in so many different ways and sometimes, I'm sorry to say, I just didn't fully appreciate him. I guess it's no secret that sometimes our relationship was pretty stormy but, let me tell you, no matter who started the argument, we always made up and even up to today, we stayed the best of friends. I'm hurting too much to say anything more but there is one thing I don't want to leave unsaid and that is, everything that has been good in my life I owe to Flo Ziegfeld. Right now, I'm feeling very empty and very, very sad.

The entertainment world and theatre lovers from coast to coast publicly mourned his passing with condolences and eulogies of praise numbering in the many hundreds. A Will Rogers letter to the *New York Times* with obvious heartfelt pathos expressed what Ziegfeld's death really meant to his beloved world of show business. The Oklahoma Cowboy wrote

> Our world of make-believe is sad. Scores of comedians are not funny. Hundreds of America's most beautiful girls are not gay, our benefactor has passed away. He picked us from all walks of life. He led us into what little fame we achieved. He remained our friend regardless of our usefulness to him as an entertainer. He brought beauty into the entertainment world. The profession of acting must be necessary, for it exists in every race, and in every language, and to have been the master amusement provider of your generation, surely a life's work was accomplished. And he left something on earth that hundreds of us will treasure until our curtain falls, and that was a "badge," a badge of which we were proud: I worked for Ziegfeld. So, goodbye, Flo. Save a spot for me for you will put on a show someday that will knock their eyes out! Yours, Will Rogers.

Eight months following his death, over eight hundred friends and Ziegfeld "alumnae" gathered at the deceased producer's magnificent show palace on Sixth Avenue and 54th Street in Manhattan. It was a dual occasion, not only commemorating Ziegfeld's passing but marking the reopening of the theatre as a first-run movie house, Loew's Ziegfeld Theatre. This was not the movie house known currently as the Ziegfeld Theatre on West 54th Street between Sixth and Seventh Avenues.

It had been eight years earlier when Ziegfeld, after several unsuccessful attempts, finally struck gold with William Randolph Hearst and secured financial backing for construction of his very own theatre. In their *Ziegfeld Touch*, Richard and Paulette Ziegfeld describe the birth of the Hearst/Ziegfeld business alliance:

> Ziegfeld and Hearst realized that they had a mutual interest in building a theatre at 54th Street and Sixth Avenue, opposite to Hearst's already constructed Warwick Hotel. The theatre district was still concentrated around 42nd Street and Times Square. The Warwick was a bit far north but Hearst wanted a cultural attraction nearby his own property to draw hotel patrons. Aware of Ziegfeld's aspirations, Hearst and his right-hand man, Arthur Brisbane, agreed to finance a Ziegfeld Theatre across the street from the Warwick.

That Hearst had fallen for Marion Davies, a blonde and blue-eyed beauty, when he spotted her in the Ziegfeld *Follies* chorus line in 1916, was the sustaining bond between William Randolph Hearst and Florenz Ziegfeld. Marion became Hearst's mistress and constant companion until his death. His wife, a devout Catholic with five sons, would never divorce him.

The Ziegfeld Touch further describes Flo's venue, which so ironically became the showplace for his memorial service: "Costing two million dollars, it was opulent and elegantly appointed, its equipment provided cutting edge technology...the egg-shaped auditorium housed a $500,000 stage and was capped by a magnificent [Joseph] Urban designed mural depicting romances and myths from all epochs. It was the only theatre mural in New York that covered the entire ceiling." The film chosen for the gala reopening was Metro-Goldwyn-Mayer's historical drama of the Russian Revolution, *Rasputin and the Empress*, starring John, Lionel and Ethel Barrymore.

Although this day the distinguished assemblage had gathered to honor the greatest showman of his time, it escaped no one that in the very place they were now seated, the curtain had fallen on the fruits of his creative genius, and that front-and-center footlights had succumbed to 35-millimeter projectors perched high in the dark recesses of the last balcony. For the legitimate and musical theatre it was an ominous sign of the times.

The roll call of celebrities for the 1933 Ziegfeld memorial was of such magnitude that the Scripps-Howard *New York World Telegram* aptly dubbed it "a show that no sponsor could afford." The by-invitation-only audience was an amalgam of glorified girls, wardrobe mistresses, writers, composers, designers and stagehands. The glittering assemblage of big-name headliners included Fanny Brice, Eddie Cantor, Jimmy Durante, Ruth Etting, Gladys Glad, Marilyn Miller, Ann Pennington, Harry Richman, Ethel Shutta, Ed Wynn and, of course, Lillian Lorraine.

Eddie Cantor took the stage in a rarely-seen somber mood. The press reported, "It was one of the rare occasions when Eddie Cantor was seen without a smile on his face and a jest on his lips. There was a burst of applause when he stepped on the stage and it took only a few moments for the audience to become as responsive to his serious remarks as it would to his clowning and witticisms. The comedian praised Mr. Ziegfeld as a producer we all loved and respected."

Marilyn Miller sang "Look for the Silver Lining," bringing back memories of her hit show, *Sally*. Jimmy Durante sang a selection from *Show Girl*, while Dennis King and Norma Terris sang "Why Do I Love You?" from the 1932 *Show Boat* revival. From the same show, Jules Bledsoe offered up a stirring and powerful rendition of "Old Man River," and Irving Berlin came forward to sing one of his own compositions from the early *Follies*. Abe Lyman and his orchestra played many of the more popular *Follies* show tunes. Annie Hart, who had ended her fifty-five-year career with *Show Boat*, was the oldest of the Ziegfeld alums in the audience. The youngest attendee was eight-year-old Evelyn Eaton, who was introduced by Dowling as the last person to have a written contract with Ziegfeld. The oldest member present was the ninety-one-year-old Shakespearean actress, Alice Brooks.

Speculation was widespread concerning the absence of Billie Burke. "A prior film commitment" was the official explanation, but many still wondered out loud if the presence of former rivals Marilyn Miller and Lillian Lorraine might not have been the real deterrent. At any rate, a scroll of over 800 signatures was sent to Billie as a memento of a very special afternoon in New York City. Both Marilyn and Lillian, of course, were signatories on this scroll.

New York press accounts of the service reported:

> When Miss Lillian Lorraine, a former Ziegfeld star and once the toast of Broadway, was discovered in the audience by Eddie Dowling, acting as master of ceremonies, she was urged to come forward and sing "By the Light of the Silvery Moon."
> Rather reluctantly Miss Lorraine walked down the aisle while Gus Edwards took his place at the piano on the stage. He played a few strains. Miss Lorraine stood by the orchestra pit, facing the audience; suddenly she collapsed and was unable to sing, being overcome by the emotion. After she was assisted back to her seat, Rita Gould, also seated in the audience, volunteered to sing the old-time favorite.

Filled with grief, fraught with the pain of arthritis, forty-one-year-old Lillian ultimately departed the service — no more than a living symbol of her glory days on Broadway. This had been her last significant live performance and it was not a good one. Not so for some of her fellow Ziegfeldian contemporaries: Fanny Brice, Eddie Cantor, Gladys Glad, Marilyn Miller and Will Rogers would all move on to additional fame and fortune in the celluloid jungle known as Hollywood.

During the late twenties and early thirties, Lillian was no stranger to the West Coast movie Mecca. On September 6th, 1933, Hollywood friends were dismayed to open their *Los Angeles Examiner* and see a quarter-page photograph of Lillian with the caption, "Lillian Lorraine, who was admittedly the most beautiful of all Ziegfeld's showgirls, is hiding in poverty, singing table songs in hidden away cafes." Ten days later she was seen and photographed with a group of friends at the Hollywood Music Box Revue. Early in October, Peter Gary spotted her among the party guests at the Mullholland Drive home of ex-*Follies* girl Peggy Fears. There was no predicting where or how Lillian would turn up. Nothing had changed. Her life continued to be a mass of contradicting ups and downs.

Peter Gary told me about a sad personal encounter he had with Lillian during those Hollywood days. I met Peter in the fall of 1995 at a social function of the Episcopal Actors' Guild in New York City. He was an extraordinarily versatile man with a good many notches in his belt — actor, playwright, lyricist, ex-vaudevillian, high-wire aerialist and confidant of actresses Mary Boland, Lillian Gish and Peggy Fears. Over drinks and dinner, Peter recalled for me his first of two encounters with Lillian. "You know," he said, "Lillian Lorraine was still a beautiful woman and the men at Peggy's affair moved around her like moths attracted to a flame. Several days after the party, I dropped in at a neighborhood restaurant called Cooper's Bar and Grille on Los Palmas, off Hollywood Boulevard. As soon as I walked in I saw Lillian, alone at the bar. She was having a heated argument with the bartender, who had '86ed' her after she'd run up a pretty good-sized tab. She identified herself and the bartender sassed her back, saying something like, 'Don't give me that bullshit about being Lillian Lorraine!'"

Gary, being the gentleman that he was, said he stepped in and confirmed that she was who she said she was. With that, he paid her bill and she accepted his offer to walk her home at to a nearby hotel. Peter continued, "Lillian, after a few drinks, was pretty good with the four-letter words, and was a far cry from the gracious charmer I'd first met at Peggy's party. My God! I really got stuck because on the way to her hotel she wanted to stop at every bar along the way. I remember we did go into Bradley's Five and Dime, a sleazy dive, but that was it. I was lucky to get her back to the hotel without any more problems."

Back on the East Coast, in New York and New Jersey, Lillian's contacts with the show business community were virtually nonexistent. Winnie Dunn was now happily married, living and raising a family on Long Island, but continuing to stay in touch with Lillian, and through Winnie, so did my mother and Marie Wallace DeSylva. There were times, however, in the forties that it was not always possible to know Lillian's exact whereabouts. Sometime during that period, Lillian did find religion. Winnie Dunn's daughter told me in 1997 that her mother had been responsible for bringing Lillian back into the Roman Catholic Church. It will be seen, though, her zest for the high life had not yet dampened completely.

On those occasions when Lillian did appear in public she could still raise the antennae of the media newshawks. On December 5, 1935, *New York Evening Graphic* columnist Ed (Toast of the Town) Sullivan wrote the following piece:

> Lillian Lorraine at forty-three. Not all of the veterans of Broadway cling to the stem with the tenacity of Lillian Lorraine, one of the most famous of the Ziegfeld pretties. Today, at the age when most of the glorified have settled down to the comforts of home, this former Broadway Belle is still active in the life of the world's most advertised thoroughfare. Strangest of all, La Lorraine is still

extremely pretty. In fact, the boys even now permit themselves a fast once-over when she walks into the late spots or the local scotch and soda fountains. Whereas most of the moderns can alibi their thirst on prohibition, Lillian has no such feeble excuse to offer. She was thirsty long before Volstead inserted blotters into the Congressional Record, and to her credit, be it said, La Lorraine never disguised her drinking. "That's my business," she told protestants, and that was that.

For several years nothing had been heard of Lillian's old beau, Coca-Cola tycoon Joseph Whitehead, from the days of the Bessie Poole tragedy. Whitehead had gone on to his great reward, but not, according to the *New York Daily Mirror*, before tricking his estranged wife into signing away her rights to his eight-million-dollar estate. The divorce had never been finalized, and now the widow, Laura Whitehead, was suing for the entire estate. Again, Lillian's pretty features were on display, but for no other reason than to justify the caption: "Lillian Lorraine was his companion."

31

Frazzled Silver Lining

From the mid-twenties well into the next decade, many Ziegfeld stars had migrated west and with varying degrees of success were becoming movie stars. Among the early pioneers were Anna Held, Mae Murray, Olive Thomas, Billie Burke and Lillian Lorraine. Soon to follow, the list of names read like a payroll for a lavish MGM spectacular: Lina Bassquette, Louise Brooks, Ina Claire, Hazel Dawn, Billie Dove, three of the Eaton clan (Doris, Mary and Charles), Ruth Etting, Gilda Gray, Helen Morgan, Ann Pennington, Vivienne Segal, Marion Davies, Justine Johnston, Martha Mansfield, and many more. The roster of those who achieved super-stardom and longevity is not quite so long: Fanny Brice, Eddie Cantor, W.C. Fields, Will Rogers, Ruby Keeler, Barbara Stanwyck, and composer George Gershwin.

It was 1930 when Marilyn Miller took the plunge and made her way into the celluloid jungle of talking pictures. Her screen debut was in a film adaptation of her immensely popular stage hit *Sally*, and happily, the film was equally successful. Her romantic lead co-star was the handsome matinee idol Alexander Gray, while wide-mouth comedian Joe. E. Brown more than held his own in the third lead position. Jack L. Warner, one of Marilyn's numerous West Coast lovers, was vice-president in charge of production and more than any other one individual was the greatest influence on her movie career. Within days of the *Sally* release, Warner Brothers signed Marilyn for two additional pictures. *Sunny* was another musical comedy, but much to the surprise of star and studio alike, it was a financial failure, more than likely due, at least partially, to the 1929 stock market crash and the resultant Depression era.

In an effort to salvage their investment in the blonde dancer, the Warner Brothers publicity department was instructed to create a new image for Marilyn, something that would promote her as a love goddess in the genre of Theda Bara, Greta Garbo and Marlene Dietrich. Marilyn's third motion picture undertaking was titled *Her Majesty Love*. Daryl F. Zanuck, at the time Warner's production chief, acquiesced to Marilyn's insistence that Ben Lyon be signed as her leading man and that W.C. Fields be brought onboard to play her screen father. Marilyn and Fields had a continuing friendship dating back to when they had both appeared in the 1918 *Ziegfeld Follies*. Despite the attempted image makeover and a saturation-level promotional campaign, *Her Majesty Love* was a total box office disaster. Studio executive Hal Wallis placed the blame squarely at Marilyn's feet, arguing that "the magic she projected on stage, that indefinable charm that made up for her tiny voice and moderate acting talent, utterly vanished on camera." The end result was nonrenewal of her contract and a cooling-down of her romantic dalliance with Jack Warner, but not before he helped her to negotiate a seventy-five-thousand-dollar severance package. The big winner, however, was W.C. Fields, previously written off as all washed-up and a has-been. The film jump-started his movie career into high gear with a momentum that would last through to the next decade.

Marilyn returned to New York, where her career continued to languish until 1933, when her fortunes took a dramatic upswing as a result of her having secured the starring role in a new Irving Berlin musical, *As Thousands Cheer*. With music and lyrics by Berlin and a supporting cast composed of Clifton Webb, Ethel Waters, Helen Broderick and Jerome Cowan, it was a show that just couldn't miss. It had a Broadway run of four hundred performances. Due to her increasingly serious health and drinking problems, Marilyn was replaced in the last eighty performances by Dorothy Stone.

During her recently past Hollywood interlude, Marilyn had found romantic solace in the arms of not only Jack Warner but, after that episode, with actors Ben Lyon, Alexander Gray and dancer Don Alvarado. Now, back in New York, her frequent escort and companion was the bisexual multimillionaire playboy Jimmy Donahue, a cousin of Woolworth heiress Barbara Hutton. It was Donahue who directed Marilyn's attention to twenty-four-year-old Chester O'Brien. With his twin brother, Mortimer, the good-looking, dark-haired Chester was at the time a dancer in the chorus of *As Thousands Cheer*. In backstage circles, Marilyn's penchant for casual sexcapades with young and "straight" chorus boys was a frequent subject of common gossip. In O'Brien's case, he soon acquired the title of "assistant stage manager," and, according to Warren Harris, Marilyn's biographer, this elevated status gave Chester easier access to Marilyn than if he had been just another member of the male ensemble. Marilyn was ten years his senior, but the age difference was not a problem. She was in love again. Her 1927 divorce from Jack Pickford was history, and her greatest love, Frank Carter, was dead fourteen years. So it was, in October of 1934, Marilyn chose to dance down the matrimonial path for a third and final time.

At midnight on October 1, Marilyn, along with a cousin and Chester, motored twenty-five miles north of New York City to Westchester County and the posh suburban hamlet of Harrison. Locating and persuading Town Clerk William Wilding to leave a local dance party and issue a marriage license, they then proceeded to awaken Town Justice Leo Mintzer, who, while still in his sleeping attire, performed the nuptials. When I was active in Westchester County politics in the early 1960s, Judge Mintzer's wife, Mae, recalled to me that "Marilyn and Chet were behaving like two teen-agers, eloping without parental consent!" Marilyn was the talk of the town after local newspapers announced that she had come to Harrison for her wedding.

With the intention of enhancing Chet's theatrical credentials, Marilyn put up twenty-five thousand dollars to finance a new musical revue, *Fools Rush In*, with the proviso that her new husband be retained as dance director for the show. Rehearsals were a disaster, as were the opening night notices. Jimmy Donahue paid for additional advertising and Marilyn wrote another check for six thousand dollars, but no amount of money could keep the show afloat. It survived only fourteen performances.

Marilyn and Lillian, both, were about to induce major headaches for MGM.

Within three years of Ziegfeld's demise, Metro-Goldwyn-Mayer had a signed agreement with his widow, Billie Burke, to move ahead with plans to produce *The Great Ziegfeld*. It was to be a gigantic and lavish musical tribute to her already legendary husband. For such a production, no other Hollywood studio could muster the resources at Metro's command. The MGM roster of contract mega-stars was larger than the rosters of all other studios combined. For starters, there was Clark Gable, Greta Garbo, Joan Crawford, Jean Harlow, Spencer Tracy, Jeanette MacDonald, Nelson Eddy, Marie Dressler, Wallace Beery, and the "Nick and Nora" of *Thin Man* fame, William Powell and Myrna Loy. These latter two stars, their box office potency already well established, were signed for the lead characters of Ziegfeld and Billie Burke. A Viennese-born, heretofore unknown, Luise Rainer, was the perfect choice for Anna Held. The brilliance and wisdom of this particular casting was confirmed when the following spring, Luise Rainer won the 1936 Best Actress Academy Award.

At the outset, with a record-breaking-two-million-dollar budget in place, it was obvious Louis B. Mayer intended this film to be the most opulently expensive musical of all time. The lush sets and lavish production numbers would exceed anything ever before seen on a motion picture screen.

Now, with the casting of two out of three Ziegfeld love interests, the two wives, Anna Held and Billie Burke, studio chiefs were confronted with the problem of who would, or could, portray the third point of the love triangle — Lillian Lorraine. Frederic Santon, costume historian and author of *MGM's Ziegfeld Trilogy*, provides fascinating insight and background as to just how that particular dilemma was approached. In the early 1980s, Santon was given unrestricted access to MGM's Ziegfeld files by the studio's legal advisor, Fred Nussbaum. Santon wrote me, "He [Nussbaum] opened up whatever files I wanted to research and I was even free to run films and precious outtakes."

With the first announcement of MGM's intention to make the Ziegfeld film, Lillian was adamant that neither her name nor character be used or portrayed. Santon's research unearthed correspondence and telegrams depicting the quandary with which the studio was faced. Early on in pre-production days, March 10, 1935, L.B. Mayer sent the following telegram to Florence Browning in MGM's New York casting office: "Need for Ziegfeld, young Billie Burke and Lillian Lorraine around twenty years of age. Must be able to act."

At this early juncture the intent for integrity in casting and story line was still present. However, within hours, that intent disappeared, as evidenced by producer Hunt Stromberg's same-date memorandum to Mayer, stating: "We have dropped plans to include W.C. Fields and Eddie Cantor in Ziegfeld because of enormous salary involved. We have signed Fanny Brice and Ann Pennington and contemplating other Ziegfeld performers." Stromberg made the decision to substitute the fictitious character "Audrey Lane" for Lillian. The film was dealt serious blows by the omissions of Lorraine, Fields and Cantor, especially Lorraine. Film critics had a field day questioning the integrity and accuracy of the story line.

The studio's legal guru's awareness of the probable ramifications resulting from the use of the character Audrey Lane is clearly evident in a September 15, 1935, telegram sent to Stromberg from attorney J. Robert Rubin of MGM's New York office: "As soon as you wrote us about *The Great Ziegfeld* we made investigation about the name Audrey Lane and we cannot find any actress in real life who had this name but it is still dangerous since it can be linked to Lillian Lorraine who firmly denied the use of her name in the picture." Again, three months later, on December 13, Rubin cautioned Stromberg, "Suggest name Audrey Lane be changed because confusing Lillian Lorraine. It is risky and can become libel."

Nevertheless, Mayer and the studio legal team decided to ignore Rubin's warnings, throw caution to the winds and stay with the name Audrey Lane.

For the part, they selected Virginia Bruce, a pretty but mature-appearing twenty-eight-year-old blonde who had at one time actually been a dancer in one of the later editions of the *Follies*. Her besotted portrayal of the character as a perpetually drunk, money-grubbing tart bore little resemblance to the dark-haired, exquisitely beautiful seventeen-year-old who in real life had captured Ziegfeld's heart. However, in the characterization there was just enough innuendo to leave no doubt in theatre-savvy minds as to just who Audrey Lane was supposed to be. Upon release of the film, which did go on to win the Academy Award for Best Picture, Lillian made good on her threat and brought suit against MGM. According to syndicated columnist Leonard Lyons, the case was settled out of court "for a nice chunk of dough."

They ran into another snag with the character of Marilyn Miller. Neither stage nor screen offers were in profusion for thirty-five-year-old Marilyn, who was battling a longtime affliction with acute sinusitis. On the heels of the first media mention of MGM's proposed Ziegfeld film, Marilyn and Chet O'Brien headed for California with every expectation that she would be approached to play herself in the film. She had not, however, taken into consideration that Billie Burke, who, it was known, had no love for Marilyn, was already signed on as a technical advisor with all-important final script approval. Billie raised no objection to Marilyn's being featured in one or two of the musical numbers, but did veto Marilyn's insistence that she be given further prominence in the cast billing lineup. After much back-and-forth haggling with studio chiefs, Marilyn withdrew and, as had Lillian, threatened legal action if her name was even so much as mentioned in the film. It was not.

In the final analysis, *The Great Ziegfeld* was a magnificent, highly fictionalized epic of glorified girls and pink fluff. Critics of the film's biographical authenticity questioned how the Flo Ziegfeld story could be told without including the character of Lillian Lorraine. This, they queried, especially since Billie Burke was listed in the credits as a technical consultant. Did Billie intentionally cause the characters of Lillian and Marilyn to be absent from the telling of her husband's story? Despite its almost three-hour running time, the phenomenal box office returns left little doubt the Ziegfeld name had lost none of its magical luster. *Motion Picture Guide* reported, "MGM spent almost two million dollars, a king's ransom, and every penny is up there on the screen."

The financial returns on their investment in *The Great Ziegfeld* sent Louis Mayer and the Metro hierarchy scrambling to ensure the momentum not be lost, and within the next decade there was *The Ziegfeld Girl* (1941), starring three of the then-reigning MGM glamour queens, Lana Turner, Hedy Lamarr and Judy Garland. Then came *The Ziegfeld Follies* (1946), with William Powell in a cameo, reprising the title role. Specialty production numbers featured appearances by Fred Astaire, Gene Kelly, Judy Garland, Fanny Brice, Lena Horne, Red Skelton and Lucille Ball. Their purchase of the rights to Ziegfeld's greatest masterpiece, *Show Boat*, capped their control of the Ziegfeld legacy. First produced by Universal in 1936, *Show Boat* was remade by MGM in 1951.

Marilyn Miller's problems with ill health and a waning career accelerated at an alarming pace. The MGM rejection of her bid for a movie comeback had been an unexpected blow and one from which she would never truly recover. She and Chet had become familiar fixtures on the Hollywood party circuit and alcohol was becoming more and more of a quick fix to dull Marilyn's physical distress. The twosome were often guests of Marion Davies and William Randolph Hearst at their San Simeon and Malibu beach house compounds. Davies, a former *Follies* girl and longtime friend, convinced Marilyn to undergo corrective surgery, which did temporarily alleviate the bothersome and painful nasal sinus condition. The relief, however, was only short-term, and Marilyn turned to so-called miracle doctors, one of whom prescribed insulin injections to lessen her emotional distress. Again, according to Warren G. Harris, this erroneous diagnosis put her into New York City's Doctors' Hospital on March 26, 1936. Within days her condition had so deteriorated that she fell into an eleven-day coma. The same doctor who had previously prescribed the insulin treatment now announced that she had developed a serious toxic condition. Following a brief three-week period of remission, at the age of 37, Marilyn Miller, Broadway's golden girl, died. Chet O'Brien and Marilyn's sister Claire were at her bedside.

The funeral service was held in New York City's magnificent Saint Bartholomew's Episcopal Church, where an overflow congregation filled every pew in the twelve-hundred-seat nave and transept. The *New York Daily News* estimated that more than five thousand fans and curiosity seekers had jammed Park Avenue between 50th and 51st Streets. Former Mayor Jimmy Walker and his wife, former showgirl Betty Compton, led the delegation of public officials. The immediate family was represented by Marilyn's sister, Claire Montgomery, and on the O'Brien side were Chester, two of his brothers, Mortimer and Jay, two sisters, Frances and Alice, and their mother, Mrs. Edward Marsh. Billie Burke, Vivienne Segal, Bea Lillie, Ben Lyon, Bebe Daniels and Lillian Lorraine were among the many hundreds of mourners from the theatre and film communities.

At the conclusion of the 45-minute service, Chester and Marilyn's personal maid, Carrie Wallace, escorted the silver-bronze casket to the waiting hearse. Within minutes the funeral cortege proceeded to Woodlawn Cemetery in the Bronx, where Marilyn's casket was placed across from that of Frank Carter in the miniature Greek-temple-style mausoleum she had constructed for him sixteen years earlier. Regrettably, today, after years of neglect, large pieces of concrete from the ceiling of the poorly-maintained mausoleum have fallen, and have chipped away at the outer casements of the two caskets—grim testimony to fleeting fame and subsequent disregard.

In 1994, during the course of a telephone conversation with me, Chester O'Brien denounced with rancor the man he termed "the quack doctor" who had performed the initial surgery for Marilyn's sinus condition, as well as the second doctor responsible for the insulin prescription. He also complained bitterly that Marilyn's sister had deprived him of any share in Marilyn's estate, which at the time of her death had dwindled to less than fifty thousand dollars. Chester married twice again and died at his Long Island home in 1995, less than one year after our telephone conversation.

32

Lillian Hits the Skids
— Ziegfeld Redux

By 1939 media mentions of Lillian Lorraine sightings were almost nonexistent. Former *Follies* girl Kitty Mack Roland, an influential director of the Ziegfeld Club and close friend of Lillian's, recalled to me in 1995, "Lillian always had a lot of pride. Whenever she was down and broke she disappeared from the Broadway scene but she'd be back as soon as she could pay her own way."

Bernard Sobel in his memoir, *Ziegfeld and Me*, had another view; namely, that Lillian was a recipient of the Club's assistance program. My thorough search of the Club records does not confirm Sobel's assertion. Furthermore, the late Dana O'Connell, former Ziegfeld Club president, told me in 1998 she had no recollection of Lillian's ever having been involved with the Club, its activities or the assistance program, neither contributing to, nor benefiting from, the Club. With conviction, Dana declared, "If she had been a recipient, I'd have known it!"

During one memorable meeting with Kitty Roland, at a time when she was near death at the Cabrini Hospital Hospice, and in spite of her rapidly declining physical condition and all of the life-saving equipment she was painfully connected to, she retained her wonderful sense of humor. She joked with me about an incident that had occurred decades earlier involving an Irish priest that Kitty and Lillian were friendly with. Lillian had been arrested for driving while intoxicated, and in desperation, she put through a call to Kitty. The priest was visiting Kitty at the time. He told Kitty, "I'm going to get her." Kitty laughingly said the charges were dropped and that the real reason must have been because everyone involved was Irish: the police, the priest, even Lillian, who was half-Irish on her mother's side. The day following this unforgettable exchange, Kitty insisted she be taken home from hospice. Within several days she passed away at her Sutton Place residence on Manhattan's East Side.

In September of 1939, Lillian resurfaced as a Broadway presence, and the Great White Way was reminded that Lillian was not completely *passe*. The International News Service carried photos picturing her at the Gotham Hospital recovering from a bout of pneumonia. In a bedside interview with the *New York Daily Mirror's* Jean Adams, she defiantly announced she would be returning to the legitimate theatre in a new play written by Robert Hanna and Mary Cerf. "I had given up the stage," she said, "but recently I began to feel I'd like to show people I'm not dead yet!"

Lillian's physical condition had been an ongoing concern dating back to the 1921 fracture of her cervical vertebrae. She went on to tell Jean Adams:

When I look back and recall the golden opportunities I threw away — oh well, I've made up my mind to come back, and I will. This time I'll put my money in the bank. I've had my ups and downs but there'll be no more downs for me. You know, it's sad, but many of my old friends have passed away but I feel enough of them are left who will be glad to see me come back. One friend

181

who just can't be replaced is Flo Ziegfeld. He was very, very special. I don't have any living relatives—not even a cousin.

Lillian's comeback pronouncement, as with her earlier declaration following her appendectomy, turned out to be more wishful thinking than actual fact. Producers were not knocking at Lillian's door.

Although she was under doctor's orders to rest and avoid overexertion, at the first opportunity, Lillian packed her bags and headed for the West Coast, visiting friends and rejoining the film colony's social swim, now far more glamorous and sophisticated than in the days of her past film stardom. She was especially happy for the opportunity to renew her longstanding friendship with ex-*Follies* girl Marie Wallace DeSylva, now a socially prominent member of Hollywood's Blue Book "A" list. Marie's husband, Buddy, was chief executive of Paramount Pictures, and in collaboration with Lew Brown, Nacio Herb Brown and Arthur Freed, was a prolific songwriter of great note.

On her return to the East Coast, Lillian retreated again to her old stamping grounds in Atlantic City, where she was a familiar but lonely figure in the local nightspots and favorite haunts of brighter and happier days. The New York City press reported that at the end of January 1941, she moved back to New York and took a furnished $15-a-week apartment at 17 West 64th Street. Fellow tenants, completely unaware of her past celebrity status, said she was rarely seen and very seldom left her room.

On February 18, Julia Daniels plugged in her switchboard cord and was startled to hear a woman's voice screaming, "Fire, fire!" Building employees rushed up a flight of stairs to a second-floor one-room apartment where they found a white-haired woman, crippled with arthritis, flat on the floor beside a blazing davenport. The sparsely furnished room was strewn with empty liquor bottles and cigarette butts. As the building staff attempted to pick her up, she pleaded, "Just one more drink!" Fellow second-floor tenants said Lillian's most frequent visitor was a delivery boy from the neighborhood liquor store. Amid strenuous protestations—"I'm wealthy and I have a thirteen-week radio contract," she insisted—Lillian was carried, blue eyes flashing angrily, reportedly kicking and screaming, from the smoke-filled room into which she had moved only two weeks earlier. Attending police were told Lillian had been lying on the couch and fallen asleep while smoking a cigarette. Despite her protests that "the whole affair was just a foolish accident," she was removed by ambulance to Bellevue Hospital's Psychiatric Ward, where she was booked as Mary Ann Brennan, age 49.

The following day, tabloid headlines blazed, "Fame Gone, Bellevue Gets Lillian Lorraine." The more sedate and conservative *New York Herald Tribune* reported, "Lillian Lorraine taken to Hospital after Fire; Suffers Smoke Poisoning in Slight Blaze at Home."

Up and down Broadway, former friends and old-time theatre buffs shook their heads with a deep sense of resignation and dismay. Lillian's descent into ignominy was complete and there was nothing anyone could do to alter the pattern of self-destruction put in motion so many years earlier when the fifteen-year-old beauty from San Francisco first set foot on the Great White Way. Some few old friends came forward but, as in the past, were rebuffed by a very proud woman who refused to see them or admit her need for help. Among them were my mother, Winnie Dunn, and Marie Wallace DeSylva.

Following a period of drying out, Lillian was discharged from Bellevue and once again disappeared from public view.

Lillian and Marie Wallace had maintained a close friendship since working together in the 1918 *Follies*. Marie was long since retired from the stage. After nineteen years of relatively happy married life, it came as a shock to the film colony when the Paramount press office announced that Marie and Buddy DeSylva were separating. No reason was given, nor was it disclosed whether divorce was contemplated. Buddy and Marie first met in a music publisher's office while Marie was still a dancer in the *Follies*. A few weeks later, as the story goes, Buddy proposed marriage. Marie conditioned her acceptance on Buddy's promise to write a song—just for her. He agreed, and that song was "Somebody Loves Me." Very shortly thereafter, Buddy had a hit song and a brand-new bride as well.

Buddy DeSylva succumbed to a heart attack on July 11, 1950. The bulk of his estimated three-million-dollar estate was left to Marie and David Shelley, her son by a first marriage. The Shelley bequest was looked upon as strange, since Buddy, throughout the nineteen-year marriage, had refused to acquiesce to Marie's wish that he formally adopt David and treat him as his own son. A second and even more surprising item in Buddy's will was creation of a fifty-thousand-dollar trust for a six-year-old biological son, Stephan, fathered out of wedlock and born to a former secretary, Marie Ballentine.

The cause for the split with Marie was now public knowledge and the stage was set for a nasty and long-drawn-out contest of the will by Marie Ballentine. Buddy had stipulated that if Marie Ballentine did choose to contest the will, the child was to get nothing. Nevertheless, California Supreme Court Judge Raymond McIntosh ruled that the boy should receive a settlement of eighty-two thousand five hundred dollars from his father's estate. Marie Wallace DeSylva never remarried and died from a heart attack in Hollywood on December 22, 1961. Her son and heir, David Shelley, married film actress Martha Stewart.

Forty-six years after his death, a reincarnated version of Flo Ziegfeld arrived on home television sets in a three-hour miniseries enticingly titled *Ziegfeld: The Man and His Women*. Ziegfeld's character was played by Paul Shenar, actor, director and founder of the American Conservatory Theatre in San Francisco. All of the key characters of this production, in real life, were long since deceased, thereby eliminating the probabilities of numerous lawsuits and extended litigation relating to the accuracy of the film's content and the highly fictionalized use of the life stories of Ziegfeld and his three love interests. The production was a lavish, expensive and imaginative depiction of the Ziegfeld love triangle as seen through the camera lens of TV producer Mike Frankovich. In its review of May 21, 1978, the *New York Daily News* described the television special as

> a big, colorful, old-fashioned musical with all the assets and liabilities of that endangered species of entertainment. For starved televiewers longing for a taste of Hollywood musicals of the past, it was a visual feast, with scantily dressed showgirls, music striking familiar chords, vast production numbers, stunning sets and fabulous costumes. But there are also moments in this production that would make the late showman turn in disgust from the railing which he used to stand behind in back of his theatre during performances. One such scene comes when Valerie Perrine, a twenty-seven-year-old [*sic*] former Las Vegas showgirl cast as Lillian Lorraine, the beautiful but talentless showgirl and the woman "Ziggy" loved, is placated with a spot in the *Follies*. Since she could neither sing or dance he devises a production number with a large chorus of long-stemmed beauties and lots of balloons which in this TV version is meant to be comical. It, unfortunately, goes one step beyond and borders on the disastrous. Miss Perrine, who looks more like a big overgrown kid, is hardly convincing as a fabulously beautiful showgirl who can dangle the great showman on a string."

James Wolcott of *The Village Voice* on June 5, 1978, required only two words to describe the choice of Perrine to play the Lorraine character: "disastrously miscast!" It was almost a cry back to 1936, when 28-year-old Virginia Bruce was also disastrously miscast by MGM as the fictitious Audrey Lane in *The Great Ziegfeld*. In fact, Ziegfeld had been smitten with Lillian as a 16-year-old beauty in a Shubert chorus line who, by his own description, "had a magnetic personality and stage presence"—none of which were on display in the Bruce or Perrine characterizations. To Kay Gardella of the *Daily News*, Valerie Perrine showed abysmally limited knowledge of her subject when she sat for an interview and stated, "Lillian Lorraine was an easy character for me to play. She was flirtatious and a gal who wanted to get somewhere. She was mean, though. Not a nice lady. She treated Ziegfeld badly in the end. She loved him and left him. Once I read the line, 'All you have to do is make me a star,' I knew it was a part I could walk through." And that's just about all she did!

33

Excommunication

"The year was 1945. Lillian Lorraine's personal life was in free-fall. A hopeless alcoholic, arthritically crippled and, for the most part, bound to and dependent on wheelchair transport, her quality of life could best be measured on the lowest possible decibel. Home was a dingy back room apartment on New York City's upper west side. It was here NY DAILY NEWS staff writer Ruth Turner discovered the long-forgotten former Follies dazzler Flo Ziegfeld had touted as "the most beautiful woman in the world.""

A partial, uncensored text of Lillian's last and totally destructive public interview never saw the light of day, or printers' ink, until the 1986 publication of theater great Ruth Gordon's autobiography, *My Side*—thirty-one years after Lillian's passing.

Lillian Lorraine was old and broke and living up Broadway at 96th. Some paper sent the lady interviewer up to do a piece. "What do you think happened, Miss Lorraine? Ziegfeld said you were the greatest beauty he ever had in the Follies. What went wrong?"

"He was right and he was crazy about me. He had me in a tower suite at the Hotel Ansonia and he and his wife lived in the tower suite above. And I cheated on him like he cheated on Billie Burke. I had a whirl! I blew a lot of everybody's money. I got loaded. I was on the stuff, I got the syphilis, I tore around, stopped at nothing. If I wanted to do it, I did it and I did not give a damn. I got knocked up, I had abortions, I broke up homes, I gave fellers the clap. So that's what happened!"

"Well, Miss Lorraine," gasped the lady reporter, "if you had it to do over would you do anything different?"

"Yes," said Lillian Lorraine. "I never shoulda cut my hair!"

The filth and gutter talk most probably continued. No good purpose can be served in continuing to further relate this drunken diatribe from an embittered and hapless shadow of a woman who had once been the adored and undisputed toast of Broadway.

Lillian had committed the unpardonable cardinal sin by disgracing not only herself and the Ziegfeld *Follies* name but, most importantly, maligning the character of the most important figure in Broadway musical history—the man who had in every sense of the word been her creator. Her name, her photographs and innumerable other memorabilia were subsequently all removed from the Ziegfeld Club archives.

Now, the question I had raised early on—why no one in the Ziegfeld Club would return my calls or discuss her association with the Ziegfeld *Follies*—was finally answered. Lillian Lorraine had quite simply been excommunicated by her own peers. The Ziegfeld Diva successfully brought down the curtain on any good memories associated with a lustrous, albeit tumultuous career.

34

Final Curtain — Oblivion

For more than a decade, from 1941 to 1955, Lillian Lorraine virtually disappeared from public view. This was in stark contrast to countless other former Ziegfeld stars. There were those who had married wealthy suitors and remained very much in the public eye through social connections and volunteer work with charitable organizations. Others entered the ranks of professional women at a time when business career opportunities for the fair sex were flourishing and were rapidly becoming almost commonplace. Then, there were those who chose the path of homemaker, raising families and involving themselves in activities typical of that particular station in life. There was, however, one common denominator and bond for all — "once a Ziegfeld Girl, always a Ziegfeld Girl!" The glamour and glitz of bygone days was still enough of a driving force to strengthen and carry forward the mission of the National Ziegfeld Club to the present day.

No such bond existed in the life pattern of Lillian Lorraine. She elected to choose anonymity through the use of her mother's maiden name, Mary Ann Brennan, and to become a veritable recluse, moving from one cheap boarding house to another, like the lost soul which she had actually become. Only as an occasional aside to a Ziegfeldian point of reference, one might see her name in the newspaper columns of Walter Winchell, Leonard Lyons, Ed Sullivan and Louis Sobol.

Saturday evening, April 16, 1955, on Manhattan's Upper West Side, Doctor Quintin Rosenthal was called to the apartment of the Jack O'Briens at 235 West 97th Street. Lillian O'Brien had been his patient since January of 1948. The precise nature of her indisposition that night is not known, but subsequent newspaper reports stated that following his evening house call, Dr. Rosenthal told Jack O'Brien he would return the following morning.

The next day, Sunday, April 17, at ten o'clock in the morning, Lillian Lorraine O'Brien died in her sleep. Dr. Rosenthal signed the death certificate, which carried the standard printed notation, "Death due to natural causes." Noted as "informant" was "John W. O'Brien, husband." Within hours, Lillian's body was removed to the Joseph T. Kennedy Funeral Chapel at 981 Amsterdam Avenue, and three days later, on April 20, to Holy Name Roman Catholic Church on Amsterdam Avenue and 96th Street. At the time, neither the funeral director nor the priest who offered the requiem Mass, Father Gerard Micera, had any inkling that Lillian O'Brien and Lillian Lorraine were one and the same person. The Mass was attended only by O'Brien and two friends. Lillian's body was transferred to a Calvary Cemetery "free grave" for burial.

Lillian's passing was not publicly known until a day later, April 21, when newspapers from New York to San Francisco carried detailed accounts of her former celebrity status and, for the first time, a surprise mention that she had married "Jack O'Brien, accountant, some nine years prior to her death." My exhaustive searches of municipal records in New York and New Jersey failed to yield any corroborative evidence of that marriage, and I am left with no other source than John O'Brien's declaration to Dr. Rosenthal for insertion (husband) on Lil-

Top: A cautionary tale. Unmarked free grave, St. Patrick's Cathedral section, Range 22, Plot Q, Grave 16. Lillian Lorraine's field grave, in shadow of Long Island Expressway, Calvary Cemetery, prior to her being transferred to St. Raymond's Cemetery, Bronx, New York, on May 18, 1955. *Left:* Watercolor of Lillian Lorraine by the late Gilbert Spurgeon, a gift to the author (photograph courtesy of Grace Griparich). *Right:* Lillian Lorraine (Lillian O'Brien) gravestone, Dunn family grave plot, St. Raymond Cemetery, Bronx County, New York.

Lillian Lorraine death certificate (died April 17, 1955).

lian's death certificate. There is no record of the marriage in New York or New Jersey marriage registries. I am therefore led to believe the relationship was a common-law marriage. John W. O'Brien was never listed in a New York City telephone directory or New York State registry of accountants. He was apparently without sufficient funds to provide Lillian a proper burial. He appealed to the Roman Catholic Archdiocese of New York, and a "free grave"—identified

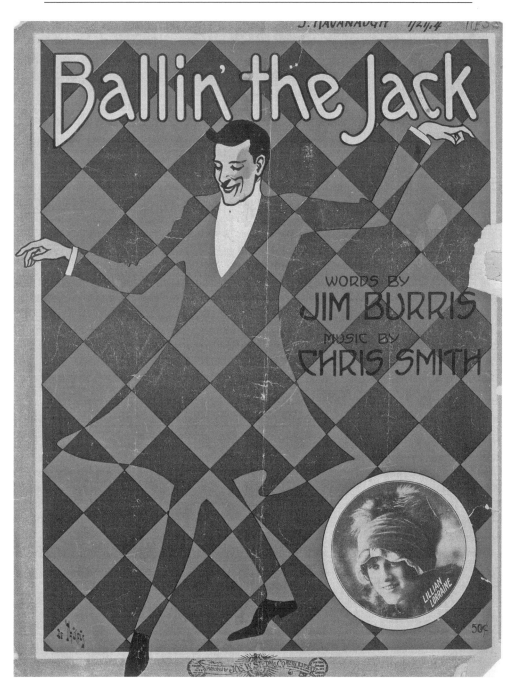

Sheet music cover, "Ballin' the Jack," introduced by Lillian Lorraine, 1913.

only by the number 16 — was provided at Calvary Cemetery in Queens, New York. The location of these free grave sites is commonly known as a "potter's field."

Lillian, for the last time, was a hot copy item in newspapers from coast to coast. A sampling of the death notice headlines reads like the story of her life. In New York, the *Herald Tribune* headed their obituary notice, "Lillian Lorraine, Ziegfeld's Most Beautiful Actress

Dies"; the *New York Times*. "Lillian Lorraine, Star of Ziegfeld Follies and Other Broadway Musicals Dead at 63"; the *New York Daily News*, "Lonely Grave for a Ziegfeld Beauty"; the *San Francisco Chronicle*, "Early Ziegfeld Beauty Buried in Obscurity"; the *Philadelphia Inquirer*, "Curtain Rings Down on Lillian Lorraine"; and the *Chicago Tribune*, "Girl Ziegfeld Billed as Most Beautiful, Dies."

The name Lillian Lorraine certainly was mentioned from time to time in our home, even though my father insisted, and my mother ultimately agreed, when I was just a boy, that it would be best to shield their children from the influence of the Broadway crowd, including breaking contact with Lillian. Mother even had my father bring home the *New York Journal American* from Grand Central Terminal on his way home from work at Swedish American Line in Manhattan's Rockefeller Center. Dorothy Kilgallen and Cholly Knickerbocker, who wrote for the *Journal American*, would mention Lillian from time to time, and Mother was interested. At that time, of course, I had little or no interest in the goings-on of this person in my mother's past. However, because my parents were in Europe at the time of Lillian's passing, I did save her obituaries from the *New York Times* and the *New York Herald Tribune* for them. My mother was heartbroken when she read the obituaries, and she immediately contacted Winnie Dunn. Using the information contained in the obituaries, they were able to make contact with Jack O'Brien and secure his permission to have Lillian's body exhumed and transferred to the Dunn family plot in St. Raymond's Cemetery in the Bronx, New York.

Thus, Lillian Lorraine, one of the most brilliant lights in Florenz Ziegfeld's galaxy of stars, a tempestuous, often neurotic, fun-loving free spirit, was finally at peace, rescued from the ignominy of a potter's field grave by two old friends who still cared, my mother Nanny Elsie Johnson Hanson and Winifred Dunn.

* * *

Fast forward to the year 2000. The place: the stage of the magnificently restored New Amsterdam Theatre, home to the *Ziegfeld Follies* from 1913 to 1927. On this stage, after the passage of eighty years, ninety-six-year-old Doris Eaton Travis, a vision of loveliness in a sparkling dress of blue, green and silver sequins, moves downstage to introduce the musical number she and brother Charles will sing and dance for some 1,800 cheering and stomping souls of the Broadway theatre community.

Doris announces, "I want to turn back the clock and sing a song introduced by Lillian Lorraine in 1913, 'Ballin' the Jack.'…"

Sitting in back-row balcony seats, twenty-year-old dancers Scott Taylor and Susan Reilly pick up on the words just spoken. Turning to Susan and whispering softly, Scott asks, "Who the heck was Lillian Lorraine?" Susan's response, "Darned if I know."

35

Coda to Lillian and Her Times

Lillian Lorraine's tortured and erratic descent from the tenuous pinnacle of fame and adulation to the depths of despair, poverty and anonymity was not an uncommon phenomenon in the jaded Jazz Age of the Roaring Twenties. The glamorous world of show business had a dark and tragic underside often overlooked in the bright glare of the high-powered publicists' domain of make-believe. Many a newly discovered ingénue, consciously or subconsciously, immediately entered into a flat-out footrace with the devil of time ticking over her shoulder. This was nothing more than an attempt to squeeze in all the life she could before her youth and beauty disappeared, signaling the end of however lustrous a career, and the inevitable fading of the spotlight. Perhaps Lillian was just more sensitive to those hands of time nipping at her heels. To be sure, Dame Good Fortune did cast her smile in the direction of the luckier Ziegfeld alumnae — but then, there were the others....

Although she appeared in the 1908, 1909, 1915 and 1920 *Follies*, **Mae Murray** is far better known for her hugely successful career in silent films, most notable of which was *The Merry Widow,* in which she co-starred with matinee idol John Gilbert. She became one of the highest paid film actresses of her time, reportedly earning more than three million dollars over the course of her Hollywood years. Her fall from grace began when, at the insistence of her fourth husband, Prince David Mixivani, she broke her contract with Metro-Goldwyn-Mayer, the studio that had made her a star. The legal maneuvering and public recriminations had been nasty and from that point on, film offers were few and far between. She had obviously not endeared herself to the moguls of the celluloid jungle. Mae returned to the vaudeville stage, but never regained the prominence she had previously enjoyed. After four divorces, a failed court battle for custody of her son, and a filing for bankruptcy, she was literally destitute. In 1964 the Salvation Army reported finding her aimlessly wandering the streets of St. Louis. One year later, a lonely and forgotten figure, she died at the Motion Picture Home in Woodland Hills, California.

Flame-haired **Peggy Davis**, a pretty showgirl in the 1919 *Follies*, had not yet reached the prime of her young life when she abruptly turned her back on a promising show business career. Instead, she chose marriage to David Townsend, a wealthy American entrepreneur. During a European holiday on the French Riviera, near the resort town of Ezy-sur-mer, a stone's throw from Nice, witnesses reported seeing Peggy drive her small sports coupe over a cliff and drop five hundred feet to her death. Although no note was ever found, French police listed her death as a probable suicide. There was, however, a further element of mystery when a hint of scandal was introduced by the gendarme who had made the perilous descent down the wall of the cliff to recover Peggy's body. A man's overcoat was found in the wreckage. Inside one pocket was sewed a label containing the name of Pierre Purvis de Chavaness, a descendant of France's most famous mural painter and friend of the Townsend couple.

If one were called upon in the twenties and thirties to define the term "torch singer," the response required only two words: **Helen Morgan**. She had appeared in the 1928 *Midnight*

Frolic and the 1931 *Follies*, but it was the role of Julie in Ziegfeld's *Show Boat* that catapulted her into superstardom. Prior to this she had achieved notable success as a cabaret and nightclub proprietress and entertainer. In her last years she was plagued with continuing ill health caused primarily by heavy drinking. Nonetheless, at the peak of her fame as a single attraction in vaudeville, Helen was earning twenty-five hundred dollars a week, and although some accounts have her income at well over one hundred thousand dollars a year, she died penniless in 1941 from a liver ailment.

Titian-haired *Follies* dancer **Mary Lygo** became involved in a torrid love affair with wealthy Chicago socialite Gordon C. Thorne. When it became obvious his intentions did not include marriage, Mary unsuccessfully sued him for breach of promise. Several hours after an unfavorable court verdict, Mary swallowed a fatal dose of poison and within days had succumbed to a horribly painful death. Then there was the case of blonde and beautiful *Follies* principal **Allyn King**. Discouraged and depressed over her inability to control a weight problem, she plunged to her death from a New York City hotel window. This was at a time when the weight-reducing fad was in full swing and the demand for slim and boyish forms had destroyed the careers of more than one of the previously famous glamour queens.

Yvonne (Evelyn) Hughes joined the *Follies* when she was seventeen years old. After two years she moved to Hollywood and a promising career in silent films. In two of them she was Rudolf Valentino's dance partner. In 1928 she married Harvard-educated society playboy Gordon Godowsky. His parents, very much opposed to the marriage, cut him off from the family fortune. The marriage was rocky, and after four years, Godowsky, despondent over financial losses, committed suicide. Yvonne dabbled in the stock market, at first meeting with considerable success—but it was short-lived. In the 1929 crash she lost everything, turned to drinking and ended up living with a taxi cab driver in a four-year common-law relationship. She died a violent death in New York City, where, according to newspaper accounts, after an all-day drinking binge with an itinerant Swedish lumberjack, she was found strangled to death with her own silk stockings.

In 1931, *Follies* principal **Harry Richman** invited two Ziegfeld pretties, **Virginia Biddle** and **Helen Walsh**, for a weekend cruise on his luxury motor yacht. While they were anchored in a Greenport, Long Island, marina, escaping gas fumes accidentally ignited, causing a massive explosion and fire, severely burning the two girls and one other male guest. Helen Walsh sustained burns over 95% of her body, and within one day of the accident she was dead at the age of twenty-three. Her funeral was attended by many hundreds of her peers, but Flo Ziegfeld, true to form, was not among the mourners. A tremendous spray of orchids was the only evidence that he wanted to participate in some way. Virginia Biddle recovered to rejoin the *Follies* after many months of rehabilitation. In her years of retirement, she married and had a daughter. She resided in Old Saybrook, Connecticut, and in 2003 was seriously injured in an automobile accident and died shortly thereafter at the age of 93. Virginia told me that when she and Helen were burned in the explosion they were put in the same hospital room, and Helen lay dead for a full day in the bed next to Virginia's before her body was removed.

Pearl Eaton, eldest of the Eaton siblings, was found bludgeoned to death on the floor of her apartment in Manhattan Beach, California. She had been a dancer and choreographer in Ziegfeld's *Follies* and *Frolics*. Following a successful but brief involvement with the film industry, then several disappointing business ventures, Pearl, heretofore a social butterfly, turned to excessive consumption of alcohol. Eventually, up to the time of her unsolved 1958 murder, she became a veritable recluse.

Blonde and beautiful **Mary Eaton**, youngest of the Eaton sisters, died in Hollywood at the age of forty-seven after ingesting a lethal combination of drugs and alcohol. She had been a major star in the Ziegfeld galaxy and appeared to be headed for equal stature in the film world, but Mary did not choose wisely in the field of matrimony. Each of her three husbands was an alcoholic and a meddler in her career, which no doubt was a contributing factor to her tragic demise in 1948. Her husbands' chronic and unreasonable demands of the studio bosses for more money led, finally, to studio refusals to employ her. She ultimately succumbed to her addictions.

Cute and perky *Follies* tap-dancing star **Ann Pennington** ended her days destitute in New York City. Throughout her adult life, Ann was a habitual attendee at the local race tracks, and in her later years squandered whatever money she was able to borrow or earn from sporadic club dates. She was an active member of the Ziegfeld Club and also, from time to time, a recipient of their financial assistance program. Dana O'Connell told me, "In her heyday Penny was the most generous girl you'd ever want to know. One night I was going out on a date and Penny, out of the blue, gave me, not loaned, but gave me a mink jacket and diamond wristwatch." In the end, however, Ann was a familiar and sad figure in the lobby of the Times Square Hotel on Eighth Avenue and West Forty-Third Street and the Forty-Sixth Street and Broadway Horn & Hardart Automat, sitting alone with a cup of coffee and just watching the world go by. Her burial is in the Actors' Fund plot at Kensico Cemetery in Valhalla, New York.

Jenny Dolly, of the famed Dolly Sisters duo, was seriously injured and badly disfigured in an automobile accident outside of Paris. Despite extensive plastic surgery she never truly recovered from the shock of losing her beauty. In 1941, still in a state of depression, she hanged herself.

Jessie Reed was generally acknowledged to have been one of Ziegfeld's most beautiful showgirls. Married and divorced at least five times, she lived her life on a continuous fast track, running through fortunes in money and jewelry at breakneck speed. After several unsuccessful attempts at theatrical comebacks, she settled for employment as a nightclub hostess: After many years of heavy drinking, at the age of forty-five, alone and friendless, she died of pneumonia.

Lupe Velez achieved such fame and fortune in her film career as the "Mexican Spitfire" that few theatre buffs recall she starred with Bert Lahr and Charles "Buddy" Rogers in Florenz Ziegfeld's last Broadway production, *Hot Cha*. Lupe's personal life was a series of revolving-door romantic dalliances with some of Hollywood's biggest names. In 1933 she wed Johnny "Tarzan" Weismuller. From the beginning, their public squabbles were grist for the tabloid press. After five years, their marriage was acrimoniously terminated and Lupe returned to her former lifestyle of blatant promiscuity. In 1944, finding herself pregnant with a child fathered by a lover reluctant to become a groom, Lupe ended her life by devouring a full bottle of sleeping pills.

Fame is generally short-lived and ordinarily not easily acquired. More often than not it is fleeting. Two thousand years ago, Roman historian Gaius Sallustius Crispus wrote, "The fame which is based on wealth or beauty is a frail and fleeting thing, but virtue shines for ages with undiminished lustre."

Epilogue

It is now fifty-five years since the earthly remains of Lillian Lorraine were rescued from the ignominy of a potter's field burial site and reentered in century-old St. Raymond's Cemetery, Bronx County, State of New York. Lillian Lorraine's infamous *New York Daily News* interview exposed the seamy side of a Lillian Lorraine never before known to followers of the Broadway theater world. The image of this embittered and besotted former glamour queen could never be reconciled with a woman who had once been one among the most famous fashion plates of her time. From the text of the interview one can easily surmise Lillian was most probably in a state of extreme intoxication, delighted at this surprise opportunity, this one last time, to publicly express her resentment against a world that had long ago relegated her to the forgotten world of has-beens.

Throughout the writing of this book I have cited many instances of what I perceived to be Lillian's true nature, examples provided by the men and women who perhaps knew her best — her peers. The question arises: why did my mother, Elsie Hanson, Winnie Dunn and Marie Wallace stand by her to the bitter end?

The fact that my mother, Winnie Dunn and Marie Wallace DeSylva did stand by Lillian to the bitter end is definitive and stark testimony to the fact that she was indeed far more than an irresponsible, self-destructive, fun-loving vamp with an insatiable lust for life on the fast track. Showgirl Grace LaRue's aforementioned account of the diamond bracelet incident is illustrative of Lillian's well-known generosity and compassion for her fellow performers.

One could make a case that she was perhaps the first true diva — a forerunner of today's Whitney Houstons, Madonnas, Lindsay Lohans and Lady Gagas, and a by-product of the volatile cocktail that was, and in large part continues to be ... show business: with a jigger here of the inherent pressures to measure up and continue to exceed expectation, a generous splash there of talent, a kicker of high emotion, and served up in attempts to quench the thirst of an adoring public.

Ultimately, a poem in Lillian's handwriting, possibly an attempt at a new song lyric, signed by Harry Leighton and Lillian Lorraine, speaks to the yearning and isolation of one who rides the roller-coaster ride of fame. A last bit salvaged from "the trunk":

Friendship

I sat thinking last night of friendship
That attribute rare in man
So often used, more often abused
By mankind, in their life's whole span.
I dreamed of an ideal friendship,
Of a life growing sweet and calm,
Where man served friends, not selfish ends,
And the lamp and I smoked on.

I pictured my friend as I'd have him
For whom I would lay down my life

A steadfast friend, on whom to depend
Through life's battle of storm and strife.
The friendship of which I was dreaming
To one does so seldom come
'Tis a greater rarity than Christian charity;
And the lamp and I dreamed on.

Lamp and pipe shall we stop our smoking
And give up the search in despair?
Or patiently look through life's great book
Till we find such a friend somewhere?
Shall we ever find one and wonder,
A friend so sturdy and strong.
Yes! Someday I mean, if not we can dream
So the lamp and I dream on.

Harry Leighton
Lillian Lorraine

Lillian Lorraine Stage Credits and Filmography

Stage Credits

1896–1905

Theatrical debut at 4 years of age as Little Eva in *Uncle Tom's Cabin*, Old Central Theatre Stock Company, San Francisco. Additional unidentified roles through 1905.

1907

First walk-on Broadway appearance in Gus Edwards's *School Boys and Girls*, Victoria Theater, Paradise Roff Garden, Aug. 10. Followed by chorus spots in *The Orchid* and *The Tourists* producers Sam and Lee Shubert, Majestic Theater, Columbus Circle, Broadway and 59th St., March 23rd.

1908

Chorus spot in *Gay White Way* with Blanche Ring and Jeff DeAngelis, produced by Sam and Lee Shubert, Casino Theater, Broadway and 39th. Minor singing/speaking role in *The Paradise of Mohamett*.

1909

Supporting role to Anna Held in Ziegfeld's *Miss Innocence*. Introduces Gus Edwards's "By the Light of the Silvery Moon."

1910

Shares starring/featured billing with Fanny Brice, Bert Williams, *Ziegfeld Follies of 1910*. Introduces Gus Edwards's "Sweet Kitty Bellairs."

1911

Featured in *Ziegfeld Follies of 1911*, with the Dolly Sisters, Vera Maxwell and Leon Errol.

1912

Co-stars with Eddie Foy in Ziegfeld-Dillingham production *Over the River* at the Globe Theatre. Stars in 1912 *Ziegfeld Follies* with Bernard Granville, Bert Williams, Leon Errol. Signs for Hippodrome Christmas fund benefit.

1913

Leaves Ziegfeld fold, with Bert Williams, for London, UK, appearances, which she later pulled out of. Replaced by Josie Collins in 1913 *Follies*. Palace Theatre headliner in November. Vaudeville headliner, Victoria Theatre, in December.

1914

Stars in Shubert's *Whirl of the World* at Winter Garden. Introduces Harry Carroll hit song, "Smother Me With Kisses."

1915

Stars in Hammerstein's *Winter Garden Revue*, March.

1917

Opens at Palace, co-starring with Jack Norworth in *Odds and Ends*.

1918

Rejoins Ziegfeld fold for 1918 *Follies*, *Nine O'Clock Revue* and *Midnight Frolic* at New Amsterdam Theatre and Roof.

1919

Co-stars with Bernard Granville in *Little Blue Devil* with Winnie Dunn.

1920

Last year with Ziegfeld in *Nine O'Clock Revue* and *Ziegfeld Girls of 1920*. Stars in Washington, D.C., production of *Sonny* with Emma Dunn and Robert Ames at the Selwyn.

1922

Returns to Broadway (after 8-month spinal fracture recuperation) in Arthur Hammerstein's *The Blue Kitten* with Joseph Cawthorne at 42nd Street Selwyn Theatre.

1923

Headliner, *Ted Lewis Frolic*, with Joe Morton, New York City and Boston. Headliner and hostess at Beaux Arts Cabaret restaurant, 80 W 40th St., New York City.

1924

Headlines *Fay Follies* with Dottie Wilson and the Arthur Lange Orchestra at West 54th St.

1925

Headlines Ciro's *Rhapsody in Blue* revue at 141 West 56th St.

1927

Female lead in Charlton Andrews's comedy *Get Me Into the Movies*. Pre-Broadway tryouts Hartford, CT, March 7, and Mamaroneck, New York, March 17.

1933

Last public appearance of record, April 21, Ziegfeld Theatre memorial to Ziegfeld.

Filmography

(supplemental material via imdb.com)

1912

The Immigrant's Violin, as Lora. Directed by Otis Turner. Also starring King Baggot as Albert Radley, Vivian Prescott as Mrs. Albert Radley, and William Robert Daly.

Dublin Dan. Directed by Edward Warren, Herbert Blaché (uncredited). Produced by Alice Guy. Also starring Barney Gilmore as Dublin Dan, Darwin Karr as John Forsythe, John Roberts as Robert Forsythe, James Sterling as Bill Steele, Blanche Cornwall as Rosalie Forsythe, Ray Leanski as Juno Savage, Lee Beggs as Matt, and George Paxton as a sailor.

The Face at the Window. Directed by Alice Guy. Also starring Lee Beggs, Darwin Karr, Blanche Cornwall, and Vinnie Burns.

1913

Flowers in Japan. 1st Kinemacolor film.

The Detective's Santa Claus, as Miss Steele. Also starring Will E. Sheerer as Tom Steele, Clara Horton as Molly Steele, Willie Gibbons as Frank Steele, Mimi Yvonne as Fanny Steele, George Larkin as Bill Tempest.

The Old Parlor. Directed by William Robert Daly. Written by C.B. Hoadley. Also starring Irene Wallace, Frank Smith, and John Webster.

1915

Neal of the Navy, as Annette Illington. Directed by William Bertram and W.M. Harvey. Written by Douglas Bronston (screenplay), Will-

iam Hamilton Osborne (story). Produced by E.D. Horkheimer, H.M. Horkheimer. Also starring William Courtleigh Jr. as Neal Hardin, William Conklin as Thomas Illington, Ed Brady as Hernandez, Henry Stanley as Ponto, Richard Johnson as Joe Welcher, Charles Dudley, Helen Lackaye as Mrs. Hardin, Bruce Smith as Captain John Hardin, Lucy Blake, and Philo McCullough.

Should a Wife Forgive?, as La Belle Rose. Directed by Henry King. Written by Joseph E. Howard (scenario). Produced by E.D. Horkheimer, H.M. Horkheimer. Also starring Mabel Van Buren as Mary Holmes, Henry King as Jack Holmes, Lew Cody as Alfred Bedford, William Lampe as Dr. Charles Hoffman, Mollie McConnell as Mrs. Forrester, Daniel Gilfether as Henry Wilson, Marie Osborne as Robert Holmes, and Fred Whitman as Reggy Stratford.

1917

The Prima Donna's Special (aka *The Hazards of Helen #118: The Prima Donna's Special*), as the Prima Donna. Directed by Walter Morton. Written by Herman A. Blackman (story). Also starring Helen Gibson as Helen and George A. Williams.

1918

Playing the Game. Directed by Victor Schertzinger. Presented by Thomas H. Ince. Written by Julien Josephson (story), R. Cecil Smith (scenario). Cinematography by Chester Lyons. Art Direction by G. Harold Percival. Also starring Charles Ray as Larry Prentiss, Doris May as Moya Shannon, Harry L. Rattenberry as Matt Shannon, Robert McKim as "Flash" Jim Purdy,

William Elmer as Hodges, Leota Lorraine as "Babe" Fleur de Lis, Charles Perley as Hickey Trent, and Melbourne MacDowell as Jeremiah Prentiss.

1920

The Flaming Disk. Directed by Robert F. Hill. Written by Arthur Henry Goodson. Also starring Elmo Lincoln as Elmo Gray/Jim Gray, Louise Lorraine as Helen, Monte Montague as Bat, Lee Kohlmar as Prof. Wade, George B. Williams as Stanley Barrows, Jenks Harris as Con, Ray Watson as Rodney Stanton, Fred Hamer as Briggs, Fay Holderness, and Bob Reeves.

1922

Lonesome Corners, as Martha Forrest. Directed, written and produced by Edgar Jones. Also starring Edgar Jones as Grant Hamilton, Henry Van Bousen as Henry Warburton, Edna May Sperl as Nola, Walter P. Lewis as Jake Fowler.

Bibliography

Books

Alpert, Hollis. *Broadway! 125 Years of Musical Theatre*. New York: Arcade Publishing, 1991.

Atkinson, Brooks. *Broadway*. New York: Macmillan, 1970.

Baral, Robert. *Revue: The Great Broadway Period*. New York: Fleet Press, 1962.

Berliner, Louise. *Texas Guinan, Queen of the Nightclubs*. Austin: University of Texas Press, 1993.

Blum, Daniel. *Great Stars of the American Stage*. New York: Greenberg, 1952.

_____. *A Pictorial History of the Silent Screen*. New York: Grosset & Dunlap, 1953.

Bordman, Gerald. *American Musical Theatre*. New York: Oxford University Press, 1978, 1992.

Brown, Gene. *Showtime*. New York: Macmillan, 1997.

Burke, Billie. *With a Feather on My Nose*. New York: Appleton-Century-Crofts, 1949.

_____. *With Powder on My Nose*. New York: Coward/McCann, 1959.

Burke, John. *Duet in Diamonds: The Flamboyant Saga of Lillian Russell and Jim Brady in America's Gilded Age*. New York: G.P. Putnam's Sons, 1972.

Cantor, Eddie. *Ziegfeld, The Great Glorifier*. New York: Alfred H. King, 1934.

Carter, Randolph. *The World of Flo Ziegfeld*. New York: Praeger, 1974.

Castle, Irene. *Castles in the Air*. New York: Da Capo Press, 1980.

Churchill, Allen. *The Great White Way*. New York: E.P. Dutton, 1962.

_____. *The Theatrical 20s*. New York: McGraw-Hill, 1975.

Cole, Carter. *Joseph Urban: Architecture, Theatre, Opera, Film*. New York: Abbeville Press, 1992.

Curtis, James. *W.C. Fields: A Biography*. New York: Alfred A. Knopf, 2003.

Davis, Lee. *Scandals and Follies: The Rise and Fall of the Great Broadway Revue*. Limelight Editions, 2000.

Dressler, Marie. *My Own Story*. New York: Hurst and Blackett, 1935.

Earle, Marcelle, Arthur Homme Jr. *Midnight Frolic: A Ziegfeld Girl's True Story*. Basking Ridge, NJ: Twin Oaks, 1999.

Everson, William K. *The Art of W.C. Fields*. Indianapolis: Bobbs-Merrill, 1967.

Ewen, David. *New Complete Book of the American Musical Theatre*. New York: Henry Holt, 1970.

Farnsworth, Marjorie. *The Ziegfeld Follies: A History in Text and Pictures*. New York: Bonanza Books, 1956.

Fowler, Gene. *Timber Line: A Story of Bonfils and Tammen*. New York: Blue Ribbon Books, 1933.

Gaines, Steven. *The Sky's the Limit: Passion and Property in Manhattan*. New York: Little, Brown & Co., 2005.

Golden, Eve. *Ann Held and the Birth of Ziegfeld's Broadway*. Lexington: University Press of Kentucky, 2000.

Goldman, Herbert. *Fanny Brice: The Original Funny Girl*. New York: Oxford University Press, 1992.

Gordon, Ruth. *My Side*. New York: Harper & Row, 1976.

Green, Abel, and Joe Laurie, Jr. *Showbiz: From Vaude to Video*. New York: Henry Holt, 1954.

Harris, Warren G. *The Other Marilyn: A Biography of Marilyn Miller*. New York: Arbor House, 1985.

Held, Anna, and Liane Carrera. *Anna Held and Flo Ziegfeld*. Hicksville, NY: Exposition Press, 1979.

Henderson, Mary. *The New Amsterdam: The Biography of a Broadway Theatre*. New York: Roundtable Press, 1991.

Higham, Charles. *Ziegfeld*. Chicago: Henry Regnery, 1972.

Jasen, David A. *Tin Pan Alley*. London: Omnibus Press, 1988.

Jura, Jean-Jacques, and Rodney N. Bardin II. *Balboa Films: A History and Filmography of the Silent Film Studio*. Jefferson, NC: McFarland, 1999.

Katkov, Norman. *The Fabulous Fanny*. New York: Alfred A. Knopf, 1953.

Kaye, Lenny. *You Call It Madness: The Sensuous Song of the Croon*. New York: Villard, 2004.

Lee, Casey, ed. *Denver Murders*. New York: Duell, Sloan & Pearce, 1946.

Lissauer, Robert. *Lissauer's Encyclopedia of American Popular Music: 1888 to the Present*. New York: Paragon House, 1991.

Louvish, Simon. *Man on the Flying Trapeze: The Life and Times of W.C. Fields*. New York: W.W. Norton, 1997.

Maxwell, Gilbert. *Helen Morgan: Her Life and Legend*. New York: Hawthorn Books, 1967.

Mizejewski, Linda. *Ziegfeld Girl: Image and Icon in Culture and Cinema*. Durham, NC: Duke University Press, 1999.

Monti, Carlotta. *W.C. Fields and Me*. Englewood Cliffs, NJ: Prentice-Hall, 1971.

Morrell, Parker. *Diamond Jim: The Life and Times of James Buchanan Brady*. Garden City, NY: Garden City Publishing, 1934.

Morris, Lloyd. *Curtain Time: The Story of the American Theatre*. New York: Random House, 1953.

Paris, Barry. *Louise Brooks*. New York: Alfred A. Knopf, 1989.

Ragan, David. *Who's Who in Hollywood 1900–1976*. New Rochelle, NY: Arlington House, 1976.

Riker, Eleanor Deuel. *S.I.S.— Simply Incredible Sisters: The Story of the Deuel Sisters*. Manchester, CT: Grames, 1993.

Slide, Anthony. *Encyclopedia of Vaudeville*. Westport, CT: Greenwood Press, 1994.

Sobel, Bernard. *A Pictorial History of Vaudeville*. New York: Bonanza Books, 1961.

_____. *Ziegfeld and Me*. Unpublished, 1930s.

Sobol, Louis. *The Longest Street*. New York: Crown, 1968.

Spitzer, Marian. *The Palace: The Lively and Intimate Story of the Theatre that Became Legend*. New York: Atheneum, 1969.

Stein, Charles W. *American Vaudeville As Seen by Its Contemporaries*. New York: Alfred A. Knopf, 1984.

Taylor, Robert L. *W.C. Fields, His Follies and Fortunes*. Garden City, NY: Doubleday, 1949.

Toll, Robert C. *On With the Show: The First Century of Show Business in America*. New York: Oxford University Press, 1976.

Traub, James. *The Devil's Playground: A Century of Pleasure and Profit in Times Square*. New York: Random House, 2004.

Tucker, Sophie. *Some of These Days*. Garden City, NY: Doubleday, 1945.

Van Hoogstraten, Nicholas. *Lost Broadway Theatres*. New York: Princeton Architectural Press, 1991.

Vazzana, Eugene M. *Silent Film Necrology*. McFarland, 1995.

Werthem, Arthur F. *Will Rogers at the Ziegfeld Follies*. Norman: University of Oklahoma, 1992.

Whitfield, Ellen. *Pickford: The Woman Who Made Hollywood*. Lexington: University of Kentucky Press, 1997.

Wilson, Earl. *The Show Business Nobody Knows*. Chicago: Cowles, 1971.

Ziegfeld, Patricia. *The Ziegfelds' Girl: Confessions of an Abnormally Happy Childhood*. Boston: Little, Brown, 1964.

Ziegfeld, Richard, and Paulette Ziegfeld. *The Ziegfeld Touch*. New York: Harry N. Abrams, 1993.

Periodicals

Boston Herald
Bystander
Chicago Daily Tribune
Cleveland Leader
Denver Post
Motion Picture World
New York American
New York Daily News
New York Dramatic News
New York Evening Graphic
New York Herald Tribune
New York Morning Graphic
New York Morning Telegraph
New York Post
New York Review
New York Sun
New York Telegraph
New York Times
New York World
New York World Telegram and Sun
Philadelphia Inquirer
Photo-Play Preview Weekly
San Francisco Chronicle

Index

Numbers in **bold italics** indicate pages with photographs.

Index